<small>PHENOMENAL PRAISE FOR</small>

# *Before I Go to Sleep*

"An exceptional thriller. It left my nerves jangling for hours after I finished the last page."
—Dennis Lehane

"The summer's single most suspenseful plot belongs to *Before I Go to Sleep*. . . . Pure page-turner."
—*New York Times*

"A deft, perceptive exploration of a fascinating neurological condition, and a cracking good thriller."
—Lionel Shriver

"Brilliant in its pacing, profound in its central question, suspenseful on every page, and satisfying in its thriller ending."
—Anita Shreve

"Explosive tension."
—*Wall Street Journal*

"A brilliant, nasty noir. It drags you down into deep, dark, and disturbing waters. It entertains while touching on complex questions of the meaning of identity and memory. . . . Certain books are so good that they remind you of the vast pleasures good writers can give you if you're willing to pay them attention. If you can stand the chill, *Before I Go to Sleep* is a delicious treat."
—*Los Angeles Times*

"The structure of the novel is heart-racing. We can never really tell what is real and what is invented, and as any keen reader of thrillers knows, the blurry line between truth and fiction can be scarier than blood and gore."
—NPR.org

"This debut novel is a haunting page-turner of the literary sort."
—*Christian Science Monitor*

"Every few summers comes a thriller like this—one that should be slapped with a 'May cause sunburn' sticker because readers could easily lose all track of time, hunger, and sun exposure. . . . S. J. Watson succeeds in keeping readers tense and off-kilter—but deliciously so."
—*Parade*

"A deeply unsettling debut that asks the most terrifying question—what do you have left when you lose yourself?"
—Val McDermid

# Before I Go to Sleep

A NOVEL

S. J. Watson

HARPER

NEW YORK · LONDON · TORONTO · SYDNEY

HARPER

A hardcover edition of this book was published in 2011 by HarperCollins Publishers.

BEFORE I GO TO SLEEP. Copyright © 2011 by S. J. Watson. All rights reserved. Printed in the United States of America. No part of this book may be used or reproduced in any manner whatsoever without written permission except in the case of brief quotations embodied in critical articles and reviews. For information address HarperCollins Publishers, 195 Broadway, New York, NY 10007.

HarperCollins books may be purchased for educational, business, or sales promotional use. For information please e-mail the Special Markets Department at SPsales@harpercollins.com.

FIRST HARPER PERENNIAL EDITION PUBLISHED 2012.
FIRST HARPER PAPERBACK PUBLISHED 2014.

*Designed by Fritz Metsch*

The Library of Congress has catalogued the hardcover edition as follows:

Watson, S.J. (Steven J.)
Before I go to sleep : a novel / S.J. Watson. — 1st ed.
p. cm.
ISBN: 978-0-06-206055-6 (hardback)
1. Women authors—Fiction. 2. Memory disorders—Fiction. 3. Life change events—Fiction. 4. Identity (Psychology)—Fiction. 5. Psychological fiction. I. Title.
PR6123.A884B44 2011
823'.92—dc22
2010043159

ISBN 978-0-06-235388-7 (Harper paperback)

14  15  16  17  18    OV/RRD    10  9  8  7  6  5  4  3  2  1

*For my mother, and for Nicholas.*

*I was born tomorrow*
*today I live*
*yesterday killed me.*

—PARVIZ OWSIA

# Part I

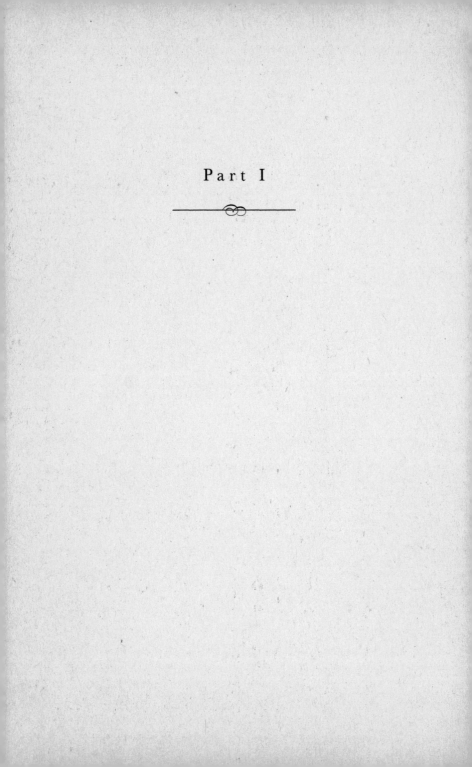

# Today

THE BEDROOM IS strange. Unfamiliar. I don't know where I am, how I came to be here. I don't know how I'm going to get home.

I have spent the night here. I was woken by a woman's voice—at first I thought she was in bed with me, but then realized she was reading the news and I was hearing a radio alarm—and when I opened my eyes found myself here. In this room I do not recognize.

My eyes adjust and I look around in the near-dark. A dressing gown hangs off the back of the closet door—suitable for a woman, but for one much older than I am—and some dark-colored trousers are folded neatly over the back of a chair at the dressing table, but I can make out little else. The alarm clock looks complicated, but I find a button and manage to silence it.

It is then that I hear a juddering intake of breath behind me and realize I am not alone. I turn around. I see an expanse of skin and dark hair, flecked with white. A man. He has his left arm outside the covers and there is a gold band on the third finger of the hand. I suppress a groan. *So this one is not only old and gray,* I think, *but also married. Not only have I screwed a married man, but I have done so in what I am guessing is his home, in the bed he must usually share with his wife.* I lie back to gather myself. *I ought to be ashamed.*

I wonder where the wife is. Do I need to worry about her arriving back at any moment? I imagine her standing at the other side of the room, screaming, calling me a slut. A medusa. A mass of snakes. I wonder how I will defend myself, if she does appear. The guy in the bed does not seem concerned, though. He has turned over and snores on.

I lie as still as possible. Usually I can remember how I get into situations like this, but not today. There must have been a party, or a trip to a bar or a club. I must have been pretty wasted. Wasted enough that I don't remember anything at all. Wasted enough to have gone home with a man with a wedding ring and hairs on his back.

I fold back the covers as gently as I can and sit on the edge of the bed. First, I need to use the bathroom. I ignore the slippers at my feet—after all, fucking the husband is one thing, but I could never wear another woman's shoes—and creep barefoot onto the landing. I am aware of my nakedness, fearful of choosing the wrong door, of stumbling in on a lodger, a teenage son. Relieved, I see the bathroom door is ajar and go in, locking it behind me.

I sit, use the toilet, then flush it and turn to wash my hands. I reach for the soap, but something is wrong. At first I can't work out what it is, but then I see it. The hand gripping the soap does not look like mine. Its skin is wrinkled, the nails are unpolished and bitten to the quick and, like that of the man in the bed I have just left, the third finger wears a plain gold wedding ring.

I stare for a moment, then wriggle my fingers. The fingers of the hand holding the soap move also. I gasp, and the soap thuds into the sink. I look up at the mirror.

The face I see looking back at me is not my own. The hair has no volume and is cut much shorter than I wear it; the skin on the cheeks and under the chin sags; the lips are thin; the mouth turned down. I cry out, a wordless gasp that would turn into a shriek of shock were I to let it, and then notice the eyes. The skin around them is lined, yes, but despite everything else, I can see that they are mine. The person in the mirror is me, but I am twenty years too old. Twenty-five. More.

This isn't possible. I begin to shake and grip the edge of the sink. Another scream begins to rise in my chest and this one erupts as a strangled gasp. I step back, away from the mirror, and it is then that I see them. Photographs. Taped to the wall, to the mirror itself. Pictures, interspersed with yellow pieces of gummed paper, felt-tipped notes, damp and curling.

I choose one at random. *Christine*, it says, and an arrow points to a photograph of me—this new me, this old me—in which I am sitting on a bench on the side of a quay, next to a man. The name seems familiar, but only distantly so, as if I am having to make an effort to believe that it is mine. In the photograph we are both smiling at the camera, holding hands. He is handsome, attractive, and when I look closely, I can see that it is the same man I slept with, the one I left in the bed. The word *Ben* is written beneath it, and next to it, *Your husband*.

I gasp, and rip it off the wall. *No*, I think. *No! It cannot be . . .* I scan the rest of the pictures. They are all of me, and him. In one I am wearing an ugly dress and unwrapping a present, in another both of us wear matching weatherproof jackets and stand in front of a waterfall as a small dog sniffs at our feet. Next to it is a picture of me sitting beside him, sipping a glass of orange juice, wearing the dressing gown I have seen in the bedroom next door.

I step back farther, until I feel cold tiles against my back. It is then I get the glimmer that I associate with memory. As my mind tries to settle on it, it flutters away, like ashes caught in a breeze, and I realize that in my life there is a then, a before, though before what I cannot say, and there is a now, and there is nothing between the two but a long, silent emptiness that has led me here, to me and him, in this house.

.  .  .

I GO BACK into the bedroom. I still have the picture in my hand—the one of me and the man I had woken up with—and I hold it in front of me.

"What's going on?" I say. I am screaming; tears run down my face. The man is sitting up in bed, his eyes half-closed. "Who are you?"

"I'm your husband," he says. His face is sleepy, without a trace of annoyance. He does not look at my naked body. "We've been married for years."

"What do you mean?" I say. I want to run, but there is nowhere to go. " 'Married for years'? What do you mean?"

He stands up. "Here," he says, and passes me the dressing gown, waiting while I put it on. He is wearing pajama trousers that are too big for him, a white T-shirt. He reminds me of my father.

"We got married in 1985," he says. "Twenty-two years ago. You—"

"What—?" I feel the blood drain from my face, the room begin to spin. A clock ticks somewhere in the house, and it sounds as loud as a hammer. "But—?" He takes a step toward me. "How—?"

"Christine, you're forty-seven now," he says. I look at him, this stranger who is smiling at me. I don't want to believe him, don't want to even hear what he is saying, but he carries on. "You had an accident," he says. "A bad accident. You suffered head injuries. You have problems remembering things."

"What things?" I say, meaning, *surely not the last twenty-five years?* "What things?"

He steps toward me again, approaching me as if I am a frightened animal. "Everything," he says. "Sometimes starting from your early twenties. Sometimes even earlier than that."

My mind spins, whirring with dates and ages. I don't want to ask, but know that I must. "When . . . when was my accident?"

He looks at me, and his face is a mixture of compassion and fear.

"When you were twenty-nine . . ."

I close my eyes. Even as my mind tries to reject this information, I know, somewhere, that it is true. I hear myself start to cry again, and as I do so this man, this *Ben*, comes over to where I stand in the doorway. I feel his presence next to me, do not move as he puts his arms around my waist, do not resist as he pulls me into him. He holds me. Together we rock gently, and I realize the motion feels familiar somehow. It makes me feel better.

"I love you, Christine," he says, and though I know I am supposed to say that I love him too, I don't. I say nothing. How can I love him? He is a stranger. Nothing makes sense. I want to know so many things. How I got here, how I manage to survive. But I don't know how to ask.

"I'm scared," I say.

"I know," he replies. "I know. But don't worry, Chris. I'll look after you. I'll always look after you. You'll be fine. Trust me."

.    .    .

HE SAYS HE will show me around the house. I feel calmer. I have put on a pair of panties and an old T-shirt that he gave me, then put the robe over my shoulders. We go out onto the landing. "You've seen the bathroom," he says, opening the door next to it. "This is the office."

There is a glass desk with what I guess must be a computer,

though it looks ridiculously small, almost like a toy. Next to it is a filing cabinet in gunmetal gray, above it a wall planner. All is neat, orderly. "I work in there, now and then," he says, closing the door. We cross the landing and he opens another door. A bed, a dressing table, more closets. It looks almost identical to the room in which I woke. "Sometimes you sleep in here," he says, "when you feel like it. But usually you don't like waking up alone. You get panicked when you can't work out where you are." I nod. I feel like a prospective tenant being shown around a new flat. A possible housemate. "Let's go downstairs."

I follow him down. He shows me a living room—a brown sofa and matching chairs, a flat screen bolted to the wall, which he tells me is a television—and a dining room and kitchen. None of it is familiar. I feel nothing at all, not even when, sitting on a sideboard, I see a framed photograph of the two of us. "There's a garden out the back," he says, and I look through the glass door that leads off the kitchen. It is just beginning to get light, the night sky starting to turn an inky blue, and I can make out the silhouette of a large tree, and a shed sitting at the far end of the small garden, but little else. I realize I don't even know what part of the world we are in.

"Where are we?" I say.

He stands behind me. I can see us both, reflected in the glass. Me. My husband. Middle-aged.

"North London," he replies. "Crouch End."

I step back. Panic begins to rise. "Jesus," I say. "I don't even know where I bloody live . . ."

He takes my hand. "Don't worry. You'll be fine." I turn around to face him, to wait for him to tell me how, how I will be fine, but he does not. "Shall I make you your coffee?"

For a moment I resent him, but then say, "Yes. Yes please." He fills a kettle. "Black, please," I say. "No sugar."

"I know," he says, smiling at me. "Want some toast?"

I say yes. He must know so much about me, yet still this feels like the morning after a one-night stand: breakfast with a stranger in his house, plotting how soon it would be acceptable to make an escape, to go back home.

But that's the difference. Apparently this *is* my home.

"I think I need to sit down," I say. He looks up at me.

"Go and sit yourself down in the living room," he says. "I'll bring this in a minute."

I leave the kitchen.

A few moments later, Ben follows me in. He gives me a book. "This is a scrapbook," he says. "It might help." I take it from him. It is bound in plastic that is supposed to look like worn leather but does not, and has a red ribbon tied around it in an untidy bow. "I'll be back in a minute," he says, and leaves the room.

I sit on the sofa. The scrapbook weighs heavy in my lap. To look at it feels like snooping. I remind myself that whatever is in there is about me, was given to me by my husband.

I untie the bow and open it at random. A picture of me and Ben, looking much younger.

I slam it closed. I run my hands around the binding, fan the pages. *I must have to do this every day.*

I cannot imagine it. I am certain there has been a terrible mistake, yet there cannot have been. The evidence is there—in the mirror upstairs, in the creases on the hands that caress the book in front of me. I am not the person I thought I was when I woke this morning.

*But who was that?* I think. When was I that person, who woke in a stranger's bed and thought only of escape? I close my eyes. I feel as though I am floating. Untethered. In danger of being lost.

I need to anchor myself. I close my eyes and try to focus on something, anything, solid. I find nothing. *So many years of my life*, I think. *Missing.*

This book will tell me who I am, but I don't want to open it. Not yet. I want to sit here for a while, with the whole past a blank. In limbo, balanced between possibility and fact. I am frightened to discover my past. What I have achieved, and what I have not.

Ben comes back in and sets a tray in front of me. Toast, two cups of coffee, a jug of milk. "You okay?" he says. I nod.

He sits beside me. He has shaved, dressed in trousers and a shirt and tie. He does not look like my father anymore. Now he looks as though he works in a bank, or an office. *Not bad, though*, I think, then push the thought from my mind.

"Is every day like this?" I say. He puts a piece of toast on a plate, smears butter on it.

"Pretty much," he says. "You want some?" I shake my head and he takes a bite. "You seem to be able to retain information while you're awake," he says. "But then, when you sleep, most of it goes. Is your coffee okay?"

I tell him it's fine, and he takes the book from my hands. "This is a sort of scrapbook," he says, opening it. "We had a fire a few years ago so we lost a lot of the old photos and things, but there are still a few bits and pieces in here." He points to the first page. "This is your degree certificate," he says. "And here's a photo of you on your graduation day." I look at where he points; I am smiling, squinting into the sun, wearing a black gown and a felt hat with a gold tassel. Just behind me stands a man in a suit and tie, his head turned away from the camera.

"That's you?" I say.

He smiles. "No. I didn't graduate at the same time as you. I was still studying then. Chemistry."

I look up at him. "When did we get married?" I say.

He turns to face me, taking my hand between his. I am surprised by the roughness of his skin, used, I suppose, to the softness of youth. "The year after you got your PhD. We'd been dating for a few years, then, but you—we—we both wanted to wait until your studies were out of the way."

That makes sense, I think, though it feels oddly practical of me. I wonder if I had been keen to marry him at all.

As if reading my mind, he says, "We were very much in love," and then adds, "we still are."

I can think of nothing to say. I smile. He takes a swig of his coffee before looking back at the book in his lap. He turns over some more pages.

"You studied English," he says. "Then you did a few jobs, once you'd graduated. Just odd things. Secretarial work. Sales. I'm not sure you really knew what you wanted to do. I left with a bachelor's and did teacher training. It was a struggle, for a few years, but then I was promoted and well, we ended up here."

I look around the living room. It is smart, comfortable. Blandly middle-class. A framed picture of a woodland scene sits on the wall above the fireplace, china figurines next to the clock on the mantelpiece. I wonder if I helped to choose the decor.

Ben goes on. "I teach in a high school nearby. I'm head of department, now." He says it with no hint of pride.

"And me?" I say, though, really, I know the only possible answer. He squeezes my hand.

"You had to give up work. After your accident. You don't do anything." He must sense my disappointment. "You don't need to. I earn a good enough wage. We get by. We're okay."

I close my eyes, put my hand to my forehead. This all feels too much, and I want him to shut up. I feel as if there is only so much

I can process, and if he carries on adding more then eventually I will explode.

*Then what do I do all day?* I want to say but, fearing the answer, I say nothing.

He finishes his toast and takes the tray out to the kitchen. When he comes back in, he is wearing an overcoat.

"I have to leave for work," he says. I feel myself tense.

"Don't worry," he says. "You'll be fine. I'll call you. I promise. Don't forget today is no different from every other day. You'll be fine."

"But—" I begin.

"I have to go," he says. "I'm sorry. I'll show you some things you might need, before I leave."

In the kitchen he shows me which things are in which cabinet, points out some leftovers in the fridge that I can have for lunch, and an eraser board screwed to the wall next to a black marker pen tied to a piece of string. "I sometimes leave messages here for you," he says. I see that he has written FRIDAY on it in neat, even capitals, and beneath it the words *laundry? walk? (take phone!) tv?* Under the word *lunch*, he has noted that there is some leftover salmon in the fridge and added, *salad?* Finally, he has written that he should be home by six. "You also have a diary," he says. "In your bag. It has important phone numbers in the back of it, and our address, in case you get lost. And there's a cell phone—"

"A what?" I say.

"A phone," he says. "It's cordless. You can use it anywhere. Outside the house, anywhere. It'll be in your handbag. Make sure you take it with you if you go out."

"I will," I say.

"Right," he says. We go into the hall and he picks up a battered leather briefcase by the door. "I'll be off, then."

"Okay," I say. I am not sure what else to say. I feel like a child kept out of school, left alone at home while her parents go to work. *Don't touch anything,* I imagine him saying. *Don't forget to take your medicine.*

He comes over to where I stand. He kisses me, on the cheek. I do not stop him, but neither do I kiss him back. He turns toward the front door, and is about to open it when he stops.

"Oh!" he says, looking back at me. "I almost forgot!" His voice sounds suddenly forced, the enthusiasm affected. He is trying too hard to make it seem natural; it is obvious he has been building up to what he is about to say for some time.

In the end it is not as bad as I feared. "We're going away this evening," he says. "Just for the weekend. It's our anniversary, so I thought I'd book something. Is that okay?"

I nod. "That sounds nice," I say.

He smiles, looks relieved. "Something to look forward to, eh? A bit of sea air? It'll do us good." He turns back to the door and opens it. "I'll call you later," he says. "See how you're getting on?"

"Yes," I say. "Do. Please."

"I love you, Christine," he says. "Never forget that."

He closes the door behind him, and I turn. I go back into the house.

.   .   .

LATER, MID-MORNING. I sit in an armchair. The dishes are done and neatly stacked on the drainer, the laundry is in the machine. I have been keeping myself busy.

But now I feel empty. It's true, what Ben said. I have no memory. Nothing. There is not a thing in this house that I remember seeing before. Not a single photograph—either around the mirror or in the scrapbook in front of me—that triggers a recollection of when it was taken, not a moment with Ben that I can recall, other than those since we met this morning. My mind feels totally empty.

I close my eyes, try to focus on something. Anything. Yesterday. Last Christmas. Any Christmas. My wedding. There is nothing.

I stand up. I move through the house, from room to room. Slowly. Drifting, like a wraith, letting my hand brush against the walls, the tables, the backs of the furniture, but not really touching any of it. *How did I end up like this?* I think. I look at the carpets, the patterned rugs, the china figurines on the mantelpiece and ornamental plates arranged on the display racks in the dining room. I try to tell myself that this is mine. All mine. My home, my husband, my life. But these things do not belong to me. They are not part of me. In the bedroom I open the closet door and see a row of clothes I do not recognize, hanging neatly, like empty versions of a woman I have never met. A woman whose home I am wandering through, whose soap and shampoo I have used, whose dressing gown I have discarded and slippers I am wearing. She is hidden to me, a ghostly presence, aloof and untouchable. This morning I had selected my underwear guiltily, searching through the pairs of panties, balled together with tights and stockings, as if I was afraid of being caught. I held my breath as I found panties in silk and lace at the back of the drawer, items bought to be seen as well as worn. Rearranging the unused ones exactly as I had found them, I chose a pale blue pair that seemed to have a matching bra and slipped them both on, before pulling a heavy pair of tights over the top, and then trousers and a blouse and finally a sweater.

I had sat down at the dressing table to examine my face in the mirror, approaching my reflection cautiously. I traced the lines on my forehead, the folds of skin under my eyes. I smiled and looked at my teeth, and at the wrinkles that bunched around the edge of my mouth, the crow's feet that appeared. I noticed the blotches on my skin, a discoloration on my forehead that looked like a bruise that had not quite faded. I found some makeup, and put a little on. A light powder, a touch of blush. I pictured a woman—my mother, I realize now—doing the same, calling it her *war paint*, and this morning, as I blotted my lipstick on a tissue and recapped the mascara, the word felt appropriate. I felt that I was going into some kind of battle, or that some battle was coming to me.

Sending me off to school. Putting on her makeup. I tried to think of my mother doing something else. Anything. Nothing came. I saw only a void, vast gaps between tiny islands of memory, years of emptiness.

Now, in the kitchen, I open cabinets: packages of pasta, packets of a rice labeled ARBORIO, cans of kidney beans. I do not recognize this food. I remember eating cheese on toast, macaroni and cheese, corned beef sandwiches. I pull out a can labeled CHICKPEAS, a packet of something called couscous. I do not know what these things are, less how to cook them. How, then, do I survive as a wife?

I look up at the eraser board that Ben had shown me before he left. It is a dirty gray color; words have been scrawled on it and wiped out, replaced, amended, each leaving a faint residue. I wonder what I would find if I could go back and decipher the layers, if it were possible to delve into my past that way, but realize that, even if it were possible, it would be futile. I am certain that all I would find are messages and lists, groceries to buy, tasks to perform.

*Is this really my life?* I think. *Is this all I am?* I take the pen and add another note to the board. *Pack bag for tonight?* it says. Not much of a reminder, but my own.

I hear a noise. A tune, coming from my bag. I open it and empty its contents onto the sofa. My purse, some tissues, pens, a lipstick. A powder compact, a receipt for two coffees. A diary, just a couple of inches square and with a floral design on the front and a pencil in its spine.

I find something that I guess must be the phone that Ben described—it is small, plastic, with a keypad that makes it look like a toy. It is ringing, the screen flashing. I press what I hope is the right button.

"Hello?" I say. The voice that replies is not Ben's.

"Hi," it says. "Christine? Is that Christine Lucas?"

I do not want to answer. My last name seems as strange as my first name had. I feel as though any solid ground I had attained has vanished again, replaced by quicksand.

"Christine? Are you there?"

Who can it be? Who knows where I am, who I am? I realize it could be anyone. I feel panic rise in me. My finger hovers over the button that will end the call.

"Christine? It's me. Dr. Nash. Please answer."

The name means nothing to me, but still I say, "Who is this?"

The voice takes on a new tone. Relief? "It's Dr. Nash," he says. "Your doctor?"

Another flash of panic. "My doctor?" I say. *I'm not ill,* I want to add, but I do not know even this. I feel my mind begin to spin.

"Yes," he says. "But don't worry. We've just been doing some work on your memory. Nothing's wrong."

I notice the tense he has used. *Have been.* So this is someone else I have no memory of.

"What kind of work?" I say.

"I've been trying to help you to improve things," he says. "Trying to work out exactly what's caused your memory problems, and whether there's anything we can do about them."

It makes sense, though another thought comes to me. Why had Ben not mentioned this doctor before he left this morning?

"How?" I say. "What have we been doing?"

"We've been meeting over the last few weeks. A couple of times a week, give or take."

It does not seem possible. Another person I see regularly who has left no impression on me whatsoever.

*But I've never met you before,* I want to say. *You could be anyone.*

I say nothing. The same could be said of the man I woke up with this morning, and he turned out to be my husband.

"I don't remember," I say instead.

His voice softens. "Don't worry. I know." If what he says is true then he must understand that as well as anyone. He explains that our next appointment is today.

"Today?" I say. I think back to what Ben told me this morning, to the list of jobs written on the board in the kitchen. "But my husband hasn't mentioned anything to me." I realize it is the first time I have referred in this way to the man I woke up with.

There is a pause, and then Dr. Nash says, "I'm not sure Ben knows you're meeting me."

I notice that he knows my husband's name, but say, "That's ridiculous! How can he not? He would have told me!"

There is a sigh. "You'll have to trust me," he says. "I can explain everything, when we meet. We're really making progress."

When we meet. How can we do that? The thought of going out, without Ben, without him even knowing where I am or who I am with, terrifies me.

"I'm sorry," I say. "I can't."

"Christine," he says. "It's important. If you look in your diary you'll see what I'm saying is true. Do you have it? It should be in your bag."

I pick up the floral book from where it had fallen onto the sofa and register the shock of seeing the year printed on the front in gold lettering. 2007. Twenty years later than it should be.

"Yes."

"Look at today's date," he says. "November thirtieth. You should see our appointment?"

I don't understand how it can be November—December tomorrow—but still I skim through the leaves, thin as tissue, to today's date. There, tucked between the pages, is a piece of paper, and on it, printed in handwriting I don't recognize, are the words *November 30th—seeing Dr. Nash*. Beneath them, are the words *Don't tell Ben*. I wonder if he has read them, whether he looks through my things.

I decide there is no reason he would. The other days are blank. No birthdays, no nights out, no parties. Does this really describe my life?

"Okay," I say. He explains that he will come and pick me up, that he knows where I live and will be there in an hour.

"But my husband—" I say.

"It's okay. We'll be back long before he gets in from work. I promise. Trust me."

The clock on the mantelpiece chimes and I glance at it. It is old-fashioned, a large dial in a wooden case, edged with roman numerals. It reads eleven thirty. Next to it sits a silver key for winding it, something that I suppose Ben must remember to do every evening. It looks old enough to be an antique, and I wonder how we came to own such a clock. Perhaps it has no history, or none with us at least, but is simply something we saw once, in a shop or at a market, and one of us liked it. Probably Ben, I think. I realize I don't like it.

I'll see him just this once, I decide. And then, tonight, when he gets home, I will tell Ben. I cannot believe I am keeping something like this from him. Not when I rely so utterly on him.

But there is an odd familiarity to Dr. Nash's voice. Unlike Ben, he does not seem entirely alien to me. I realize I almost find it easier to believe that I have met him before than I do my husband.

*We're making progress,* he'd said. I need to know what kind of progress he means.

"Okay," I say. "Come."

.  .  .

WHEN HE ARRIVES, Dr. Nash suggests we go for a cup of coffee. "Are you thirsty?" he says. "I don't think there's much point in driving all the way to the office. I mostly wanted to talk to you today, anyway."

I nod and say yes. I was in the bedroom when he arrived, and watched him park his car and lock it, saw him rearrange his hair, smooth his jacket, pick up his briefcase. *Not him,* I thought as he nodded to the workmen who were unloading tools from a van, but then he walked up the path to our house. He looked young——too young to be a doctor——and, though I don't know what I had been expecting him to be wearing, it was not the sports jacket and gray corduroy trousers that he had on.

"There's a park at the end of the street," he says. "I think it has a café. We could go there?"

We walk together. The cold is biting and I pull my scarf tight around my neck. I am glad I have in my bag the cell phone that

Ben has given me. Glad, too, that Dr. Nash has not insisted we drive somewhere. There is some part of me that trusts this man, but another, larger part tells me he could be anyone. A stranger.

I am an adult, but a damaged one. It would be easy for this man to take me somewhere, though I don't know what he would want to do. I am as vulnerable as a child.

We reach the main road that separates the end of the street from the park opposite, and wait to cross. The silence between us feels oppressive. I had intended to wait until we were sitting down before asking him, but find myself speaking. "What sort of doctor are you?" I am saying. "What do you do? How did you find me?"

He looks over at me. "I'm a neuropsychologist," he says. He is smiling. I wonder if I ask him the same question every time we meet. "I specialize in patients with brain disorders, with an interest in some of the newer functional neuroimaging techniques. For a long time I've been particularly interested in researching memory process and function. I heard about you through the literature on the subject, and tracked you down. It wasn't too difficult."

A car rounds the bend farther up the road and heads toward us. "The literature?"

"Yes. There have been a couple of case studies written about you. I got in touch with the place where you were being treated before you came to live at home."

"Why? Why did you want to find me?"

He smiles. "Because I thought I could help you. I've been working with patients with these sorts of problems for a little while. I believe they can be helped; however, they require more intensive input than the usual one hour per week. I had a few ideas about how real improvements could be effected and wanted to try some of them out." He pauses. "Plus I've been writing a paper on your case. The definitive work, you might say." He begins to laugh, but cuts it short when I do not join in. He clears his throat. "Your case is unusual. I believe we can discover a lot more about the way memory works than we already know."

The car passes and we cross the road. I feel myself get anxious, uptight. *Brain disorders. Researching. Tracked you down.* I try to breathe, to relax, but find I cannot. There are two of me, now, in the same body; one is a forty-seven-year-old woman, calm, polite, aware of what kind of behavior is appropriate and what is not, and the other is in her twenties, and screaming. I cannot decide which is me, but the only noise I hear is that of distant traffic and the shouts of children from the park, and so I guess it must be the first.

On the other side, I stop and say, "Look, what's going on? I woke up this morning in a place I've never seen but that's apparently my home, lying next to a man I've never met who tells me I've been married to him for years. And you seem to know more about me than I know about myself."

He nods slowly. "You have amnesia," he says, putting his hand on my arm. "You've had amnesia for a long time. You can't retain new memories, so you've forgotten much of what's happened to you for your entire adult life. Every day you wake up as if you are a young woman. Some days you wake as if you are a child."

Somehow it seems worse, coming from him. A doctor. "So it's true?"

"I'm afraid so. Yes. The man at home is your husband. Ben. You've been married to him for years. Since long before your amnesia began." I nod. "Shall we go on?"

I say yes, and we walk into the park. A path circles its edge, and there is a children's playground nearby, next to a hut from which

I see people emerge carrying trays of snacks. We head there, and I take a seat at one of the chipped Formica tables while Dr. Nash orders our drinks.

When he returns, he is carrying two plastic cups filled with strong coffee, mine black, his white. He adds sugar from the bowl on the table but offers none to me, and it is that, more than anything, that convinces me we have met before. He looks up and asks me how I hurt my forehead.

"What—?" I say at first, but then I remember the bruise I saw this morning. My makeup has clearly not covered it. "That?" I say. "I'm not sure. It's nothing, really. It doesn't hurt."

He does not answer. He stirs his coffee.

"So my husband looks after me at home?" I say.

He looks up. "Yes, though he hasn't always. At first your condition was so severe that you required round-the-clock care. It has only been fairly recently that Ben felt he could look after you alone."

So the way I feel at the moment is an improvement, then. I am glad I cannot remember the time when things were worse.

"He must love me very much," I say, more to myself than to Nash.

He nods. There is a pause. We both sip our drinks. "Yes. I think he must."

I smile and look down, at my hands holding the hot drink, at the gold wedding band, at the short nails, at my legs, crossed politely. I do not recognize my own body.

"Why doesn't my husband know that I'm seeing you?" I say.

He sighs and closes his eyes. "I'll be honest," he says, clasping his hands together and leaning forward in his seat. "Initially I asked you not to tell Ben that you were seeing me."

A jolt of fear goes through me, almost an echo. Yet he does not look untrustworthy.

"Go on," I say. I want to believe he can help me.

"Several people—doctors, psychiatrists, psychologists, and so on—have approached you and Ben in the past, wanting to work with you. But he has always been extremely reluctant to let you see these professionals. He has made it very clear that you have had extensive treatment before, and in his opinion it has achieved nothing other than to upset you. Naturally he wanted to spare you—and himself—from any more upset."

Of course; he doesn't want to raise my hopes. "So you persuaded me to come and see you without him knowing?"

"Yes. I did approach Ben first. We spoke on the phone. I even asked him to meet with me so that I could explain what I had to offer, but he refused. So I contacted you directly."

Another jolt of fear, as if from nowhere. "How?" I say.

He looked down at his drink. "I came to see you. I waited until you came out of the house and then introduced myself."

"And I agreed to see you? Just like that?"

"Not at first. No. I had to persuade you that you could trust me. I suggested that we should meet once, just for one session. Without Ben's knowledge if that was what it took. I said I would explain to you why I wanted you to come and see me, and what I thought I could offer you."

"And I agreed . . ."

He looks up. "Yes," he says. "I told you that after that first visit it was entirely up to you whether you chose to tell Ben or not, but if you decided not to I would call you to make sure you remembered our appointments, and so on."

"And I chose not to."

"Yes. That's right. You've spoken about wanting to wait until we were making progress before telling him. You felt that was better."

"And are we?"

"What?"

"Making progress?"

He swallows some more coffee, then puts his cup back on the table. "I believe so, yes. Though progress is somewhat difficult to quantify exactly. But lots of memories seem to have come back to you over the last few weeks—many of them for the first time, as far as we know. And there are certain truths that you are aware of more often, where there were few before. For example, you occasionally wake up and remember that you're married, now. And—"

He pauses. "And?" I say.

"And, well, you're gaining independence, I think."

"Independence?"

"Yes. You don't rely on Ben as much as you did. Or me."

That's it, I think. That is the progress he is talking about. Independence. Perhaps he means I can make it to the shops or a library without a chaperone, though right now I am not even sure that much is true. In any case, I have not yet made enough progress for me to wave it proudly in front of my husband. Not even enough for me to always wake up remembering I have one.

"But that's it?"

"It's important," he says. "Don't underestimate it, Christine."

I don't say anything. I take a sip of my drink and look around the café. It is almost empty. There are voices from a small kitchen at the back, the occasional rattle as the water in an urn reaches boiling point, the noise of children playing in the distance. It is difficult to believe that this place is so close to my home and yet I have no memory of ever being here before.

"You say we've been meeting for a few weeks," I say to Dr. Nash. "So what have we been doing?"

"Do you remember anything of our previous sessions? Anything at all?"

"No," I say. "Nothing. As far as I know I am meeting you for the first time today."

"Forgive me asking," he says. "As I said, you have flashes of memory, sometimes. It seems you know more on some days than on others."

"I don't understand," I say. "I have no memory of ever meeting you before, or of what happened yesterday, or the day before, or last year for that matter. Yet I can remember some things from years ago. My childhood. My mother. I remember being at university, just. I don't understand how these old memories could have survived when everything else has been wiped clean."

He nods throughout my question. I don't doubt he has heard it before. Possibly I ask the same thing every week. Possibly we have exactly the same conversation.

"Memory is a complex thing," he says. "Human beings have a short-term memory that can store facts and information for about a minute or so, but also a long-term memory. Here we can store huge quantities of information, and retain it for a seemingly indefinite length of time. We now know that these two functions seem to be controlled by different parts of the brain, with some neural connections between them. There is also a part of the brain that seems to be responsible for taking short-term, transient memories and coding them as long-term memories for recall much later."

He speaks easily, quickly, as if he is now on solid territory. I would have been like that once, I suppose; sure of myself.

"There are two main types of amnesia," he says. "Most commonly the affected person cannot recall past events, with more recent events being most severely affected. So if, for example, the sufferer has a motor accident, they may not remember the accident, or the days or weeks preceding it, but can remember everything up to, say, six months before the accident perfectly well."

I nod. "And the other?"

"The other is rarer," he says. "Sometimes there is an inability to transfer memories from short-term storage into long-term storage. People with this condition live in the moment, able to recall only the immediate past, and then only for a small amount of time."

He stops talking, as if waiting for me to say something. It is as if we each have our lines, have rehearsed this conversation often.

"I have both?" I say. "A loss of the memories I had, plus an inability to form new ones?"

He clears his throat. "Yes, unfortunately. It's not common, but perfectly possible. What's unusual in your case, however, is the pattern of your amnesia. Generally you have no consistent memory of anything that happened since your early childhood, but you seem to process new memories in a way I have never come across before. If I left this room now and returned in two minutes, most people with anterograde amnesia would not remember having met me at all, certainly not today. But you seem to remember whole chunks of time—up to twenty-four hours—which you then lose. That's not typical. To be honest, it doesn't make any sense, considering the way we believe that memory works. It suggests you are able to transfer things from short-term to long-term storage perfectly well. I don't understand why you can't retain them."

I may be leading a shattered life, but at least it is shattered into pieces large enough for me to maintain a semblance of independence. I guess that means I am lucky.

"Why?" I say. "What has caused it?"

He does not say anything. The room goes quiet. The air feels still and sticky. When he speaks, his words seem to echo off the walls. "Many things can cause an impairment of memory," he says. "Either long-term or short-term. Disease, trauma, drug use. The exact nature of the impairment seems to differ, depending on the part of the brain that has been affected."

"Yes," I say. "But what has caused mine?"

He looks at me for a moment. "What has Ben told you?"

I think back to our conversation in the bedroom. *An accident,* he had said. *A bad accident.*

"He didn't really tell me anything," I say. "Nothing specific, anyway. He just said I'd had an accident."

"Yes," he says, reaching for his bag that sits under the table. "Your amnesia was caused by trauma. That's true, at least partly." He opens his bag and takes out a book. At first, I wonder if he is going to consult his notes, but instead he passes it across the table to me. "Look. I want you to have this," he says. "It will explain everything. Better than I can. About what has caused your condition, especially. But other things as well."

I take it from him. It is brown, bound in leather. I open it at random. The paper is heavy and faintly lined, with a red margin, and the pages are filled with dense handwriting. "What is it?" I say.

"It's a journal," he says. "One that you've been keeping over the past few weeks."

I am shocked. "A journal?" I wonder why he has it.

"Yes. A record of what we've been doing recently. I asked you to keep it. We've been doing a lot of work trying to find out exactly how your memory behaves. I thought it might be helpful for you to keep a record of what we've been doing."

I look at the book in front of me. "So I've written this?"

"Yes. I told you to write whatever you like in it. Many amnesiacs have tried a similar approach, but usually it's not as helpful as you might think, as they have such a short window of memory. But as there are some things that you can remember for the whole day, I didn't see why you shouldn't jot down some notes in a book every evening. I thought it might help you to maintain a thread of memory from one day to the next. Plus I felt that memory might be like a muscle, something that can be strengthened through exercise."

"And you've been reading it, as we've been going along?"

"No," he says. "You've been writing it in private."

"But how—?" I begin, and then say, "Ben's been reminding me to write in it?"

He shakes his head. "I suggested that you keep it secret," he says. "You've been hiding it, at home. I've been calling you to tell you where it is hidden."

"Every day?"

"Yes. More or less."

"Not Ben?"

He pauses, then says, "No. Ben hasn't read it."

I wonder why not, what it might contain that I do not want my husband to see. What secrets might I have? Secrets I do not even know myself.

"But you've read it?"

"You left it with me a few days ago," he says. "You said you wanted me to read it. That it was time."

I look at the book. I am excited. A journal. A link back to a lost past, albeit only recent.

"Have you read it all?"

"Yes," he says. "Most of it. I think I've read everything important, anyway." He pauses, and looks away from me, scratching the back of his neck. Embarrassed, I think. I wonder if he is telling me the truth, what the book contains. He drains the last of his cup of coffee, and says, "I didn't force you to let me see it. I want you to know that."

I nod, and finish the rest of my drink in silence, flicking through the pages of the book as I do. On the inside of the front cover is a list of dates. "What are these?" I say.

"They're the dates we've been meeting," he says. "As well as the ones we had planned. We've been arranging them as we go along. I've been calling to remind you, asking you to look in your journal."

I think of the yellow note tucked between the pages of my diary today. "But today?"

"Today I had your journal," he says. "So we wrote a note instead."

I nod and look through the rest of the book. It is filled with a dense handwriting that I don't recognize. Page after page. Days and days' worth of work.

I wonder how I found the time, but then think of the board in the kitchen, and the answer is obvious: I have had nothing else to do.

I put it back on the table. A young man wearing jeans and a T-shirt comes in and glances over to where we sit, before ordering a drink and settling at a table with the newspaper. He does not look up at me again, and the twenty-year-old me is upset. I feel as though I am invisible.

"Shall we go?" I say.

We walk back the way we had come. The sky has clouded over, and a thin mist hangs in the air. The ground is soggy underfoot; it feels like walking on quicksand. On the playground, I see a merry-go-round, turning slowly even though no one is riding it.

"We don't normally meet here?" I say, when we reach the road. "In the café, I mean?"

"No. No, we normally meet in my office. We do exercises. Tests and things."

"So why here today?"

"I really just wanted to give you your book back," he says. "I was worried about you not having it."

"I've come to rely on it?" I say.

"In a way, yes."

We cross the road and walk back down to the house I share with Ben. I can see Dr. Nash's car, still parked where he left it, the tiny garden outside our window, the short path and neat flower beds. I still cannot quite believe this is the place in which I live.

"Do you want to come in?" I say. "Another drink?"

He shakes his head. "No. No, I won't, thanks. I have to get going. Julie and I have plans this evening."

He stands for a moment, looking at me. I notice his hair, cut short, neatly parted, and the way his shirt has a vertical stripe that clashes with the horizontal one on his pullover. I realize that he is only a few years older than I thought I was when I woke this morning. "Julie is your wife?"

He smiles and shakes his head. "No, my girlfriend. Actually, my fiancée. We got engaged. I keep forgetting."

I smile back at him. These are the details I should remember, I suppose. The little things. Perhaps it is these trivialities I have been writing down in my book, these small hooks on which a whole life is hung.

"Congratulations," I say, and he thanks me.

I feel like I ought to ask more questions, ought to show more interest, but there is little point. Anything he tells me now I will have forgotten by the time I wake tomorrow. Today is all I have.

"I ought to get back anyway," I say. "We're going away this weekend. To the coast. I need to pack later . . ."

He smiles. "Good-bye, Christine," he says. He turns to leave, but then looks back at me. "Your journal has my numbers written in it," he says. "At the front. Call me, if you'd like to see me again. To carry on with your treatment, I mean. Okay?"

"If?" I say. I remember my journal, the appointments that we had penciled in between now and the end of the year. "I thought we had more sessions booked?"

"You'll understand when you read your book," he says. "It will all make sense. I promise."

"Okay," I say. I realize I trust him, and I am glad. Glad that I do not only have my husband to rely on.

"It's up to you, Christine. Call me, whenever you like."

"I will," I say, and then he waves and gets into his car and, checking over his shoulder as he does, he pulls out into the road and is gone.

I make a cup of coffee and carry it into the living room. From outside I hear the sound of whistling, punctured by heavy drilling and an occasional burst of staccato laughter, but even that recedes to a gentle buzz as I sit in the armchair. The sun shines weakly through the net curtains and I feel its dull warmth on my arms and thighs. I take the journal out of my bag.

I feel nervous. I do not know what this book will contain. What shocks and surprises. What mysteries. I see the scrapbook on the coffee table. In that book is a version of my past, but one chosen by Ben. Does the book I hold contain another? I open it.

The first page is unlined. I have written my name in black ink across its center. CHRISTINE LUCAS. It's a wonder I haven't written PRIVATE! beneath it. Or KEEP OUT!

Something has been added. Something unexpected, terrifying. More terrifying than anything else I have seen today. There, beneath my name, in blue ink and capital letters, are three words.

DON'T TRUST BEN.

There is nothing I can do but turn the page.
I begin to read my history.

## Part II

—∞—

# The Journal of
# Christine Lucas

# Friday, November 9

My name is Christine Lucas. I am forty-seven. An amnesiac. I am sitting here, in this unfamiliar bed, writing my story dressed in a silk nightie that the man downstairs—who tells me that he is my husband, that he is called Ben—apparently bought me for my forty-sixth birthday. The room is silent and the only light comes from the lamp on the bedside table—a soft orange glow. I feel as if I am floating, suspended in a pool of light.

I have the bedroom door closed. I am writing this in private. In secret. I can hear my husband in the living room—the soft sigh of the sofa as he leans forward or stands up, an occasional cough, politely stifled—but I will hide this book if he comes upstairs. I will put it under the bed, or the pillow. I don't want him to see I am writing in it. I don't want to have to tell him how I got it.

I look at the clock on the bedside table. It is almost eleven; I must write quickly. I imagine that soon I will hear the TV silenced, a creak of a floorboard as Ben crosses the room, the flick of a light switch. Will he go into the kitchen and make a sandwich or pour himself a glass of water? Or will he come straight to bed? I don't know. I don't know his rituals. I don't know my own.

Because I have no memory. According to Ben, according to the doctor I met this afternoon, tonight, as I sleep, my mind will erase everything I know today. Everything I did today. I will wake up tomorrow as I did this morning. Thinking I am still a child. Thinking I still have a whole lifetime of choice ahead of me.

And then I will find out, again, that I am wrong. My choices have already been made. Half my life is behind me.

The doctor was called Nash. He called me this morning, collected me in his car, drove me to an office. He asked me and I told him that I had never met him before; he smiled—though not unkindly—and opened the lid of the computer that sat on his desk.

He played me a film. A video clip. It was of me and him, sitting in different clothes but the same chairs, in the same office. In the film he handed me a pencil and asked me to draw shapes on a piece of paper, but by looking only in a mirror so that everything appeared backward. I could see that I found it difficult, but watching it now all I could see was my wrinkled fingers and the glint of the wedding ring on my left hand. When I had finished, he seemed pleased. "You're getting faster," he said on the video, then added that somewhere, deep, deep down, I must be remembering the effects of my weeks of practice even if I did not remember the practice itself. "That means your long-term memory must be working on some level," he said. I smiled then, but did not look happy. The film ended.

Dr. Nash closed his computer. He said we have been meeting for the last few weeks, that I have a severe impairment of something called my episodic memory. He explained that this means I can't remember events, or autobiographical details, and told me that this is usually due to some kind of neurological problem. Structural, or chemical, he said. Or a hormonal imbalance. It is very rare, and I seem to be affected particularly badly. When I asked him how badly, he told me that some days I can't remember much beyond my early childhood. I thought of this morning, when I had woken with no adult memories at all.

"Some days?" I said. He did not answer, and his silence told me what he really meant:

*Most days.*

There are treatments for persistent amnesia, he said—drugs, hypnosis—but most have already been tried. "But you're uniquely placed to help yourself, Christine," he said, and when I asked him why, he told me it was because I am different from most amnesiacs. "Your pattern of symptoms does not suggest that your memories are lost forever," he said. "You can recall things for hours. Right up until you go to sleep. You can even doze and still remember things when you wake up, as long as you haven't been in a deep sleep. That's very unusual. Most amnesiacs lose their new memories every few seconds . . ."

"And?" I said. He slid a brown notebook across the desk toward me.

"I think it might be worth you documenting your treatment, your feelings, any impressions or memories that come to you. In here."

I reached forward and took the book from him. Its pages were blank.

*So this is my treatment?* I thought. *Keeping a journal? I want to remember things, not just record them.*

He must have sensed my disappointment. "I'm also hoping the act of writing your memories might trigger some more," he said. "The effect might be cumulative."

I was silent for a moment. What choice did I have, really? Keep a journal or stay as I am, forever.

"Okay," I said. "I'll do it."

"Good," he said. "I've written my numbers in the front of the book. Call me if you get confused."

I took the book from him and said I would. There was a long pause, and he said, "We've been doing some good work recently around your early childhood. We've been looking at pictures. Things like that." I said nothing, and he took a photograph out of the file in front of him. "Today I'd like you to take a look at this," he said. "Do you recognize it?"

The photograph was of a house. At first it seemed totally unfamiliar to me, but then I saw the worn step that led to the front door and suddenly knew. It was the house in which I had grown up, the one that, this morning, I had thought I was waking up in. It had looked different, somehow less real, but was unmistakable. I swallowed hard. "It's where I lived as a child," I said.

He nodded and told me that most of my early memories are unaffected. He asked me to describe the inside of the house.

I told him what I remembered: that the front door opened directly into the living room, that there was a small dining room at the back of the house, that visitors were encouraged to use the alley that separated our house from the neighbors and go straight into the kitchen at the back.

"More?" he said. "How about upstairs?"

"Two bedrooms," I said. "One at the front, one at the back. The bath and toilet were through the kitchen, at the very back of the house. They'd been in a separate building until it was joined to the rest of the house with two brick walls and a roof of corrugated plastic."

"More?"

I did not know what he was looking for. "I'm not sure . . ." I said.

He asked me if I remembered any small details.

It came to me then. "My mother kept a jar in the pantry with the word *Sugar* written on it," I said. "She used to keep money in there. She'd hide it on the top shelf. There were jams up there, too. She made her own. We used to pick the berries from a wood that we drove to. I don't remember where. The three of us would walk deep into the forest and pick blackberries. Bags and bags. And then my mother would boil them to make jam."

"Good," he said, nodding. "Excellent!" He was writing in the file in front of him. "What about these?"

He showed me a couple more pictures. One of a woman who, after a few moments, I recognized as my mother. One of me. I told him what I could. When I finished, he put them away. "That's good. You've remembered a lot more of your childhood than usual. I think because of the photographs." He paused. "Next time I'd like to show you a few more."

I said yes. I wondered where he had got these photos, how much he knew of my life that I did not know myself.

"Can I keep it?" I said. "That picture of my old house?"

He smiled. "Of course!" He passed it over and I slipped it between the pages of the notebook.

He drove me back. He'd already explained that Ben does not know we are meeting, but now he told me I ought to think carefully about whether I wanted to tell him about the journal I was to keep. "You might feel inhibited," he said. "Reluctant to write about certain things. I think it very important that you feel able to write whatever you want. Plus Ben might not be happy to find that you've decided to attempt treatment, once again." He paused. "You might have to hide it."

"But how will I know to write in it?" I said. He said nothing. An idea came to me. "Will you remind me?"

He told me he would. "But you'll have to tell me where you're going to hide it," he said. We were pulling up in front of a house. A moment after he stopped the car, I realized it was my own.

"The closet," I said. "I'll put it in the back of the closet." I thought back to what I'd seen this morning, as I'd dressed. "There's a shoebox in there. I'll put it in that."

"Good idea," he said. "But you'll have to write in it tonight. Before you go to sleep. Otherwise tomorrow it'll be just another blank notebook. You won't know what it is."

I said I would, that I understood. I got out of the car.

"Take care, Christine," he said.


Now I sit in bed. Waiting for my husband. I look at the photo of the home in which I grew up. It looks so normal, so mundane. And so familiar.

*How did I get from there to here?* I think. *What happened? What is my history?*

I hear the clock in the living room chime. Midnight. Ben is coming up the stairs. I will hide this book in the shoebox I have found. I will put it in the closet, right where I have told Dr. Nash it will be. Tomorrow, if he calls, I will write more.

# Saturday, November 10

I am writing this at noon. Ben is downstairs, reading. He thinks I am resting but, even though I am tired, I am not. I do not have time. I have to write this down, before I lose it. I have to write my journal.

I look at my watch and note the time. Ben has suggested we go for a walk this afternoon. I have a little over an hour.

This morning I woke not knowing who I am. When my eyes flicked open, I expected to see the hard edges of a bedside table, a yellow lamp. A boxy bureau in the corner of the room and wallpaper with a muted pattern of ferns. I expected to hear my mother downstairs cooking bacon, or my father in the garden whistling as he trims the hedge. I expected the bed I was in to be single, to contain nothing except me and a stuffed rabbit with one torn ear.

I was wrong. *I am in my parents' room,* I thought first, then realized I recognized nothing. The bedroom was completely foreign. I lay back in bed. *Something is wrong,* I thought. *Terribly, terribly wrong.*

By the time I went downstairs, I had seen the photographs around the mirror, read their labels. I knew I was not a child, not even a teenager, and had worked out that the man I could hear cooking breakfast and whistling along to the radio was not my father, or a roommate, or boyfriend, but he was called Ben, and he was my husband.

I hesitated outside the kitchen. I felt scared. I was about to meet him, as if for the first time. What would he be like? Would he look as he did in the pictures? Or were they, too, an inaccurate representation? Would he be older, fatter, balder? How would he sound? How would he move? How well had I married?

A vision came from nowhere. A woman—my mother?—telling me to be careful. *Marry in haste . . .*

I pushed the door open. Ben had his back to me, nudging bacon with a spatula as it spat and sizzled in the pan. He had not heard me come in.

"Ben?" I said. He turned around quickly.

"Christine? Are you okay?"

I did not know how to answer, and so I said, "Yes. I think so."

He smiled then, a look of relief, and I did the same. He looked older than in the pictures upstairs—his face carried more lines, his hair was beginning to gray and receding slightly at the temples— but this had the effect of making him more, rather than less, attractive. His jaw had a strength that suited an older man, his eyes shone mischief. I realized he resembled a slightly older version of my father. *I could have done worse,* I thought. *Much worse.*

"You've seen the pictures?" he said. I nodded. "Don't worry. I'll explain everything. Why don't you go and sit down?" He gestured back toward the hallway. "The dining room's there. I won't be a moment. Here, take this."

He handed me a pepper mill and I went to the dining room. A few minutes later, he followed me with two plates. A pale sliver of bacon swam in grease, an egg and some bread had been fried and sat on the side. As I ate, he explained how I survive my life.

Today is Saturday, he said. He works during the week; he is a teacher. He explained about the phone I have in my bag, the board tacked on the wall in the kitchen. He showed me where we keep our emergency fund—two twenty-pound notes, rolled tightly and tucked behind the clock on the mantelpiece—and the scrapbook in which I can glimpse snatches of my life. He told me that, together, we manage. I was not sure I believed him, yet knew I must.

We finished eating and I helped him tidy away the breakfast things. "We should go for a stroll, later," he said. "If you like?" I said that I would and he looked pleased. "I'm just going to read the paper," he said. "Okay?"

I came upstairs. Once I was alone, my head spun, full and empty at the same time. I felt unable to grasp anything. Nothing seemed real. I looked at the house I was in—the one I now knew was my home—with eyes that had never known it before. For a moment I felt like running. I had to calm myself.

I sat on the edge of the bed in which I had slept. *I should make it,* I thought. *Tidy up. Keep myself busy.* I picked up the pillow to plump it and as I did, something began to buzz.

I wasn't sure what it was. It was low, insistent. A tune, thin and quiet. My bag was at my feet and when I picked it up I realized the buzz seemed to come from there. I remembered Ben telling me about the phone I have.

When I found it the phone was lit up. I stared at it for a long moment. Some part of me, buried deep, or somewhere at the very edge of memory, knew exactly what the call was about. I answered it.

"Hello?" A man's voice. "Christine? Christine, are you there?"

I told him I was.

"It's your doctor. Are you okay? Is Ben around?"

"No," I said. "He's— What's this about?"

He told me his name and that we have been working together for a few weeks. "On your memory," he said, and when I didn't reply, he said, "I want you to trust me. I want you to look in the closet in your bedroom." Another pause then, before he went on, "There's a shoebox on the floor in there. Have a look inside that. There should be a notebook."

I glanced at the closet in the corner of the room.

"How do you know all this?"

"You told me," he said. "I saw you yesterday. We decided you should keep a journal. That's where you told me you'd hide it."

*I don't believe you,* I wanted to say, but it seemed impolite and was not entirely true.

"Will you look?" he said. I told him I would, then he added, "Do it now. Don't say anything to Ben. Do it now."

I did not end the call but went over to the closet. He was right. Inside, on the floor, was a shoebox—a blue box with the word SCHOLL on the ill-fitting lid—and inside that a book wrapped in tissue.

"Do you have it?" said Dr. Nash.

I lifted it out and unwrapped it. It was brown leather and looked expensive.

"Christine?"

"Yes. I have it."

"Good. Have you written in it?"

I opened it to the first page. I saw that I had. *My name is Christine Lucas,* it began. *I am forty-seven. An amnesiac.* I felt nervous, excited. It felt like snooping, but on myself.

"I have," I said.

"Excellent!" he said, and then he said he would phone me tomorrow and we ended the call.

I did not move. There, crouching on the floor by the open closet, the bed still unmade, I began to read.

At first, I felt disappointed. I remembered nothing of what I had written. Not Dr. Nash, nor the offices I claim that he took me to, the puzzles I say that we did. Despite having just heard his voice, I could not picture him, or myself with him. The book read like fiction. But then, tucked between two pages near the back of the book, I found a photograph. The house in which I had grown up, the one in which I expected to find myself when I woke this morning. It was real, this was my evidence. I had seen Dr. Nash, and he had given me this picture, this fragment of my past.

I closed my eyes. Yesterday I had described my old home, the sugar jar in the pantry, picking berries in the woods. Were those memories still there? Could I conjure more? I thought of my mother, my father, willing something else to come. Images formed silently. A dull orange carpet, an olive-green vase. A yellow romper with a pink duck sewn onto the breast and snaps up the middle. A plastic car seat in navy blue and a faded pink potty.

Colors and shapes, but nothing that described a life. Nothing. *I want to see my parents,* I thought, and it was then, for the first time, I realized that somehow I knew that they were dead.

I sighed and sat on the edge of the unmade bed. A pen was tucked between the pages of the journal, and almost without thinking I took it out, intending to write more. I held it, poised over the page, and closed my eyes to concentrate.

It was then that it happened. Whether that realization—that my parents are gone—triggered others, I don't know, but it felt as if my mind woke up from a long, deep sleep. It came alive. But not gradually; this was a jolt. A spark of electricity. Suddenly I was not sitting in a bedroom with a blank page in front of me but somewhere else. Back in the past—a past I thought I had lost— and I could touch and feel and taste everything. I realized I was remembering.

I saw myself coming home, to the house I grew up in. I am thirteen or fourteen, eager to get on with a story I am writing, but I find a note on the kitchen table. *We've had to go out*, it says. *Uncle Ted will pick you up at six.* I get a drink and a sandwich and sit down with my notebook. Mrs. Royce has said that my stories are 'strong' and 'moving'; she thinks I could turn them into a career. But I cannot think what to write, cannot concentrate. I seethe in silent fury. It is their fault. *Where are they? What are they doing? Why aren't I invited?* I screw up the paper and throw it away.

The image vanished, but straight away there was another. Stronger. More real. My father is driving us home. I am sitting in the back of the car, staring at a fixed spot on the windshield. A dead fly. A piece of dirt. I cannot tell. I speak, not sure what I am going to say.

"When were you going to tell me?"

Nobody answers.

"Mum?"

"Christine," says my mother. "Don't."

"Dad? When were you going to tell me?" Silence. "Will you die?" I ask, my eyes still focused on the spot on the window. "Daddy? Will you die?"

He glances over his shoulder and smiles at me. "Of course not, angel. Of course not. Not until I'm an old, old man. With lots and lots of grandchildren!"

I know he's lying.

"We're going to fight this," he says. "I promise."

A gasp. I opened my eyes. The vision had ended, was gone. I

sat in a bedroom, the bedroom I had woken up in this morning, yet for a moment it looked different. Completely flat. Colorless. Devoid of energy, as if I was looking at a photograph that had faded in the sun. It was as if the vibrancy of the past had leached all the life from the present.

I looked down, at the book in my hand. The pen had slipped from my fingers, marking the page with a thin blue line as it slid to the floor. My heart raced in my chest. I had remembered something. Something huge, important. It was not lost. I picked the pen off the floor and started writing this.

I will finish there. When I close my eyes and try to will the image back, I can. Myself. My parents. Driving home. It is still there. Less vivid, as if it has faded with time, but still there. Even so, I am glad I have written it down. I know that eventually it will disappear. At least now it is not completely lost.

Ben must have finished his paper. He has called upstairs, asked if I am ready to go out. I told him I was. I will hide this book in the closet, find a jacket and some boots. I will write more later. If I remember.

*   *   *

That was written hours ago. We have been out all afternoon, but are back at home now. Ben is in the kitchen, cooking fish for our dinner. He has the radio on and the sound of jazz drifts up to the bedroom where I sit, writing this. I did not offer to make our meal—I was too eager to come upstairs and record what I saw this afternoon—but he did not seem to mind.

"You have a nap," he said. "It'll be about forty-five minutes before we eat." I nodded. "I'll call you, when it's ready."

I look at my watch. If I write quickly, I should have time.

———

We left the house just before one o'clock. We did not go far, and parked the car by a low, squat building. It looked abandoned; a single gray pigeon sat in each of the boarded windows; the door was hidden with corrugated iron. "That's the outdoor pool," said Ben as he got out of the car. "It's open in summer, I think. Shall we walk?"

A concrete path curved toward the brow of the hill. We walked in silence, hearing only the occasional shriek of one of the crows that sat on the empty football field or a distant dog's plaintive bark, children's voices, the hum of the city. I thought of my father, of his death and the fact that I had remembered a little of it at least. A lone jogger padded around a running track and I watched her for a while before the path took us beyond a tall hedge and up toward the top of the hill. There I could see life; a little boy flew a kite while his father stood behind him, a girl walked a small dog on a long leash.

"This is Parliament Hill," said Ben. "We come here often."

I said nothing. The city sprawled before us under the low cloud. It seemed peaceful. And smaller than I imagined; I could see all the way across it to low hills in the distance. I could see the thrust of the Telecom tower, St. Paul's dome, the power station at Battersea, shapes I recognized, though dimly and without knowing why. There were other, less familiar, landmarks, too: a glass building shaped like a fat cigar, a giant wheel, way in the distance. Like my own face, the view seemed both alien and somehow familiar.

"I feel I recognize this place," I said.

"Yes," said Ben. "Yes. We've been coming here for a while, though the view changes all the time."

We continued walking. Most of the benches were occupied by people, alone, or in couples. We headed for one just past the top of the hill, and sat down. I smelled ketchup; a half-eaten burger lay under the bench in a cardboard box.

Ben picked it up carefully and put it in one of the garbage bins, then returned to sit next to me. He pointed out some of the landmarks. "That's Canary Wharf," he said, gesturing toward a building that, even at this distance, looked immeasurably tall. "It was built in the early nineties, I think. They're all offices, things like that."

The nineties. It was odd to hear summed up in two words a decade that I could not remember living through. I must have missed so much. So much music, so many films and books, so much news. Disasters, tragedies, wars. Whole countries might have fallen to pieces as I wandered, oblivious, from one day to the next.

So much of my own life, too. So many views I do not recognize, despite seeing them every day.

"Ben?" I said. "Tell me about us."

"Us?" he said. "What do you mean?"

I turned to face him. The wind gusted up the hill, cold against my face. A dog barked somewhere. I wasn't sure how much to say; he knows I remember nothing of him at all.

"I'm sorry," I said. "I don't know anything about me and you. I don't even know how we met, or when we got married, or anything."

He smiled, and shuffled along the bench so that we were touching. He put his arm around my shoulder. I began to recoil, then remembered he is not a stranger but the man I married. "What do you want to know?"

"I don't know," I said. "How did we meet?"

"Well, we were both at university," he said. "You had just started your PhD. Do you remember that?"

I shook my head. "Not really. What did I study?"

"You'd graduated in English," he said, and an image flashed in front of me, quick and sharp. I saw myself in a library and recalled vague ideas of writing a thesis concerning feminist theory and early twentieth-century literature, though really it was just something I could be doing while I worked on novels, something my mother might not understand but would at least see as legitimate. The scene hung for a moment, shimmering, so real I could almost touch it, but then Ben spoke and it vanished.

"I was doing my degree," he said, "in chemistry. I would see you all the time. At the library, in the bar, whatever. I would always be amazed at how beautiful you looked, but I could never bring myself to speak to you."

I laughed. "Really?" I could not imagine myself as intimidating.

"You always seemed so confident. And intense. You would sit for hours, surrounded by books, just reading and taking notes, sipping from cups of coffee or whatever. You looked so beautiful. I never dreamed you would ever be interested in me. But then one day I happened to be sitting next to you in the library, and you accidentally knocked your cup over, and your coffee went all over my books. You were so apologetic, even though it hardly mattered anyway, and we mopped up the coffee and then I insisted on buying you another. You said it ought to be you buying me one, to say sorry, and I said okay then, and we went for coffee. And that was that."

I tried to picture the scene, to remember the two of us, young, in a library, surrounded by soggy papers, laughing. I could not, and felt the hot stab of sadness. I imagined how every couple must love the story of how they met—who first spoke to whom, what was said—yet I have no recollection of ours. The wind whipped the tail of the little boy's kite; a sound like a death rattle.

"What happened then?" I said.

"Well, we dated. The usual, you know? I finished my degree, and you finished your PhD, and then we got married."

"How? Who asked who?"

"Oh," he said. "I asked you."

"Where? Tell me how it happened."

"We were totally in love," he said. He looked away, into the distance. "We spent all our time together. You shared a house, but you were hardly there at all. Most of your time you would spend with me. It made sense for us to live together, to get married. So, one Valentine's Day, I bought you a bar of soap. Expensive soap, the kind you really liked, and I took off the cellophane wrapper and I pressed the engagement ring into the soap, and then I wrapped it back up and gave it to you. As you were getting ready that evening, you found it, and you said yes."

I smiled to myself. It sounded messy, a ring caked in soap and fraught with the possibility that I might not have used the bar, or found the ring, for weeks. But still, it was not an unromantic story.

"Who did I share a house with?" I said.

"Oh," he said, "I don't really remember. A friend. Anyway, we got married the following year. In a church in Manchester, near where your mother lived. It was a lovely day. I was training to be a teacher by then, so we didn't have much money, but it was still lovely. The sun shone, everyone was happy. And then we went for our honeymoon. To Italy. The lakes. It was wonderful."

I tried to picture the church, my dress, the view from a hotel room. Nothing would come.

"I don't remember any of it," I said. "I'm sorry."

He looked away, turning his head so that I couldn't see his face. "It doesn't matter. I understand."

"There aren't many photographs," I said. "In the scrapbook, I mean. There aren't any photos of us from our wedding."

"We had a fire," he said. "In the last place we were living."

"A fire?"

"Yes," he said. "Our house pretty much burned down. We lost a lot of things."

I sighed. It did not seem fair, to have lost both my memories and my souvenirs of the past.

"What happened then?"

"Then?"

"Yes," I said. "What happened? After the marriage, the honeymoon?"

"We moved in together. We were very happy."

"And then?"

He sighed and said nothing. *That can't be it,* I thought. *That can't describe my whole life. That can't be all I amounted to. A wedding, a honeymoon, a marriage.* But what else was I expecting? What else could there have been?

The answer came suddenly. Children. Babies. I realized with a shudder that that was what seemed to be missing from my life, from our home. There were no pictures on the mantelpiece of a son or daughter—clutching a degree certificate, white-water rafting, even just posing, bored, for the camera—and none of grandchildren either. I had not had a baby.

I felt the slap of disappointment. The unsatisfied desire was burned into my subconscious. Even though I had woken up not even knowing how old I was, some part of me must have known I had wanted to have a child.

Suddenly I heard my own mother, describing the biological clock as if it were a bomb. "Get busy achieving all the things in life you want to achieve," she said, "because one day you'll be fine and the next . . ."

I knew what she meant: Boom! My ambitions would disappear and all I would want to do would be to have children. "It's what happened to me," she said. "It'll happen to you. It happens to everyone."

But it hadn't, I suppose. Or something else had happened instead. I looked at my husband.

"Ben?" I said. "What then?"

He looked at me and squeezed my hand.

"Then you lost your memory," he said.

My memory. It all came back to that, in the end. Always.

I looked out across the city. The sun hung low in the sky, shining weakly through the clouds, casting long shadows on the grass. I realized that it would be dark soon. The sun would set, finally, the moon would rise in the sky. Another day would end. Another lost day.

"We never had children," I said. It was not a question.

He did not answer but turned to look at me. He held my hands in his, rubbing them as if against the cold.

"No," he said. "No. We didn't."

Sadness etched his face. For himself, or me? I could not tell. I let him rub my hands, hold my fingers between his. I realized that, even despite the confusion, I felt safe there, with this man. I could see that he was kind, and thoughtful, and patient. No matter how awful my situation, it could be so much worse.

"Why?" I said.

He said nothing. He looked at me, the expression on his face one of pain. Pain and disappointment.

"How did it happen, Ben?" I said. "How did I get to be like this?"

I felt him tense. "You're sure you want to know?" he said.

I fixed my eyes on a little girl riding a tricycle in the distance. I knew this couldn't be the first time I have asked him this question, the first time he has had to explain these things to me. Possibly I ask him every day.

"Yes," I said. I realized this time was different. This time I would write down what he told me.

He took a deep breath. "It was December. Icy. You'd been out for the day, at work. You were on your way home, a short walk. There were no witnesses. We don't know if you were crossing the street at the time or if the car that hit you mounted the sidewalk, but either way you must have gone over the hood. You were very badly injured. Both legs were broken. An arm and your collarbone."

He stopped talking. I could hear the low beat of the city. Traffic, a plane overhead, the murmur of the wind in the trees. Ben squeezed my hand.

"They said your head must have hit the ground first, which is why you lost your memory."

I closed my eyes. I could remember nothing of the accident, and so did not feel angry or even upset. I was filled instead with a kind of quiet regret. An emptiness. A ripple across the surface of the lake of memory.

He squeezed my hand, and I put mine over his, feeling the cold, hard band of his wedding ring. "You were lucky to survive," he said.

I felt myself go cold. "What happened to the driver?"

"He didn't stop. It was a hit-and-run. We don't know who hit you."

"But who would do that?" I said. "Who would run someone over and then just drive away?"

He said nothing. I didn't know what I had expected. I thought of what I had read of my meeting with Dr. Nash. A neurological problem, he had told me. Structural, or chemical. A hormonal imbalance. I assumed he had meant an illness. Something that had just happened, had come out of nowhere. *One of those things.*

But this seemed worse; it was done to me by someone else, it had been avoidable. If I had taken a different route home that evening—or if the driver of the car that hit me had done so—I would have still been normal. I might even have been a grandmother by now, just.

"Why?" I said. "Why?"

It was not a question Ben could answer, and so he said nothing. We sat in silence for a while, our hands locked together. It grew dark. The city was bright, the buildings lit. *It will be winter soon,* I thought. *We will soon be halfway through November. December will follow, and then Christmas.* I couldn't imagine how I would get from here to there. I couldn't imagine living through a whole string of identical days.

"Shall we go?" said Ben. "Back home?"

I didn't answer him. "Where was I?" I said. "The day that I was hit by the car. What had I been doing?"

"You were on your way home from work," he said.

"What job, though? What was I doing?"

"Oh," he said. "You had a temporary job as a secretary—well, personal assistant, really—at some lawyer's, I think it was."

"But why—" I began.

"You needed to work so that we could pay the mortgage," he said. "It was tough, for a while."

That wasn't what I meant, though. What I wanted to say was, *You told me I had a PhD. Why had I settled for that?*

"But why was I working as a secretary?" I said.

"It was the only job you could get. Times were hard."

I remembered the feeling I had earlier. "Was I writing?" I said. "Books?"

He shook his head. "No."

So it was a transitory ambition, then. Or maybe I had tried and failed. As I turned to ask him, the clouds lit up and, a moment later, there was a loud bang. Startled, I looked out; sparks in the distant sky, raining down on the city below.

"What was that?" I said.

"A firework," said Ben. "It was Guy Fawkes Night this week."

A moment later, another firework lit the sky, another loud bang.

"It looks like there'll be a display," he said. "Shall we watch?"

I nodded. It could do no harm, and though part of me wanted to rush home to my journal, to write down what Ben had told me, another part of me wanted to stay, hoping he might tell me more. "Yes," I said. "Let's."

He grinned and put his arm around my shoulders. The sky was dark for a moment, and then there was a crackle and fizz, and a thin whistle as a tiny spark shot high. It hung for a slow moment before exploding in orange brilliance with an echoing bang. It was beautiful.

"Usually we go to see the fireworks," said Ben. "One of the big organized displays. But I forgot it was tonight." He nuzzled my neck with his chin. "Is this okay?"

"Yes," I said. I looked out over the city, at the explosions of color in the air above it, at the screeching lights. "This is fine. This way we get to see all the shows."

He sighed. Our breath misted in the air in front of us, each mingled with that of the other, and we sat in silence, watching the sky turn to color and light. The smoke rose from the gardens of the city, lit with violence—with red and orange, blue and purple— and the night air turned smoky, shot through with a flinty smell, dry and metallic. I licked my lips, tasted sulfur, and as I did so, another memory struck.

It was needle-sharp. The sounds were too loud, the colors too bright. I felt not like an observer but instead as though I was still in the middle of it. I had the sensation I was falling backward. I gripped Ben's hand.

I saw myself with a woman. She has red hair, and we are standing on a rooftop, watching fireworks. I can hear the rhythmic throb of music that plays in the room beneath our feet, and a cold wind blows, sending acrid smoke floating over us. Even though I am wearing only a thin dress, I feel warm, buzzing with alcohol and the joint that I am still holding between my fingers. I feel gravel under my feet and remember I have discarded my shoes and left them in this girl's bedroom downstairs. I look across at her as she turns to face me and feel alive, dizzily happy.

"Chrissy," she says, taking the joint. "Fancy a tab?"

I don't know what she means, and tell her.

She laughs. "You know!" she says. "A tab. A trip. Acid. I'm pretty sure Nige has brought some. He told me he would."

"I'm not sure," I say.

"C'mon! It'd be fun!"

I laugh and take the joint back, inhaling a lungful as if to prove that I am not boring. We have promised ourselves that we will never be boring.

"I don't think so," I say. "It's not my scene. I think I just want to stick to this. And beer. Okay?"

"I suppose so," she says, looking back over the railing. I can tell she is disappointed, though not angry with me, and wonder whether she will do it anyway. Without me.

I doubt it. I have never had a friend like her before. One who knows everything about me, whom I trust, sometimes even more than I trust myself. I look at her now, her red hair wind-whipped, the end of the joint glowing in the dark. Is she happy with the way her life is turning out? Or is it too early to say?

"Look at that!" she says, pointing to where a Roman candle has exploded, throwing the trees into silhouette in front of its red glare. "Fucking beautiful, isn't it?"

I laugh, agreeing with her, and then we stand in silence for a few more minutes, passing the joint between us. Eventually she offers me what is left of the soggy roach and, when I refuse, grinds it into the asphalt with her booted foot.

"We should go downstairs," she says, grabbing my arm. "There's someone I want you to meet."

"Not again!" I say, but I go anyway. We step over a couple kissing on the stairs. "It's not going to be another one of those pricks from your course, is it?"

"Fuck off!" she says, trotting down the stairs. "I thought you'd love Alan!"

"I did!" I said. "Right up until the moment he told me he was in love with a guy called Kristian."

"Yes, well." She laughs. "How was I supposed to know that Alan would decide to choose you to come out to? This one's different. You'll love him. I know it. Just say hello. There's no pressure."

"Okay," I say. I push the door open and we go into the party.

The room is large, with concrete walls and unshaded lightbulbs hanging from the ceiling. We make our way to the kitchen area and get ourselves a beer, then find a spot over by the window. "So where's this guy, then?" I say, but she does not hear me. I feel the buzz of the alcohol and the weed and begin to dance. The room is full of people, dressed mostly in black. *Fucking art students,* I think.

Someone comes over and stands in front of us. I recognize him. Keith. We've met before, at a different party, where we ended up kissing in one of the bedrooms. Now, though, he is talking to my friend, pointing to one of her paintings, which hangs on the wall in the living room. I wonder whether he's decided to ignore me, or cannot remember having met me before. Either way, I think, he's a jerk. I finish my beer.

"Want another?" I say.

"Yeah," says my friend. "Want to get them while I deal with Keith? And then I'll introduce you to that guy I mentioned. Okay?"

I laugh. "Okay. Whatever." I wander off, into the kitchen.

A voice, then. Loud in my ear. "Christine! Chris! Are you okay?" I felt confused; the voice sounded familiar. I opened my eyes. With a start, I realized I was outside, in the night air, on Parliament Hill, with Ben calling my name and fireworks in front of me turning the sky the color of blood. "You had your eyes closed," he said. "What's the matter? What's wrong?"

"Nothing," I said. My head spun; I could hardly breathe. I turned away from my husband, pretending to watch the rest of the display. "I'm sorry. Nothing. I'm fine. I'm fine."

"You're shivering," he said. "Are you cold? Do you want to go home?"

I realized I was. I did. I wanted to record what I had just seen.

"Yes," I said. "Do you mind?"

On the way home, I thought back to the vision I had seen as we watched the fireworks. It had shocked me with its clarity, its hard edges. It had caught me, sucked me into it as if I were living it

again. I felt everything, tasted everything. The cool air and the
fizz of the beer. The burn of the weed at the back of my throat.
Keith's saliva, warm on my tongue. It felt real, almost more real
than the life I had opened my eyes to when it vanished.

I didn't know exactly when it was from. University, I supposed,
or just after. The party I had seen myself at was the kind I imagined a student would enjoy. It did not have the feel of responsibil-
ity. It was carefree. Light.

And, though I could not remember her name, this woman was
important to me. My best friend. *Forever,* I had thought, and even
though I didn't know who she was, I had felt a sense of security
with her, of safety.

I wondered briefly if we might still be close, and tried to talk
to Ben about it as we drove. He was quiet—not unhappy, but dis-
tracted. For a moment I considered telling him everything about
the vision, but instead I asked him who my friends were, when we
met.

"You had lots of friends," he said. "You were very popular."

"Did I have a best friend? Someone special?"

He glanced over at me then. "No," he said. "I don't think so.
Not particularly."

I wondered why I could not remember this woman's name, yet
had recalled Keith and Alan.

"You're sure?" I said.

"Yes," he said. "I'm sure." He turned back to face the road.
It began to rain. Lights from the shops, and from the neon signs
above them, were reflected in the road. *There is so much I want to ask
him,* I thought, but I said nothing and, after a few more minutes,
it was too late. We were home, and he had begun cooking. It was
too late.

\* \* \*

As soon as I had finished writing that, Ben called me down to our dinner. He had set the table and poured glasses of white wine, but I was not hungry and the fish was dry. I left most of my meal. Then—since Ben had cooked—I offered to wash up. I carried the plates into the kitchen and ran hot water into the sink, all the time hoping that later I would be able to make an excuse and come upstairs to read my journal and perhaps write some more. But I could not—to spend so much time alone in our room would arouse suspicion—and so we spent the evening in front of the television.

I could not relax. I thought of my journal and watched the hands of the clock on the mantelpiece creep from nine to ten to ten thirty. Finally, as they approached eleven, I realized I would have no more time tonight, and said, "I think I'm going to turn in. It's been a long day."

He smiled, tilting his head. "Okay darling," he said. "I'll be up in a moment."

I nodded, and said okay, but as I left the room, I felt a creeping dread. *This man is my husband,* I told myself, *I am married to him,* yet still I felt somehow as if going to bed with him was wrong. I could not remember ever having done so before, and did not know what to expect.

In the bathroom, I used the toilet and brushed my teeth without looking at the mirror or the photos arranged around it. I went into the bedroom and found my nightie folded on my pillow and began to get undressed. I wanted to be ready before he came in, to be under the covers. For a moment, I had the absurd idea that I could pretend to be asleep.

I took off my pullover and looked at myself in the mirror. I saw the cream bra I had put on this morning and, as I did so, had a fleeting vision of myself as a child, asking my mother why she wore one when I did not, and her telling me that one day I would.

And now that day was here, and it had not come gradually but instantly. Here, even more obviously than the lines on my face and wrinkles on my hands, was the fact that I was not a girl anymore but a woman. Here, in the soft plumpness of my breasts.

I pulled the nightie over my head and flattened it down. I reached underneath it and unhooked my bra, feeling the weight of my chest as I did so, and then unzipped my trousers and stepped out of them. I did not want to examine my body further, not tonight, and so, once I had peeled off the tights and panties I had put on this morning, I slipped between the covers and, closing my eyes, turned onto my side.

I heard the clock downstairs chime, then, a moment later, Ben came into the room. I did not move but listened to him undress, then felt the sag of the bed as he sat on its edge. He was still for a moment, and then I felt his hand, heavy on my hip.

"Christine?" he said, half-whispering. "Are you awake?" I murmured that I was. "You remembered a friend today?" he said. I opened my eyes and turned onto my back. I could see the broad expanse of his bare back, the fine hair that was scattered over his shoulders.

"Yes," I said. He turned to me.

"What did you remember?"

I told him, though only vaguely. "A party," I said. "We were both students, I think."

He stood up then and turned to get into bed. I saw that he was naked. His penis swung from its dark nest of hair and I had to suppress the urge to giggle. I could not remember ever seeing male genitals before, not even in books, yet they were not unfamiliar to me. I wondered how much of them I knew, what experiences I might have had. Almost involuntarily, I looked away.

"You've remembered that party before," he said as he pulled

back the bedclothes. "It comes to you fairly often, I think. You have certain memories that seem to crop up regularly."

I sighed. *So it's nothing new,* he seemed to be saying. *Nothing to get excited about.* He lay beside me and pulled the covers over us both. He did not turn out the light.

"Do I remember things often?" I said.

"Yes. A few things. Most days."

"The same things?"

He turned to face me, propping himself on his elbow. "Sometimes," he said. "Usually. Yes. It's rare there's a surprise."

I looked away from his face and up to the ceiling. "Do I ever remember you?"

He turned to me. "No," he said. He took my hand. Squeezed it. "But that's okay. I love you. It's okay."

"I must be a dreadful burden to you," I said.

He moved his hand and began to stroke my arm. There was a crackle of static. I flinched. "No," he said. "Not at all. I love you."

He twisted his body into mine then, and kissed my lips.

I closed my eyes. Confused. Did he want to have sex? To me he was a stranger; though intellectually I knew we got into bed together every night, had done so since we were married, still my body had known him for less than a day.

"I'm very tired, Ben," I said.

He lowered his voice, and began to murmur. "I know, my darling," he said. He kissed me, softly, on the cheek, my lips, my eyes. "I know." His hand moved lower, beneath the covers, and I felt a wave of anxiety begin to build within me, almost panic.

"Ben," I said. "I'm sorry." I grabbed his hand and stopped its descent. I resisted the urge to fling it away as if it were revolting, and stroked it instead. "I'm tired," I said. "Not tonight. Okay?"

He said nothing, but withdrew his hand and lay on his back.

Disappointment came off him in waves. I did not know what to say. Some part of me thought I should apologize, but some larger part told me I had done nothing wrong. And so we lay in silence, in bed but not touching, and I wondered how often this happens. How often he comes to bed and craves sex, whether I ever want it myself, or even feel able to give it to him, and if this is always what happens, this awkward silence, if I do not.

"Good night, darling," he said, after a few more minutes, and the tension lifted. I waited until he was snoring softly and slipped out of bed and here, in the spare room, sat down to write this.

I would like so much to remember him. Just once.

# Monday, November 12

The clock has just chimed four; it is beginning to get dark. Ben will not be home just yet but, as I sit and write, I listen for his car. The shoebox sits on the floor next to my feet, the tissue paper in which this journal was wrapped spills out of it. If he comes in, I will put my book in the closet and tell him I have been resting. It is dishonest, but not terribly so, and there is nothing wrong with wanting to keep the contents of my journal a secret. I must write down what I have seen. What I have learned. But that doesn't mean I want someone—anyone—to read it.

I saw Dr. Nash today. We were sitting opposite each other, on either side of his desk. Behind him was a filing cabinet, on top of which sat a plastic model of the brain, sliced down the middle, parted like an orange. He asked me how I'd been getting on.

"Okay," I said. "I suppose." It was a difficult question to answer—the few hours since I had woken that morning were the only ones I could clearly remember. I met my husband, as if for the first time though I knew it was not, was called by my doctor who told me about my journal. Then, after lunch, he picked me up and drove me here to his office.

"I wrote in my journal," I said. "After you called. On Saturday."

He seemed pleased. "Do you think it helped at all?"

"I think so," I said. I told him about the memories I'd had. The vision of the woman at the party, of learning of my father's illness. He made notes as I spoke.

"Do you still remember those things now?" he said. "Or did you when you woke up this morning?"

I hesitated. The truth was I did not. Or only some of it, at least. This morning I had read my entry for Saturday—of the breakfast I shared with my husband, of the trip to Parliament Hill. It had felt as unreal as fiction, nothing to do with me, and I found myself reading and rereading the same section, over and over, trying to cement it in my mind, to fix it. It took me more than an hour.

I read of the things Ben had told me, of how we met and married, of how we lived, and I felt nothing. Yet other things stayed with me. The woman, for example. My friend. I could not recall specifics—the fireworks party, being on the roof with her, meeting a man called Keith—but her memory still existed within me, and this morning, as I read and reread my entry for Saturday, more details had come. The vibrant red of her hair, the black clothes that she preferred, the studded belt, the scarlet lipstick, the way that she used to make smoking look as though it was the coolest thing in the world. I could not remember her name but now recalled the night we met, in a room that was shrouded in a thick fug of cigarette smoke and alive with the whistles and bangs of pinball machines and a tinny jukebox. She had given me a light when I asked her for one, then introduced herself and suggested I join her and her friends. We drank vodka and lager and, later, she held my hair out of the toilet bowl as I vomited most of it back up. "I guess we're definitely friends now!" she said, laughing, as I pulled myself back to my feet. "I wouldn't do that for just anyone, you know?"

I thanked her and, for no reason I knew, and as if it explained what I had just done, told her my father was dead. "Fuck . . ." she said, and, in what must have been the first of her many switches from drunken stupidity to compassionate efficiency, she took me back to her room and we ate crackers and drank black coffee, all the while listening to records and talking about our lives, until it began to get light.

She had paintings propped up against the wall and at the end of the bed, and sketchbooks littered the room. "You're an artist?" I said, and she nodded. "It's why I'm here at university," she said. I remembered her telling me she was studying fine art. "I'll end up a teacher, of course, but in the meantime one has to dream. Yes?" I laughed. "What about you? What are you studying?" I told her. English. "Ah!" she said. "So do you want to write novels or teach, then?" She laughed, not unkindly, but I didn't mention the story I had worked on in my room before coming down. "Dunno," I said, instead, "I guess I'm the same as you." She laughed again, and said, "Well, here's to us!" and as we toasted each other with coffee, I felt, for the first time in months, that things might finally be all right.

I remembered all this. It exhausted me, this effort of will to search the void of my memory, trying to find any tiny detail that might trigger a recollection. But my memories of my life with my husband? They were gone. Reading those words had not stirred even the smallest residue of memory. It was as if not only had the trip to Parliament Hill not happened, but neither had the things he told me there.

"I remember some things," I said to Dr. Nash. "Things from when I was younger, things that I remembered yesterday. They're still there. And I can remember more details, too. But I can't remember what we did yesterday at all. Or on Saturday. I can try to construct a picture of the scene I described in my journal, but I know it isn't a memory. I know I'm just imagining it."

He nodded. "Is there anything you remember from Saturday? Any small detail that you wrote down that you can still recall? The evening, for example?"

I thought of what I had written about going to bed. I realized I felt guilty. Guilty that, despite his kindness, I had not been able to give myself to my husband. "No," I lied. "Nothing."

I wondered what he might have done differently for me to want to take him in my arms, to let him love me? Flowers? Chocolates? Does he need to make romantic overtures every time he'd like to have sex, as if it were the first time? I realized how closed the avenues of seduction are to him. He cannot even play the first song we danced to at our wedding, or re-create the meal we enjoyed the first time we ate out together, because I don't remember what they are. And in any case, I am his wife; he should not have to seduce me, as if we have just met, every time he wants us to have sex.

But is there ever a time when I let him make love to me, or perhaps, even, want to make love to him? Do I ever wake and know enough for desire to exist, unforced?

"I don't even remember Ben," I said. "I had no idea who he was this morning."

He nodded. "You'd like to?"

I almost laughed. "Of course!" I said. "I want to remember my past. I want to know who I am. Who I married. It's all part of the same thing—"

"Of course," he said. He paused, then leaned his elbows on the desk and clasped his hands in front of his face, as if thinking carefully about what to say, or how to say it. "What you've told me is encouraging. It suggests that the memories aren't lost completely. The problem is not one of storage but of access."

I thought for a moment, then said, "You mean my memories are there, I just can't get to them?"

He smiled. "If you like," he said. "Yes."

I felt frustrated. Eager. "So how do I remember more?"

He leaned back and looked in the file in front of him. "Last week," he said, "on the day I gave you your journal. Did you write that I showed you a picture of your childhood home? I gave it to you, I think."

"Yes," I said. "I did."

"You seemed to remember much more, having seen that photo, than when I asked you about the place where you used to live without showing you a picture of it first." He paused. "Which, again, isn't surprising. But I'd like to see what happens if I show you pictures from the period you definitely don't remember. I want to see if anything comes back to you then."

I was hesitant, unsure of where this avenue might lead, but certain it was a road I had no choice but to take.

"Okay," I said.

"Good! We'll look at just one picture today." He took a photograph from the back of the file and then walked around the desk to sit next to me. "Before we look, do you remember anything of your wedding?"

I already knew there was nothing there; as far as I was concerned, my marriage to the man I had woken up with this morning had simply not happened.

"No," I said. "Nothing."

"You're sure?"

I nodded. "Yes."

He put the photograph on the desk in front of me. "You got married here," he said, tapping it. It was of a church. Small, with a low roof and a tiny spire. Totally unfamiliar.

"Anything?"

I closed my eyes and tried to empty my mind. A vision of water. My friend. A tiled floor, black and white. Nothing else.

"No. I don't remember ever having seen it before."

He looked disappointed. "You're sure?"

I closed my eyes again. Blackness. I tried to think of my wedding day, tried to imagine Ben, me, in a suit and a wedding dress, standing on the grass in front of the church, but nothing came. No memory. Sadness rose in me. Like any bride, I must have spent weeks planning my wedding, choosing my dress and waiting anxiously for the alterations, booking a hairdresser, thinking about my makeup. I imagined myself agonizing over the menu, choosing the hymns, selecting the flowers, all the time hoping that the day would live up to my impossible expectations. And now I have no way of knowing whether it did. It has all been taken from me, every trace erased. Everything apart from the man I married.

"No," I said. "There's nothing."

He put the photograph away. "According to the notes taken during your initial treatment, you were married in Manchester," he said. "The church is called Saint Mark's. That was a recent photograph—it's the only one I could get—but I imagine it looks pretty much the same now as it did then."

"There are no photographs of our wedding," I said. It was both a question and a statement.

"No. They were lost. In a fire at your home, apparently."

I nodded. Hearing him say it cemented it somehow, made it seem more real. It was almost as if the fact he was a doctor gave his words an authority that Ben's did not have.

"When did I get married?" I said.

"It would have been in the mid-eighties."

"Before my accident——" I said.

Dr. Nash looked uncomfortable. I wondered if I had ever spoken to him about the accident that left me with no memory.

"You know about what caused your amnesia?" he said.

"Yes," I said. "I spoke to Ben. The other day. He told me everything. I wrote it in my journal."

He nodded. "How do you feel about it?"

"I'm not sure," I said. The truth was that I had no memory of the accident, and so it did not seem real. All I had were its effects. The way it had left me. "I feel like I ought to hate the person that did this to me," I said. "Especially as they've never been caught, never been punished for leaving me like this. For ruining my life. But the odd thing is I don't, really. I can't. I can't imagine them, or picture what they look like. It's like they don't even exist."

He looked disappointed. "Is that what you think?" he said. "That your life is ruined?"

"Yes," I said after a few moments. "Yes. That's what I think." He was silent. "Isn't it?"

I don't know what I expected him to do, or say. I suppose part of me wanted him to tell me how wrong I am, to try and convince me that my life is worth living. But he didn't. He just looked straight at me. I noticed how striking his eyes were. Blue, flecked with gray.

"I'm sorry, Christine," he said. "I'm sorry. But I'm doing everything I can, and I think I can help you. I really do. You have to believe that."

"I do," I said. "I do."

He put his hand on top of mine, where it lay on the desk between us. It felt heavy. Warm. He squeezed my fingers, and for a second I felt embarrassed, for him, and also for me, but then I looked into his face, at the expression of sadness I saw there, and realized that his action was that of a young man comforting an older woman. Nothing more.

"I'm sorry," I said. "I need to use the bathroom."

When I returned, he had poured coffee and we sat on opposite sides of the desk, sipping at our drinks. He seemed reluctant to make eye contact, instead leafing through the papers on his desk, shuffling awkwardly. At first, I thought he was embarrassed about squeezing my hand, but then he looked up and said, "Christine. I wanted to ask you something. Two things, really." I nodded. "First, I've decided to write up your case. It's pretty unusual in the field, and I think it would be really beneficial to get the details out there in the wider scientific community. Do you mind?"

I looked at the journals, stacked in haphazard piles on the shelves around the office. Is this how he intended to further his career, or make it more secure? *Is that why I am here?* For a moment, I considered telling him I'd rather he didn't use my story, but in the end I simply shook my head and said, "No. It's fine."

He smiled. "Good. Thank you. Now, I have a question. More of a sort of idea, really. Something I'd like to try. Would you mind?"

"What's your idea?" I said. I felt nervous but relieved he was finally about to tell me what was on his mind.

"Well," he said. "According to your files, after you and Ben were married, you continued to live together in the house in East London that you shared." He paused. Out of nowhere came a voice that must have been my mother's. *Living in sin*—a tut, a shake of her head that said everything. "And then, after a year or so, you moved to another house. You stayed there pretty much until you were hospitalized." He paused. "It's quite near where you live now." I began to understand what he might be suggesting. "I thought we could leave now and visit it on the way home. What do you think?"

What did I think? I did not know. It was an almost unanswerable question. I knew it was a sensible thing to do, that it might help me in some undefinable way that neither of us could yet understand, but still I was reluctant. It was as if my past suddenly felt dangerous. A place it might be unwise to visit.

"I'm not sure," I said.

"You lived there for a number of years," he said.

"I know, but—"

"We can just go and look at it. We don't have to go inside."

"Go inside?" I said. "How—?"

"Yes," he said. "I've written to the couple who live there now. We've spoken on the phone. They said that if it might help they'd be more than happy to let you have a look around."

I was surprised by this. "Really?" I said.

He looked slightly away—quickly, but enough for it to register as embarrassment. I wondered what he might be hiding. "Yes," he said, and then, "I don't go to this much trouble for all my patients." I said nothing. He smiled. "I really think it might help, Christine."

What else could I do?

On the way there I had intended to write in my journal, but the journey was not long and I had barely finished reading the last entry when we parked outside a house. I closed the book and looked up. The house was similar to the one we'd left that morning—the one that I had to remind myself I live in now—with its red brick and painted woodwork and the same bay window and well-tended garden. If anything, this house looked bigger, and a window in the roof suggested a loft conversion that we did not have. I found it hard to understand why we'd left this place to move what must be only a couple of miles away to an almost identical house. After a moment, I realized: memories. Memories of a better time, before my accident, when we were happy, living a normal life. Ben would have had them, even if I did not.

I felt suddenly positive that the house would reveal things to me. Reveal my past.

"I want to go in," I said.

I pause, there. I want to write the rest, but it is important—too important to be rushed—and Ben will be home very soon. He is late already; the sky is dark, the street echoing to the sounds of slammed doors as people arrive home from work. Cars slow outside the house—soon one of them will be Ben's. It is better if I finish now, if I put my book away, hide it safely in the closet.

I will continue later.

\* \* \*

I was replacing the lid of the shoebox when I heard Ben's key in the lock. He called out when he came into the house, and I told him I would be down in a moment. Though I have no reason to pretend I have not been looking in the closet, I closed its door softly, then went to see my husband.

The evening was fractured. My journal called to me. As we ate, I wondered if I could write in it before washing up; as I washed up, I wondered if I should feign a headache and write when I finished. But then, after I had tidied in the kitchen, Ben said he had a little work to do and went into his office. I sighed, relieved, and told him I would go to bed.

That's where I am now. I can hear Ben—the tap tap tap of his keyboard—and I admit the sound is comforting. I have read what

I wrote before Ben got home and can now once again picture my-self as I was this afternoon: sitting outside a house in which I once lived. I can take up my story.

It happened in the kitchen.

A woman—Amanda—had answered the doorbell's insistent buzz, greeting Dr. Nash with a handshake and me with a look that hovered between pity and fascination. "You must be Chris-tine," she'd said, tilting her head to one side and holding out her manicured hand. "Do come in!"

She closed the door behind us. She was wearing a cream blouse, gold jewelry. She introduced herself and said, "You stay as long as you like, okay? As long as you need. Yes?"

I nodded and looked around. We were standing in a bright, carpeted hallway. The sun streamed through the glass panels in the window to pick out a vase of red tulips that sat on a side table. The silence was long and uncomfortable. "It's a lovely house," Amanda said, eventually, and for a moment I felt as if Dr. Nash and I were prospective purchasers and she a real estate agent keen to negotiate a deal. "We bought it about ten years ago. We just adore it. It's so bright. Do you want to go into the living room?"

We followed her into the lounge. The room was sparse, taste-ful. I felt nothing, not even a dull sense of familiarity; it could have been any room in any house in any city.

"Thank you so much for letting us look around," said Dr. Nash.

"Oh, nonsense!" she said, with a peculiar snort. I imagined her riding horses or arranging flowers.

"Have you done a lot of decorating since you were here?" he said.

"Oh, some," she said. "Bits and pieces."

I looked around at the sanded floorboards and white walls, at the cream sofa, the modern art prints that hung on the wall. I thought of the house I had left this morning; it could not have looked more different.

"Do you remember how it looked when you moved in?" said Dr. Nash.

She sighed. "Only vaguely, I'm afraid. It was carpeted. A kind of biscuit color, I think. And there was wallpaper. Sort of striped, if I remember." I tried to picture the room as she'd described it. Nothing came. "There was a fireplace we had removed, too. I wish we hadn't, now. It was an original feature."

"Christine?" said Dr. Nash. "Anything?" When I shook my head he turned to Amanda. "Do you think we could look around the rest of the house?"

We went upstairs. There were two bedrooms. "Giles works from home a good deal," she said as we went in the one at the front of the house. It was dominated by a desk, filing cabinets, and books. "I think the previous owners must have used this as their bedroom." She looked at me, but I said nothing. "It's a little bigger than the other room, but Giles can't sleep in here. Because of the traffic." There was a pause. "He's an architect." Again, I said nothing. "It's quite a coincidence," she continued, "because the man we bought the house off was also an architect. We met him when we came by to look at the place. They got on quite well. I think we knocked him down by a few thousand just because of the connection." Another pause. I wondered if she was expecting to be congratulated. "Giles is setting up his own practice."

*An architect*, I thought. *Not a teacher, like Ben*. These can't have been the people that he had sold the house to. I tried to imagine the room with a bed instead of the glass-topped desk, carpet and wallpaper replacing the stripped boards and white walls.

Dr. Nash turned to face me. "Anything?"

I shook my head. "No. Nothing. I don't remember anything."

We looked in the other bedroom, the bathroom. Nothing came to me, and so we went downstairs, into the kitchen. "Would you like a cup of tea?" said Amanda. "It's really not a problem. It's made already."

"No, thank you," I said. The room was harsh. Hard-edged. The appliances were chrome and white, and the countertop looked like poured concrete. A bowl of limes provided the only color. "I think we ought to leave soon," I said.

"Of course," said Amanda. Her breezy efficiency seemed to have vanished, replaced by a look of disappointment. I felt guilty; she had obviously hoped that a visit to her home would be the miracle that cured me. "Could I have a glass of water?" I said.

She brightened immediately. "Of course!" she said. "Let me get you one!" She handed me a glass and it was then, as I took it from her, that I saw it.

Amanda and Dr. Nash had both disappeared. I was alone. On the countertop, I saw an uncooked fish, wet and glistening, lying on an oval plate. I heard a voice. A man's voice. It was Ben's voice, I thought, but younger, somehow. "White wine?" it said. "Or red?"—and I turned and saw him coming into a kitchen. It was the same kitchen—the one I was standing in with Dr. Nash and Amanda—but it had different-colored paint on the walls. Ben was holding a bottle of wine in each hand, and it was the same Ben but slimmer, with less gray in his hair, and he had a mustache. He was naked, and his penis was semierect, bobbing comically as he walked. His skin was smooth, taut over the muscles of his arms and chest, and I felt the sharp tug of lust. I saw myself gasp, but I was laughing.

"White, I think?" he said, and he laughed with me, and then he put both bottles down on the table and came over to where

I stood. His arms encircled me, and then I was closing my eyes, and my mouth opened, as if involuntarily, and I was kissing him, and he me, and I could feel his penis pressing into my crotch and my hand moving toward it. And, even as I was kissing him, I was thinking, *I must remember this, how this feels. I must put this in my book. This is what I want to write.*

I fell into him then, pressing my body against his, and his hands began to tear at my dress, groping for the zipper. "Stop it!" I said. "Don't—" But even though I was saying no, asking him to stop, I felt as though I wanted him more than I had ever wanted anyone before. "Upstairs," I said, "quick," and then we were leaving the kitchen, tearing at our clothes as we went, and heading up to the bedroom with the gray carpet and blue patterned wallpaper, and all the time I was thinking, *Yes, this is what I ought to be writing about in my next novel, this is the feeling I want to capture.*

I stumbled. The sound of breaking glass, and the image in front of me vanished. It was as if the reel of film had run through, the images on the screen replaced with a flickering light and the shadows of dust motes. I opened my eyes.

I was still there, in that kitchen, but now it was Dr. Nash standing in front of me, and Amanda a little way past him, and they were both looking at me, concerned and anxious. I realized I had dropped the glass.

"Christine," said Dr. Nash. "Christine. Are you okay?"

I did not answer. I did not know what to feel. It was the first time—as far as I knew—I had ever remembered my husband.

I closed my eyes and tried to will the vision back. I tried to see the fish, the wine, my husband, with a mustache, naked, his penis bobbing, but nothing would come. The memory had gone, evaporated as if it had never existed, or had been burned away by the present.

"Yes," I said. "I'm fine. I—"

"What's wrong?" said Amanda. "Are you all right?"

"I remembered something," I said. I saw Amanda's hands fly to her mouth, her expression change to one of delight.

"Really?" she said. "That's wonderful! What? What did you remember?"

"Please—" said Dr. Nash. He stepped forward, taking my arm. Broken glass crunched at his feet.

"My husband," I said. "Here. I remembered my husband—"

Amanda's expression fell. *Is that all?* she seemed to be saying.

"Dr. Nash?" I said. "I remembered Ben!" I began to shake.

"Good," said Dr. Nash. "Good! That's excellent!"

Together, they led me to the living room. I sat on the sofa. Amanda handed me a mug of hot tea, a cookie on a plate. *She does not understand,* I thought. *She cannot. I have remembered Ben. Me, when I was young. The two of us, together. I know we were in love. I no longer have to take his word for it. It is important. Far more important than she can ever know.*

I felt excited, all the way home. Lit with nervous energy. I looked at the world outside—the strange, mysterious, unfamiliar world—and in it, I did not see threat, but possibility. Dr. Nash told me he thought we were really getting somewhere. He seemed excited. *This is good,* he kept saying. *This is good.* I wasn't sure whether he meant it was good for me or for him, for his career. He said he'd like to arrange a scan and, almost without thinking, I agreed. He gave me a cell phone, too, telling me it used to belong to his girlfriend. It looked different from the one Ben had given me. It was smaller, and the casing flipped open to reveal a keypad and screen inside. *A spare,* he said. *You can ring me anytime. Any time it's important. And keep it with you. I'll call you on it to remind you about your journal.* That was hours ago. Now I realize he gave it to me so that he can phone me without Ben knowing. He'd even said as much. *I rang the other day and Ben answered. It might get awkward. This will make things easier.* I took it without question.

I have remembered Ben. Remembered that I loved him. Perhaps later, when we go to bed, I will make amends for last night's neglect. I feel alive. Buzzing with potential.

# Tuesday, November 13

It is the afternoon. Soon Ben will be home from another day at work. I sit with this journal in front of me. A man—Dr. Nash—called me at lunchtime and told me where to find it. I was sitting in the living room when he rang, and at first did not believe that he knew who I was. *Look in the shoebox in the closet,* he'd said eventually. *You'll find a book.* I had not believed him, but he had stayed on the line while I looked, and he was right. My journal was there, wrapped in tissue. I lifted it out as if it were fragile, and then, once I had said good-bye to Dr. Nash, I knelt by the closet and read it. Every word.

I was nervous, though I did not know why. The journal felt forbidden, dangerous, though this was perhaps only because of the care with which I'd hidden it. I glanced up repeatedly from its pages to check the time, even closed it quickly and put it back in its tissue when there was the sound of a car outside the house. But now I am calm. I am writing this in the window of the bedroom, in the bay. It feels familiar here, somehow, as if this is a place where I sit often. I can see down the street: in one direction, to a row of tall trees behind which a park can be glimpsed; in the other, to a row of houses and another, busier, road. I realize that, though I may choose to keep my journal secret from Ben, nothing terrible would happen if he were to find it. He is my husband. I can trust him.

I read again of the excitement I felt on the way home yesterday. It has disappeared. Now I feel content. Still. Cars pass. Occasionally someone walks by—a man, whistling, or a young mother taking her child to the park and then, later, away from it. In the distance, a plane, coming in to land, seems almost to be stationary.

The houses opposite are empty, the street quiet apart from the whistling man and the bark of an unhappy dog. The commotion of the morning, with its symphony of closing doors and singsong good-byes and revved engines, has disappeared. I feel alone in the world.

It begins to rain. Large droplets spatter the window in front of my face, hang for a moment, and then, joined by others, begin their slow slide down the pane. I put my hand up to the cold glass.

So much separates me from the rest of the world.

I read of visiting the home I had shared with my husband. Was it really only yesterday those words were written? They do not feel as if they belong to me. I read of the day I had remembered, too. Of kissing my husband—in the house we bought together, so long ago—and when I close my eyes, I can see it again. It is dim at first, unfocused, but then the image shimmers and resolves, snapping to sharpness with an almost overwhelming intensity. My husband, tearing at my clothes. Ben, holding me, his kisses becoming more urgent, deeper. I remember we neither ate the fish nor drank the wine; instead, when we had finished making love, we stayed in bed for as long as we could, our legs entwined, my head on his chest, his hand stroking my hair, semen drying on my stomach. We were silent. Happiness surrounded us like a cloud.

"I love you," he said. He was whispering, as if he had never said those words before, and, though he must have done so many times, they sounded new. Forbidden and dangerous.

I looked up at him, at the stubble on his chin, the flesh of his lips, and the outline of his nose above them. "I love you too," I said, whispering into his chest as if the words were fragile. He squeezed my body to his, then, and kissed me softly. The top of my head, my brow. I closed my eyes and he kissed my eyelids, barely brushing them with his lips. I felt safe, at home. I felt as if here, against his body, was the only place in which I belonged. The only place I had ever wanted to be. We lay in silence for a while, holding each other, our skin merging, our breathing synchronized. I felt as if silence might allow the moment to last forever, which would still not be enough.

Ben broke the spell. "I have to leave," he said, and I opened my eyes and took his hand in mine. It felt warm. Soft. I brought it to my mouth and kissed it. The taste of glass, and earth.

"Already?" I said.

He kissed me again. "Yes. It's later than you think. I'll miss my train."

I felt my body plunge. Separation seemed unthinkable. Unbearable. "Stay a bit longer?" I said. "Get the next one?"

He laughed. "I can't, Chris," he said. "You know that."

I kissed him again. "I know," I said. "I know."

I showered after he left. I took my time, soaping myself slowly, feeling the water on my skin as if it were a new sensation. In the bedroom, I sprayed myself with perfume and put on my nightdress and a robe, and then I went downstairs, into the dining room.

It was dark. I turned on the light. On the table in front of me was a typewriter, threaded with blank paper, and next to it a shallow stack of pages, turned facedown. I sat down, in front of the machine. I began to type. *Chapter Two.*

I paused then. I could not think what to write next, how to begin. I sighed, resting my fingers on the keyboard. It felt natural beneath me, cool and smooth, contoured to my fingertips. I closed my eyes and typed again.

My fingers danced across the keys, automatically, almost without thought. When I opened my eyes, I had typed a single sentence.

*Lizzy did not know what she had done, or how it could be undone.*

I looked at the sentence. Solid. Sitting there, on the page.

*Nonsense,* I thought. I felt angry. I knew I could do better. I had done so before, two summers previously, when the words had flown out of me, scattering my story onto the page like confetti. But now? Now something was wrong. Language had become solid, stiff. Hard.

I took a pencil and drew a line through the sentence. I felt a little better with it scored out, but now I had nothing again; nowhere to start.

I stood up and lit a cigarette from the pack that Ben had left on the table. I drew the smoke deep into my lungs, held it, exhaled. For a moment, I wished it was weed, wondered where I could get some from, for next time. I poured myself a drink— neat vodka into a whiskey tumbler—and took a mouthful. It would have to do. *Writer's block,* I thought. *How did I become such a fucking cliché?*

Last time. How did I do it last time? I went over to the bookcases that lined the wall of the dining room and, with the cigarette dangling between my lips, took down a book from the top shelf. *There must be clues here. Surely?*

I put the vodka down and turned the book over in my hands. I rested my fingertips on the cover, as if the book were delicate, and brushed them gently over the title. *For the Morning Birds,* it said. *Christine Lucas.* I opened the cover and flicked through the pages.

The image vanished. My eyes opened. The room I was in looked drab and gray, but my breathing was ragged. I dimly registered the surprise that I had once smoked, but it was replaced by something else. Was it true? Had I written a novel? Had it been published? I stood up; my journal slid from my lap. If so, I had been someone, someone with a life, with goals and ambitions and achievements. I ran down the stairs.

Was it true? Ben had said nothing to me this morning. Nothing about being a writer. This morning, I had read of our trip to Parliament Hill. There, he had told me I had been working as a secretary when I had my accident.

I scanned the bookshelves in the living room. Dictionaries. An atlas. A guide to do-it-yourself. A few novels, hardcover and, from their condition, I guessed unread. But nothing by me. Nothing to suggest I had had a novel published. I spun around, half-crazy. *It must be here,* I thought. *It must.* But then another thought struck me. Perhaps my vision was not memory but invention. Perhaps, without a true history to hold and ponder, my mind had created one of its own. Perhaps my subconscious decided that I was a writer because that is what I always wanted to be.

I ran back upstairs. The shelves in the office were filled with box files and computer manuals, and I had seen no books in either bedroom as I explored the house that morning. I stood, for a moment, then saw the computer in front of me, silent and dark. I knew what to do, though I did not know how I knew. I switched it on and it whirred into life beneath the desk, the screen lighting up a moment later. A swell of music from the rattling speaker by the side of the screen, and then an image appeared. A photograph of Ben and me, both smiling. Across the middle of our faces, there was a box. USER-NAME, it said, and beneath it there was another. PASSWORD.

In my vision, I was touch-typing, my fingers dancing over the keys as if powered by instinct. I positioned the flashing cursor in the box marked USERNAME and held my hands above the keyboard. Was it true? Had I learned to type? I let my fingers rest on the raised letters. They moved, effortlessly, my little fingers seeking the keys over which they belonged, the rest falling into place beside them. I closed my eyes and, without thinking, began to type, listening only to the sound of my breathing and the plastic clatter of the keys. When I had finished, I looked at what I had done, at what was written in the box. I expected nonsense, but what I saw shocked me.

*The quick brown fox jumps over the lazy dog.*

I stared at the screen. It was true. I could touch-type. Maybe my vision was not invention but memory.

Maybe I had written a novel.

I ran into the bedroom. It did not make sense. For a moment, I had the almost overwhelming feeling that I was going mad. The novel seemed to exist and not exist at the same time, to be real and also totally imaginary. I could remember nothing of it, nothing about its plot or characters, not even the reason I had given it its title, yet still it felt real, as if it beat within me like a heart.

And why had Ben not told me? Not kept a copy on display? I pictured it, hidden in the house, wrapped in tissue, stored in a box in the loft or the cellar. Why?

An explanation came to me. Ben had told me I had been working as a secretary. Perhaps that was why I could type: the only reason.

I dug one of the phones out of my bag, not caring which one, hardly even caring who I called. My husband or my doctor? Both seemed equally alien to me. I flipped it open and scrolled through the menu until I saw a name I recognized, then pressed the CALL button.

"Dr. Nash?" I said, when the call was answered. "It's Christine." He began to say something, but I interrupted him. "Listen. Did I ever write anything?"

"Sorry?" he said. He sounded confused, and for a moment I had the sense I had done something terribly wrong. I wondered whether he even knew who I was, but then he said, "Christine?"

I repeated what I had said. "I just remembered something. That I was writing something, years ago, when I first knew Ben, I think. A novel. Did I ever write a novel?"

He did not seem to understand what I meant. "A novel?"

"Yes," I said. "I seem to remember wanting to be a writer, when I was little. I just wondered whether I ever wrote anything. Ben told me I worked as a secretary, but I was just thinking—"

"He hasn't told you?" he said then. "You were working on your second novel when you lost your memory. Your first was published. It was a success. I wouldn't say it was a bestseller, but it was certainly a success."

The words spun in on each other. A novel. A success. Published. It was true, my memory had been real. I did not know what to say. What to think.

I said good-bye, then came upstairs to write this.

*  *  *

The bedside clock reads ten thirty. I imagine Ben will come to bed soon, but still I sit here on the edge of the bed, writing. I spoke to him after dinner. I had spent the afternoon fretful, pacing from one room to another, looking at everything as if for the first time, wondering why he would so thoroughly remove evidence of even this modest success? It did not make sense. Was he ashamed? Embarrassed? Had I written about him, our life together? Or was the reason something worse? Something darker I could not yet see?

By the time he got home, I had resolved to ask him directly, but now? Now that did not seem possible. It felt like I would be accusing him of lying.

I spoke as casually as I could. "Ben?" I said. "What did I do for a living?" He looked up from the newspaper. "Did I have a job?"

"Yes," he said. "You worked as a secretary for a while. Just after we were married."

I tried to keep my voice even. "Really? I have the feeling I used to want to write."

He folded his pages together, giving me his full attention.

"A feeling?"

"Yes. I definitely remember loving books as a child. And I seem to have a vague memory of wanting to be a writer." He held out his hand across the dinner table and took mine. His eyes seemed sad. Disappointed. *What a shame,* they seemed to say. *Bad luck. I don't suppose you ever will now.* "Are you sure?" I began. "I seem to remember—"

He interrupted me. "Christine," he said. "Please. You're imagining things . . ."

For the rest of the evening, I was silent, hearing only the thoughts that echoed in my head. *Why would he do that? Why would he pretend I had never written a word? Why?* I watched him, asleep on the sofa, snoring softly. Why had I not told him that I knew I had written a novel? Did I really trust him so little? I had remembered us lying in each other's arms, murmuring our love for each other as the sky grew darker. How had we gone from that to this?

But then I began to imagine what would happen if I did stumble upon a copy of my novel in a cupboard or at the back of a high shelf. What would it say to me, other than *Look how far you have fallen. Look what you could do, before a car on an icy road took it all from you, leaving you worse than useless.*

It would not be a happy moment. I saw myself becoming hysterical—much more so than this afternoon, when at least the realization was gradual, triggered by a longed-for memory—screaming, crying. The effect might be devastating.

No wonder Ben might want to hide it from me. I picture him now, removing all the copies, burning them in the metal barbecue on the back porch, before deciding what to tell me. How best to reinvent my past to make it tolerable. What I needed to believe for the remainder of my years.

But that is over now. I know the truth. My own truth, one I have not been told but have remembered. And it is written now, etched in this journal rather than my memory, but permanent nevertheless.

I know that the book I am writing—my second, I realize with pride—may be dangerous, as well as necessary. It is not fiction. It may reveal things best left undiscovered. Secrets that ought not to see the light of day.

But still my pen moves across the page.

# Wednesday, November 14

This morning, I asked Ben if he'd ever grown a mustache. I was still feeling confused, unsure of what was true and what was not. I had woken early and, unlike previous days, had not thought that I was still a child. I had felt adult. Sexual. The question in my mind was not *Why am I in bed with a man?* but, instead, *Who is he?* and *What did we do?* In the bathroom, I looked at my reflection with horror, but the pictures around it seemed to resonate with truth. I saw the man's name—Ben—and it was familiar somehow. My age, my marriage, these facts seemed to be things I was being reminded of, not told about for the first time. Buried, but not deeply.

Dr. Nash called me almost as soon as Ben left for work. He reminded me about my journal and then—once he had told me that he would be picking me up later to take me for my scan—I read it. There were a few things in it I could perhaps recall, and maybe whole passages I could remember writing. It was as if some residue of memory had survived the night.

Perhaps that was why I had to be sure the things contained within it were true. I called Ben.

"Ben," I said, once he'd told me he wasn't busy. "Did you ever have a mustache?"

"That's an odd question!" he said. I heard the clink of a spoon against a cup and pictured him spooning sugar into his coffee, a newspaper spread in front of him. I felt awkward. Unsure how much to say.

"I just—" I began. "I had a memory. I think."

Silence. "A memory?"

"Yes," I said. "I think so." My mind flashed on the things I had written about the other day—his mustache, his naked body, his erection—and those I had remembered yesterday. The two of us in bed. Kissing. Briefly, they were illuminated, before sinking back into the depths. Suddenly I felt afraid. "I just seem to remember you with a mustache."

He laughed, and I heard him put down his drink. I felt solid ground begin to slip away. Maybe everything I had written was a lie. *I am a novelist, after all,* I thought. Or I used to be.

The futility of my logic hit me. I used to write fiction, therefore my assertion that I had been a novelist might be one of those fictions. In which case, I had not written fiction. My head spun.

It had felt true, though. I told myself that. Plus I could touch-type. Or I had written that I could, at least . . .

"Did you?" I asked, desperate. "It's just . . . it's important . . ."

"Let's think," he said. I imagined him closing his eyes, biting his bottom lip in a parody of concentration. "I suppose I might have done, once," he said. "Very briefly. It was years ago. I forget . . ." A pause, then, "Yes. Actually, yes. I think I probably did. For a week or so. A long time ago."

"Thank you," I said, relieved. The ground on which I stood felt a little more secure.

"You okay?" he asked, and I said that I was.

Dr. Nash picked me up at midday. He'd told me to have some lunch first, but I wasn't hungry. Nervous, I suppose. "We're meeting a colleague of mine," he said in the car. "Dr. Paxton." I said nothing. "He's an expert in the field of functional imaging of patients with problems like yours. We've been working together."

"Okay," I said, and now we sat in his car, stationary in stuck traffic. "Did I call you yesterday?" I asked. He said that I had.

"You read your journal?"

"Most of it. I skipped bits. It's already quite long."

He seemed interested. "What sections did you skip?"

I thought for a moment. "There are parts that seem familiar to me. I suppose they feel as if they're just reminding me of things I already know. Already remember . . ."

"That's good." He glanced at me. "Very good."

I felt a glow of pleasure. "So what did I call about? Yesterday?"

"You wanted to know if you'd really written a novel," he said.

"And had I?" I said. "Have I?"

He turned back to me. He was smiling. "Yes," he said. "Yes, you have."

The traffic moved again and we pulled away. I felt relief. I knew what I had written was true. I relaxed into the journey.

Dr. Paxton was older than I expected. He was wearing a tweed jacket, and white hair sprouted unchecked from his ears and nose. He looked as though he ought to have retired.

"Welcome to the Vincent Hall Imaging Center," he said once Dr. Nash had introduced us, and then, without taking his eyes off mine, he winked and shook my hand. "Don't worry," he added. "It's not as grand as it sounds. Here, come in. Let me show you around."

We made our way into the building. "We're attached to both the hospital and the university, here," he said as we went through the main entrance. "Which can be both a blessing and a curse." I did not know what he meant and waited for him to elaborate, but he said nothing. I smiled.

"Really?" I said. He was trying to help me. I wanted to be polite.

"Everyone wants us to do everything." He laughed. "No one wants to pay us for any of it."

We walked into a waiting room. It was dotted with empty chairs, copies of the same magazines Ben had left for me at home—*Radio Times, Hello!*, now joined by *Country Life* and *Marie Claire*—and discarded plastic cups. It looked like there had recently been a party that everyone had left in a hurry. Dr. Paxton paused at another door. "Would you like to see the control room?"

"Yes," I said. "Please."

"Functional MRI is a fairly new technique," he said, once we'd gone in. "Have you heard of MRI? Magnetic resonance imaging?"

We were standing in a small room, lit only by the ghostly glow from a bank of computer monitors. One wall was taken up by a window, beyond which was another room, dominated by a large cylindrical machine, a bed protruding from it like a tongue. I began to feel afraid. I knew nothing of this machine. Without memory, how could I?

"No," I said.

He smiled. "I'm sorry. MRI is a fairly standard procedure. It's a little like taking an X ray through the body. Here we're using some of the same techniques but actually looking at how the brain works. At function."

Dr. Nash spoke then—the first time in a while he had done so—and his voice sounded small, almost timid. I wondered whether he was in awe of Dr. Paxton, even desperate to impress him.

"If someone has a brain tumor, then we need to scan their head to find out where the tumor is, what part of the brain is affected. That's looking at structure. What functional MRI allows us to see is which part of the brain you use when you do certain tasks. We want to see how your brain processes memory."

"Which parts light up, as it were," said Paxton. "Where the juices are flowing."

"That will help?" I asked.

"We hope it will help us to identify where the damage is," said Dr. Nash. "What's gone wrong. What's not working properly."

"And that will help me to get my memory back?"

He paused, and then said, "We hope so."

I took off my wedding ring and my earrings and put them in a plastic tray. "You'll need to leave your bag in here, too," said Dr. Paxton, and then he asked me if I had anything else pierced. "You'd be surprised, my dear," he said when I shook my head. "Now, she's a bit of a noisy old beast. You'll need these." He handed me some yellow earplugs. "Ready?"

I hesitated. "I don't know." Fear was beginning to creep over me. The room seemed to shrink and darken, and through the glass the scanner itself loomed. I had the sense I had seen it before, or one just like it. "I'm not sure about this," I said.

Dr. Nash came over to me then. He placed his hand on my arm.

"It's completely painless," he said. "Just a little noisy."

"It's safe?"

"Perfectly. I'll be here, just on this side of the glass. We'll be able to see you all the way through."

I must have still looked unsure, because then Dr. Paxton added,

"Don't worry. You're in safe hands, my dear. Nothing will go wrong." I looked at him, and he smiled and said, "You might want to think of your memories as being lost somewhere in your mind. All we're doing with this machine is trying to find out where they are."

It was cold, despite the blanket they had wrapped around me, and dark, except for a red light blinking in the room and a mirror hung from a frame a couple of inches above my head, angled to reflect the image of a computer screen that sat somewhere else. As well as the earplugs, I was wearing a set of headphones, through which they said they would talk to me, but for now they were silent. I could hear nothing but a distant hum, the sound of my breathing, hard and heavy, the dull thud of my heartbeat.

In my right hand, I clutched a plastic bulb filled with air. "Squeeze it, if you need to tell us anything," Dr. Paxton had said. "We won't be able to hear you if you speak." I caressed its rubbery surface and waited. I wanted to close my eyes, but they had told me to keep them open, to look at the screen. Foam wedges kept my head perfectly still; I could not have moved even if I'd wanted to. The blanket over me, like a shroud.

A moment of stillness, and then a click. So loud that I startled, despite the earplugs, and followed by another, and a third. A deep noise, from within the machine, or my head. I couldn't tell. A lumbering beast, waking, the moment of silence before the attack. I clutched the rubber bulb, determined that I would not squeeze it, and then a noise, like an alarm or a drill, over and over again, impossibly loud, so loud that the whole of my body shook with each new shock. I closed my eyes.

A voice in my ear. "Christine," it said. "Can you open your eyes, please?" They could see me, then, somehow. "Don't worry, it's all fine."

*Fine?* I thought. *What do they know about fine? What do they know about what it's like to be me, lying here, in a city I do not remember, with people I've never met? I am floating,* I thought, *completely without anchor, at the mercy of the wind.*

A different voice. Dr. Nash's. "Can you look at the pictures? Think what they are, say it, but only to yourself. Don't say anything out loud."

I opened my eyes. Above me, in the little mirror, were drawings, one after the other, white on black. A man. A ladder. A chair. A hammer. I named each one as it came, and then the screen flashed the words THANK YOU! NOW RELAX! and I said that to myself, too, to keep myself busy, wondering at the same time how anyone could relax in the belly of a machine like this.

More instructions flashed on the screen. RECALL A PAST EVENT, it said, and then beneath it flashed the words A PARTY.

I closed my eyes.

I tried to think of the party I had remembered as Ben and I watched the fireworks. I tried to picture myself on the roof next to my friend, to hear the noise of the party beneath us, to taste the fireworks on the air.

Images came, but they did not seem real. I could tell I was not remembering but inventing them.

I tried to see Keith, to remember him ignoring me, but nothing would come. Those memories were lost again to me. Buried, as if forever, though now at least I know that they exist, that they are in there, somewhere, locked away.

My mind turned to childhood parties. Birthdays, with my

mother and aunt and my cousin Lucy. Twister. Musical chairs. Musical statues. My mother with bags of candy to wrap up as prizes. Peanut butter and jelly sandwiches with the crusts removed.

I remembered a white dress with ruffles at the sleeves, ruffled socks, black shoes. My hair is still blond, and I am sitting at a table in front of a cake, with candles. I take a deep breath, lean forward, blow. Smoke rises in the air.

Memories of another party crowded in then. I saw myself at home, looking out of my bedroom window. I am naked, about seventeen. There are trestle tables out in the street, arranged in long rows, loaded with trays of sandwiches, jugs of iced tea. Flags are everywhere, bunting hangs from every window. Blue. Red. White.

There are children in fancy dress—pirates, wizards, Vikings— and the adults are trying to organize them into teams for an egg-and-spoon race. I can see my mother on the other side of the street fastening a cape around Matthew Soper's neck and, just below my window, my father sits in a deck chair with a glass of juice.

"Come back to bed," says a voice. I turn around. Dave Soper sits in my single bed, underneath my poster of The Slits. The white sheet is twisted around him, spattered with blood. I had not told him it was my first time.

"No," I say. "Get up! You have to get dressed before my parents come back!"

He laughs, though not unkindly. "Come on!"

I pull on my jeans. "No," I say, reaching for a T-shirt. "Get up. Please?"

He looks disappointed. I didn't think this would happen— which does not mean I didn't want it to—and now I would like to be alone. It is not about him at all.

"Okay," he says, standing up. His body looks pale and skinny, his penis almost absurd. I look away as he dresses, out of the window. *My world has changed,* I think. *I have crossed a line, and I cannot go back.* "Bye, then," he says, but I don't speak. I do not look back until he has left.

A voice in my ear brought me back to the present. "Good. More pictures now, Christine," said Dr. Paxton. "Just look at each one and tell yourself what, or who, it is. Okay? Ready?"

I swallowed hard. *What would they show me?* I thought. *Who? How bad could it be?*

*Yes,* I thought to myself, and we began.

The first photograph was black-and-white. A child—a girl, four, five years old—in the arms of a woman. The girl was pointing to something, and they were both laughing, and in the background, slightly out of focus, was a fence with a tiger resting on the other side of it. *A mother,* I thought to myself. *A daughter. At a zoo.* And then, with a shock of recognition, I looked at the child's face and realized that the little girl was me, the mother my own. Breath caught in my throat. I could not remember ever going to a zoo, yet here we were, here was evidence that we had. *Me,* I said silently, remembering what I had been told. *Mother.* I stared at the screen, trying to burn her image into my memory, but the picture faded and was replaced by another, also of my mother, now older yet not seeming old enough to need the walking stick on which she is leaning. She was smiling but looked exhausted, her eyes sunk deep in her thin face. *My mother,* I thought again, and other words came, unbidden: *in pain.* I closed my eyes involuntarily, had to force them open again. I began to grip the bulb in my hand.

The images came quickly then, and I recognized only a few.

One was of the friend I had seen in my memory, and, with a thrill, I knew her almost straight away. She looked as I had imagined her, dressed in old blue jeans and a T-shirt, smoking, her red hair loose and untidy. Another picture showed her with her hair cut short and dyed black, and a pair of sunglasses pushed high on her head. It was followed by a photograph of my father—the way he looked when I was a little girl, smiling, happy, reading a newspaper in our front room—and then one of me and Ben, standing with another couple I didn't recognize.

Other photos were of strangers. A black woman in a nurse's uniform; another woman dressed in a suit, sitting in front of a bookcase, peering with a grave expression over the top of her half-moon glasses. A man with ginger hair and a round face; another with a beard. A child, six or seven—a boy eating an ice cream and then, later, the same boy, sitting at a desk, drawing. A group of people, arranged loosely, looking at the camera. A man, attractive, his hair black and slightly longish, with a pair of dark-rimmed glasses framing narrowed eyes and a scar running down the side of his face. They went on and on, these photographs, and as they did, I looked at them all and tried to place them, to remember how—or even whether—they were woven into the tapestry of my life. I did as I had been asked. I was good, and yet I felt myself begin to panic. The whir of the machine seemed to rise in pitch and volume until it became an alarm, a warning, and my stomach clenched. I could not breathe, and I closed my eyes, and the weight of the blanket began to press down on me, heavy as a marble slab, so that it felt like I was drowning.

I squeezed my right hand, but it balled itself into a fist, closing on nothing. Nails bit into flesh; I had dropped the bulb. I called out, a wordless cry.

"Christine," came a voice in my ear. "Christine."

I could not tell who it was, or what they wanted me to do, and I cried out again, and began kicking the blanket off my body.

"Christine!"

Louder now, and then the siren noise whirred to a halt, a door crashed open, and there were voices in the room, and hands on me, on my arms and legs, and across my chest, and I opened my eyes.

"It's okay," said Dr. Nash in my ear. "You're okay. I'm here."

Once they'd calmed me down with reassurances that everything was fine—and given me back my handbag, my earrings, and my wedding ring—Dr. Nash and I went to a coffee bar. It was along the corridor, small, with orange plastic chairs and yellow-ing Formica-topped tables. Trays of tired pastries and sandwiches sat wilting in the harsh light. I had no money in my purse, but I let Dr. Nash buy me a cup of coffee and a piece of carrot cake and then selected a seat by the window while he paid. Outside was sunny, the shadows long in the courtyard of grass. Purple flowers dotted the lawn.

Dr. Nash scraped his chair under the table. He seemed much more relaxed, now that the two of us were alone together. "There you go," he said, setting the tray in front of me. "Hope that's okay."

I saw that he had selected tea for himself; the bag still floated in the syrupy liquid as he added sugar from the bowl in the center of the table. I took a sip of my drink and grimaced. It was bitter and too hot.

"It's fine," I said. "Thank you."

"I'm sorry," he said after a moment. At first, I thought he was talking about the coffee. "I had no idea that you would find it so distressing in there."

"It's very claustrophobic," I said. "And noisy."

"Yes, of course."

"I dropped the emergency button."

He said nothing, but instead stirred his drink. He fished the tea bag out and deposited it on the tray. He took a sip.

"What happened?" I said.

"Difficult to say. You panicked. It's not that uncommon. It isn't comfortable in there, as you said."

I looked down at my slice of cake. Untouched. Dry. "The photographs. Who were they? Where did you get them?"

"They were a mixture. Some of them I got from your medical files. Ben had donated them, years ago. I asked you to bring a couple from home for the purposes of this exercise—you said they'd been arranged around your mirror. Some I provided—of people you've never met. What we call controls. We mixed them all up together. Some of the images were people you knew at a very young age, people you should, or might, remember. Family. Friends from school. The rest were people from the era of your life that you definitely can't remember. Dr. Paxton and I are trying to find out whether there's a difference in the way you attempt to access memories from these different periods. The strongest reaction was to your husband, of course, but you reacted to others. Even though you don't remember the people from your past, the patterns of neural excitation are definitely there."

"Who was the woman with red hair?" I said.

He smiled. "An old friend, perhaps?"

"Do you know her name?"

"I'm afraid I don't. The photos were in your file. They weren't labeled."

I nodded. *An old friend.* I knew that, of course—it was her name I so wanted.

"You said that I reacted to the pictures, though?"

"Some of them, yes."

"That's good?"

"We'll need to look at the results in more detail before we really know what conclusions we can draw. This work is very new," he said. "Experimental."

"I see." I cut off a corner of the carrot cake. It, too, was bitter; the icing too sweet. We sat in silence for a while. I offered him my cake and he declined, patting his stomach. "Have to watch this!" he said, even though I could see no reason for him to worry yet. His stomach was mostly flat, though it looked to be the sort that would develop a paunch. For now, though, he was young, and age had hardly touched him.

I thought of my own body. I am not fat, not even overweight, yet still it surprises me. When I sit, it takes a different shape from the one I am expecting. My buttocks sag, my thighs rub together as I cross them. I lean forward to reach for my mug and my breasts shift in my bra, as if reminding me that they exist. I shower and feel a slight wobbling of the skin under my arms, barely perceptible. There is more of me than I think; I take up more space than I realize. I am not a little girl, compact, my skin tight on my bones; not even a teenager, my body beginning to lay down its fat.

I looked at the uneaten cake and wondered what will happen in the future. Perhaps I will continue to expand. I will grow pudgy and then fat, bloating up and up like a party balloon. Or else I will stay the same size as I am now, never getting used to it, instead watching as the lines on my face deepen and the skin on my hands grows as thin as that of an onion, and I turn into an old woman, stage by stage, in the bathroom mirror.

Dr. Nash looked down to scratch the top of his head. Through his hair I could see his scalp, more obvious in a circle at the crown.

He won't have noticed that yet, I thought, but one day he will. He will see a photograph of himself taken from behind, or surprise himself in a changing room, or his hairdresser will make a comment, or his girlfriend. *Age catches us all out,* I thought as he looked up. *In different ways.*

"Oh," he said, with a cheeriness that sounded forced. "I brought you something. A gift. Well, not really a gift, just something you might like to have." He reached down and retrieved his briefcase from the floor. "You've probably already got a copy," he said, opening it. He took out a package. "Here you go."

I knew what it was even as I took it. What else could it be? It felt heavy in my hand. He had wrapped it in a padded envelope, sealed it with tape. My name was written in heavy black marker pen. CHRISTINE. "It's your novel," he said. "The one you wrote."

I did not know what to feel. *Evidence,* I thought. *Proof that what I had written was true, should I need it tomorrow.*

Inside the envelope was a single copy of a book. I took it out. It was a paperback, not new. There was a coffee ring on the front and the edges of the pages were yellowed with age. I wondered if Dr. Nash had given me his own copy, whether it was even still in print. As I held it, I saw myself again as I had the other day; younger, much younger, reaching for this novel in an effort to find a way into the next. Somehow I knew it hadn't worked—the second novel had never been completed.

"Thank you," I said. "Thank you."

He smiled. "Don't mention it."

I put it underneath my coat, where, all the way home, it beat like a heart.

\* \* \*

As soon as I got back to the house, I looked at my novel, but only quickly. I wanted to write as much as I could remember in my journal before Ben came home, but once I'd finished and put it away, I hurried back downstairs to look properly at what I had been given.

I turned the book over. On the cover was a pastel drawing of a desk, upon which sat a typewriter. A crow was perched on its carriage, its head cocked to one side, almost as if it were reading the paper threaded there. Above the crow was written my name, and above that, the title.

FOR THE MORNING BIRDS, it said. CHRISTINE LUCAS.

My hands began to shake as I opened the book. Inside was a title page, a dedication. *For my father*—and then, *I miss you.*

I closed my eyes. A fluttering of memory. I saw my father, lying in a bed under bright white lights, his skin translucent, filmed with sweat so that he almost shone. I saw a tube in his arm, a bag of clear liquid hung from an IV stand, a cardboard tray and a tub of pills. A nurse, checking his pulse, his blood pressure, and he not waking up. My mother, sitting on the other side of his bed, trying not to cry while I tried to force the tears to come.

A smell came then. Cut flowers and low, dirty earth. Sweet and sickly. I saw the day we cremated him. Me wearing black—which I somehow know is not unusual—but this time without makeup. My mother, sitting next to my grandmother. The curtains open, the coffin slides away, and I cry, picturing my father turning to dust. My mother, squeezing my hand, and then we go home and drink cheap, fizzy wine and eat sandwiches as the sun goes down and she dissolves in the half-light.

I sighed. The image disappeared, and I opened my eyes. My novel, in front of me.

I turned to the title page, the opening line. *It was then,* I had written, *with the engine whining and her right foot pressed hard against the accelerator pedal, that she let go of the wheel and closed her eyes. She knew what would happen. She knew where it would lead. She always had.*

I flicked to the middle of the novel. I read a paragraph there, and then one from near the end.

I had written about a woman called Lou, a man—her husband, I guessed—called George, and the novel seemed to be rooted in a war. I felt disappointed. I don't know what I had been hoping for—autobiography, perhaps?—but it seemed any answers this novel could give me would be limited.

Still, I thought as I turned it over to look at the back cover, I had at least written it, got it published.

Where there might have been an author photograph, there was none. Instead, there was a short biography.

*Christine Lucas was born in 1960, in the north of England,* it said. *She majored in English at University College London, and has now settled in that city. This is her first novel.*

I smiled to myself, feeling a swell of happiness and pride. *I did this.* I wanted to read it, to unlock its secrets, but at the same time I did not. I was worried the reality might take my happiness away. Either I would like the novel and feel sad that I would never write another, or I would not, and feel frustrated that I never developed my talent. I could not say which was more likely, but I knew that one day, unable to resist the pull of my only achievement, I would find out. I would make that discovery.

But not today. Today I had something else to discover, something far worse than sadness, more damaging than mere frustration. Something that might rip me apart.

I tried to slip the book back in the envelope. There was something else in there. A note, folded into four, the edges crisp. Dr. Nash had written on it: *I thought this might interest you!*

I unfolded the paper. Across the top, he'd written *Standard, 1986.* Beneath it was a copy of a newspaper article, next to a photograph. I looked at the page for a second or two before I realized that the article was a review of my novel and the picture was of me.

I shook as I held the page. I didn't know why. This was an artifact from years ago; good or bad, whatever its effects had been, they were long gone. It was history now, its ripples vanished completely. But it was important to me. How was my work received, all those years ago? Had I been successful?

I scanned the article, hoping to understand its tone before being forced to analyze the specifics. Words jumped out at me. Positive, mostly. *Studied. Perceptive. Skilled. Humanity. Brutal.*

I looked at the photograph. Black-and-white, it showed me sitting at a desk, my body angled toward the camera. I am holding myself awkwardly. Something is making me uncomfortable, and I wondered if it was the person behind the camera or the position I am sitting in. Despite this, I am smiling. My hair is long and loose, and although the photograph is black-and-white, it seems darker than it is now, as if I have dyed it black, or it is damp. Behind me, there are patio doors, and through them, just visible in the corner of the frame, is a leafless tree. There is a caption beneath the photograph. *Christine Lucas, at her North London home.*

I realized it must be the house I had visited with Dr. Nash. For a second, I had an almost overwhelming desire to go back there, to take this photograph with me and convince myself that yes, it was true; I had existed, then. It had been me.

But I knew that already, of course. Though I couldn't remember it anymore, I knew that there, standing in the kitchen, I had remembered Ben. Ben and his bobbing erection.

I smiled and touched the photograph, running my fingertips over it, looking for hidden clues as a blind man might. I traced the edge of my hair, ran my fingers over my face. In the photograph, I look uncomfortable, but also radiant in some way. It is as if I am keeping a secret, holding it like a charm. My novel has been published, yes, but there is something else, something more than that.

I looked closely. I could see the swell of my breasts in the loose dress I am wearing, the way I am holding one arm across my stomach. A memory bubbles up from nowhere—me, sitting for the picture, the photographer in front of me behind his tripod, the journalist with whom I have just discussed my work hovering in the kitchen. She yells in, asking how it's going, and both of us reply with a cheery "Fine!" and laugh. "Not long now," he says, changing his film. The journalist has lit a cigarette and yells to ask not if I mind but whether we have an ashtray. I feel annoyed, but only slightly. The truth is, I am yearning for a cigarette myself, but I have given up, ever since I found out that—

I looked at the picture again, and I knew. In it, I am pregnant.

My mind stopped for a moment, and then began to race. It tripped over itself, caught on the sharp edges of the realization, the fact that not only had I been carrying a baby as I sat in the dining room and had my picture taken, but I had known it, was happy about it.

It did not make sense. What had happened? The child ought to be—how old now? Eighteen? Nineteen? Twenty?

*But there is no child,* I thought. *Where is my son?*

I felt my world tip again. That word: *son.* I had thought it, said it to myself with certainty. Somehow, from somewhere deep within me, I knew that the child I had been carrying was a boy.

I gripped the edge of the chair to try and steady myself, and as I did, another word bubbled to the surface and exploded. *Adam.* I felt my world slip out of one groove and into another.

I had had the child. We called him Adam.

I stood up and the package containing the novel skidded to the floor. My mind raced like a whirring engine that has at last caught, energy ricocheted within me as if desperate for release. He was absent from the scrapbook in the living room. I knew that. I would have remembered seeing a picture of my own child as I leafed through it this morning. I would have asked Ben who he was. I would have written about it in my journal. I crammed the clipping back into the envelope along with the book and ran upstairs. In the bathroom, I stood in front of the mirror. I did not even glance at my face but looked around it, at the pictures of the past, the photographs that I must use to construct myself when I don't have memory.

Me and Ben. Me, alone, and Ben, alone. The two of us with another couple, older, who I take to be his parents. Me, much younger, wearing a scarf, petting a dog, smiling happily. But there is no Adam. No baby, no toddler. No photos taken on his first day of school, or at sports day, or on holiday. No pictures of him building castles in the sand. Nothing.

It did not make sense. Surely these are pictures that every parent takes and none discards?

*They must be here,* I thought. I lifted pictures up to see if there were others taped beneath them, layers of history overlain like strata. There was nothing. Nothing but the pale blue tiles on the wall, the smooth glass of the mirror. A blank.

*Adam.* The name spun in my head. My eyes closed and more memories hit, each one striking violently, shimmering for a moment before disappearing, triggering the next. I saw Adam, his blond hair that I knew would one day turn brown, the Spiderman T-shirt that he insisted on wearing until it was far too small for him and had to be thrown out. I saw him in a stroller, sleeping, and remembered thinking that he was the most perfect baby, the most perfect thing, I had ever seen. I saw him riding a blue bike—a plastic tricycle—and somehow knew that we had bought it for him on his birthday, and that he would ride it everywhere. I saw him in a park, his head hunched over handlebars, grinning as he flew down an incline toward me and, a second later, tipping forward and slamming to the ground as the bike hit something on the path and twisted beneath him. I saw myself holding him as he cried, mopping blood from his face, finding one of his teeth on the ground next to a still-spinning wheel. I saw him showing me a picture he'd painted—a blue strip for the sky, green for the ground, and between them three blobby figures and a tiny house—and I saw the toy rabbit that he carried everywhere.

I snapped back to the present, to the bathroom in which I stood, but closed my eyes again. I wanted to remember him at school, or as a teenager, or to picture him with me or his father. But I could not. When I tried to organize my memories, they fluttered and vanished, like a feather caught on the wind that changes direction whenever a hand snatches at it. Instead, I saw him holding a dripping ice cream, then with licorice over his face, then sleeping in the backseat of a car. All I could do was watch as these memories came and then went, just as quickly.

It took all my strength not to tear at the photos in front of me. I wanted to rip them from the wall, looking for evidence of my son. Instead, as if fearing that any movement at all might result in my limbs betraying me, I stood perfectly still in front of the mirror, every muscle in my body tensed.

No photographs on the mantelpiece. No teenage bedroom with posters of pop stars on the wall. No T-shirts in the laundry or among the piles of ironing. No tattered sneakers in the cupboard under the stairs. Even if he had left home, there would still be some evidence of his existence, surely? Some trace?

But no, he isn't in this house. With a chill, I realized it was as if he didn't exist, and never had.

I don't know how long I stood there in the bathroom, looking at his absence. Ten minutes? Twenty? An hour? At some point, I heard a key in the front door, the swoosh as Ben wiped his feet on the mat. I did not move. He went into the kitchen, then the dining room, and then called upstairs, asking if I was all right. He sounded anxious, his voice had a nervous fluting to it that I had not heard this morning, but I only mumbled that yes, yes I was. I heard him go into the living room, the television flick on.

Time stopped. My mind emptied of everything. Everything except the need to know what had happened to my son, balanced perfectly with a dread at what I might find out.

I hid my novel in the closet and went downstairs.

I stood outside the living room door. I tried to slow down my breathing but could not; it came in hot gasps. I did not know what to say to Ben: how I could tell him that I knew about Adam? He would ask me how, and what would I say then?

It didn't matter, though. Nothing did. Nothing other than knowing about my son. I closed my eyes and, when I felt as calm as I thought I would ever feel, gently pushed the door open. I felt it slide against the rough carpet.

Ben did not hear me. He was sitting on the sofa, watching television, a plate balanced on his lap, half a cookie on it. I felt a wave of anger. He looked so relaxed and happy, a smile played across his mouth. He began to laugh. I wanted to rush over, to grab him and shout until he told me everything, told me why he had kept my novel from me, why he had hidden evidence of my son. I wanted to demand he give back to me everything that I had lost.

But I knew that would do no good. Instead, I coughed. A tiny, delicate cough. A cough that said *I don't want to disturb you, but . . .*

He saw me and smiled. "Darling!" he said. "There you are!"

I stepped into the room. "Ben," I said. My voice was strained. It sounded alien to me. "Ben? I need to talk to you."

His face melted into anxiety. He stood up and came toward me, the plate sliding to the floor. "What is it, love? Are you all right?"

"No," I said. He stopped a couple of feet from where I stood. He held out his arms for me to fall into, but I did not.

"Whatever's wrong?"

I looked at my husband, at his face. He appeared to be in control, as if he had been here before, was used to these moments of hysteria.

I could go no longer without saying the name of my son. "Where's Adam?" I said. The words came out in a gasp. "Where is he?"

Ben's expression changed. Surprise? Or shock? He swallowed. "Tell me!" I said.

He took me in his arms. I wanted to push him away, but did not. "Christine," he said. "Please. Calm down. I can explain everything. Okay?"

I wanted to tell him that no, things weren't okay at all, but I said nothing. I hid my face from him, burying it in the folds of his shirt.

I began to shake. "Tell me," I said. "Please, tell me now."

We sat on the sofa. Me at one end. Him at the other. It was as close as I wanted us to be.

We'd been talking. For minutes. Hours. I couldn't tell. I didn't want him to speak, to say it again, but he did.

"Adam is dead."

I felt myself clench. Tight as a mollusk. His words, sharp as razor wire.

I thought of the fly on the windshield on the way home from my grandmother's house.

He spoke again. "Christine, love. I'm so sorry."

I felt angry. Angry with him. *Bastard,* I thought, even though I knew it wasn't his fault.

I forced myself to speak. "How?"

He sighed. "Adam was in the army."

I went numb. Everything receded, until I was left with pain, and nothing else. Pain. Reduced to a single point.

A son I did not even know that I had, and he had become a soldier. A thought ran through me. Absurd. *What will my mother think?*

Ben spoke again, in staccato bursts. "He was a Royal Marine. He was stationed in Afghanistan. He was killed. Last year."

I swallowed. My throat, dry.

"Why?" I said, and then, "How?"

"Christine—"

"I want to know," I said. "I need to know."

He reached across to take my hand, and I let him, though I was relieved when he moved no closer on the sofa.

"You don't want to know everything, surely?"

My anger surged. I couldn't help it. Anger and panic. "He was my son!"

He looked away, toward the window.

"He was traveling in an armored vehicle," he said. He spoke

slowly, almost whispering. "They were escorting troops. There was a bomb, on the roadside. One soldier survived. Adam and one other didn't."

I closed my eyes, and my voice dropped to a whisper, too. "Did he die straight away? Did he suffer?"

Ben sighed. "No," he said, after a moment. "He didn't suffer. They think it would have been very quick."

I looked across to where he sat. He did not look at me.

*You're lying*, I thought.

I saw Adam, bleeding to death by a roadside, and pushed the thought out, focusing instead on nothing, on blankness.

My mind began to spin. Questions. Questions that I dared not ask in case the answers killed me. *What was he like as a boy, a teenager, a man? Were we close? Did we argue? Was he happy? Was I a good mother?*

And, *How did the little boy who had ridden a plastic tricycle end up being killed on the other side of the world?*

"What was he doing in Afghanistan?" I said. "Why there?"

Ben told me we were at war. A war against terror, he said, though I don't know what that means. He said there was an attack, an awful attack, in America. Thousands were killed.

"And now my boy ends up dead in Afghanistan?" I said. "I don't understand . . ."

"It's complicated," he said. "He always wanted to join the army. He thought he was doing his duty."

"His duty? Did you think that was what he was doing? His duty? Did I? Why didn't you persuade him to do something else? Anything?"

"Christine, it was what he wanted."

For an awful moment, I almost laughed. "To get himself killed? Is that what he wanted? Why? I never even knew him."

Ben was silent. He squeezed my hand, and a single tear rolled down my face, hot as acid, and then another, and then more. I wiped them away, frightened that to start to cry would be never to stop.

I felt my mind begin to close down, to empty itself, to retreat into nothingness. "I never even knew him," I said.

Later, Ben brought down a box and put it on the coffee table in front of us.

"I keep these upstairs," he said. "For safety."

*From what?* I thought. The box was gray, made of metal. The kind of box in which one might keep money or important documents.

Whatever it contained must be dangerous. I imagined wild animals, scorpions and snakes, hungry rats, venomous toads. Or an invisible virus, something radioactive.

"For safety?" I said.

He sighed. "There are some things it wouldn't be good for you to stumble on when you're by yourself. Some things that it's better if I explain to you."

He sat next to me and opened the box. I could see nothing inside but paper.

"This is Adam as a baby," he said, taking out a handful of photographs and handing one to me.

It was a picture of me, on a street. I am walking toward the camera, with a baby—Adam—strapped to my chest in a pouch. His body is facing mine, but he is looking over his shoulder at whoever is taking the picture, the smile on his face a toothless approximation of my own.

"You took this?"

Ben nodded. I looked at it again. It was torn, its edges stained, the colors fading as if it were slowly bleaching to white.

Me. A baby. It did not seem real. I tried to tell myself I was a mother.

"When?" I said.

Ben looked over my shoulder. "He would have been about six months old, then," he said. "So, let's see. That must be about 1987."

I would have been twenty-seven. A lifetime ago.

My son's lifetime.

"When was he born?"

He dug his hand into the box again, passed me a slip of paper. "January," he said. It was yellow, brittle. A birth certificate. I read it in silence. His name was there. Adam.

"Adam Wheeler," I said, out loud. To myself as much as to Ben.

"Wheeler is my last name," he said. "We decided he should have my name."

"Of course," I said. I brought the paper up to my face. It felt too light to be a vessel for so much meaning. I wanted to breathe it in, for it to become part of me.

"Here," said Ben. He took the paper from me and folded it. "There are more pictures," he said. "Do you want to see them?"

He handed me a few more photographs.

"We don't have that many," he said, as I looked at them. "A lot were lost."

He made it sound as if they had been left on trains or given to strangers for safekeeping.

"Yes," I said. "I remember. We had a fire." I said it without thinking.

He looked at me oddly, his eyes narrowed, pinched tight.

"You remember?" he said.

Suddenly I wasn't sure. Had he told me about the fire this morning or was I remembering him telling me the other day? Or was it just that I had read it in my journal after breakfast?

"Well, you told me about it."

"I did?" he said.

"Yes."

"When?"

When was it? Had it been that morning, or days ago? I thought of my journal, remembered reading it after he'd gone to work. He'd told me about the fire as we sat on Parliament Hill.

I could have told him about my journal then, but something held me back. He seemed less than happy that I had remembered something. "Before you left for work?" I said. "When we looked through the scrapbook. You must have, I suppose."

He frowned. It felt terrible to be lying to him, but I did not feel able to cope with more revelations. "How would I know otherwise?"

He looked directly at me. "I suppose so."

I paused for a moment, looking at the handful of photographs in my hand. They were pitifully few, and I could see that the box did not contain many more. Were they really all I would ever have to describe my son's life?

"How did the fire start?" I said.

The clock on the mantelpiece chimed. "It was years ago. In our old house. The one we lived in before we came here." I wondered if he meant the one I'd been to. "We lost a lot of things. Books, papers. That kind of stuff."

"But how did it start?" I said.

For a moment, he said nothing. His mouth began to open and close, and then he said, "It was an accident. Just an accident."

I wondered what he was not telling me. Had I left a cigarette burning, or the iron plugged in, or a pot to boil dry? I imagined myself in the kitchen I had stood in the day before yesterday, with its concrete countertop and white appliances, but years ago. I saw myself standing over a sizzling fryer, shaking the wire basket that contained the sliced potatoes that I was cooking, watching as they floated to the surface before rolling and sinking back under the oil. I saw myself hear the phone ring, wipe my hands on the apron I had tied around my waist, go into the hall.

What then? Had the oil burst into flames as I took the call, or had I wandered back into the living room, or up to the bathroom, with no recollection of ever having begun to cook dinner?

I don't know, can never know. But it was kind of Ben to tell me that it had been an accident. Domesticity has so many dangers for someone without a memory, and another husband might have pointed out my mistakes and deficits, might have been unable to resist taking the moral high ground. I touched his arm, and he smiled.

I thumbed through the handful of photographs. There was one of Adam wearing a plastic cowboy hat and a yellow bandanna, aiming a plastic rifle at the person with the camera, and in another he was a few years older; his face thinner, his hair beginning to darken. He was wearing a shirt, buttoned to the neck, and a child's tie.

"That was taken at school," said Ben. "An official portrait." He pointed to the photograph and laughed. "Look. It's such a shame. The picture's ruined!"

The elastic of the tie was visible, not tucked under the collar. I ran my hands over the picture. It wasn't ruined, I thought. It was perfect.

I tried to remember my son, tried to see myself kneeling in front of him with an elasticated tie, or combing his hair, or wiping dried blood from a grazed knee.

Nothing came. The boy in the photograph shared a fullness of mouth with me, and had eyes that resembled, vaguely, my mother's, but otherwise he could have been a stranger.

Ben took out another picture and gave it to me. In it, Adam was a little older—maybe seven. "Do you think he looks like me?" he said.

He was holding a football, dressed in shorts and a white T-shirt. His hair was short, spiked with sweat. "A little," I said. "Perhaps."

Ben smiled, and together we continued looking at the photographs. They were mostly of me and Adam, the occasional one of him alone; Ben must have taken the majority. In a few, he was with friends, a couple showed him at a party, wearing a pirate costume, carrying a cardboard sword. In one, he held a small black dog.

There was a letter, tucked among the pictures. It was addressed to Santa Claus and written in blue crayon. The jerky letters danced across the page. He wanted a bike, he said, or a puppy, and promised to be good. It was signed, and he had added his age. Four.

I do not know why, but as I read it, my world seemed to collapse. Grief exploded in my chest like a grenade. I had been feeling calm—not happy, not even resigned, but calm—and that serenity vanished, as if vaporized. Beneath it, I was raw.

"I'm sorry," I said, handing the bundle back to Ben. "I can't. Not now."

He hugged me. I felt nausea rise in my throat, but swallowed it down. He told me not to worry, told me I would be fine, reminded me that he was here for me, that he always would be. I

clung to him, and we sat there, rocking together. I felt numb, totally removed from the room in which we sat. I watched him get
me a glass of water, watched as he closed the box of photographs. I
was sobbing. I could see that he was upset, too, yet already his expression seemed tinged with something else. Resignation, it could
have been, or acceptance, but not shock.

With a shudder, I realized that he has done all this before. His
grief is not new. It has had the time to bed down within him, to
become part of his foundations, rather than something that rocks
them.

It is only my grief that is fresh, every day.

I made an excuse. I came upstairs, to the bedroom. Back to the
closet. I wrote on.

\* \* \*

These snatched moments. Kneeling in front of the closet or leaning on the bed. Writing. I am feverish. It floods out of me, almost
without thought. Pages and pages. I am here again now, while
Ben thinks I am resting. I cannot stop. I want to write down everything.

I wonder if this is what it was like when I wrote my novel, this
pouring onto the page. Or had that been slower, more considered?
I wish I could remember.

After I went downstairs, I made us both a cup of tea. As I stirred
in the milk, I thought of how many times I must have made meals
for Adam, pureeing vegetables, mixing juice. I took the tea back to
Ben. "Was I a good mother?" I said, handing it to him.

"Christine—"

"I have to know," I said. "I mean, how did I cope? With a
child? He must have been very little when I—"

"—had your accident?" he interrupted. "He was two. You were a wonderful mother, though. Until then. Afterward, well—"

He stopped talking, letting the rest of the sentence disappear, and turned away. I wondered what it was he was leaving unsaid, what he'd thought better of telling me.

I knew enough to fill in some of the blanks, though. I might not be able to remember that time, but I can imagine it. I can see myself being reminded every day that I was married and a mother, being told that my husband and son were coming to visit me. I can imagine myself greeting them both every day as if I had never seen them before, slightly frostily, perhaps, or simply bewildered. I can see the pain we must have been in. All of us.

"It's okay," I said. "I understand."

"You couldn't look after yourself. You were too ill for me to look after you at home. You couldn't be left alone, even for a few minutes. You would forget what you were doing. You used to wander off. I was worried you might run yourself a bath and leave the water running, or try and cook yourself some food and forget you'd started it. It was too much for me. So I stayed at home and looked after Adam. My mother helped. But every evening we would come and see you, and—"

I took his hand.

"Sorry," he said. "I just find it hard, thinking of that time."

"I know," I said. "I know. How about my mother, though? Did she help? Did she enjoy being a grandmother?" He nodded and looked about to speak. "She's dead, isn't she?" I said.

He took my hand. "She died a few years ago. I'm sorry."

I had been right. I felt my mind begin to close down, as if it could not process any more grief, any more of this scrambled past, but I knew I would wake up tomorrow and remember none of this.

What could I write in my journal that would get me through tomorrow, the next day, the one after that?

An image floated in front of me. A woman with red hair. Adam in the army. A name came, unbidden. *What will Claire think?*

And there it was. The name of my friend. *Claire.*

"And Claire?" I said. "My friend, Claire. Is she still alive?"

"Claire?" said Ben. He looked puzzled for a long moment, and then his face changed. "You remember Claire?"

He seemed surprised. I reminded myself that—according to my journal, at least—it had been a few days since I had told him I had remembered her at the party on the roof.

"Yes," I said. "We were friends. What happened to her?"

Ben looked at me, sadly, and for a moment I froze. He spoke slowly, but his news was not as bad as I feared. "She moved away," he said. "Years ago. Must be nearly twenty years, I think. Just a few years after we got married, in fact."

"Where to?"

"New Zealand."

"Are we in touch?"

"You were for a while, but no. Not anymore."

It doesn't seem possible. *My best friend,* I had written, after remembering her on Parliament Hill, and I had felt the same sensation of closeness when I had thought of her today. Otherwise, why would I care what she thought?

"We argued?"

He hesitated, and again I sensed a calculation, an adjustment. I realized that, of course, Ben knows what will upset me. He has had years to learn what I will find acceptable and what is dangerous ground for us to tread. After all, this is not the first time he has had this conversation. He has had the opportunity to practice, to learn how to navigate routes that will not rip through the land-scape of my life and send me tumbling somewhere else.

"No," he said. "I don't think so. You didn't argue. Or not that you ever told me anyway. I think you just drifted apart, and then Claire met someone, and she married him, and they moved away."

An image came then. Claire and I joking that we would never marry. "Marriage is for losers!" she was saying as she raised a bottle of red wine to her lips, and I was agreeing, though at the same time knew that one day I would be her bridesmaid, and she mine, and we would sit in hotel rooms, dressed in organza, sipping champagne from a flute while someone did our hair.

I felt a sudden flush of love. Though I have barely remembered any of our time, our life, together—and tomorrow even that will be gone—I sensed somehow that we were still connected, that for a while she had meant everything to me.

"Did we go to the wedding?" I said.

"Yes." He nodded, opening the box on his lap and digging through it. "There are a couple of photos here."

They were wedding pictures, though not formal shots; these were blurred and dark, taken by an amateur. By Ben, I guessed. I approached the first one cautiously.

She was as I had imagined her. Tall, thin. More beautiful, if anything. She was standing on a cliff top, her dress diaphanous, blowing in the breeze, the sun setting over the sea behind her. I put the picture down and looked through the rest. In some she was with her husband—a man I didn't recognize—and in others I had joined them, dressed in pale blue silk, looking only slightly less beautiful. It was true; I had been a bridesmaid.

"Are there any of our wedding?" I said.

He shook his head. "They were in a separate album," he said. "It was lost."

Of course. The fire.

I handed the photos back to him. I felt like I was looking at another life, not my own. I desperately wanted to get upstairs, to write about what I had discovered.

"I'm tired," I said. "I need to rest."

"Of course," he said. He held out his hand. "Here." He took the bundle of photographs from me and put them back in the box.

"I'll keep these safe," he said, closing the lid, and I came up here to my journal, and wrote this.

* * *

Midnight. I am in bed. Alone. Trying to make sense of all that has happened today. All that I have learned. I don't know whether I can.

I decided to take a bath before dinner. I locked the bathroom door behind me and looked quickly at the pictures arranged around the mirror, now seeing only what was missing. I turned on the hot tap.

Most days I realize I don't remember Adam at all, yet today he had come to me after I saw just one picture. Are these photographs selected so they will anchor me in my self without reminding me of what I have lost?

The room began to fill with hot steam. I could hear my husband downstairs. He had turned on the radio and the sound of jazz floated up to me, hazy and indistinct. Beneath it, I could hear the rhythmic slice of a knife on a board. He would be chopping carrots, onions, peppers. Making dinner, as if this were a normal day.

For him, it is a normal day, I realized. I am filled with grief, but not he.

I don't blame him for not telling me, every day, about Adam, my mother, Claire. In his position, I would do the same. These things are painful, and if I can go a whole day without remembering them, then I am spared the sorrow and he the pain of causing it. How tempting it must be for him to keep quiet, and how difficult life must be for him, knowing that I carry these jagged shards of memory with me always, everywhere, like tiny bombs, and at any moment one might pierce the surface and force me to go through the pain as if for the first time, taking him with me.

I undressed slowly, folded my clothes, placed them on the chair by the side of the bath. Naked, I stood in front of the mirror and looked at my alien body. I forced myself to look at the wrinkles in my skin, at my sagging breasts. *I do not know myself,* I thought. *I recognize neither my body nor my past.*

I stepped closer to the mirror. They were there, across my stomach, on my buttocks and breasts. Thin, silvery streaks, the jagged scars of history. I had not seen them before, because I had not looked for them. I pictured myself charting their growth, willing them to disappear as my body expanded. Now I am glad they are there; a reminder.

My reflection began to disappear in the mist. *I am lucky,* I thought. Lucky to have Ben, to have someone to look after me, here, in what is my home, even if I don't remember it as such. I am not the only one suffering. He has been through what I have, today, but will go to bed knowing that tomorrow he might have to do it all again. Another husband might have felt unable to cope, or unwilling. Another husband might have left me. I stared into my own face, as if trying to burn the image into my brain, to leave it near the surface so that when I wake up tomorrow it will not be so alien to me, so shocking. When it had completely vanished, I turned away from myself and stepped into the water. I fell asleep.

I did not dream—or did not think I had—but when I woke, I was confused. I was in a different bathroom, the water still warm, a tapping on the door. I opened my eyes and recognized nothing. The mirror was plain and unadorned, bolted to white tiles rather than blue. A shower curtain hung from a rail above me, two glasses were facedown on a shelf above the sink, and a bidet sat next to the toilet bowl.

I heard a voice. "I'm coming," it said, and I realized it was mine. I sat up in the bath and looked over to the bolted door. Two dressing gowns hung off hooks on the opposite wall, both white, matching, monogrammed with the letters RGH. I stood up.

"Come on!" came a voice from outside the door. It sounded like Ben, but at the same time not Ben. It became singsong. "Come on! Come on, come on, come on!"

"Who is it?" I said, but it did not stop. I stepped out of the bath. The floor was tiled, black and white diagonals. It was wet; I felt myself slip, my feet, my legs giving way. I crashed to the floor, pulling the shower curtain down on top of me. My head hit the sink as I fell. I cried out, "Help me!"

I woke for real, then, with another, different voice calling me. "Christine! Chris! Are you okay?" it said, and with relief I realized it was Ben and I had been dreaming. I opened my eyes. I was lying in a bath, my clothes folded on a chair beside me, pictures of my life taped to the pale blue tiles above the sink.

"Yes," I said. "I'm fine. I just had a bad dream."


I got up, ate dinner, then went to bed. I wanted to write, to get down all I had learned before it disappeared. I wasn't sure I would have time to do so before Ben came to bed.

But what could I do? *I have spent so long today writing,* I thought. Surely he will be suspicious, will wonder what I have been doing, upstairs, alone. I have been telling him I am tired, that I need to rest, and he has believed me.

I cannot say I don't feel guilty. I have heard him, creeping around the house, opening and closing doors softly so as not to wake me, while I have been hunched over my journal, writing furiously. But I have no choice. I have to record these things. To do so seems almost more important than anything, because otherwise I will lose them forever. I must make my excuses and return to my book.

"I think I'll sleep in the spare room tonight," I'd said. "I'm upset. You understand?"

He'd said yes, told me that he would check on me in the morning to make sure that I was all right before he went to work, then kissed me good night. I hear him now, switching off the television, turning the key in the front door. Locking us in. It would do no good for me to wander, I suppose. Not in my condition.

I cannot believe that in a few moments, when I fall asleep, I will forget about my son all over again. The memories of him had seemed—still seem—so real, so vivid. And I had remembered him even after dozing in the bath. It does not seem possible that a longer sleep will erase everything, yet Ben and Dr. Nash tell me that this is exactly what will happen.

Do I dare hope that they are wrong? I am remembering more each day, waking knowing more of who I am. Perhaps things are going well, writing in this journal is bringing my memories to the surface.

Perhaps today is the day I will one day look back on and recognize as a breakthrough. It is possible.

I am tired now. I will stop writing soon, and then hide my journal, turn off the light. Sleep. Pray that tomorrow I may wake and remember my son.

# Thursday, November 15

I was in the bathroom. I didn't know how long I'd been standing there. Just looking. All those pictures of me and Ben smiling happily together, when there should have been three of us. I stared at them, unmoving, as if I thought that might make Adam's image emerge, willed into being. But it did not. He remained invisible.

I had woken with no memory of him. None at all. I still believed motherhood to be something that sat in the future, gleaming and disquieting. Even after I had seen my own middle-aged face, learned that I was a wife, old enough to soon be having grandchildren—even after those facts had sent me reeling—I was unprepared for the journal that Dr. Nash told me, when he called, that I kept in the closet. I did not imagine that I would discover that I am a mother, too. That I have had a child.

I held the journal in my hand. As soon as I read it, I knew it to be true. I had had a son. I felt it, almost as if he were still with me, inside my pores. I read it over and over again, trying to fix it in my mind.

And then I read on, and discovered that he is dead. It did not seem real. Did not seem possible. My heart resisted the knowledge, tried to reject it even as I knew it was true. Nausea hit me. Bile rose in my throat, and as I swallowed it down, the room began to swim. For a moment, I felt myself begin to fall forward to the floor. The journal slid from my lap and I stifled a scream of pain. I stood up, propelling myself out of the bedroom.

I went into the bathroom, to look again at the pictures in which he ought to be. I felt desperate, did not know what I was going to do when Ben came home. I imagined him coming in, kissing me, making dinner; I thought of us eating it together. And then we would watch television, or whatever it is that we do most evenings, and all the time I would have to pretend that I didn't know I had lost a son. And then we would go to bed, together, and after that—

It seemed more than I could bear. I couldn't stop myself. I didn't really know what I was doing. I began to claw at the pictures, ripping, pulling. It seemed to take no time at all, and then they were gone. Scattered on the bathroom floor. Floating in the water in the toilet bowl.

I grabbed this journal and put it in my bag. My purse was empty, and so I took one of the two twenty-pound notes that I had read were hidden behind the clock on the mantelpiece and ran out of the house. I did not know where I was going. I wanted to see Dr. Nash, but had no idea where he was, or how I could get there even if I did. I felt helpless. Alone. And so I ran.

On the street, I turned left, toward the park. It was a sunny afternoon. The orange light reflected off the parked cars and the pools of water left by the morning's storm, but it was cold. My breath misted around me. I pulled my coat tight, my scarf over my ears, and hurried on. Leaves fell from the trees, blew in the wind, piled against the gutter in a brown mush.

I stepped off the curb. The sound of brakes. A car crunched to a halt. A man's voice, muffled, from behind glass.

*Get out of the way!* it said. *Stupid fucking bitch!*

I looked up. I was in the middle of the road, a stalled car in front of me, its driver screaming with fury. I had a vision—myself, metal on bone, crumpling, buckling, and then sliding, up and over the hood of the car, or under it, to lie, a tangled mess, the end of a ruined life.

Could it really be that simple? Would a second collision end what was started by the first, all those years ago? I feel as if I have already been dead for twenty years, but is that where all this has to lead, eventually?

Who would miss me? My husband. A doctor, perhaps, though to him I am only a patient. But there is no one else. Can my circle have drawn so tight? Did my friends abandon me, one by one? How quickly I would be forgotten, were I to die.

I looked at the man in the car. He, or someone like him, did this to me. Robbed me of everything. Robbed me even of myself. Yet there he was, still living.

*Not yet*, I thought. *Not yet*. However my life was to end, I did not want it to be like this. I thought of the novel I had written, the child I had raised, even the fireworks party with my best friend all those years ago. I still have memories to unearth. Things to discover. My own truth to find.

I mouthed "Sorry," and ran on, over the road, through a gate and into the park.

There was a hut, in the middle of the grass. A café. I went in and bought myself coffee and then sat on one of the benches, warming my hands on the Styrofoam cup. Opposite was a playground. A slide, swings, a carousel. A small boy sat on a seat shaped like a ladybug, which was fixed to the ground by a heavy spring. I watched him rock himself back and forth, an ice cream in one hand, despite the cold.

My mind flashed on a vision of myself and another young girl in the park. I saw the two of us, climbing stairs to a wooden cage from where we would glide to the ground on a metal slide. How high it had felt, all those years ago, yet looking at the playground now, I saw that it must have been only a little higher than I am tall. We would muddy our dresses and be told off by our mothers, and skip home, clutching bags of candy or potato chips.

Was this memory? Or invention?

I watched the boy. He was alone. The park seemed empty. Just the two of us, in the cold, under a sky roofed with a dark cloud. I took a mouthful of my coffee.

"Hey!" said the boy. "Hey! Lady!"

I looked up, then down at my hands.

"Hey!" he shouted more loudly. "Lady! You help! You spin me!"

He got up and went over to the carousel. "You spin me!" he said. He tried to push the metal contraption, but despite the effort evident in his face it barely moved. He gave up, looking disappointed. "Please?" he said.

"You'll be okay," I called. I took a sip of my coffee. I would wait here, I decided, until his mother came back from wherever she was. I would keep an eye on him.

He climbed onto the carousel, shifting himself until he stood right in its center. "You spin me!" he said again. His voice was lower. Pleading. I wished I had not come here, could make him go away. I felt removed from the world. Unnatural. Dangerous. I thought of the photos I had ripped off the wall and left scattered in the bathroom. I had come here for peace. Not this.

I looked at the boy. He had moved, was trying once again to push himself around, his legs barely reaching the ground from where he stood on the carousel's platform. He looked so fragile. Helpless. I went over to him.

"You push me!" he said. I put my coffee on the ground and grinned.

"Hold tight!" I said. I heaved my weight against the bar. It was surprisingly heavy, but I felt it begin to give, and walked around with it so that it gained speed. "Here we go!" I said. I sat on the edge of the platform.

He grinned excitedly, clutching the metal bar with his hands as though we were spinning far more quickly than we were. His hands looked cold, almost blue. He was wearing a green coat that looked far too thin, a pair of jeans, turned up at the ankle. I wondered who had sent him out without gloves, or a scarf, or a hat.

"Where's your mummy?" I said. He shrugged. "Your daddy?"

"Dunno," he said. "Mummy says Daddy's gone. She says he doesn't love us no more."

I looked at him. He had said it with no sense of pain, or disappointment. For him it was a simple statement of fact. For a moment the carousel felt perfectly still, the world spinning around the two of us rather than us within it.

"I bet your mummy loves you, though?" I said.

He was silent for a few seconds. "Sometimes," he said.

"But sometimes she doesn't?"

He paused. "I don't think so." I felt a thudding in my chest, as if something was turning over. Or waking. "She says not. Sometimes."

"That's a shame," I said. I watched the bench I had been sitting on come toward us, then recede. We spun, again and again.

"What's your name?"

"Alfie," he said. We were slowing down, the world coming to a halt behind his head. My feet connected with the ground and I kicked off, spinning us again. I said his name, as if to myself. *Alfie.*

"Mummy says sometimes she'd be better off if I lived somewhere else," he said.

I tried to keep smiling, my voice cheery. "I bet she's joking though?"

He shrugged.

My whole body tensed. I saw myself asking him if he would like to come with me. Home. To live. I imagined how his face would brighten, even as he said he wasn't supposed to go anywhere with strangers. *But I'm not a stranger,* I would say. I would lift him up— he would be heavy and smell sweet, like chocolate—and together we would go into the café. *What juice do you want?* I would say, and he would ask for apple. I would buy him a drink, and some candy, too, and we would leave the park. He would be holding my hand as we walked back home, back to the house I shared with my husband, and that night I would cut his meat for him and mash his potatoes, and then, once he was in his pajamas, I would read him a story before tucking the covers under his sleeping body and kissing him softly on the top of his head. And tomorrow—

*Tomorrow? I have no tomorrow,* I thought. Just as I had no yesterday.

"Mummy!" he called out. For a moment, I thought he was talking to me, but he leaped off the carousel and ran toward the café.

"Alfie!" I called out, but then I saw a woman walking over, clutching a plastic cup in each hand.

She crouched down as he reached her. "Y'all right, Tiger?" she said as he ran into her arms, and she looked up, past him, at me. Her eyes were narrowed, her face set hard. *I've done nothing wrong!* I wanted to shout. *Leave me alone!*

But I didn't. Instead I looked the other way and then, once she had led Alfie away, I got off the carousel. The sky was darkening now, turning to an inky blue. I sat on a bench. I didn't know what time it was, or how long I'd been out. I knew only that I couldn't go home, not yet. I couldn't face Ben. I couldn't face having to pretend I knew nothing about Adam, that I had no idea I'd had a child. For a moment, I wanted to tell him everything. About my journal, Dr. Nash. Everything. But I pushed the thought from my mind. I did not want to go home, but had nowhere else to go.

I stood and began to walk as the sky turned black.

The house was in darkness. I did not know what to expect when I pushed open the front door. Ben would be missing me; he had said he would be home by five. I pictured him pacing up and down the living room—for some reason, even though I had not seen him smoke this morning, my imagination added a lit cigarette to this scene—or maybe he was out, driving the streets, looking for me. I imagined teams of police and volunteers out there, going from door to door with a photocopied picture of me, and felt guilty. I tried to tell myself that, even though I had no memory, I was not a child, I was not a missing person, not yet, but still I went into the house ready to make an apology.

I called out. "Ben?" There was no answer, but I felt, rather than heard, movement. A creak of a floorboard, somewhere above me, an almost imperceptible shift in the equilibrium of the house. I called out, again, louder this time. "Ben?"

"Christine?" came a voice. It sounded weak, cracked open.

"Ben," I said. "Ben, it's me. I'm here."

He appeared above me, standing at the top of the stairs. He looked as though he'd been sleeping. He was still wearing the clothes he'd put on that morning to go to work, but now his shirt was creased and hung loose from his trousers, and his hair stood out in all directions, emphasizing his look of shock with an almost comical hint of electricity. A memory floated through me—science lessons and Van de Graaff generators—but did not emerge.

He started to come down the stairs. "Chris, you're home!"

"I . . . I had to get some air," I said.

"Thank God," he said. He came over to where I stood and took my hand. He gripped it, as if to shake it, or to make sure it was real, but did not move it. "Thank God!"

He looked at me, his eyes wide, glowing. They glistened in the dim light as though he'd been crying. *How much he loves me*, I thought. My feeling of guilt intensified.

"I'm sorry," I said. "I didn't mean to—"

He interrupted me. "Oh, let's not worry about that, shall we?"

He brought my hand to his lips. His expression changed, became one of pleasure, of happiness. All traces of anxiety disappeared. He kissed me.

"But—"

"You're back, now. That's the main thing." He flicked on the light and then smoothed his hair into a semblance of order. "Right!" he said, tucking in his shirt. "What say you go and freshen up? And then I thought we could go out? What do you think?"

"I don't think so," I said. "I—"

"Oh, Christine. We should! You look like you need cheering up!"

"But, Ben, I don't feel like it."

"Please?" he said. He took my hand again, squeezing it gently. "It would mean a lot to me." He took my other hand and brought them both together, between his. "I don't know if I told you this morning. It's my birthday today."

What could I do? I did not want to go out. But then, I did not want to do anything. I told him I would do as he asked, would freshen up, and then see how I felt. I went upstairs. His mood had disturbed me. He had seemed so concerned, but, as soon as I appeared safe and well, that concern evaporated. Did he really love me so much? Trust me so much that all he cared about was that I was safe, not where I had been?

I went into the bathroom. Perhaps he hadn't seen the photos scattered all over the floor, genuinely believed I had been out for a walk. There was still time for me to cover my tracks. To hide my anger and my grief.

I locked the door behind me. I pulled the cord and turned on the light. The floor had been swept clean. There, arranged around the mirror as if they had never been moved, were the photographs, every one perfectly restored.

I told Ben I would be ready in half an hour. I sat in the bedroom and, as quickly as I could, wrote this.

# Friday, November 16

I do not know what happened after that. What did I do after Ben told me that it was his birthday? After I went upstairs and discovered the photographs, replaced just as they had been before I ripped them down? I don't know. Perhaps I showered and got changed, maybe we went out, for a meal, to the movies. I cannot say. I did not write it down and do not remember, despite it being only a few hours ago. Unless I ask Ben, it is lost completely. I feel like I am going mad.

This morning, in the early hours, I woke with him lying next to me. A stranger, again. The room was dark, silent. I lay, rigid with fear, not knowing who, or where, I was. I could think only of running, of escape, but could not move. My mind felt scooped out, hollow, but then words floated to the surface. Ben. Husband. Memory. Accident. Death. Son.

Adam.

They hung in front of me, in and out of focus. I could not connect them. Did not know what they meant. They whirled in my mind, echoing, a mantra, and then the dream came back to me, the dream that must have woken me up.

I was in a room, in a bed. In my arms was a body, a man. He lay on top of me, heavy, his back broad. I felt peculiar, odd, my head too light, my body too heavy; the room rocked beneath me, and when I opened my eyes, its ceiling would not swim into focus.

I could not tell who the man was—his head was too close to mine for me to see his face—but I could feel everything, even the hairs on his chest, rough against my naked breasts. There was a taste on my tongue, furry, sweet. He was kissing me. He was too rough; I wanted him to stop, but said nothing. "I love you," he said, murmuring, his words lost in my hair, the side of my neck. I knew I wanted to speak—though I did not know what I wanted to say—but I could not understand how to do so. My mouth did not seem connected to my brain, and so I lay there as he kissed me and spoke into my hair. I remembered how I had both wanted him and wanted him to stop, how I had told myself, as he began to kiss me, that we would not have sex, but his hand had moved down the curve of my back to my buttocks and I had let it. And again, as he had lifted my blouse and put his hand beneath it, I thought, *This, this is as far as I will let you go. I will not stop you, not now, because I am enjoying this. Because your hand feels warm on my breast, because my body is responding with tiny shudders of pleasure. Because, for the first time, I feel like a woman. But I will not have sex with you. Not tonight. This is as far as we will go, this far and no further.* And then he had taken off my blouse and unhooked my bra, and it was not his hand on my breast but his mouth, and still I thought I would stop him, soon. The word "no" had even begun to form, cemented itself in my mind, but by the time I had spoken it, he was pushing me back toward the bed and sliding down my underwear, and it had turned into something else, into a moan of something that I dimly recognized as pleasure.

I felt something between my knees. It was hard. "I love you," he said again, and I realized it was his knee, that he was forcing my legs apart with one of his own. I did not want to let him, but at the same time knew that somehow I ought to, that I had left it too late, watched my chances to say something, to stop this, disappear one by one. And now I had no choice. I had wanted it then, as he unzipped his trousers and stepped clumsily out of his underwear, and so I must still want it now, now that I am beneath his body.

I tried to relax. He arched up and moaned—a low, startling noise that started deep within him—and I saw his face. I didn't recognize it, not in my dream, but now I knew it. Ben. "I love you," he said, and I knew that I should say something, that he was my husband, even though I felt I had met him for the first time just that morning. I could stop him. I could trust him to stop himself.

"Ben, I—"

He silenced me with his wet mouth, and I felt him tear into me. Pain, or pleasure. I could not tell where one ended and the other began. I clung to his back, moist with sweat, and tried to open myself to him, tried first to enjoy what was happening, and then, when I found I could not, tried to ignore it. *I asked for this,* I thought, at the same time as *I never asked for this.* Is it possible to both want and not want something at the same time? For desire to ride with fear?

I closed my eyes. I saw a face. A stranger, with dark hair, a beard. A scar down his cheek. He looked familiar, yet I had no idea from where. As I watched him, his smile disappeared, and that was when I cried out, in my dream. That was the moment I woke up to find myself in a still, quiet bed, with Ben lying next to me and no idea where I was.

I got out of bed. To use the bathroom? To escape? I did not know where I was going, what I would do. If I had somehow known of its existence, I would have opened the closet door, as quietly as I could, and lifted out the shoebox that contained my journal, but I did not. And so, I went downstairs. The front door was locked, the moonlight blue through the frosted glass. I realized I was naked.

I sat on the bottom of the stairs. The sun rose, the hall turned from blue to burned orange. Nothing made sense; the dream least of all. It felt too real, and I had woken in the same bedroom I had dreamed myself in, next to a man I was not expecting to see.

And now, now I have read my journal after Dr. Nash called me, a thought forms. *Might it have been a memory?* A memory I had retained from the previous night?

I do not know. If so, then it is a sign of progress, I suppose. But also it means Ben forced himself on me and, worse, as he did so, I saw an image of a bearded stranger, a scar running down his face. Of all possible memories, this seems a cruel one to retain.

But perhaps it means nothing. It was just a dream. Just a nightmare. Ben loves me and the bearded stranger does not exist.

But how can I ever know for sure?

Later, I saw Dr. Nash. We were sitting at a traffic light, Dr. Nash tapping his fingers on the rim of the steering wheel, not quite in time to the music that played from the stereo—pop that I neither recognized nor enjoyed—while I stared ahead. I'd called him this morning, almost as soon as I had finished reading my journal, finished writing about the dream that might have been a memory. I had to speak to someone—the news that I was a mother had felt like a tiny rip in my life, which now threatened to snag, tearing it apart—and he'd suggested we move our next meeting to today. He asked me to bring my journal. I hadn't told him what was wrong, intending to wait until we were in his offices, but now didn't know whether I could.

The light changed. He stopped tapping and we jerked back

into motion. "Why doesn't Ben tell me about Adam?" I heard my-self say. "I don't understand. Why?"

He glanced at me but said nothing. We drove a little farther. A plastic dog sat in the back window of the car in front of us, its head bobbing comically, and beyond it I could see the blond hair of a toddler. I thought of Alfie.

Dr. Nash coughed. "Tell me what happened."

It was true, then. Part of me was hoping he would ask me what I was talking about, but as soon as I had said "Adam," I had real-ized how futile that hope had been, how misguided. Adam feels real. He exists, within me, within my consciousness, taking up space in a way that no one else does. Not Ben, or Dr. Nash. Not even myself.

I felt angry. He had known all along.

"And you," I said. "You gave me my novel. So why didn't you tell me about Adam?"

"Christine," he said. "Tell me what happened."

I stared out of the front window. "I had a memory," I said.

He glanced across at me. "Really?" I didn't say anything. "Christine," he said. "I'm trying to help."

I told him. "It was the other day," I said. "After you'd given me my novel. I looked at the photograph that you'd put with it and, suddenly, I remembered the day it was taken. I can't say why. It just came to me. And I remembered that I'd been pregnant."

He said nothing.

"You knew about him?" I said. "About Adam?"

He spoke slowly. "Yes," he said. "I did. It's in your file. He was a couple of years old when you lost your memory." He paused. "Plus, we've spoken about him before."

I felt myself go cold. I shivered, despite the warmth in the car. I knew it was possible, even probable, that I had remembered Adam before, but this bare truth—that I had gone through all this before and would therefore go through it all again—shook me.

He must have sensed my surprise.

"A few weeks ago," he said, "you told me you'd seen a child, out in the street. A little boy. At first you had the overwhelming sense that you knew him, that he was lost but was coming home, to your house, and you were his mother. Then it came back to you. You told Ben, and he told you about Adam. Later that day you told me."

I remembered nothing of this. I reminded myself that he was not talking about a stranger, but about me.

"But you haven't told me about him since?"

He sighed. "No—"

Without warning, I remembered what I had read this morning, of the images they had shown me as I lay in the scanner.

"There were pictures of him!" I said. "When I had my scan! There were pictures . . ."

"Yes," he said. "From your file . . ."

"But you didn't mention him! Why? I don't understand."

"Christine, you must accept that I can't begin every session by telling you all the things I know but you don't. Plus, in this case, I decided it wouldn't necessarily benefit you."

"Benefit me?"

"No. I knew it would be very upsetting for you to know that you had a child and have forgotten him."

We were pulling into an underground parking lot. The soft daylight faded, replaced by harsh fluorescence and the smell of gasoline and concrete. I wondered what else he might feel it unethical to tell me, what other time bombs I am carrying in my head, primed and ticking, ready to explode.

"There aren't any more—?" I said.

"No," he interrupted. "You only had Adam. He was your only child."

The past tense. Then Dr. Nash knew he was dead, too. I did not want to ask, but knew that I must.

"You know he was killed?"

He stopped the car and turned off the engine. The parking lot was dim, lit only by pools of fluorescent light, and silent. I heard nothing but the occasional door slamming, the rattle of an elevator. For a moment, I thought there was still a chance. Maybe I was wrong. Adam was alive. My mind lit with the idea. Adam had felt real to me as soon as I read about him this morning, yet still his death did not. I tried to picture it, or to remember how it must have felt to be given the news that he had been killed, yet I could not. It did not seem right. Grief should surely overwhelm me. Every day would be filled with constant pain, with longing, with the knowledge that part of me has died and I will never be whole again. Surely my love for my son would be strong enough for me to remember my loss. If he really were dead, then surely my grief would be stronger than my amnesia.

I realized I did not believe my husband. I did not believe my son was dead. For a moment, my happiness hung, balancing, but then Dr. Nash spoke.

"Yes," he said. "I know."

Excitement discharged within me like a tiny explosion, turned to its opposite. Something worse than disappointment. More destructive, shot through with pain.

"How . . . ?" was all I could say.

He told me the same story as Ben. Adam, in the army. A roadside bomb. I listened, determined to find the strength not to cry. When he had finished, there was a pause, a moment of stillness, before he put his hand on mine.

"Christine," he said softly. "I'm so sorry."

I didn't know what to say. I looked at him. He was leaning toward me. I looked down at his hand, covering mine, crisscrossed with tiny scratches. I saw him at home, later. Playing with a kitten, perhaps a small dog. Living a normal life.

"My husband does not tell me about Adam," I said. "He keeps all of the photographs of him locked away in a metal box. For my own protection." Dr. Nash said nothing. "Why would he do that?"

He looked out of the window. I saw the word CUNT sprayed onto the wall in front of us. "Let me ask you the same question. Why do you think he would do that?"

I thought. I thought of all the reasons I could. So that he can control me. Have power over me. So that he can deny me this one thing that might make me feel complete. I realized I didn't believe any of those were true. I was left only with the mundane fact. "I suppose it's easier for him. Not to tell me, if I don't remember."

"Why is it easier for him?"

"Because I find it so upsetting? It must be a horrible thing to have to do, to tell me every day that not only have I had a child but that he has died. And in such a horrible way."

"Any other reasons, do you think?"

I was silent, and then realized. "Well, it must be hard for him too. He was Adam's father and, well . . ." I thought how he must be managing his own grief, as well as mine.

"This is difficult for you, Christine," Dr. Nash said. "But you must try to remember that it is difficult for Ben, too. More difficult, in some ways. He loves you very much, I expect, and—"

"—and yet I don't even remember he exists."

"True," he said.

I sighed. "I must have loved him, once. After all, I married him." He said nothing. I thought of the stranger I had woken up with that morning, of the photos of our lives together I had seen, of the dream—or the memory—I had had in the middle of the night. I thought of Adam, and of Alfie, of what I had done, or thought about doing. A panic rose in me. I felt trapped, as though there was no way out, my mind skittering from one thing to another, searching for freedom and release.

*Ben,* I thought to myself. *I can cling to Ben. He is strong.*

"What a mess," I said. "I just feel overwhelmed."

He turned back to face me. "I wish I could do something to make this easier for you."

He looked as though he really meant it, as though he would do anything he could to help me. There was a tenderness in his eyes, in the way he rested his hand on mine, and there, in the dim half-light of the underground parking lot, I found myself wondering what would happen if I put my hand on his, or moved my head slightly forward, holding his gaze, opening my mouth as I did so, just a touch. Would he, too, lean forward? Would he try to kiss me? Would I let him, if he did?

Or would he think me ridiculous? Absurd? I may have woken this morning thinking I am in my twenties, but I am not. I am almost fifty. Nearly old enough to be his mother. And so, instead, I looked at him. He sat perfectly still, looking at me. He seemed strong. Strong enough to help me. To get me through.

I opened my mouth to speak, without knowing what I was going to say, but the muffled ringing of a telephone interrupted me. Dr. Nash didn't move, other than to take his hand away, and I realized the phone must be one of mine.

I retrieved the ringing phone from my bag. It was not the one that flipped open but the one my husband has given me. BEN, it said on the screen.

When I saw his name, I realized how unfair I was being. He was bereaved, too. And he had to live with it, every day, without being able to speak to me about it, without being able to come to his wife for support.

And he did all that for love.

And here was I, sitting in a parking lot with a man he barely knew existed. I thought of the photos I had seen that morning, in the scrapbook. Me and Ben, over and over again. Smiling. Happy. In love. If I were to go home and look at them now, I might only see in them the thing that was missing. Adam. But they are the same pictures, and in them we look at each other as if no one else in the world exists.

We had been in love; it was obvious.

"I'll call him back, later," I said. I put the phone back in my bag. *I will tell him tonight,* I thought. *About my journal. Dr. Nash. Everything.*

Dr. Nash coughed. "We should go up to the office. Make a start?"

"Of course," I said. I did not look at him.

* * *

I began to write that in the car as Dr. Nash drove me home. Much of it is barely legible, a hasty scrawl. Dr. Nash said nothing as I wrote, but I saw him glancing at me as I searched for the right word or a better phrase. I wondered what he was thinking— before we left his office, he had asked me to consent to him discussing my case at a conference he had been invited to attend. "In Geneva," he said, unable to disguise a flash of pride. I said yes, and I imagined he would soon ask me if he could take a photocopy of my journal. *For research.*

When we arrived back at the house, he said good-bye, adding, "I'm surprised you wanted to write your book in the car. You

seem very . . . determined. I suppose you don't want to miss anything out."

I know what he meant, though. He meant frantic. Desperate.
Desperate to get everything down.

And he is right. I am determined. Once I got in, I finished the
entry at the dining table and closed my journal and put it back
in its hiding place before slowly undressing. Ben had left me a
message on the phone. *Let's go out tonight,* he'd said. *For dinner. It's
Friday . . .*

I stepped out of the navy blue trousers I had found in the closet
that morning. I peeled off the pale blue blouse that I had decided
matched them best. I was bewildered. I had given Dr. Nash my
journal during our session—he'd asked if he could read it and I'd
said yes. This was before he'd mentioned his invite to Geneva,
and I wonder now if that's why he asked. "This is excellent!" he'd
said when he finished. "Really good. You're remembering lots of
things, Christine. Lots of memories are coming back. There's no
reason that won't continue. You should feel very encouraged . . ."

But I did not feel encouraged. I felt confused. Had I flirted with
him, or he with me? It was his hand on mine, but I had let him
put it there, and let him keep it. "You should continue to write,"
he said, when he gave me the journal back, and I told him that I
would.

Now, in my bedroom, I tried to convince myself I had done
nothing wrong. I still felt guilty. Because I had enjoyed it. The attention, the feeling of connection. For a moment, in the middle of
everything else that was going on, there had been a tiny pinprick
of joy. I had felt attractive. Desirable.

I went to my underwear drawer. There, tucked at the back, I
found a pair of black silk panties, and a matching bra. I put them
on—these clothes that I know must be mine even though they do

not feel as though they are—all the time thinking of my journal hidden within the closet. What would Ben think, if he found it? If he read all that I had written, all that I had felt? Would he understand?

I stood in front of the mirror. He would, I told myself. He must. I examined my body with my eyes and my hands. I explored it, ran my fingers over its contours and undulations as if it were something new, a gift. Something to be learned from scratch.

Though I knew that Dr. Nash had not been flirting with me, for that brief space in which I thought he was, I had not felt old. I had felt alive.

I do not know how long I stood there. For me time stretches, is almost meaningless. Years have slipped through me, leaving no trace. Minutes do not exist. I only had the chime of the clock downstairs to show me that time was passing at all. I looked at my body, at the weight in my buttocks and on my hips, the dark hairs on my legs, under my arms. I found a razor in the bathroom and soaped my legs, then drew the cold blade across my skin. I must have done this before, I thought, countless times, yet still it seemed an odd thing to be doing, faintly ridiculous. I nicked the skin on my calf—a tiny stab of pain and then a red plush welled, quivering before it began to trickle down my leg. I stemmed it with a finger, smearing the blood like treacle, brought it to my lips. The taste of soap and warm metal. It did not clot. I let it bleed down my skin, newly smooth, then mopped it with a damp tissue.

Back in the bedroom, I put on stockings and a tight black dress. I selected a gold necklace from the box on the dresser, a pair of matching earrings. I sat at the dresser and put on makeup, and curled and gelled my hair. I sprayed perfume on my wrists and behind my ears. And all the time I did this, a memory was floating through me. I saw myself rolling on stockings, snapping home the fasteners on a garter belt, hooking up a bra, but it was a different me, in a different room. The room was quiet. Music played, but softly, and in the distance I could hear voices, doors opening and closing, the faint buzz of traffic. I felt calm and happy. I turned to the mirror, examined my face in the glow of the candlelight. *Not bad*, I thought. *Not bad at all.*

The memory was just out of reach. It shimmered, under the surface, and while I could see details, snatched images, moments, it lay too deep for me to follow where it led. I saw a champagne bottle on a bedside table. Two glasses. A bouquet of flowers on the bed, a card. I saw that I was in a hotel room, alone, waiting for the man I loved. I heard a knock, saw myself stand up, walk toward the door, but then it ended, as if I had been watching television and, suddenly, the aerial had been disconnected. I looked up and saw myself back in my own home. Even though the woman I saw in the mirror was a stranger—and with the makeup and gelled hair that unfamiliarity was even more pronounced than it must usually be—I felt ready. For what, I could not say, but I felt ready. I went downstairs to wait for my husband, the man I married, the man I loved.

*Love*, I remind myself. *The man I love.*

I heard his key in the lock, the door pushed open, feet being wiped on the mat. A whistle? Or was that the sound of my breathing, hard and heavy?

A voice. "Christine? Christine, are you all right?"

"Yes," I said. "I'm in here."

A cough, the sound of his jacket being hung up, a briefcase being put down.

He called upstairs. "Everything okay?" he said. "I phoned you earlier. I left a message."

The creak of the stairs. For a moment, I thought he was going straight up, to the bathroom or his study, without coming in to see me first, and I felt foolish, ridiculous to be dressed as I was, wearing someone else's clothes, waiting for my husband of who knows how many years. I wished I could peel off the outfit, scrape away the makeup, and transform myself back into the woman I am, but I heard a grunt as he levered a shoe off, and then the other, and I realized he was sitting down to put on his slippers. The stair creaked again, and he came into the room.

"Darling—" he began, and he stopped. His eyes traveled over my face, down my body, back up to meet mine. I could not tell what he thought.

"Wow," he said. "You look—" He shook his head.

"I found these clothes," I said. "I thought I would dress up a little. It's Friday night after all. The weekend."

"Yes," he said, still standing in the doorway. "Yes. But . . ."

"Do you want to go out somewhere?"

I stood up then, and went over to him. "Kiss me," I said, and, though I hadn't exactly planned it, it felt like the right thing to do, and so I put my arms around his neck. He smelled of soap, and sweat, and work. Sweet, like crayons. A memory floated through me—kneeling on the floor with Adam, drawing—but it did not stick.

"Kiss me," I said again. His hands circled my waist.

Our lips met. Brushing, at first. A kiss good-night or good-bye, a kiss for being in public, a kiss for your mother. I didn't release my arms, and he kissed me again. The same.

"Kiss me, Ben," I said. "Properly."

"Ben," I said later. "Are we happy?"

We were sitting in a restaurant, one we'd been to before, he said, though I had no idea, of course. Framed photographs of people who I assumed were minor celebrities dotted the walls; an oven gaped at the back, awaiting pizza. I picked at the plate of melon in front of me. I couldn't remember ordering it.

"I mean," I continued. "We've been married . . . how long?"

"Let's see," he said. "Twenty-two years." It sounded an impossibly long time. I thought of the vision I'd had as I got ready this afternoon. Flowers in a hotel room. I can only have been waiting for him.

"Are we happy?"

He put down his fork and sipped at the dry white wine he'd ordered. A family arrived and took their seats at the table next to us. Elderly parents, a daughter in her twenties. Ben spoke.

"We're in love, if that's what you mean. I certainly love you."

And there it was; my cue to tell him that I loved him, too. Men always say *I love you* as a question.

What could I say, though? He is a stranger. Love doesn't happen in the space of twenty-four hours, no matter how much I might once have liked to believe that it does.

"I know you don't love me," he said. I looked at him, shocked for a moment. "Don't worry. I understand the situation you're in. We're in. You don't remember, but we were in love, once. Totally, utterly. Like in the stories, you know? Romeo and Juliet, all that crap." He tried to laugh, but instead looked awkward. "I loved you and you loved me. We were happy, Christine. Very happy."

"Until my accident."

He flinched at the word. Had I said too much? I'd read my journal but was it today he'd told me about the hit-and-run? I didn't know but, still, *accident* would have been a reasonable guess to make for anyone in my situation. I decided not to worry about it.

"Yes," he said sadly. "Until then. We were happy."

"And now?"

"Now? I wish things could be different, but I'm not unhappy, Chris. I love you. I wouldn't want anyone else."

*How about me?* I thought. *Am I unhappy?*

I looked across at the table next to us. The father was holding a pair of glasses to his eyes, squinting at the laminated menu, while his wife arranged their daughter's hat and removed her scarf. The girl sat without helping, looking at nothing, her mouth slightly open. Her right hand twitched under the table. A thin string of saliva hung from her chin. Her father noticed me watching, and I looked away, back to my husband, too quickly to make it seem as if I hadn't been staring. They must be used to that—to people looking away, a moment too late.

I sighed. "I wish I could remember what happened."

"What happened?" he said. "Why?"

I thought of all the other memories that had come to me. They had been brief, transitory. They were gone now. Vanished. But I had written them down; I knew they had existed—still did exist, somewhere. They were just lost.

I felt sure that there must be a key, a memory that would unlock all the others.

"I just think that if I could remember my accident, then maybe I could remember other things, too. Not everything, maybe, but enough. Our wedding, for example, our honeymoon. I can't even remember that." I sipped my wine. I had nearly said our son's name before remembering that Ben did not know I had read about him. "Just to wake up and remember who I am would be something."

Ben locked his fingers, resting his chin on his balled fist. "The doctors said that wouldn't happen."

"But they don't know, do they? Surely? They could be wrong?"

"I doubt it."

I put down my glass. He was wrong. He thought all was lost, that my past had vanished completely. Maybe this was the time to tell him about the snatched moments I still had, about Dr. Nash. My journal. Everything.

"But I am remembering things, occasionally," I said. He looked surprised. "I think things are coming back to me, in flashes."

He unlaced his hands. "Really? What things?"

"Oh, it depends. Sometimes nothing very much. Just odd feelings, sensations. Visions. A bit like dreams, but they seem too real for me to be making them up." He said nothing. "They must be memories."

I waited, expecting him to ask me more, to want me to tell him everything I had seen, as well as how I even knew what memories I had experienced.

But he did not speak. He continued looking at me sadly. I thought of the memories I had written about, the one in which he had offered me wine in the kitchen of our first home. "I had a vision of you," I said. "Much younger . . ."

"What was I doing?" he said.

"Not much," I replied. "Just standing in the kitchen." I thought of the girl, her mother and father, sitting a few feet away. My voice dropped to a whisper. "Kissing me."

He smiled then.

"I thought that if I am capable of having one memory, then maybe I am capable of having lots—"

He reached across the table and took my hand. "But the thing is, tomorrow you won't remember that memory. That's the problem. You have no foundation on which to build."

I sighed. What he was saying is true; I can't keep writing down everything that happens to me for the rest of my life, not if I also have to read it every day.

I looked across at the family next to us. The girl spooned minestrone clumsily into her mouth, soaking the cloth bib that her mother had tucked around her neck. I could see their lives, broken, trapped by the role of caregivers, a role they had expected to be free of years before.

*We are the same,* I thought. I need to be spoon-fed, too. And, I realized, rather like them and their child, Ben loves me in a way that can never be reciprocated.

And yet, maybe, we were different. Maybe we still had hope.

"Do you want me to get better?" I said.

He looked surprised. "Christine," he said. "Please . . ."

"Maybe if there was someone I could see? A doctor?"

"We've tried before—"

"But maybe it's worth trying again? Things are improving all the time. Maybe there's a new treatment?"

He squeezed my hand. "Christine, there isn't. Believe me. We've tried everything."

"What?" I said. "What have we tried?"

"Chris, please. Don't—"

"What have we tried?" I said. "What?"

"Everything," he said. "Everything. You don't know what it was like." He looked uncomfortable. His eyes darted left and right as if he expected a blow and didn't know from what direction it might come. I could have let the question go then, but I didn't.

"What, Ben? I need to know. What was it like?"

He said nothing.

"Tell me!"

He lifted his head and swallowed hard. He looked terrified, his face red, his eyes wide. "You were in a coma," he said. "Everyone thought you were going to die. But not me. I knew you were strong, that you'd make it through. I knew you'd get better. And then, one day, the hospital called me and said you'd woken up. They thought it was a miracle, but I knew it wasn't. It was you, my Chris, coming back to me. You were dazed. Confused. You didn't know where you were, and couldn't remember anything about the accident, but you recognized me, and your mother, though you didn't really know who we were. They said not to worry, that memory loss was normal after such severe injuries, that it would pass. But then——" He shrugged, looked down to the napkin he held in his hands. For a moment, I thought he wasn't going to continue.

"Then what?"

"Well, you seemed to get worse. I went in one day and you had no idea who I was. You presumed I was a doctor. And then you forgot who you were, too. You couldn't remember your name, what year you were born. Anything. They realized that you had stopped forming new memories, too. They did tests, scans. Everything. But it was no good. They said your accident had damaged your memory. That it would be permanent. That there was no cure, nothing they could do."

"Nothing? They didn't do anything?"

"No. They said your memory would either come back or it wouldn't, and that the longer you went without it coming back the less likely it was that it would. They told me that all I could do was look after you. And that's what I've been trying to do." He took both my hands in his, stroking my fingers, brushing the hard band of my wedding ring.

He leaned forward so that his head was only inches from mine. "I love you," he whispered, but I couldn't reply, and we ate the rest of our meal in near-silence. I could feel a resentment growing within me. An anger. He seemed so determined that I could not be helped. So adamant. Suddenly I did not feel so inclined to tell him about my journal or Dr. Nash. I wanted to keep my secrets for a little longer. I felt they were the only thing I had that I could say was mine.

We came home. Ben made himself coffee and I went to the bathroom. There I wrote as much as I could of the day so far, then took off my clothes and makeup. I put on my dressing gown. Another day was ending. Soon I will sleep, and my brain will begin to delete everything. Tomorrow I will go through it all again.

I realized I do not have ambition. I cannot. All I want is to feel normal. To live like everybody else, with experience building on experience, each day shaping the next. I want to grow, to learn things, and from things. There, in the bathroom, I thought of my old age. I tried to imagine what it will be like. Will I still wake up, in my seventies or eighties, thinking myself to be at the beginning of my life? Will I wake with no idea that my bones are old, my joints stiff and heavy? I cannot imagine how I will cope when I discover that my life is behind me, has already happened, and I have nothing to show for it. No treasure house of recollection, no wealth of experience, no accumulated wisdom to pass on. What are we, if not an accumulation of our memories? How will I feel when I look in a mirror and see the reflection of my grandmother? I do not know, but I cannot allow myself to think of that now.

I heard Ben go into the bedroom. I realized I would not be able to replace my journal in the closet, and so put it on the chair next to the bath, under my discarded clothes. I will move it later, I thought, once he is asleep. I switched off the light and went into the bedroom.

Ben sat in bed, watching me. I said nothing but climbed in next to him. I realized he was naked. "I love you, Christine," he said, and he began to kiss me, my neck, my cheek, my lips. His breath was hot and had the bite of garlic. I did not want him to kiss me, but did not push him away. *I have asked for this*, I thought. By wearing that stupid dress, by putting on the makeup and perfume, by asking him to kiss me before we went out.

I turned to face him and, though I did not want to, kissed him back. I tried to imagine the two of us in the house we had just bought together, tearing at our clothes on the way to the bedroom, our uncooked lunch spoiling in the kitchen. I told myself that I must have loved him then—or else why would I have married him?—and so there is no reason why I shouldn't love him now. I told myself that what I was doing was important, an expression of love and of gratitude, and when his hand moved to my breast, I didn't stop him but told myself it was natural, normal. Neither did I stop him when he slipped his hand between my legs and cupped me, and only I knew that later, much later, when I began to moan softly, it wasn't because of what he was doing. It wasn't pleasure at all, it was fear, because of what I saw when I closed my eyes.

*Me, in a hotel room. The same one I had seen as I got ready earlier that evening. I see the candles, the champagne, the flowers. I hear the knock at the door, see myself put down the glass I have been drinking from, stand up to open it. I feel excitement, anticipation, the air is heavy with promise. Sex and redemption. I reach out, take the handle of the door, cold and hard. I breathe deeply. Finally things will be all right.*

A hole, then. A blank in my memory. *The door, opening, swinging toward me, but I cannot see who is behind it.* There, in bed with my husband, panic slammed into me, from nowhere. "Ben!" I cried out, but he did not stop, did not even seem to hear me. "Ben!" I said again. I closed my eyes and clung to him. I spiraled back into the past.

*He is in the room. Behind me. This man, how dare he? I twist around but see nothing. Pain, searing. A pressure on my throat. I cannot breathe. He is not my husband, not Ben, but still his hands are on me, all over, his hands and his flesh, covering me. I try to breathe, but cannot. My body, shuddering, pulped, turns to nothing, to ash and air. Water, in my lungs. I open my eyes and see nothing but crimson. I am going to die, here, in this hotel room. Dear God, I think. I never wanted this. I never asked for this. Someone must help me. Someone must come. I have made a terrible mistake, yes, but I do not deserve this punishment. I do not deserve to die.*

*I feel myself disappear. I want to see Adam. I want to see my husband. But they are not here. No one is here but me and this man, this man who has his hands around my throat.*

*I am sliding, down, down. Toward blackness. I must not sleep. I must not sleep. I. Must. Not. Sleep.*

The memory ended, suddenly, leaving a terrible, empty void. My eyes flicked open. I was back in my own home, in bed, my husband inside me. "Ben!" I cried out, but it was too late. With tiny, muffled grunts, he ejaculated. I clung to him, holding him as tight as I could, and then, after a moment, he kissed my neck and told me again that he loved me, and then said, "Chris, you're crying . . ."

The sobs came, uncontrollable. "What's wrong?" he said. "Did I hurt you?"

What could I say to him? I shook as my mind tried to process what it had seen. A hotel room full of flowers. Champagne and candles. A stranger with his hands around my neck.

What could I say? All I could do was cry harder, and push him away, and then wait. Wait until he slept, and I could creep out of bed and write it all down.

## Saturday — 2:07 a.m.

I cannot sleep. Ben is upstairs, back in bed, and I am writing this in the kitchen. He thinks I am drinking a cup of cocoa that he has just made for me. He thinks I will come back to bed soon.

I will, but first I must write again.

The house is quiet and dark now, but earlier everything seemed alive. Amplified. I had hidden my journal in the closet and crept back into bed after writing about what I had seen as we made love, but still felt restless. I could hear the ticking of the clock downstairs, its chimes as it marked the hours, Ben's gentle snores. I could feel the press of the duvet cover on my chest, see nothing but the glow of the alarm clock by my side. I turned on my back and closed my eyes. All I could see was myself, with hands clamped tight around my throat so that I could not breathe. All I could hear was my own voice, echoing. I am going to die.

I thought of my journal. Would it help to write more? To read it again? Could I really take it from its hiding place without waking Ben?

He lay, barely visible in the shadows. *You are lying to me,* I thought. Because he is. Lying about my novel, about Adam. And now I feel certain he is lying about how I came to be here, trapped like this.

I wanted to shake him awake. I wanted to scream, *Why? Why are you telling me I was knocked over by a car on an icy road?* I wonder what he is protecting me from. How bad the truth might be.

And what else is there, that I do not know?

My thoughts turned from my journal to the metal box, the one in which Ben keeps the photos of Adam. Maybe there will be more answers in there, I thought. Maybe I will find the truth.

I decided to get out of bed. I folded the duvet back so that I didn't wake my husband. I grabbed my journal from its hiding place and crept, barefoot, onto the landing. The house felt different, now, sheened in the bluish moonlight. Frozen, and still.

I pulled the bedroom door closed behind me, a soft scrape of wood on carpet, a subtle click as it fastened shut. There, on the landing, I skimmed through what I had written. I read about Ben telling me I was hit by a car. I read about him denying I had written a novel. I read about our son.

I had to see a photograph of Adam. But where would I look? "I keep these upstairs," he had said. "For safety." I knew that. I had written it down. But where, exactly? The spare bedroom? The office? How would I begin to look for something I could not recall ever seeing before?

I put the journal back where I had found it and went into the office, closing that door behind me, too. Moonlight shone through the window, casting a grayish glow around the room. I did not dare to switch on the light, could not risk Ben finding me in there, searching. He would ask me what I was looking for, and I had nothing to tell him, no reason to give for being in there. There would be too many questions to answer.

The box was metal, I had written, and gray. I looked on the desk, first. A tiny computer, with an impossibly flat screen, pens and pencils in a mug, papers arranged in tidy piles, a ceramic paperweight in the shape of a seahorse. Above the desk was a wall-planner, dotted with colored stickers, circles, and stars. Under the desk was a leather briefcase and a wastepaper basket, both empty, and next to it a filing cabinet.

I looked there first. I pulled out the top drawer slowly, quietly. It was full of papers, in files labeled HOME, WORK, FINANCE. I flicked past the binders. Behind them was a plastic bottle of pills, though I couldn't make out the name in the semidarkness. The second drawer was full of stationery—boxes, pads of paper, pens—and I closed it gently before crouching down to open the bottom drawer.

A blanket, or a towel; it was difficult to tell in the dim light. I raised one corner, felt beneath, touched cold metal. I lifted it out. Underneath was the metal box, larger than I had imagined it, so big it almost filled the drawer. I maneuvered my hands around it and realized it was heavier than I expected, too, and I almost dropped it as I lifted it out and put it on the floor.

The box sat in front of me. For a moment, I did not know what I wanted to do, whether I even wanted to open it. What new shocks might it contain? Like memory itself, it might hold truths that I could not even begin to conceive of. Unimagined dreams and unexpected horrors. I was afraid. But, I realized, these truths are all I have. They are my past. They are what makes me human. Without them, I am nothing. Nothing but an animal.

I breathed deeply, closing my eyes as I did, and began to lift the lid.

It moved a little way but no farther. I tried it again, thinking it was jammed, and then once more, before I realized. It was locked. Ben had locked it.

I tried to remain calm, but an anger came then, unbidden. Who was he to have locked this box of memories? To keep me from what was mine?

The key would be near, I was sure of it. I looked in the drawer. I opened out the towel and shook it loose. I stood up, tipped the pens and pencils out of the mug on the desk, and looked in there. Nothing.

Desperate, I searched the other drawers as well as I could in the half-light. I could find no key, and realized it might be anywhere. Anywhere at all. I sank to my knees.

A sound, then. A creak, so quiet I thought it might be my own body. But then another noise. Breathing. Or a sigh.

A voice. Ben's. "Christine?" it said, and then, louder, "Christine!"

What to do? I was sitting there, in his office, with the metal box that Ben thought I had no memory of on the floor in front of me. I began to panic. A door opened, the landing light flicked on, illuminating the crack around the door. He was coming.

I moved quickly. I put the box back and, sacrificing silence for speed, slammed the drawer closed.

"Christine?" he said again. Footsteps on the landing. "Christine, love? It's me. Ben." I shoved the pens and pencils back in the mug on the desk and then sank to the floor. The door began to open.

I did not know what I was about to do until I did it. I reacted instinctively, from a level lower than gut.

"Help me!" I said as he appeared at the open door. He was silhouetted against the light on the landing, and for a moment I really did feel the terror that I was affecting. "Please! Help me!"

He switched on the light and came toward me. "Christine! What's wrong?" he said. He began to crouch down.

I skirted back, away from him, until I was pressed against the wall under the window. "Who are you?" I said. I found I had begun to cry, to shake hysterically. I clawed at the wall behind me, clutched at the curtain that hung above me as if trying to pull myself upright. Ben stayed where he was, on the other side of the room. He held out his hand to me, as if I was dangerous, a wild animal.

"It's me," he said. "Your husband."

"My what?" I said, and then, "What's happening to me?"

"You have amnesia," he said. "We've been married for years." And then, as he made me the cup of cocoa that still sits in front of me, I let him tell me, from scratch, what I already knew.

## Sunday, November 18

That happened in the early hours of Saturday morning. Today is Sunday. Midday, or thereabouts. A whole day has gone unrecorded. Twenty-four hours, lost. Twenty-four hours spent believing everything Ben told me. Believing that I have never written a novel, never had a son. Believing it was an accident that robbed me of my past.

Maybe, unlike today, Dr. Nash did not call, and I did not find this journal. Or perhaps he did but I chose not to read it. I feel a chill. What would happen if one day he decides never to call again? I would never find it, never read it, never even know it existed. I would not know my past.

It would be unthinkable. I know that now. My husband is telling me one version of how I came to have no memory, my feelings another. I wonder if I have ever asked Dr. Nash what happened. Even if I have, can I believe what he says? The only truth I have is what is written in this journal.

Written by me. I must remember that. Written by me.


I think back to this morning. I remember the sun slammed through the curtains, waking me suddenly. My eyes flicked open on an unfamiliar scene and I was confused. Yet, though particular events did not come to me, I had the sense of looking back on a wealth of history, not just a few short years. And I knew, however dimly, that that history contained a child of my own. In that fraction of a second before I was fully conscious, I knew that I was a mother. That I had borne a child, that mine was no longer the only body that I had a duty to nurture and protect.

I turned over, aware of another body in the bed, an arm draped over my waist. I did not feel alarmed, but secure. Happy. I woke more fully and the images and feelings began to coalesce into truth and memory. First I saw my little boy, heard myself calling his name—Adam—and saw him running toward me. And then I remembered my husband. His name. I felt deeply in love. I smiled.

The feeling of peace did not last. I looked over at the man next to me, and his face was not the one I expected to see. A moment later, I realized that I did not recognize the room in which I had slept, could not remember getting there. And then, finally, I understood that I could remember nothing clearly. Those brief, disconnected snatches had not been representative of my memories but their sum total.

Ben explained it to me, of course. Or parts of it, at least. And this journal explained the rest, once Dr. Nash phoned me and I found it. I did not have time to read it all—I had called down, feigning a headache, and then listened for the slightest movement downstairs, worried that Ben might come up at any moment with an aspirin and a glass of water—and skimmed over whole passages. But I read enough. The journal told me who I am, how I came to be here, what I have, and what I have lost. It told me that all is not lost. That my memories are coming back, however slowly. Dr. Nash told me so, on the day that I watched him read my journal. *You're remembering lots of things, Christine,* he'd said. *There's no reason that won't continue.* And the journal told me that the hit-and-run was a lie, that somewhere, hidden deep, I can remember what happened to me on the night I lost my memory. That it did not involve a car and icy roads but champagne and flowers and a knock on the door of a hotel room.

And now I have a name. The name of the person I had expected to see when I opened my eyes this morning was not Ben.

Ed. I woke expecting to be lying next to someone called Ed.

At the time, I did not know who he was, this *Ed*. I thought perhaps he was nobody, it was a name I invented, plucked from nowhere. Or perhaps he was an old lover, a one-night stand that I have not quite forgotten. But now I have read this journal. I have learned that I was assaulted in a hotel room. And so I know who this *Ed* is.

He is the man who was waiting on the other side of the door that night. The man who attacked me. The man who stole my life.

This evening, I tested my husband. I did not want to, did not even plan to, but I had spent the whole day worrying. *Why had he lied to me? Why? And does he lie to me every day? Is there only one version of the past that he tells me, or several?* I need to trust him, I thought. I have no one else.

We were eating lamb; a cheap joint, fatty, and overcooked. I was pushing the same mouthful around my plate, dipping it in gravy, bringing it to my mouth, putting it down again. "How did I get to be like this?" I asked. I had tried to summon up the vision of the hotel room, but it had remained elusive, just out of reach. In a way, I was glad.

Ben looked up from his own plate, his eyes wide with surprise. "Christine," he said. "Darling. I don't—"

"Please," I interrupted him. "I need to know."

He put his knife and fork down. "Very well," he said.

"I need you to tell me everything," I said. "Everything."

He looked at me, his eyes narrow. "You're sure?"

"Yes," I said. I hesitated, but then I decided to say it. "Some people might think it would be better not to tell me all the details. Especially if they were upsetting. But I don't think that. I think you should tell me everything, so that I can decide for myself what to feel. Do you understand?"

"Chris," he said. "What do you mean?"

I looked away. My eyes rested on the photograph of the two of us that sat on the sideboard. "I don't know," I said. "I know I wasn't always like this. And now I am. So something must have happened. Something bad. I'm just saying that I know that. I know it must have been something awful. But even so, I want to know what. I have to know what it was. What happened to me. Don't lie to me, Ben," I said. "Please."

He reached across the table and took my hand. "Darling. I would never do that."

And then he began. "It was December," he said. "Icy roads . . ." and I listened, with a mounting sense of dread, as he told me about the car accident. When he had finished, he picked up his knife and fork and carried on eating.

"You're sure?" I said. "You're sure it was an accident?"

He sighed. "Why?"

I tried to calculate how much to say. I did not want to reveal that I was writing again, keeping a journal, but wanted to be as honest as I could.

"Earlier today I got an odd feeling," I said. "Almost like a memory. Somehow it felt like it had something to do with why I'm like this."

"What sort of feeling?"

"I don't know."

"A memory?"

"Sort of."

"Well, did you remember specific things about what happened?"

I thought of the hotel room, the candles, the flowers. The feeling that they had not been from Ben, that it was not him I had opened the door to in that room. I thought, too, of the feeling that I could not breathe. "What sort of thing?" I said.

"Any details, really. The type of car that hit you? Even just the color? Whether you saw who was driving it?"

I wanted to scream at him, *Why are you asking me to believe I was hit by a car? Can it really be that it is an easier story to believe than whatever did happen?*

*An easier story to hear,* I thought, *or an easier one to tell?*

I wondered what he would do if I was to say, *Actually, no. I don't even remember being hit by a car. I remember being in a hotel room, waiting for someone who wasn't you.*

"No," I said. "Not really. It was more just a general impression."

"A general impression?" he said. "What do you mean, 'a general impression'?"

He had raised his voice, sounded almost angry. I was no longer sure I wanted to continue the discussion.

"Nothing," I said. "It was nothing. Just an odd feeling, as if something really bad were happening, and a feeling of pain. But I don't remember any details."

He seemed to relax. "It's probably nothing," he said. "Just the mind playing tricks on you. Try to just ignore it."

*Ignore it?* I thought. How could he ask me to do that? Was he frightened of me remembering the truth?

It is possible, I suppose. He has already told me today that I was hit by a car. He cannot enjoy the thought of being exposed as a liar, even for the rest of the one day that I could hold on to the memory. Particularly if he is lying for my benefit. I can see how believing I was hit by a car would be easier for both of us. But how will I ever find out what really happened?

And who I had been waiting for, in that room?

"Okay," I said, because what else could I say? "You're probably right." We went back to our lamb, now cold. Another thought came then. Terrible, brutal. *What if he is right? It was a hit-and-run? What if my mind had invented the hotel room, the attack?* It might all be invention. Imagination, not memory. Was it possible that, unable to comprehend the simple fact of an accident on an icy road, I had made it all up?

If so, then my memory is not working. Things are not coming back to me. I am not getting better at all, but going mad.

I found my bag and upended it over the bed. Things tumbled out. My coin purse, my floral diary, a lipstick, a powder compact, some tissues. A mobile phone, and then another. A packet of mints. Some loose coins. A yellow square of paper.

I sat on the bed, searching through the detritus. I fished out the tiny diary first, and thought I was in luck when I saw Dr. Nash's name scrawled in black ink at the back, but then I saw that the number beneath it had the word *Office* next to it in brackets. It was Sunday. He wouldn't be there.

The yellow paper was gummed along one edge, with dust and hair sticking to it, but otherwise blank. I was beginning to wonder what on earth had made me think, even for a moment, that Dr. Nash would have given me his personal number, when I remembered reading that he had written his numbers in the front of my journal. *Call me if you get confused,* he'd said.

I found it, then picked up both phones. I could not remember which one Dr. Nash had given me. The larger of the two I checked quickly, seeing that every call was from, or to, Ben. The second—the one that flipped open—had hardly been used. *Why had Dr. Nash given it to me,* I thought, *if not for this? What am I now, if not confused?* I opened it and dialed his number, then pressed CALL.

Silence, for a few moments, and then a buzzy ring, interrupted by a voice.

"Hello?" he said. He sounded sleepy, though it wasn't late. "Who is this?"

"Dr. Nash," I said, whispering. I could hear Ben downstairs where I had left him, watching some kind of talent show on the television. Singing, laughter, sprinkled with punches of applause. "It's Christine."

There was a pause. A mental readjustment.

"Oh. Okay. How—"

I felt an unexpected plunge of disappointment. He did not sound pleased to be hearing from me.

"I'm sorry," I said. "I got your number from the front of my journal."

"Of course," he said. "Of course. How are you?" I said nothing. "Is everything okay?"

"I'm sorry," I said. The words fell out of me, one after another. "I need to see you. Now. Or tomorrow. Yes. Tomorrow. I had a memory. Last night. I wrote it down. A hotel room. Someone knocked on the door. I couldn't breathe. I . . . Dr. Nash?"

"Christine," he said. "Slow down. What happened?"

I took a breath. "I had a memory. I'm sure it has something to do with why I can't remember anything. But it doesn't make sense. Ben says I was hit by a car."

I heard movement, as if he was adjusting his position, and another voice. A woman's. "It's nothing," he said quietly, and he muttered something I couldn't quite hear.

"Dr. Nash?" I said. "Dr. Nash? Was I hit by a car?"

"I can't really talk right now," he said, and I heard the woman's voice again, louder now, complaining. I felt something stir within me. Anger, or panic.

"Please!" I said. The word hissed out of me.

Silence, at first, and then his voice again, now with authority. "I'm sorry," he said. "I'm a little busy. Have you written it down?"

I didn't answer. *Busy.* I thought of him and his girlfriend, wondered what it was that I'd interrupted. He spoke again. "What you've remembered—is it written in your journal? Make sure you write it down."

"Okay," I said. "But—"

He interrupted. "We'll talk tomorrow. I'll call you. On this number? I promise."

Relief, mixed with something else. Something unexpected. Hard to define. Happiness? Delight?

No. It was more than that. Part anxiety, part certainty, suffused with the tiny thrill of pleasure to come. I still feel it as I write this, an hour or so later, but now know it for what it is. Something I don't know that I have ever felt before. Anticipation.

But anticipation of what? That he will tell me what I need to know, that he will confirm that my memories are beginning to trickle back to me, that my treatment is working? Or is it more?

I think of how I must have felt as he touched me in the parking lot, what I must have been thinking to ignore a call from my husband. Perhaps the truth is more simple. I'm looking forward to talking to him.

"Yes," I had said when he told me he would call. "Yes. Please." But by then the line was already dead. I thought of the woman's voice, realized they had been in bed.

I dismiss the thought from my mind. To chase it would be to go truly mad.

# Monday, November 19

The café was busy. One of a chain. Everything was green, or brown, and disposable, though—according to the posters that dotted the carpeted walls—in an environmentally friendly way. I drank my coffee out of a paper cup, dauntingly huge, as Dr. Nash settled himself into the armchair opposite the one into which I had sunk.

It was the first time I'd had the chance to look at him properly; or the first time today at least, which amounts to the same thing. He had called—on the phone that flips open—not long after I had cleared away the remains of my breakfast, and then picked me up an hour or so later, after I had read most of my journal. I stared out of the window as we drove to the coffee shop. I was feeling confused. Desperately so. This morning, when I woke—even though I could not be certain I knew my own name—I knew somehow that I was both an adult and a mother, although I had no inkling that I was middle-aged and my son was dead. My day so far had been brutally disorienting, one shock after another—the bathroom mirror, the scrapbook, and then, later, this journal—culminating in the belief that I do not trust my husband. I had felt disinclined to examine anything else too closely.

Now, though, I could see that Dr. Nash was younger than I

had expected, and though I had written that he did not need to worry about watching his weight, I could see that this did not mean he was as skinny as I had supposed. He had a solidness to him, emphasized by the too-large jacket that hung from his shoulders and out of which his surprisingly hairy forearms poked infrequently.

"How are you feeling today?" he said, once settled.

I shrugged. "I'm not sure. Confused, I suppose."

He nodded. "Go on."

I pushed away the cookie that Dr. Nash had given me though I hadn't asked for it. "Well, I woke up kind of knowing that I was an adult. I didn't realize I was married, but I wasn't exactly surprised that there was somebody in bed with me."

"That's good, though—" he began.

I interrupted. "But yesterday I wrote that I woke up and knew I had a husband . . ."

"You're still writing in your book, then?" he said, and I nodded. "Did you bring it today?"

I had. It was in my bag. But there were things in it I did not want him to read, did not want anyone to. Personal things. My history. The only history I have.

Things I had written about him.

"I forgot," I lied. I could not tell if he was disappointed.

"Okay," he said. "It doesn't matter. I can see it must be frustrating that one day you remember something and the next it seems to be gone again. But it's still progress. Generally you're remembering more than you were."

I wondered if what he'd said was still true. In the first few entries of this journal, I had written of remembering my childhood, my parents, a party with my best friend. I had seen my husband when we were young and first in love; myself, writing a novel. But since then? Lately I have been seeing only the son I have lost and the attack that left me like this. Things it might almost be better for me to forget.

"You said you were worried about Ben? What he's saying about the cause of your amnesia?"

I swallowed. What I had written yesterday had seemed distant, removed. Almost fictional. A car accident. Violence in a hotel bedroom. Neither had seemed like anything to do with me. Yet I had no choice but to believe that I had written the truth. That Ben had really lied to me about how I ended up like this.

"Go on . . ." he said.

I told him what I'd written down, starting with Ben's story about the accident and finishing with my recollection of the hotel room, though I mentioned neither the sex we'd been in the middle of when the memory of the hotel room came to me, nor the romance—the flowers, the candles and champagne—it had contained.

I watched him as I spoke. He occasionally murmured an encouragement and even scratched his chin and narrowed his eyes at one point, though the expression was more thoughtful than surprised.

"You knew this, didn't you?" I said when I'd finished. "You knew all of this already?"

He put down his drink. "Not exactly, no. I knew that it wasn't a car accident that caused your problems, although since reading your journal the other day I now know that Ben has been telling you that it was. I also knew that you must have been staying in a hotel on the night of your . . . of your . . . on the night you lost your memory. But the other details you mentioned are new. And as far as I know, this is the first time you've actually remembered anything yourself. This is good news, Christine."

*Good news?* I wondered if he thought I should be pleased. "So it's true?" I said. "It wasn't a car accident?"

He paused, then said, "No. No it wasn't."

"But why didn't you tell me Ben was lying? When you read my journal? Why didn't you tell me the truth?"

"Because Ben must have his reasons," he said. "And it didn't feel right to tell you he was lying. Not then."

"So you lied to me, too?"

"No," he said. "I've never lied to you. I never told you it was a car accident."

I thought of what I had read this morning. "But the other day," I said. "In your office. We talked about it . . ." He shook his head.

"I wasn't talking about an accident," he said. "You said that Ben had told you how it had happened, so I thought you knew the truth. I hadn't read your journal then, don't forget. We must have got ourselves mixed up . . ."

I could see how it might happen. Both of us skirting around an issue we didn't want to mention by name.

"So what did happen?" I said. "In that hotel room? What was I doing there?"

"I don't know everything," he said.

"Then tell me what you do know," I said. The words emerged angrily, but it was too late to snatch them back. I watched as he brushed a nonexistent crumb from his trousers.

"You're certain you want to know?" he said. I felt like he was giving me one final chance. *You can still walk away,* he seemed to be saying. *You can go on with your life without knowing what I am about to tell you.*

But he was wrong. I couldn't. Without the truth, I am living less than half a life.

"Yes," I said.

His voice was slow. Faltering. He began sentences only to abort them a few words later. The story was a spiral, as if circling around something awful, something better left unsaid. Something that made a mockery of the idle chat I imagine the café is more used to.

"It's true. You were attacked. It was . . ." He paused. "Well, it was pretty bad. You were discovered wandering. Confused. You weren't carrying any identification at all, and had no memory of who you were or what had happened. There were head injuries. The police initially thought you had been mugged." Another pause. "You were found wrapped in a blanket, covered in blood."

I felt myself go cold. "Who found me?" I said.

"I'm not sure . . ."

"Ben?"

"No. Not Ben, no. A stranger. Whoever it was calmed you down. Called an ambulance. You were admitted to a hospital, of course. There was some internal bleeding and you needed emergency surgery."

"But how did they know who I was?"

For an awful moment, I thought perhaps they had never discovered my identity. Perhaps everything, an entire history, even my name, was given to me the day I was discovered. Even Adam.

Dr. Nash spoke. "It wasn't difficult," he said. "You'd checked into the hotel under your own name. And Ben had already contacted the police to report you as missing. Even before you were found."

I thought of the man who had knocked on the door of that room, the man I had been waiting for.

"Ben didn't know where I was?"

"No," he said. "Apparently he had no idea."

"Or who I was with? Who did this to me?"

"No," he said. "Nobody was ever arrested. There was very little evidence to work with, and of course you couldn't really help the police with their investigations. It was assumed that whoever attacked you removed everything from the hotel room and then left you and fled. No one saw anyone go in, or leave. Apparently the hotel was busy that night—some kind of function in one of the ballrooms, lots of people coming and going. You were probably unconscious for some time after the attack. It was the middle of the night when you went downstairs and left the hotel. No one saw you go."

I sighed. I realized the police would have closed the case years ago. To everyone but me—even to Ben—this was old news, ancient history. I will never know who did this to me, and why. Not unless I remember.

"What happened then?" I said. "After I was taken to the hospital?"

"The operation was successful, but there were secondary effects. There was difficulty in stabilizing you after surgery. Your blood pressure in particular." He paused. "You lapsed into a coma for a while."

"A coma?"

"Yes," he said. "It was touch and go, but, well, you were lucky. You were in the right place and they treated your condition aggressively. You came around. But then it became apparent that your memory was gone. At first they thought it might be temporary. A combination of the head injury and anoxia. It was a reasonable assumption—"

"I'm sorry," I said. "Anoxia?" I had stumbled over the word.

"Sorry," he said. "Oxygen deprivation."

I felt my head begin to swim. Everything started to shrink and distort, as though it were getting smaller, or me bigger. I heard myself speak. "Oxygen deprivation?"

"Yes," he said. "You had symptoms of a severe lack of oxygen to the brain. Consistent with carbon dioxide poisoning—though there was no other evidence for this—or strangulation. There were marks on your neck that suggested this. But the most likely explanation was thought to be near-drowning." He paused as I absorbed what he was telling me. "Did you remember anything about almost drowning?"

I closed my eyes. I saw nothing but a card on a pillow, upon which I saw the words *I love you*. I shook my head.

"You recovered, but your memory did not improve. You stayed in the hospital for a couple of weeks. In the intensive care unit at first, and then the general ward. When you were well enough to be moved, you were transported back to London."

Back to London. Of course. I was found near a hotel; I must have been away from home. I asked where it was.

"In Brighton," he said. "Do you have any idea why you might have been there? Any connection to that area?"

I tried to think of holidays, but nothing came.

"No," I said. "None. None that I know of, anyway."

"It might help to go there, at some point. To see if you remember?"

I felt myself go cold. I shook my head.

He nodded. "Okay. Well, there could be any number of reasons why you'd be there, of course."

*Yes,* I thought. But only one that incorporated flickering candles and bunches of roses but didn't include my husband.

"Yes," I said. "Of course." I wondered if either of us was going to mention the word "affair," and how Ben must have felt when he realized where I had been, and why.

It struck me then. The reason Ben had not given me the real

explanation for my amnesia. Why would he want to remind me that once, however briefly, I had chosen another man over him? I felt a chill. I had chosen someone over my husband, and look at the price I had paid.

"What happened then?" I said. "Did I move back in with Ben?"

He shook his head. "No, no," he said. "You were still very ill. You had to stay in the hospital."

"For how long?"

"You were in the general ward at first. For a few months."

"And then?"

"You were moved," he said. He hesitated—I thought I would have to ask him to continue—and then said, "to a psychiatric ward."

The word shook me. "A psychiatric ward?" I imagined fearful places, full of crazy people, howling, deranged. I could not imagine myself there.

"Yes."

"But why? Why there?"

He spoke softly, but his tone betrayed annoyance. I felt suddenly convinced we had been through all this before, perhaps many times, presumably before I had begun to keep my journal. "It was more secure," he said. "You had made a reasonable recovery from your physical injuries by now, but your memory problems were at their worst. You didn't know who you were, or where. You were exhibiting symptoms of paranoia, claiming the doctors were conspiring against you. You kept trying to escape." He waited. "You were becoming increasingly unmanageable. You were moved for your own safety, as well as the safety of others."

"Of others?"

"You occasionally lashed out."

I tried to imagine what it must have been like. I pictured some-one waking up every day, confused, not sure who they were, or where, or why they'd been put in a hospital. Asking for answers and not getting them. Being surrounded by people who knew more about them than they did themselves. It must have been hell.

I remembered that we were talking about me.

"And then?"

He did not answer. I saw his eyes go up and he looked past me, toward the door, as if he were watching it, waiting. But there was no one there, it did not open, no one left or came in. I wondered if he was actually dreaming of escape.

"Dr. Nash," I said. "What happened then?"

"You stayed there for a while," he said. His voice was almost a whisper now. He has told me this before, I thought, but this time he knows I will write it down and carry it with me for more than a few hours.

"How long?"

He said nothing. I asked him again. "How long?"

He looked up at me, his face a mixture of sadness and pain. "Seven years."

He paid, and we left the coffee shop. I felt numb. I do not know what I was expecting, where I thought I had lived out the worst of my illness, but I did not think it would be there. Not in the middle of all that pain.

As we walked, Dr. Nash turned to me. "Christine," he said. "I have a suggestion." I noticed how casually he spoke, as if he was asking which flavor ice cream I would prefer. A casualness that can only be affected.

"Go on," I said.

"I think it might be helpful for you to visit the ward that you were admitted to," he said. "The place you spent all that time."

My reaction was instant. Automatic. "No!" I said. "Why?"

"You're experiencing memory," he said. "Think of what happened when we went to visit your old house." I nodded. "You remembered something then. I think it might happen again. We might trigger more."

"But—"

"You don't have to. But . . . look. I'll be honest. I've already made the arrangements with them. They'd be happy to welcome you. Us. Anytime. I only have to call to let them know we're on our way. I'd come with you. If you feel distressed or uncomfortable we can leave. It'll be fine. I promise."

"You think it might help me to get better? Really?"

"I don't know," he said. "But it might."

"When? When do you want to go?"

He stopped walking. I realized the car we were standing next to must be his.

"Today," he said. "I think we should go today." And then he said something odd. "We don't have time to lose."

* * *

I didn't have to go. Dr. Nash didn't force me to agree to the trip. But, though I can't remember doing so—can't remember much at all, in fact—I must have said yes.

The journey was not long, and we were silent. I could think of nothing. Nothing to say, nothing to feel. My mind was empty. Scooped out. I took my journal out of my bag—not caring that I had told Dr. Nash I didn't have it with me—and wrote that last entry in it. I wanted to record every detail of our conversation. I did it silently, almost without thinking, and we did not speak as he parked the car, nor as we walked through the antiseptic corridors with their smell of stale coffee and fresh paint. People were wheeled past us on gurneys, attached to IVs. Posters peeled off the walls. Overhead lights flickered and buzzed. I could think only of the seven years I had spent there. It felt like a lifetime; one I remembered nothing of.

We came to a stop outside a double door. Fisher Ward. Dr. Nash pressed a button on an intercom mounted on the wall, then mumbled something into it. *He is wrong,* I thought as the door swung open. *I did not survive that attack. The Christine Lucas who opened that hotel room door is dead.*

Another double door. "You okay, Christine?" he said as the first closed behind us, sealing us in. I said nothing. "This is a secure unit." I was hit with a sudden conviction that the door behind me was closing forever, that I would not be leaving.

I swallowed. "I see," I said. The inner door began to open. I did not know what I would see beyond it, could not believe I had ever been here before.

"Ready?" he said.

A long corridor. There were doors off each side, and as we walked I could see that they opened into glass-windowed rooms. In each was a bed—some made, some unmade, some occupied, most not. "The patients here suffer from a variety of problems," said Dr. Nash. "Many show schizoaffective symptoms, but there are those with bipolarity, acute anxiety, depression."

I looked in one window. A girl was sitting on the bed, naked, staring at the television. In another, a man sat on his haunches, rocking, his arms wrapped around his knees as if to shield himself from the cold.

"Are they locked in?" I said.

"The patients here have been committed. They're here for their own good, but against their wishes."

"Their own good?"

"Yes. They're a danger either to themselves or to others. They need to be kept secure."

We carried on walking. A woman looked up as I passed her room, and though our eyes made contact, hers betrayed no expression. Instead she slapped herself, still looking at me, and when I winced, she did it again. A vision flitted through me—visiting a zoo as a child, watching a tiger pace up and down his cage—but I pushed it away and carried on, resolving to look neither left nor right.

"Why did they bring me here?" I said.

"Before you were here, you were in the general medical ward. In a bed, just like everybody else. You would spend some weekends at home, with Ben. But you became more and more difficult to manage."

"Difficult?"

"You would wander off. Ben had to start locking the doors to the house. You became hysterical a couple of times, convinced that he had hurt you, that you were being locked in against your will. For a while you were okay when you got back to the ward, but then you started demonstrating similar behaviors there, too."

"So they had to find a way of locking me in," I said. We had reached a nursing station. A man in a uniform sat behind a desk, entering something on a computer. He looked up as we approached and said the doctor would be with us soon. He invited us to take a seat. I scanned his face—the crooked nose, the gold-stud earring—hoping something would ignite a glimmer of familiarity. Nothing. The ward seemed utterly foreign.

"Yes," said Dr. Nash. "You'd gone missing, once. For something like four and a half hours. You were picked up by the police, down by one of the canals. Dressed only in pajamas and a gown. Ben had to collect you from the station. You wouldn't go with any of the nurses. They had no choice."

He told me that, right away, Ben began to campaign to have me moved. "He felt that a psychiatric ward was not the best place for you. He was right, really. You weren't dangerous, either to yourself or to others. It's even possible that being surrounded by those who were more ill than you was making you worse. He wrote to the doctors, the head of the hospital, your MP. But nothing was available.

"And then," he said, "a residential center for people with chronic brain injuries opened. He lobbied hard, and you were assessed, and thought to be suitable, though funding was an issue. Ben had had to take a break from work to look after you and couldn't afford to fund it himself, but he wouldn't take no for an answer. Apparently he threatened to go to the press with your story. There were meetings and appeals and so on, but eventually he was successful, and you were accepted as a patient, with the state agreeing to pay for your stay for as long as you were ill. You were moved there about ten years ago."

I thought of my husband, tried to imagine him writing letters, campaigning, threatening. It did not seem possible. The man I had met that morning seemed humble, deferential. Not weak, exactly, but accepting. He did not seem like the kind of person to make waves.

*I am not the only one,* I thought, *whose personality has changed because of my injury.*

"The home was fairly small," said Dr. Nash. "A few rooms in a rehab center. There weren't many other residents. Lots of people to help look after you. You had a little more independence there. You were safe. You made improvements."

"But I wasn't with Ben?"

"No. He lived at home. He needed to carry on working, and he couldn't do that and look after you. He decided—"

A memory flashed through me, tearing me suddenly back into the past. Everything was slightly out of focus and had a haze around it, and the images were so bright I almost wanted to look away. I saw myself, walking through these same corridors, being led back toward a room that I dimly understood was mine. I am wearing slippers, a blue gown with ties up the back. The woman with me is black, wearing a uniform. "Here you go, hon," she says to me. "Look who's here to see you!" She lets go of my hand and guides me toward the bed.

A group of strangers are sitting around it, watching me. I see a man with dark hair and a woman wearing a beret, but I cannot make out their faces. *I am in the wrong room,* I want to say. *There's been a mistake.* But I say nothing.

A child—four or five years old—stands up. He had been sitting on the edge of the bed. He comes toward me, running, and he says *Mummy* and I see that he is talking to me, and only then do I realize who he is. *Adam.* I crouch down and he runs into my arms, and I hold him and kiss the top of his head, and then I stand. "Who are you?" I say to the group around the bed. "What are you doing here?"

The man looks suddenly sad; the woman with the beret stands and says, "Chris. Chrissy. It's me. You know who I am, don't you?" and then comes toward me and I see that she is crying.

"No," I say. "No! Get out! Get out!" and I turn to leave the

room and there is another woman there—standing behind me—
and I don't know who she is, or how she got there, and I begin to
cry. I begin to sink to the floor, but the child is there, holding on
to my knees, and I don't know who he is, but he keeps calling me
*Mummy*, saying it over and over again. *Mummy. Mummy. Mummy*,
and I don't know why, or who he is, or why he is holding me . . .

A hand touched my arm. I flinched as if stung. A voice. "Christine? Are you okay? Dr. Wilson is here."

I opened my eyes, looked around. A woman wearing a white
coat stood in front of us. "Dr. Nash," she said. She shook his hand,
and then turned to me. "Christine?"

"Yes," I said.

"Pleased to meet you," she said. "I'm Hilary Wilson." I took
her hand. She was a little older than me; her hair was beginning
to turn gray, and a pair of half-moon glasses dangled around her
neck on a gold chain. "How d'you do?" she said, and from nowhere I felt certain I had met her before. She nodded down the
corridor. "Shall we?"

Her office was large, lined with books, piled with boxes of spilling
papers. She sat behind a desk and indicated two chairs opposite it,
into which Dr. Nash and I sank. I watched her take a file from the
pile on her desk and open it. "Now, my dear," she said. "Let's have
a look."

Her image froze. I knew her. I had seen her picture as I lay in
the scanner, and, though I hadn't recognized it at the time, I did
now. I had been here before. Many times. Sitting where I am now,
in this chair or one like it, watching her making notes in a file as
she peered through the glasses held delicately to her eyes.

"I've met you before . . ." I said. "I remember . . ." Dr. Nash looked over at me, then back at Dr. Wilson.

"Yes," she said. "Yes you have. Though not that often." She explained that she'd only just started working here when I moved out and that at first I wasn't even on her caseload. "It's certainly most encouraging that you remember me, though," she said. "It's been a long time since you were resident here." Dr. Nash leaned forward and said it might help me to see the room in which I'd lived. She nodded and squinted at the file, then, after a minute, said she didn't know which it was. "It's possible that you moved around a fair old bit in any case," she said. "Many of the patients do. Could we ask your husband? According to the file, he and your son visited you almost every day."

I had read about Adam this morning and felt a flash of happiness at the mention of his name, and relief that I'd seen a little of him growing up, but shook my head. "No," I said. "I'd rather not call Ben."

Dr. Wilson did not argue. "A friend of yours named Claire seemed to be something of a regular, too. How about her?"

I shook my head. "We're not in touch."

"Ah," she said. "What a pity. But never mind. I can tell you a little bit of what life was like here back then." She glanced at her notes, then clasped her hands together. "Your treatment was mostly handled by a consultant psychiatrist. You underwent sessions of hypnosis, but I'm afraid any success was limited and unsustained." She read further. "You didn't receive a great deal of medication. A sedative, occasionally, though that was more to help you sleep—it can get quite noisy in here, as I'm sure you can understand," she said.

I recalled the howling I'd imagined earlier, wondering if that might have once been me. "What was I like?" I said. "Was I happy?"

She smiled. "Generally, yes. You were well liked. You seemed to make friends with one of the nurses in particular."

"What was her name?"

She scanned her notes. "I'm afraid it doesn't say. You played a lot of solitaire."

"Solitaire?"

"A card game. Perhaps Dr. Nash can explain later?" She looked up. "According to the notes, you were occasionally violent," she said. "Don't be alarmed. It's not unusual in cases like this. People who have suffered severe head trauma will often exhibit violent tendencies, particularly when there has been damage to the part of the brain that allows self-restraint. Plus, patients with amnesia such as yours often have a tendency to do something we call con-fabulation. Things around them do not seem to make sense, and so they feel compelled to invent details. About themselves and other people around them, or about their history, what has happened to them. It's thought to be due to the desire to fill gaps in the memory. Understandable, in a way. But it can often lead to violent behavior when the amnesiac's fantasy is contradicted. Life must have been very disorienting for you. Particularly when you had visitors."

Visitors. Suddenly I was afraid I might have hit my son.

"What did I do?"

"You occasionally lashed out at some of the staff," she said.

"But not at Adam? My son?"

"Not according to these notes, no." I sighed, not entirely re-lieved. "We have some pages from a sort of diary that you were keeping," she said. "Might it be helpful for you to take a look at them? You might understand your confusion better."

This felt dangerous. I glanced at Dr. Nash, and he nodded. She pushed a sheet of blue paper over to me and I took it, at first frightened to even look at it.

When I did, I saw that it was covered in an unruly scrawl. At the top, the letters were well formed, and kept neatly within the printed lines that ran across the page, but toward the bottom, they were large and messy, inches tall, just a few words across. Though dreading what I might see, I began to read.

*8:15 a.m.*, read the first entry. *I have woken up. Ben is here.* Directly underneath, I had written, *8:17 a.m. Ignore that last entry. It was written by someone else,* and underneath that, *8:20 I am awake NOW. Before I was not. Ben is here.*

My eyes flicked further down the page. *9:45 I have just woken up, FOR THE VERY FIRST TIME*, and then, a few lines later, *10:07 NOW I am definitely awake. All these entries are a lie. I am awake NOW.*

I looked up. "This was really me?" I said.

"Yes. For a long time it seemed that you were in a perpetual state of feeling that you had just woken up from a very long, very deep sleep. Look here." Dr. Wilson pointed at the page in front of me, and began quoting entries from it. *"I have been asleep forever. It was like being DEAD. I have only just woken up. I can see again, for the first time.* They apparently encouraged you to write down what you were feeling, in an effort to get you to remember what had happened before, but I'm afraid you just became convinced that all the preceding entries had been written by someone else. You began to think people here were conducting experiments on you, keeping you against your will."

I looked at the page again. The whole sheet was filled with almost identical entries, each just a few minutes apart. I felt myself go cold.

"Was I really this bad?" I said. My words seemed to echo in my head.

"For a while, yes," said Dr. Nash. "Your notes indicate that you retained memory for only a few seconds. Sometimes a minute or two. That time has gradually lengthened over the years."

I could not believe I had written this. It seemed to be the work of someone whose mind was completely fractured. Exploded. I saw the words again. *It was like being DEAD.*

"I'm sorry," I said. "I can't—"

Dr. Wilson took the sheet from me. "I understand, Christine. It's upsetting. I—"

Panic hit me then. I stood up, but the room began to spin. "I want to leave," I said. "This isn't me. It can't have been me, I—I would never hit people. I would never. I just—"

Dr. Nash stood, too, and then Dr. Wilson. She stepped forward, colliding with her desk, which sent papers flying. A photograph spilled to the floor. "Dear God—" I said, and she looked down, then crouched to cover it with another sheet. But I had seen enough.

"Was that me?" I said, my voice rising to a scream. "Was that me?"

The photograph was of the head of a young woman. Her hair had been pulled back from her face. At first, it looked as though she was wearing a Halloween mask. One eye was open and looked at the camera, the other was closed by a huge, purple bruise, and both lips were swollen, pink, lacerated with cuts. Her cheeks were distended, giving her whole face a grotesque appearance. I thought of pulped fruit. Of plums, rotten and bursting.

"Was that me?" I screamed, even though, despite the swollen, distorted face, I could see that it was.

My memory splits there, fractured in two. Part of me was calm, quiet. Serene. It watched as the other part of me thrashed and screamed and had to be restrained by Dr. Nash and Dr. Wilson. *You really ought to behave,* it seemed to be saying. *This is embarrassing.*

But the other part was stronger. It had taken over, become the real me. I shouted out, again and again, and turned and ran for the door. Dr. Nash came after me. I tore it open and ran, though where I could go I did not know. An image of bolted doors. Alarms. A man, chasing me. My son, crying. *I have done this before,* I thought. *I have done all this before.*

My memory blanks.

They must have calmed me down somehow, persuaded me to go with Dr. Nash; the next thing I can remember is being in his car, sitting next to him as he drove. The sky was beginning to cloud over, the streets looked gray, somehow flattened out. He was talking, but I could not concentrate. It was as if my mind had tripped, fallen back into something else, and now could not catch up. I looked out of the windows, at the shoppers and the dog-walkers, at the people with their strollers and their bicycles, and I wondered whether this—this search for truth—was really what I wanted. Yes, it might help me to improve, but how much can I hope to gain? I don't expect that I will ever wake up knowing everything, as normal people do, knowing what I did the day before, what plans I have for the day that follows, what circuitous route has led me to here and now, to the person I am. The best I can hope for is that, one day, looking in the mirror will not be a total shock, that I will remember I married a man called Ben and lost a son called Adam, that I will not have to see a copy of my novel to know that I had written one.

But even that much seems unattainable. I thought of what I had seen in Fisher Ward. Madness and pain. Minds that had been shattered. *I am closer to that,* I thought, *than I am to recovery. Perhaps it would be best if I learned to live with my condition, after all.* I could tell Dr. Nash I do not want to see him again and I could burn my journal, burying the truths I have already learned, hiding them as thoroughly as those I do not yet know. I would be running away from my past, but I would have no regrets—in just a few hours, I would not even know that either my journal or my doctor had ever existed—and then I could live simply. One day would follow another, unconnected. Yes, occasionally the memory of Adam would surface. I would have a day of grief and pain, would remember what I miss, but it would not last. Before long, I would sleep and, quietly, forget. *How easy that would be,* I thought. *So much easier than this.*

I thought of the picture I'd seen. The image was burned into me. *Who did that to me? Why?* I remembered the memory I'd had of the hotel room. It was still there, just under the surface, just out of reach. I had read this morning that I had reason to believe I had been having an affair, but now realized that—even if that were true—I didn't know who it had been with. All I had was a single name, remembered as I woke just a few days ago, with no promise of ever remembering more, even if I wanted to.

Dr. Nash was still talking. I had no idea what about, and interrupted him. "Am I getting better?" I said.

A heartbeat, during which I thought he had no answer, then he said, "Do you think you are?"

Did I? I couldn't say. "I don't know. Yes. I suppose so. I can remember things from my past, sometimes. Flashes of memory. They come to me when I read my journal. They feel real. I remember Claire. Adam. My mother. But they're like threads I can't keep hold of. Balloons that float into the sky before I can catch them. I can't remember my wedding. I can't remember Adam's first steps, his first word. I can't remember him starting at school, his graduation. Anything. I don't even know if I was there. Maybe Ben decided there was no point in taking me." I took a breath. "I can't even remember learning he was dead. Or burying him." I began to cry. "I feel like I'm going crazy. Sometimes I don't even think that he's dead. Can you believe that? Sometimes I think that Ben's lying to me about that, as well as everything else."

"Everything else?"

"Yes," I said. "My novel. The attack. The reason I have no memory. Everything."

"But why do you think he would do that?"

A thought came to me. "Because I was having an affair?" I said. "Because I was unfaithful to him?"

"Christine," he said. "That's unlikely, don't you think?"

I said nothing. He was right, of course. Deep down I did not believe Ben's lies could really be a protracted revenge for something that had happened years and years ago. The explanation was likely to be something much more mundane.

"You know," said Dr. Nash, "I think you are getting better. You're remembering things. Much more often than when we first met. These snatches of memory? They're definitely a sign of progress. They mean—"

I turned to him. "Progress? You call this progress?" I was almost shouting now, anger spilled out of me as if I could no longer contain it. "If that's what it is, then I don't know if I want it." The tears were flooding now, uncontrollable. "I don't want it!"

I closed my eyes and abandoned myself to my grief. It felt better, somehow, to be helpless. I did not feel ashamed. Dr. Nash was talking to me, telling me first not to be upset, that things would be all right, and then to calm down. I ignored him. I could not calm down, and did not want to.

He stopped the car. Switched off the engine. I opened my

eyes. We had left the main road, and in front of me was a park. Through the blur of my tears I could see a group of boys— teenagers, I suppose—playing soccer, with two piles of coats for goalposts. It had begun to rain, but they did not stop. Dr. Nash turned to face me.

"Christine," he said. "I'm sorry. Perhaps today was a mistake. I don't know. I thought we might trigger other memories. I was wrong. In any case, you shouldn't've seen that picture . . ."

"I don't even know if it was the picture," I said. I had stopped sobbing now, but my face was wet; I could feel a great, looping mass of mucus escaping from my nose. "Do you have a tissue?" I asked. He reached across me and began to look in the glove compartment. "It was everything," I went on. "Seeing those people, imagining that I'd been like that, once. And the diary. I can't believe that was me, writing that. I can't believe I was that ill."

He handed me a tissue. "But you're not anymore," he said. I took the tissue from him and blew my nose.

"Maybe it's worse," I said quietly. "I'd written that it was like being dead. But this? This is worse. This is like dying every day. Over and over. I need to get better," I said. "I can't imagine going on like this for much longer. I know I'll go to sleep tonight, and then tomorrow I will wake up and not know anything again, and the next day, and the day after that, forever. I can't imagine it. I can't face it. It's not life, it's just an existence, jumping from one moment to the next with no idea of the past, and no plan for the future. It's how I imagine animals must be. The worst thing is that I don't even know what I don't know. There might be lots of things, waiting to hurt me. Things I haven't even dreamed about yet."

He put his hand on mine. I fell into him, knowing what he would do, what he must do, and he did. He opened his arms and held me, and I let him embrace me. "It's okay," he said. "It's okay."

I could feel his chest under my cheek and I breathed, inhaling his scent, fresh laundry and, faintly, something else. Sweat and sex. His hand was on my back and I felt it move, felt it touch my hair, my head, lightly at first, but then more firmly as I sobbed again. "It'll be all right," he said, whispering, and I closed my eyes.

"I just want to remember what happened," I said. "On the night I was attacked. Somehow I feel that if I could only remember that, then I would remember everything."

He spoke softly. "There's no evidence that's the case. No reason—"

"But it's what I think," I said. "I know it, somehow."

He squeezed me. Gently, almost so gently that I could not feel it. I felt his body, hard against mine, and breathed in deeply, and as I did so, I thought of another time when I was being held. Another memory. *My eyes are closed, just the same, and my body is being pressed up against that of another, though this is different. I do not want to be held by this man. He is hurting me. I am struggling, trying to get away, but he is strong and pulls me to him. He speaks.* Bitch, *he says.* Slut, *and though I want to argue with him, I do not. My face is pressed against his shirt, and, just like with Dr. Nash, I am crying, screaming. I open my eyes and see the blue fabric of his shirt, a door, a dressing table with three mirrors and a picture—a painting of a bird—above it. I can see his arm, strong, muscled, a vein running down its length.* Let me go! *I say, and then I am spinning and falling—or the floor is rising to meet me, I cannot tell. He grabs a handful of my hair and drags me toward the door. I twist my head to see his face.*

It is there that memory fails me again. Though I remember looking at his face, I cannot remember what I saw. It is featureless, a blank. As if unable to cope with this vacuum, my mind cycles through faces I know, through absurd impossibilities. I see Dr. Nash. Dr. Wilson. The receptionist at Fisher Ward. My father. Ben. I even see my own face, laughing as I raise a fist to strike.

Please, *I cry*, please don't. *But my many-faced attacker hits anyway, and I taste blood. He drags me along the floor, and then I am in the bathroom, on the cold tiles, black and white. The floor is damp with condensation, the room smells of orange blossom, and I remember how I had been looking forward to bathing, to making myself beautiful, thinking that maybe I would still be in the bath when he arrived, and then he could join me, and we would make love, making waves in the soapy water, soaking the floor, our clothes, everything. Because finally, after all these months of doubt, it has become clear to me. I love this man. Finally, I know it. I love him.*

*My head slams into the floor. Once, twice, a third time. My vision blurs and doubles, then returns. A buzzing in my ears, and he shouts something, but I can't hear what. It echoes, as if there are two of him, both holding me, both twisting my arm, both grabbing handfuls of my hair as they kneel on my back. I beg him to leave me alone, and there are two of me, too. I swallow. Blood.*

*My head jerks back. Panic. I am on my knees. I see water, bubbles, already thinning. I try to speak but cannot. His hand is around my throat, and I cannot breathe. I am pitched forward, down, down, so quick that I think I will never stop, and then my head is in the water. Orange blossom in my throat.*

I heard a voice. "Christine!" it said. "Christine! Stop!" I opened my eyes. Somehow, I was out of the car. I was running. Across the park, as fast as I could, and running after me was Dr. Nash.

We sat on a bench. It was concrete, crossed with wooden slats. One was missing, and the remainder sagged beneath us. I felt the sun against the back of my neck, saw its long shadows on the ground. The boys were still playing soccer, though the game must be finishing now; some were drifting off, others talked, one of the piles of jackets had been removed, leaving the goal unmarked. Dr. Nash had asked me what had happened.

"I remembered something," I said.

"About the night you were attacked?"

"Yes," I said. "How did you know?"

"You were screaming," he said. "You kept saying, 'Get off me,' over and over."

"It was like I was there," I said. "I'm sorry."

"Please, don't apologize. Do you want to tell me what you saw?"

The truth was I did not. I felt as if some ancient instinct was telling me that this was a memory best kept to myself. But I needed his help, knew I could trust him. I told him everything.

When I had finished, he was silent for a moment, then said, "Anything else?"

"No," I said. "I don't think so."

"You don't remember what he looked like? The man who attacked you?"

"No. I can't see that at all."

"Or his name?"

"No," I said. "Nothing." I hesitated. "Do you think it might help to know who did this to me? To see him? Remember him?"

"Christine, there's no real evidence to suggest that remembering the attack would help."

"But it might?"

"It seems to be one of your most deeply repressed memories—"

"So it might?"

He was silent, then said, "I've suggested it before, but it might help to go back there . . ."

"No," I said. "No. Don't even say it."

"We can go together. You'd be fine. I promise. If you were there again . . . Back in Brighton—"

"No."

"—you might remember then—"

"No! Please?"

"—it might help?"

I looked down at my hands folded in my lap.

"I can't go back there," I said. "I just can't."

He sighed. "Okay," he said. "Maybe we'll talk about it again?"

"No," I whispered. "I can't."

"Okay," he said. "Okay."

He smiled but seemed disappointed. I felt eager to give him something, to have him not give up on me. "Dr. Nash?" I said.

"Yes?"

"The other day I wrote that something had come to me. Perhaps it's relevant. I don't know."

He turned to face me.

"Go on." Our knees touched. Neither of us drew away.

"When I woke," I said, "I kind of knew that I was in bed with a man. I remembered a name. But it wasn't Ben's name. I wondered if it was the name of the person I'd been having the affair with. The one who attacked me."

"It's possible," he said. "It might have been the beginning of the repressed memory emerging. What was the name?"

Suddenly I did not want to tell him, to say it out loud. I felt that by doing so I would be making it real, conjuring my attacker back into existence. I closed my eyes.

"Ed," I whispered. "I imagined waking up with someone called Ed."

Silence. A heartbeat that seemed to last forever.

"Christine," he said. "That's my name. I'm Ed. Ed Nash."

My mind raced for a moment. My first thought was that he had attacked me. "What?" I said, panicking.

"That's my name. I've told you that before. Maybe you've never written it down. My name is Edmund. Ed."

I realized it could not have been him. He would barely have been born.

"But—"

"You're possibly confabulating," he said. "Like Dr. Wilson explained?"

"Yes," I said. "I—"

"Or maybe you were attacked by someone with the same name?"

He smiled awkwardly as he said it, making light of the situation, but in doing so revealed he had already worked out what only later—after he had driven me home, in fact—occurred to me. I had woken that morning happy. Happy to be in bed with someone called Ed. But it was not a memory. It was a fantasy. Waking with this man called Ed was not something I had done in the past but—even though my conscious, waking mind did not know who he was—something I wanted to do in the future. I want to sleep with Dr. Nash.

And now, accidentally, inadvertently, I have told him. I have revealed the way I must feel about him. He was professional, of course. We both pretended to attach no significance to what had happened, and so revealed just how much significance there was. We walked back to the car and he drove me home. We chatted about trivialities. The weather. Ben. There are few things we can talk about; there are whole arenas of experience from which I am utterly excluded. At one point, he said, "We're going to the theater tonight," and I noted his careful use of the plural. *Don't worry,* I wanted to say. *I know my place.* But I said nothing. I did not want him to think of me as bitter.

He told me he would call me tomorrow. "If you're sure you want to continue?"

I know that I cannot stop now. Not until I have learned the truth. I owe myself that; otherwise, I am living only half a life. "Yes," I said. "I do." In any case, I need him to remind me to write in my journal.

"Okay," he said. "Good. Next time I think we should visit somewhere else from your past." He looked to where I sat. "Don't worry. Not there. I think we should go to the care home you were moved to when you left Fisher Ward. It's called Waring House." I said nothing. "It's not too far from where you live. Shall I call them?"

I thought for a moment, wondering what good it might do, but then realized there were no other options, and anything is better than nothing.

I said, "Yes. Yes. Call them."

# Tuesday, November 20

It is morning. Ben has suggested that I clean the windows. "I've written it on the board," he said, as he got into his car. "In the kitchen."

I looked. *Wash windows* he had written, adding a tentative question mark. I wondered if he thought I might not have time, wondered what he thought I did all day. He does not know I now spend hours reading my journal, and sometimes hours more writing in it. He does not know there are days when I see Dr. Nash.

I wonder what I did before my days were taken up like this. Did I really spend all my time watching television, or going for walks, or doing chores? Did I spend hour after hour sitting in an armchair, listening to the ticking of the clock, wondering how to live?

*Wash windows.* Possibly some days I read things like that and feel resentful, seeing it as an effort to control my life, but today I viewed it with affection, as nothing more sinister than the desire to keep me occupied. I smiled to myself but, even as I did, I thought how difficult it must be to live with me. He must go to extraordinary lengths to make sure I am safe, and even so must worry constantly that I will get confused, will wander off, or worse. I remembered reading about the fire that had destroyed most of our past, the one Ben has never told me that I started, even though I must have done so. I saw an image—a burning door, almost invisible in the thick smoke, a sofa, melting, turning to wax—that hovered, just out of reach, but refused to resolve itself into a memory, and remained a half-imagined dream. But Ben has forgiven me for that, I thought, just as he must have forgiven me for so much more. I looked out of the kitchen window, and through the reflection of my own face I saw the mowed lawn, the tidy borders, the shed, the fences. I realized that Ben must have known that I was having an affair—certainly once I'd been discovered in Brighton, even if not before. How much strength it must have taken to look after me—once I had lost my memory—even with the knowledge that I had been away from home, intending to fuck someone else, when it had happened. I thought of what I had seen, of the diary I had written. My mind had been fractured. Destroyed. Yet still he had stood by me, where another man might have told me that I deserved everything, left me to rot.

I turned away from the window and looked under the sink. Cleaning materials. Soap. Cartons of powders, plastic spraybottles. There was a red plastic bucket and I filled this with hot water, adding a squirt of soap and a tiny drop of vinegar. *How have I repaid him?* I thought. I took a sponge and began to soap the window, beginning at the top, working down. I have been sneaking around London, seeing doctors, having scans, visiting our old homes and the places I was treated after my accident, all without telling him. And why? Because I don't trust him? Because he has made the decision to protect me from the truth, to keep my life as simple and easy as possible? I watched the soapy water run in tiny rivulets, pooling at the bottom, and then took another cloth and polished the window to a shine.

Now I know the truth is even worse. This morning I had woken with an almost overwhelming sense of guilt, the words *You should be ashamed of yourself* spinning in my head. *You'll be sorry.* At first I'd thought I had woken with a man who was not my husband and it was only later I discovered the truth. That I have betrayed him. Twice. The first time years ago, with a man who would eventually take everything from me, and now I have done it again, with my heart if nothing else. I have developed a ridiculous, childish crush on a doctor who is trying to help me, trying to comfort me. A doctor who I cannot even begin to picture now, cannot remember even having met before, but who I know is much younger than me, has a girlfriend. And now I have told him how I feel! Accidentally, yes, but still I have told him. I feel more than guilty. I feel stupid. I cannot even begin to imagine what must have brought me to this point. I am pathetic.

There, as I cleaned the glass, I made a decision. Even if Ben does not share my belief that my treatment will work, I cannot believe he would deny me the opportunity to see for myself. Not if it was what I wanted. I am an adult; he is not a monster; surely I can trust him with the truth? I sluiced the water down the sink and refilled the bucket. I will tell my husband. Tonight. When he gets home. This cannot go on. I continued to clean the windows.

\* \* \*

I wrote that an hour ago, but now I am not so sure. I think about Adam. I have read about the photographs in the metal box, yet still there are no pictures of him on display. None. I can't believe Ben—anyone—could lose a son and then remove all traces of him from his home. It does not seem right, does not seem possible. Can I trust a man who can do that? I remembered reading about the day we sat on Parliament Hill when I had asked him straight. He had lied. I flick back through my journal now and read it again. *We never had children?* I said, and he had replied, *No. No we didn't.*

Can he really have done that just to protect me? Can he really feel that is the best thing to do? To tell me nothing, other than what he must, what is convenient?

Whatever's quickest, too. He must be so bored with telling me the same thing over and over again, every day. It occurs to me that the reason he shortens explanations and changes stories is not to do with me at all. Perhaps it's so that he doesn't drive himself crazy with the constant repetition.

I feel like I am going mad. Everything is fluid, everything shifts. I think one thing, and then, a moment later, the opposite. I believe everything my husband says, and then I believe nothing. I trust him, and then I don't. Nothing feels real, everything invented. Even myself.

I wish I knew one thing for certain. One single thing that I have not had to be told, about which I do not need to be reminded.

I wish I knew who I was with, that day in Brighton. I wish I knew who did this to me.

\* \* \*

Later. I have just finished speaking to Dr. Nash. I was dozing in the living room when the phone rang, the television was on, the sound turned down. For a moment, I could not tell where I was, whether I was asleep or awake. I thought I heard voices, getting louder. I realized one was mine, and the other sounded like Ben. But he was saying, *You fucking bitch*, and worse. I screamed at him, in anger and then in fear. A door slammed, the thud of a fist, breaking glass. It was then I realized I was dreaming.

I opened my eyes. A chipped mug of cold coffee sat on the table in front of me, a phone buzzed nervously next to it. The one that flips open. I picked it up.

It was Dr. Nash. He introduced himself, though his voice had sounded familiar anyway. He asked me if I was okay. I told him I was, and that I'd read my journal.

"You know what we talked about yesterday?" he said.

I felt a flash of shock. Horror. He had decided to tackle things then. I felt a bubble of hope—perhaps he really had felt the same way I had, the same confused mix of desire and fear—but it did not last. "About going to the place where you lived after you left the ward?" he said. "Waring House?"

I said, "Yes."

"Well, I called them this morning. It's all fine. We can go and visit. They said pretty much any time we liked." The future. Again it seemed almost irrelevant to me. "I'm pretty busy over the next couple of days," he said. "We could go on Thursday?"

"That seems fine," I said. It did not seem to matter to me when we went. I was not optimistic it would help in any case.

"Good," he said. "Well I'll call you."

I was about to say good-bye when I remembered what I had been writing before I dozed. I realized that my sleep could not have been deep, or else I would have forgotten everything.

"Dr. Nash?" I said. "Can I talk to you about something?"

"Yes?"

"About Ben?"

"Of course."

"Well, it's just that I'm confused. He doesn't tell me about things. Important things. Adam. My novel. And he lies about other things. He tells me it was an accident that caused me to be like this."

"Okay," he said. He paused for a moment, then said, "Why do you think he does this?" He emphasized the *you* rather than the *why*.

I thought for a second. "He doesn't know I'm writing things down. He doesn't know I know any different. I suppose it's easier for him."

"Just him?"

"No. I suppose it's easier for me, too. Or he thinks it is. But it isn't. It just means I don't even know if I can trust him."

"Christine, we're constantly changing facts, rewriting history to make things easier, to make them fit in with our preferred version of events. We do it automatically. We invent memories. Without thinking. If we tell ourselves often enough that something happened, we start to believe it, and then we can actually remember it. Isn't that what Ben's doing?"

"I suppose," I said. "But I feel like he's taking advantage of me. Advantage of my illness. He thinks he can rewrite history in any way that he likes and I will never know, never be any the wiser. But I do know. I know exactly what he's doing. And so I don't trust him. In the end he's pushing me away, Dr. Nash. Ruining everything."

"So," he said. "What do you think you can do about it?"

I knew the answer already. I have read what I wrote this morning, over and over. About how I should trust him. About how I don't. In the end, all I could think was: *This cannot go on.*

"I have to tell him I am writing my journal," I said. "I have to tell him I have been seeing you."

He said nothing for a moment. I don't know what I expected. Disapproval? But when he spoke, he said, "I think you might be right."

Relief flooded me. "You agree?"

"Yes," he said. "I've been thinking for a couple of days it might be wise. I had no idea that Ben's version of the past would be so different from what you're starting to remember. No idea how upsetting that might be. But it also occurs to me that we're only really getting half the picture now. From what you've said, more and more of your repressed memories are beginning to emerge. It might be helpful for you to talk with Ben. About the past. It might help that process."

"You think so?"

"Yes," he said. "I think perhaps keeping our work from Ben was a mistake. Plus, I spoke to the staff at Waring House today. I wanted to get an idea of what things were like there. I spoke to a woman who you became close to. One of the staff. Her name is Nicole. She told me that she's only recently returned to work there, but she was so happy when she found out that you'd gone back to live at home. She said no one could have loved you more than Ben. He came to see you pretty much every day. She said he would sit with you, in your room, or the gardens. And he tried so hard to be cheerful, despite everything. They all got to know him very well. They looked forward to him coming." He paused for a moment. "Why don't you suggest Ben come with us when we go and visit?" Another pause. "I probably ought to meet him, anyway."

"You've never met?"

"No," he said. "We only spoke briefly on the phone when I first approached him about meeting you. It didn't go too well . . ."

It struck me then. That was the reason he was suggesting I invite Ben. He wanted to meet him, finally. He wants to bring everything into the open, to make sure that the awkwardness of yesterday can never be repeated.

"Okay," I said. "If you think so."

He said that he did. He waited for a long time, and then he said, "Christine? You said you'd read your journal?"

"Yes," I said. He waited again.

"I didn't call this morning. I didn't tell you where it was."

I realized it was true. I had gone to the closet myself and, though I did not know what I would find inside it, I found the shoebox and opened it almost without thinking. I had found it myself. As if I had remembered it would be there.

"That's excellent," he said.

\* \* \*

I am writing this in bed. It is late, but Ben is in his office, across the landing. I can hear him work, the clatter of the keyboard, the click of the mouse. I can hear an occasional sigh, the creak of his chair. I imagine him squinting at the screen, deep in concentration. I trust that I will hear him switch off his machine in readiness for bed, that I will have time to hide my journal when he does. Now, despite what I thought this morning and agreed with Dr. Nash, I am certain that I don't want my husband to find out what I have been writing.

I talked to him this evening, as we sat in the dining room. "Can I ask you a question?" I said, and then, when he looked up, "Why did we never have children?" I suppose I was testing him. I willed him to tell me the truth, to contradict my assertion.

"It never seemed to be the right time," he said. "And then it was too late."

I pushed my plate of food to the side. I was disappointed. He had got home late, called out my name as he came in, asked me how I was. "Where are you?" he'd said. It had sounded like an accusation.

I shouted that I was in the kitchen. I was preparing dinner, chopping onions to fry in the olive oil I was heating on the stove. He stood in the doorway, as if hesitant to enter the room. He looked tired. Unhappy. "Are you okay?" I said.

He saw the knife in my hand. "What are you doing?"

"Just cooking dinner," I said. I smiled, but he did not reciprocate. "I thought we could have an omelet. I found some eggs in the fridge, and some mushrooms. Do we have any potatoes? I couldn't find any anywhere, I—"

"I had planned for us to have pork chops," he said. "I bought some. Yesterday. I thought we could have those."

"I'm sorry," I said. "I—"

"But no. An omelet is fine. If that's what you want."

I could feel the conversation slipping, down into a place I didn't want it to go. He was staring at the chopping board, above which my hand hovered, clutching the knife.

"No," I said. I laughed, but he did not laugh with me. "It doesn't matter. I didn't realize. I can always—"

"You've chopped the onions now," he said. His words were flat. A statement of fact, unadorned.

"I know, but . . . We could still have the chops?"

"Whatever you think," he said. He turned around, to go into the dining room. "I'll set the table." I did not answer. I did not know what it was that I had done, if anything. I went back to the onions.

Now we sat opposite each other. We had eaten in near-silence. I had asked him if everything was okay, but he had shrugged and said that it was. "It's been a long day," was all he would tell me, adding nothing but "at work," when I looked for more. Discussion was choked off before it had really begun, and I thought better of telling him about my journal and Dr. Nash. I picked at my food, tried not to worry—after all, I told myself, he is entitled to have bad days, too—but anxiety gnawed at me. I could feel the opportunity to speak slipping away, and did not know whether I would wake tomorrow with the same conviction that it was the right thing to do. Eventually, I could bear it no longer. "But did we want children?" I said.

He sighed. "Christine, do we have to?"

"I'm sorry," I said. I still didn't know what I was going to say, if anything. It might have been better to just let it go. But I realized I could not do that. "It's just that the oddest thing happened today," I said. I was trying to inject levity into my voice, a breeziness I did not feel. "I just thought I'd remembered something."

"Something?"

"Yes. Oh, I don't know . . ."

"Go on," he said. He leaned forward, suddenly eager. "What did you remember?"

My eyes fixed on the wall behind him. A picture hung there, a photograph. Petals of a flower, close up but black-and-white, with beads of water still clinging to them. It looked cheap, I thought. As if it belonged in a department store, not someone's home.

"I remembered having a baby."

He sat back in his chair. His eyes widened, and then closed completely. He took a breath, letting it out in a long sigh.

"Is it true?" I said. "Did we have a baby?" *If he lies now,* I thought, *then I don't know what I will do.* Argue with him, I suppose. Tell him everything in one uncontrolled, catastrophic outpouring. He opened his eyes and looked into mine.

"Yes," he said. "It's true."

He told me about Adam, and relief flooded me. Relief, but tinged with pain. All those years, lost forever. All those moments that I have no memory of, that I can never get back. I felt longing stir within me, felt it grow, so big that I felt it might engulf me. Ben told me about Adam's birth, his childhood, his life. Where he'd gone to school, the Nativity play he'd been in; his skills on the soccer field and the running track, his disappointment in his exam results. Girlfriends. The time an indiscreet roll-up had been mistaken for a joint. I asked questions and he answered them;

he seemed happy to be talking about his son, as if his mood was chased away by memory.

I found myself closing my eyes as he spoke. Images floated through me—images of Adam, and me, and Ben—but I couldn't say whether they were memories or imaginings. When he finished, I opened my eyes and for a moment was shocked at who I saw sitting in front of me, at how old he had become, how unlike the young father I had been imagining. "But there are no photographs of him," I said. "Anywhere."

He looked uncomfortable. "I know," he said. "You get upset."

"Upset?"

He said nothing. Perhaps he did not have the strength to tell me about Adam's death. He looked defeated, somehow. Drained. I felt guilty for what I was doing to him, what I did to him, every day.

"It's okay," I said. "I know he's dead."

He looked surprised. Hesitant. "You . . . know?"

"Yes," I said. I was about to tell him about my journal, that he had told me everything before, but I did not. His mood still seemed fragile, the air tense. It could wait. "I just feel it," I said.

"That makes sense. I've told you about it before."

It was true, of course. He had. Just as he had told me about Adam's life before. And yet, I realized, one story felt real and the other did not. I realized that I did not believe that my son was dead.

"Tell me again," I said.

He told me about the war, the roadside bomb. I listened, as calmly as I could. He talked about Adam's funeral, told me about the salvo of shots that had been fired over the coffin, the Union Jack that was draped over it. I tried to push my mind toward memories, even ones as difficult—as horrific—as that. Nothing would come.

"I want to go there," I said. "I want to see his grave."

"Chris," he said. "I'm not sure . . ."

I realized that, without memory, I would have to see evidence that he was dead, or else forever carry around the hope that he was not. "I want to," I said. "I have to."

I still thought he might say no. Might tell me he didn't think it was a good idea, that it might upset me far too much. What would I do then? How could I force him?

But he did not. "We'll go on the weekend," he said. "I promise."

Relief mixed with terror, leaving me numb.

We tidied away the dinner plates. I stood at the sink, dipping the dishes he passed to me into hot, soapy water, scrubbing them, passing them back to him to be dried, all the time avoiding my reflection in the window. I forced myself to think of Adam's funeral, imagined myself standing on the grass on an overcast day, next to a mound of earth, looking at a coffin suspended over the hole in the ground. I tried to imagine the volley of shots, the lone bugler, playing, as we—his family, his friends—sobbed in silence.

But I could not. It was not long ago and yet I saw nothing. I tried to imagine how I must have felt. I would have woken up that morning without any knowledge that I was even a mother; Ben must have first had to convince me that I had a son, and then that we were to spend that very afternoon burying him. I imagine not horror but numbness, disbelief. Unreality. There is only so much that a mind can take and surely none can cope with that, certainly not mine. I pictured myself being told what to wear, led from the house to a waiting car, settled in the backseat. Perhaps I wondered whose funeral we were really going to as we drove. Possibly it felt like mine.

I looked at Ben's reflection in the window. He would have had to cope with all that, at a time when his own grief was at its most acute. It might have been kinder, for all of us, if he had not taken me to the funeral at all. With a chill, I wondered if that was what he had really done.

I still did not know whether to tell him about Dr. Nash. He looked tired again, now, almost depressed. He smiled only when I caught his gaze and smiled at him. Perhaps later, I thought, though whether there might be a better time I did not know. I could not help but feel I was to blame for his mood, either through something I had done or something I had not. I realized how much I really cared for this man. I could not say whether I loved him—and still can't—but that is because I don't really know what love is. Despite the nebulous, shimmering memory I have of him, I feel love for Adam, an instinct to protect him, the desire to give him everything, the feeling that he is part of me and without him I am incomplete. For my mother, too, when my mind sees her, I feel a different love. A more complex bond, with caveats and reservations. Not one I fully understand. But Ben? I find him attractive. I trust him—despite the lies he has told me, I know that he has only my best interests at heart—but can I say I love him, when I am only distantly aware of having known him for more than a few hours?

I did not know. But I wanted him to be happy, and, on some level, I understood that I wanted to be the person to make him so. I must make more effort, I decided. Take control. This journal could be a tool to improve both our lives, not just mine.

I was about to ask how he was when it happened. I must have let go of the plate before he had gripped it; it clattered to the floor— accompanied by Ben's muttered *Shit!*—and shattered into hundreds of tiny pieces. "Sorry!" I said, but Ben did not look at me. He sank to the floor, cursing under his breath. "I'll do that," I said, but he ignored me and instead began snatching at the larger chunks, collecting them in his right hand.

"I'm sorry," I said again. "I'm so clumsy!"

I don't know what I expected. Forgiveness, I suppose, or the reassurance that it wasn't important. But, instead, Ben said, "Fuck!" He dropped the remains of the plate and began to suck the thumb of his left hand. Droplets of blood spattered the linoleum.

"Are you okay?" I said.

He looked up at me. "Yes, yes. I cut myself, that's all. Stupid fucking . . ."

"Let me see."

"It's nothing," he said. He stood up.

"Let me see," I said again. I reached for his hand. "I'll go and get a Band-Aid. Do we—?"

"For fuck's sake!" he said, batting my hand away. "Just leave it! Okay?"

I was stunned. I could see the cut was deep; blood welled at its edge and ran in a thin line down his wrist. I did not know what to do, what to say. He had not shouted, exactly, but neither had he made any attempt to hide his annoyance. We faced each other, in limbo, balanced on the edge of an argument, each waiting for the other to speak, both unsure what had happened, how much significance the moment had held.

I could not stand it. "I'm sorry," I said, even though part of me resented it.

His face softened. "It's okay. I'm sorry too." He paused. "I just feel tense, I think. It's been a very long day."

I took a paper towel and handed it to him. "You should clean yourself up."

He took it from me. "Thanks," he said, dabbing the blood on

his wrist and fingers. "I'll just go upstairs. Take a shower." He bent forward, kissed me. "Okay?"

He turned and left the room.

I heard the bathroom door close, a tap turn on. The boiler next to me fired to life. I gathered the rest of the pieces of the plate and put them in the garbage, wrapping them in paper first, then swept up the tinier fragments before finally sponging up the blood. When I had finished, I went into the living room.

The flip-top phone was ringing, muffled by my bag. I took it out. Dr. Nash.

The TV was still on. Above me, I could hear the creak of floorboards as Ben moved from room to room upstairs. I did not want him to hear me, talking on a phone he does not know I have. I whispered, "Hello?"

"Christine," came the voice. "It's Ed. Dr. Nash. Can you speak?"

While this afternoon he had sounded calm, almost reflective, now his voice was urgent. I began to feel afraid.

"Yes," I said, lowering my voice still further. "What is it?"

"Listen," he said. "Have you spoken to Ben yet?"

"Yes," I said. "Sort of. Why? What's wrong?"

"Did you tell him about your journal? About me? Did you invite him to Waring House?"

"No," I said. "I was about to. He's upstairs, I— What's wrong?"

"I'm sorry," he said. "It's probably nothing to worry about. It's just that someone from Waring House just called me. The woman I spoke to this morning? Nicole? She wanted to give me a phone number. She said that your friend Claire has apparently called there, wanting to talk to you. She left her number."

I felt myself tense. I heard the toilet flush and the sound of water in the sink. "I don't understand," I said. "Recently?"

"No," he said. "It was a couple of weeks after you left to go and live with Ben. When you weren't there she took Ben's number, but, well, they said she called again later and said she couldn't get through to him. She asked them if they'd give her your address. They couldn't do that, of course, but said that she could leave her number with them, in case you or Ben ever called. Nicole found a note in your file after we spoke this morning, and she rang back to give the number to me."

I didn't understand. "But why didn't they just mail it to me? Or to Ben?"

"Well, Nicole said they did. But they never heard back from either of you." He paused.

"Ben handles all the mail," I said. "He picks it up in the morning. Well, he did today, anyway . . ."

"Has Ben given you Claire's number?"

"No," I said. "No. He said we haven't been in touch for years. She moved away, not long after we got married. New Zealand."

"Okay," he said, and then, "Christine? You told me that before, and . . . well . . . it's not an international number."

I felt a billowing sense of dread, though still I could not say why. "So, she moved back?"

"Nicole said that Claire used to visit you all the time at Waring House. She was there almost as much as Ben was. Nicole never heard anything about her moving away. Not to New Zealand. Not anywhere."

It felt as though everything was suddenly taking off, things were moving too fast for me to keep up with them. I could hear Ben, upstairs. The water had stopped running now, the boiler was silent. *There must be a rational explanation,* I thought. *There has to be.*

I felt that all I had to do was to slow things down so that I could catch up, could work out what it was. I wanted him to stop talking, to undo the things he had said, but he did not.

"There's something else," said Nash. "I'm sorry, Christine, but Nicole asked me how you were doing, and I told her. She said she was surprised that you were back living with Ben. I asked why."

"Okay," I heard myself say. "Go on."

"I'm sorry, Christine, but listen. She said that you and Ben were divorced."

The room tipped. I gripped the arm of the chair to steady myself. It did not make sense. On the television, a blond woman was screaming at an older man, telling him she hated him. I wanted to scream, too.

"What?" I said.

"She said that you and Ben were separated. Ben left you. A year or so after you moved to Waring House."

"Separated?" I said. It felt as if the room was receding, becoming vanishingly small. Disappearing. "You're sure?"

"Yes. Apparently. That's what she said. She said she felt it might have had something to do with Claire. She wouldn't say anything else."

"Claire?" I said.

"Yes," he said. Even through my own confusion, I could hear how difficult he was finding this conversation, the hesitancy in his voice, the slow picking through possibilities to decide the best thing to say. "I don't know why Ben isn't telling you everything," he said. "I did think he believed he was doing the right thing. Protecting you. But now? I don't know. To not tell you that Claire is still local? To not mention your divorce? I don't know. It doesn't seem right, but I suppose he must have his reasons." I said nothing. "I thought maybe you should speak to Claire. She might have some answers.

She might even talk to Ben. I don't know." Another pause. "Christine? Do you have a pen? Do you want the number?"

I swallowed hard. "Yes," I said. "Yes, please."

I reached for a corner of the newspaper on the coffee table, and the pen that was next to it, and wrote down the number that he gave me. I heard the bolt on the bathroom door slide open, Ben come onto the landing.

"Christine?" said Dr. Nash. "I'll call you tomorrow. Don't say anything to Ben. Not until we've figured out what's going on. Okay?"

I heard myself agree, say good-bye. He told me not to forget to write in this journal before I went to sleep. I wrote *Claire* next to the number, still not knowing what I was going to do. I tore it off and put it in my bag.

I said nothing when Ben came downstairs, nothing as he sat on the sofa across from me. I fixed my eyes on the television. A documentary about wildlife. The inhabitants of the ocean floor. A remote-controlled submersible craft was exploring an underwater trench with jerky twitches. Two lamps shone into places that had never known light before. Ghosts in the deep.

I wanted to ask him if I was still in touch with Claire, but did not want to hear another lie. A giant squid hung in the gloom, drifting in the gentle current. This creature has never been captured on film before, said the voice-over to the accompaniment of electronic music.

"Are you all right?" he said. I nodded, without taking my eyes off the screen.

He stood up. "I have work to do," he said. "Upstairs. I'll come to bed soon."

I looked at him, then. I did not know who he was.

"Yes," I said. "I'll see you later."

# Wednesday, November 21

I have spent all morning reading this journal. Even so, I have not read it all. Some pages I have skimmed over, others I have read again and again, trying to believe them. And now I am in the bedroom, sitting in the bay, writing more.

I have the phone in my lap. Why does it feel so difficult to dial Claire's number? Neuronal impulses, muscular contractions. That is all it will take. Nothing complicated. Nothing difficult. Yet it feels so much easier to take up a pen and write about it instead.

This morning, I went into the kitchen. My life, I thought, is built on quicksand. It shifts from one day to the next. Things I think I know are wrong, things I am certain of, facts about my life, myself, belong to years ago. All the history I have reads like fiction. Dr. Nash, Ben. Adam, and now Claire. They exist, but as shadows in the dark. As strangers, they crisscross my life, connecting, disconnecting. Elusive, ethereal. Like ghosts.

And not just them. Everything. It is all invented. Conjured from nothing. I am desperate for solid ground, for something real, something that will not vanish as I sleep. I need to anchor myself.

I clicked open the lid of the garbage pail. A warmth rose from it—the heat of decomposition and decay—and it smelled, faintly. The sweet, sick smell of rotting food. I could see a newspaper, the crossword part filled in, a solitary tea bag soaking it brown. I held my breath and knelt down on the floor.

Inside the newspaper were shards of porcelain, crumbs, a fine white dust, and underneath it a plastic bag, knotted closed. I fished it out, thinking of dirty diapers, decided to tear it open later if I had to. Beneath it, there were potato peelings and a near-empty plastic bottle that was leaking ketchup. I pushed both aside.

Egg shells—four or five—and a handful of papery onion skin. The remains of a de-seeded red pepper, a large mushroom, half-rotten.

Satisfied, I replaced the things in the bin and closed it. It was true. Last night, we had eaten an omelet. A plate had been smashed. I looked in the fridge. Two pork chops lay in a polystyrene tray. In the hallway, Ben's slippers sat at the bottom of the stairs. Everything was there, exactly as I had described it in my journal last night. I hadn't invented it. It was all true.

And that meant the number was Claire's. Dr. Nash had really called me. Ben and I had been divorced.

I want to call Dr. Nash now. I want to ask him what to do, or, better, to ask him to do it for me. But for how long can I be a visitor in my own life? Passive? I need to take control. The thought crosses my mind that I might never see Dr. Nash again—not now that I have told him of my feelings, my *crush*—but I don't let it take root. Either way, I need to speak to Claire myself.

But what will I say? There seems to be so much for us to talk about, and yet so little. So much history between us, but none of it known to me.

I think of what Dr. Nash had told me about why Ben and I separated. *Something to do with Claire.*

It all makes sense. Years ago, when I needed him most but understood him least, my husband divorced me, and now we are back together he is telling me that my best friend moved to the other side of the world before any of this happened.

Is that why I can't call her? Because I am afraid that she might have more to hide than I have even begun to imagine? Is that why Ben seems less than keen for me to remember more? Is that even why he has been suggesting that any attempts at treatment are futile, so that I will never be able to link memory to memory and know what has been happening?

I cannot imagine he would do that. Nobody would. It is a ridiculous thing. I think of what Dr. Nash told me about my time in the hospital. *You were claiming the doctors were conspiring against you,* he said. *Exhibiting symptoms of paranoia.*

I wonder if that is what I am doing again now.

Suddenly a memory floods me. It strikes almost violently, rising up from the emptiness of my past to send me tumbling back, but then just as quickly disappears. Claire and me, another party. "Christ," she is saying. "It's so annoying! You know what I think is wrong? Everyone's so bloody hung up on sex. It's just animals copulating, y'know? No matter how much we try and dance around it and dress it up as something else. That's all it is."

Is it possible that with me stuck in my own hell Claire and Ben have sought solace in each other?

I look down. The phone lies dead in my lap. I have no idea where Ben really goes when he leaves every morning, or where he might stop off on the way home. It might be anywhere. And I have no opportunity to build suspicion on suspicion, to link one fact to another. Even if one day I were to discover Claire and Ben in bed, the next I would forget what I had seen. I am the perfect person on whom to cheat. Perhaps they are still seeing each other. Perhaps I have already discovered them, and forgotten.

I think this, and yet, somehow, I don't think this. I trust Ben, and yet I don't. It's perfectly possible to hold two opposing points of view in the mind at once, oscillating between them.

But why would he lie? *He just thinks he's doing the right thing.* I keep telling myself that. *He's protecting you. Keeping from you the things that you don't need to know.*

I dialed the number, of course. There was no way I could have not done so. It rang, for a while, and then there was a click, and a voice. "Hi," it said. "Please leave a message."

I knew the voice at once. It was Claire's. Unmistakable.

I left her a message. *Please call me,* I said. *It's Christine.*

I went downstairs. I had done all I could do.

* * *

I waited. For an hour that turned into two. I spent the time writing in my journal, and when she did not call, I made a sandwich and ate it in the living room. While I was in the kitchen—wiping down the countertop, sweeping crumbs into my palm, preparing to empty them into the sink—the doorbell rang. The noise startled me. I put down the sponge, dried my hands on the tea towel that hung from the handle of the oven, and went to see who it was.

Through the frosted glass I could see the outline of a man. Not uniformed; he was wearing what looked like a suit, a tie. *Ben?* I thought, before realizing he would still be at work. I opened the door.

It was Dr. Nash. I knew, partly because it could be no one else, but partly because—though when I read about him this morning, I could not picture him, and though my husband had remained unfamiliar to me even once I had been told who he was—I recognized him. His hair was short, parted, his tie loose and untidy, a sweater sat beneath a jacket with which it clashed.

He must have seen the look of surprise on my face. "Christine?" he said.

"Yes," I said. "Yes." I did not open the door more than a fraction.

"It's me. Ed. Ed Nash. Dr. Nash?"

"I know," I said. "I . . ."

"Did you read your journal?"

"Yes, but . . ."

"Are you okay?"

"Yes," I said. "I'm fine."

He lowered his voice. "Is Ben home?"

"No. No, he's not. It's just, well. I wasn't expecting you. Did we have a meeting arranged?"

He held back for a moment, a fraction of a second, enough to disrupt the rhythm of our exchange. We had not, I knew that. Or at least I had not written of one.

"Yes," he said. "Did you not write it down?"

I hadn't, but I said nothing. We stood across the threshold of the house that I still do not think of as my home, looking at each other. "Can I come in?" he asked.

I did not answer at first. I wasn't sure I wanted to invite him in. It seemed wrong somehow. A betrayal.

But of what? Ben's trust? I did not know how much that mattered to me anymore. Not after his lies. Lies that I had spent most of my morning reading.

"Yes," I said. I opened the door. He nodded as he stepped into the house, glancing left and right as he did. I took his coat and hung it on the coat rack next to a rain slicker that I guessed must be mine. "In there," I said, pointing to the living room, and he went in.

I made us both a drink, gave his to him, sat opposite with mine. He did not speak, and I took a slow sip, waiting as he did the same. He put his cup down on the coffee table between us.

"You don't remember asking me to come over?" he said.

"No," I said. "When?"

He said it then, and it chilled me. "This morning. When I rang to tell you where to find your journal."

I could remember nothing of him calling that morning, and still can't, even now he has gone.

I thought of other things I had written of. *A plate of melon I couldn't remember ordering. A cookie I hadn't asked for.*

"I don't remember," I said. A panic began to rise within me.

Concern flashed on his face. "Have you slept at all today? Anything more than a quick doze?"

"No," I said, "no. Not at all. I just can't remember. When was it? When?"

"Christine," he said. "Calm down. It's probably nothing."

"But what if— I don't—"

"Christine, please. It doesn't mean anything. You just forgot, that's all. Everyone forgets things sometimes."

"But whole conversations? It must have only been a couple of hours ago!"

"Yes," he said. He spoke softly, trying to calm me, but did not move from where he sat. "But you have been through a lot lately. Your memory has always been variable. Forgetting one thing doesn't mean that you're deteriorating, that you won't get better again. Okay?" I nodded, trying to believe him, desperate to. "You asked me here because you wanted to speak to Claire, but weren't sure you could. And you wanted me to speak to Ben on your behalf."

"I did?"

"Yes. You said you didn't think you could do it yourself."

I looked at him, thought of all the things I had written. I realized I didn't believe him. I must have found my journal myself. I had not asked him here today. I did not want him to talk to Ben. Why would I, when I had decided to say nothing to Ben myself, yet? And why would I tell him I needed him here to help me speak to Claire, when I had already phoned her myself and left a message?

*He's lying.* I wondered what other reasons he might have for coming. What he might not feel able to tell me.

I have no memory, but I am not stupid. "Why are you really here?" I said. He shifted in his chair. Possibly he just wanted to see inside the place where I live. Or possibly to see me, one more time, before I speak to Ben. "Are you worried that Ben won't let me see you after I tell him about us?"

Another thought comes. Perhaps he is not writing a research paper at all. Perhaps he has other reasons for wanting to spend so much of his time with me. I push it from my mind.

"No," he said. "That's not it at all. I came because you asked me to. Besides, you've decided not to tell Ben that you're seeing me. Not until you've spoken to Claire. Remember?"

I shook my head. I did not remember. I did not know what he was talking about.

"Claire is fucking my husband," I said.

He looked shocked. "Christine," he said. "I—"

"He's treating me like I'm stupid," I said. "Lying to me about anything and everything. Well, I'm not stupid."

"I know you're not stupid," he said. "But I don't think—"

"They've been fucking for years," I said. "It explains every-thing. Why he tells me she moved away. Why I haven't seen her even though she's supposedly my best friend."

"Christine," he said. "You're not thinking straight." He came and sat beside me on the sofa. "Ben loves you. I know. I've spoken to him, when I wanted to persuade him to let me see you. He was totally loyal. Totally. He told me that he'd lost you once and didn't want to lose you again. That he'd watched you suffer whenever people had tried to treat you and wouldn't see you in pain any-more. He loves you. It's obvious. He's trying to protect you. From the truth, I suppose."

I thought of what I had read this morning. Of the divorce. "But he left me. To be with her."

"Christine," he said. "You're not thinking. If that was true, why would he bring you back? Back here? He would have just left you in Waring House. But he hasn't. He looks after you. Every day."

I felt myself collapse, folding in on myself. I felt as if I under-stood his words, yet at the same time didn't. I felt the warmth his body gave off, saw the kindness in his eyes. He smiled as I looked at him. He seemed to become bigger, until his body was all I could see, his breathing all I could hear. He spoke, but I did not hear what he said. I heard only one word. *Love.*

I didn't intend to do what I did. I didn't plan it. It happened suddenly, my life shifting like a stuck lid that finally gives. In a moment, all I could feel were my lips on his, my arms around his neck. His hair was damp and I neither understood nor cared why. I wanted to speak, to tell him what I felt, but I did not, because to do so would have been to stop kissing him, to end the moment that I wanted to go on forever. I felt like a woman, finally. In con-trol. Though I must have done so, I can remember—have written about—no other time when I have kissed anyone but my husband; it might as well have been the first.

I don't know for how long it lasted. I don't even know how it happened, how I went from sitting there, on the sofa next to him, diminished, so small that I felt I might disappear, to kissing him. I don't remember willing it, which is not to say I don't remember wanting it. I don't remember it beginning. I remember only that I went from one state to another, with nothing in between, with no opportunity for conscious thought, no decision.

He did not push me away roughly. He was gentle. He gave me that, at least. He did not insult me by asking me what I was doing, much less what I *thought* I was doing. He simply removed first his lips from mine, then my hands from where they had come to rest on his shoulders, and, softly, said, "No."

I was stunned. At what I had done? Or his reaction to it? I cannot say. It felt only that, for a moment, I had been somewhere else and a new Christine had stepped in, taken me over completely, and then vanished. I was not horrified, though. Not even disappointed. I was glad. Glad that, because of her, something had happened.

He looked at me. "I'm sorry," he said, and I could not tell what he felt. Anger? Pity? Regret? Any of those things might be possible. Perhaps the expression I saw was a mixture of all three. He was still holding my hands and he put them back in my lap, then let them go. "I'm sorry, Christine," he said again.

I did not know what to say. What to do. I was silent, about to apologize myself, and then I said, "Ed. I love you."

He closed his eyes. "Christine," he began, "I—"

"Please," I said. "Don't. Don't tell me you haven't felt it too." He frowned. "You know you love me."

"Christine," he said. "Please, you're . . . you're . . ."

"What?" I said. "Crazy?"

"No. Confused. You're confused."

I laughed. " 'Confused'?"

"Yes," he said. "You don't love me. You remember we talked about confabulation? It's quite common with people who—"

"Oh," I said. "I know. I remember. With people who have no memory. Is that what you think this is?"

"It's possible. Perfectly possible."

I hated him then. He thought he knew everything, knew me better than I did myself. All he really knew was my condition.

"I'm not stupid," I said.

"I know. I know that, Christine. I don't think you are. I just think—"

"You must love me."

He sighed. I was frustrating him now. Wearing his patience thin.

"Why else have you been coming here so much? Driving me around London. Do you do that with all your patients?"

"Yes," he began, then, "well, no. Not exactly."

"Then why?"

"I've been trying to help you," he said.

"Is that all?"

A pause, then he said, "Well, no. I've been writing a paper, too. A scientific paper—"

"Studying me?"

"Well, sort of," he said. I tried to push what he was saying from my mind.

"But you didn't tell me that Ben and I were separated," I said. "Why? Why didn't you do that?"

"I didn't know!" he said. "No other reason. It wasn't in your file and Ben didn't tell me. I didn't know!" I was silent. He moved, as if to take my hands again, then stopped, scratching his forehead instead. "I would have told you. If I'd known."

"Would you?" I said. "Like you told me about Adam?"

He looked hurt. "Christine, please."

"Why did you keep him from me?" I said. "You're as bad as Ben!"

"Jesus, Christine," he said. "We've been through this. I did what I thought was best. Ben wasn't telling you about Adam. I couldn't tell you. It wouldn't be right. It wouldn't have been ethical."

I laughed. A hollow, snorting laugh. "Ethical? What is ethical about keeping him from me?"

"It was down to Ben to decide whether to tell you about Adam. Not me. I suggested you keep a journal, though. So that you could write down what you'd learned. I thought that was for the best."

"How about the attack, then? You were quite happy for me to go along thinking I'd been involved in a hit-and-run accident!"

"Christine, no. No, I wasn't. Ben told you that. I didn't know that's what he was saying to you. How could I?"

I thought of what I had seen. Orange blossom–scented baths and hands around my throat. The feeling that I could not breathe. The man whose face remained a mystery. I began to cry. "Then why did you tell me at all?" I said.

He spoke kindly but still did not touch me. "I didn't," he said. "I didn't tell you that you were attacked. That, you remembered yourself." He was right, of course. I felt angry. "Christine, I—"

"I want you to leave," I said. "Please." I was crying solidly now, yet felt curiously alive. I did not know what had just happened, could barely even remember what had been said, but it felt as if some awful thing had lifted, some dam within me finally burst.

"Please," I said. "Please go."

I expected him to argue. To beg me to let him stay. I almost wanted him to. But he did not. "If you're sure?" he said.

"Yes," I whispered. I turned toward the window, determined to not look at him again. Not today, which for me will mean that by tomorrow I might as well have never seen him at all. He stood up, walked to the door.

"I'll call you," he said. "Tomorrow? Your treatment. I—"

"Just go," I said. "Please."

He said nothing else. I heard the door close behind him.

I sat there for a while. A few minutes? Hours? I don't know. My heart raced. I felt empty and alone. Eventually I went upstairs. In the bathroom, I looked at the photos. My husband. Ben. *What have I done?* I have nothing, now. No one I can trust. No one I can turn to. My mind raced, out of control. I kept thinking of what Dr. Nash had said. *He loves you. He's trying to protect you.*

Protect me from what, though? From the truth. I thought the truth more important than anything. Maybe I am wrong.

I went into the study. Ben has lied about so much. There is nothing he has told me I can believe. Nothing at all.

I knew what I had to do. I had to know. Know that I could trust him, about this one thing.

The box was where I had described it, locked, as I suspected. I did not get upset.

I began to look. I told myself I would not stop until I found the key. I searched the office first. The other drawers, the desk. I did it methodically. I replaced everything where I had found it, and when I had finished, I went into the bedroom. I looked in the drawers, digging beneath his underwear, the handkerchiefs, neatly ironed, the undershirts and T-shirts. Nothing, and nothing in the drawers I used, either.

There were drawers in the bedside tables. I intended to look in each, starting with Ben's side of the bed. I opened the top drawer and rooted through its contents—pens, a watch that had stopped, a blister pack of pills I did not recognize—before opening the bottom drawer.

At first, I thought it was empty. I closed it gently, but as I did, I heard a tiny rattle, metal scraping on wood. I opened it again, my heart already beating fast.

A key.

I sat on the floor with the open box. It was full. Photographs, mostly. Of Adam, and me. Some looked familiar—I guess the ones he had shown me before—but many not. I found Adam's birth certificate, the letter he had written to Santa Claus. Handfuls of photos of him as a baby—crawling, grinning, toward the camera; feeding at my breast; sleeping, wrapped in a green blanket—and as he grew. The photo of him dressed as a cowboy, the school photographs, the tricycle. They were all here, exactly as I had described them in my journal.

I lifted them all out and spread them across the floor, looking at each one as I did. There were photographs of Ben and me, too; one in which we are in front of the Houses of Parliament, both smiling, but standing awkwardly, as if neither of us knows the other exists; another from our wedding, a formal shot. We are standing in front of a church under an overcast sky. We look happy, ridiculously so, and even more so in one that must have been taken later, on our honeymoon. We are in a restaurant, smiling, leaning in over a half-eaten meal, our faces flushed with love and the bite of the sun.

Relief began to flood me. I stared at the photograph of the woman sitting there with her new husband, gazing out at a future she could not predict and did not want to, and thought about how much I share with her. But all of it is physical. Cells and tissues. DNA. Our chemical signature. But nothing else. She is a stranger. There is nothing linking her to me, no means to thread my way back to her.

Yet she is me, and I am her, and I could see that she was in love. With Ben. The man she has just married. The man I still wake up with, every day. He did not break the vows he made on that day in the tiny church in Manchester. He has not let me down. I looked at the photograph and love welled inside me again.

But still, I put it down, carried on searching. I knew what I wanted to find—and what I also dreaded finding. The one thing that would prove my husband wasn't lying, that would give me my partner even if, in doing so, it would deny me my son.

It was there. At the bottom of the box, inside an envelope. A photocopy of a news article, folded, its edges crisp. I knew what it was, almost before I opened it, but still I shook as I read. *A British soldier who died escorting troops in Helmand Province, Afghanistan, has been named by the Ministry of Defence. Adam Wheeler,* it said, *was 19 years old. Born in London . . .* Clipped to it was a photograph. Flowers, arranged on a grave. The inscription read, ADAM WHEELER. 1987–2006.

The grief hit me then, with a force I doubt it can ever have had before. I dropped the paper and doubled up in pain, too much pain even to cry, and emitted a noise like a howl, like a wounded animal, starving, praying for its end to come. I closed my eyes and saw it then. A brief flash. An image, hanging in front of me, shimmering. A medal, given to me in a black velvet box. A coffin, a flag. I looked away from it and prayed that it would never return. There are memories I am better off without. Things better lost forever.

I began to tidy the papers away. *I should have trusted him,* I thought. *All along.* I should have believed that he was keeping things from me only because they are too painful to face, fresh, every day. All he was doing was trying to spare me this. This brutal truth. I put the photographs back, the papers, just as I had found them. I felt satisfied. I put the key back in the drawer, the box back in the filing cabinet. *I can look whenever I want, now. As often as I like.*

There was only one more thing I still had to do. I had to know why Ben had left me. And I had to know what I had been doing in Brighton, all those years ago. I had to know who had stolen my life from me. I had to try once more.

For the second time today, I dialed Claire's number.

Static. Silence. Then a two-tone ring. She will not answer, I thought. She has not responded to my message, after all. She has something to hide, something to keep from me.

I almost felt glad. This was a conversation I wanted to have only in theory. I could not see how it could be anything but painful. I prepared myself for another emotionless invitation to leave a message.

A click. Then a voice. "Hello?"

It was Claire. I knew it instantly. Her voice felt as familiar as my own. "Hello?" she said again.

I did not speak. Images flooded me, flashing. I saw her face, her hair cut short, wearing a beret. Laughing. I saw her at a wedding—my own, I suppose, though I cannot say—dressed in emerald, pouring champagne. I saw her holding a child, carrying him, giving him to me with the words "Dinner time!" I saw her sitting on the edge of a bed, talking to the figure lying in it, and realized the figure was me.

"Claire?" I said.

"Yep," she said. "Hello? Who is this?"

I tried to focus, to remind myself that we had been best friends once, no matter what had happened in the years since. I saw an image of her lying on my bed, clutching a bottle of vodka, giggling, telling me that men were *fucking ridiculous*.

"Claire?" I said. "It's me. Christine."

Silence. Time stretched so that it seemed to last forever. At first, I thought she would not speak, that she had forgotten who I was, or did not want to speak to me. I closed my eyes.

"Chrissy!" she said. An explosion. I heard her swallow, as if she had been eating. "Chrissy! My God. Darling, is that really you?"

I opened my eyes. A tear had begun its slow traverse down the unfamiliar lines of my face.

"Claire?" I said. "Yes. It's me. It's Chrissy."

"Jesus. Fuck," she said, and then again, "fuck!" Her voice was quiet. "Roger! Rog! It's Chrissy! On the phone!" Suddenly loud, she said, "How are you? Where are you?" and then, "Roger!"

"Oh, I'm at home," I said.

"Home?"

"Yes."

"With Ben?"

I felt suddenly defensive. "Yes," I said. "With Ben. Did you get my message?"

I heard an intake of breath. Surprise? Or was she smoking? "Yep!" she said. "I would have called you back but this is the landline and you didn't leave a number." She hesitated, and for a moment I wondered if there were other reasons she had not returned my call. She went on. "Anyway, how are you, darling? It's so good to hear your voice!" I did not know how to answer, and when I didn't reply Claire said, "Where are you living?"

"I don't know, exactly," I said. I felt a surge of pleasure, certain that her question meant that she was not seeing Ben, followed by the realization that she might be asking me so that I do not suspect the truth. I wanted so much to trust her—to know that Ben had not left me because of something he had found in her, some love to replace that which had been taken from me—because doing so meant that I could trust my husband as well. "Crouch End?" I said.

"Right," she said. "So how's it going? How're things?"

"Well, you know?" I said. "I can't remember a fucking thing."

We both laughed. It felt good, this eruption of an emotion that wasn't grief, but it was short-lived, followed by silence.

"You sound good," she said, after a while. "Really good." I told her I was writing again. "Really? Wow. Super. What are you working on? A novel?"

"No," I said. "It'd be kind of hard to write a novel when I can't remember anything from one day to the next." Silence. "I'm just writing about what's happening to me."

"Okay," she said, then nothing. I wondered if perhaps she did not entirely understand my situation, and worried about her tone. It sounded cool. I wondered how things had been left, the last time we saw each other. "So what is happening with you?" she said then.

What to say? I had an urge to let her see my journal, to let her read it all for herself, but of course I could not. Or not yet, anyway. There seemed to be too much to say, too much I wanted to know. My whole life.

"I don't know," I said. "It's difficult . . ."

I must have sounded upset, because she said, "Chrissy, darling. Whatever's wrong?"

"Nothing," I said. "I'm fine. I just . . ." The sentence petered out. "Darling?"

"I don't know," I said. I thought of Dr. Nash, of the things I'd said to him. Could I be sure that he wouldn't talk to Ben? "I just feel confused. I think I've done something stupid."

"Oh, I'm sure that's not true." Another silence—a calculation?—and then she said, "Listen. Can I speak to Ben?"

"He's out," I said. I felt relieved that our discussion seemed to have moved onto something concrete, factual. "At work."

"Right," said Claire. Another silence. The conversation felt suddenly absurd.

"I need to see you," I said.

"'Need'?" she said. "Not 'want'?"

"No," I began. "Obviously I want . . ."

"Relax, Chrissy," she said. "I'm kidding. I want to see you, too. I'm dying to."

I felt relieved. I had had the idea that our talk might limp to a halt, end with a polite good-bye and a vague promise to speak again in the future, and another avenue into my past would slam shut forever.

"Thank you," I said. "Thank you."

"Chrissy," she said. "I've been missing you so much. Every day. Every single day I've been waiting for this bloody phone to ring, hoping it would be you, never for a second thinking it would be." She paused. "How . . . how is your memory now? How much do you know?"

"I'm not sure," I said. "Better than it has been, I think. But I still don't remember much." I thought of all the things I'd written down, all the images of me and Claire. "I remember a party," I said. "Fireworks on a rooftop. You painting. Me studying. But nothing after that, really."

"Ah!" she said. "The big night! Jesus, that seems like a long time ago! There's a lot I need to fill you in on. A lot."

I wondered what she meant, but did not ask her. It can wait, I thought. There were more important things I needed to know.

"Did you ever move away?" I said. "Abroad?"

She laughed. "Yeah," she said. "For about six months. I met this bloke, years ago. It was a disaster."

"Where?" I said. "Where did you go?"

"Barcelona," she replied. "Why?"

"Oh," I said. "It's nothing." I felt defensive, embarrassed to not know these details of my friend's life. "It's just something someone told me. They said you'd been to New Zealand. They must have made a mistake."

"New Zealand?" she said, laughing. "Nope. Not been there. Ever."

So Ben had lied to me about that, too. I still did not know why, could not think of a reason he would feel the need to remove Claire from my life so thoroughly. Was it just like everything else he had lied about, or chosen not to tell me? Was it for my own benefit?

It was something else I would have to ask him, when we had the conversation I now knew we must. When I tell him all that I know, and how I have found it out.


We spoke some more, our conversation punctuated by long gaps and desperate rushes. Claire told me she had married, then divorced, and now was living with Roger. "He's an academic," she said. "Psychology. Bugger wants me to marry him, which I shan't in a hurry. But I love him."

It felt good to talk to her, to listen to her voice. It seemed easy, familiar. Almost like coming home. She demanded little, seeming to understand that I had little to give. Eventually, she stopped and

I thought she might be about to say good-bye. I realized that neither of us had mentioned Adam.

"So," she said instead. "Tell me about Ben. How long have you been, well . . ."

"Back together?" I said. "I don't know. I didn't even know we'd ever been apart."

"I tried to call him," she said. I felt myself tense, though could not say why.

"When?"

"This afternoon. After you called. I guessed that he must have given you my number. He didn't answer, but then I only have an old work number. They said he's not there anymore."

I felt a creeping dread. I looked around the bedroom, alien and unfamiliar. I felt sure she was lying.

"Do you speak to him often?" I said.

"No. Not lately." A new tone entered her voice. Hushed. I did not like it. "Not for a few years." She hesitated. "I've been so worried about you."

I was afraid. Afraid that Claire would tell Ben that I had called her, before I had a chance to speak to him.

"Please don't call him," I said. "Please don't tell him I've called you."

"Chrissy!" she said. "Why ever not?"

"I'd just rather you didn't."

She sighed heavily, then sounded cross. "Look. What on earth is going on?"

"I can't explain," I said.

"Try."

I could not bring myself to mention Adam, but I told her about Dr. Nash, and about the memory of the hotel room, and how Ben insists that I had a car accident. "I think he's not telling me the truth because he knows it would upset me," I said. She did not answer. "Claire?" I said. "What might I have been doing in Brighton?"

Silence stretched between us. "Chrissy," she said. "If you really want to know, then I'll tell you. Or as much as I know, anyway. But not over the phone. When we meet. I promise."

The truth. It hung in front of me, glistening, so close I could almost reach out and take it.

"When can you come over?" I said. "Today? Tonight?"

"I'd rather not come to you," she said. "If you don't mind?"

"Why not?"

"I just think . . . well . . . it's better if we meet somewhere else? I can take you for a coffee?"

There was a jollity in her voice, but it seemed forced. False. I wondered what she was frightened of, but said, "Okay."

"Alexandra Palace?" she said. "Is that all right? You should be able to get there easily enough from Crouch End."

"Okay," I said.

"Cool. Friday? I'll meet you at eleven. Is that okay?"

I told her it was. It would have to be. "I'll be fine," I said. She told me which buses I would need and I wrote the details on a slip of paper. Then, after we'd chatted for a few minutes more, we said good-bye and I took out my journal and began to write.

\* \* \*

"Ben?" I said when he got home. He was sitting in the armchair in the living room, reading the newspaper. He looked tired, as if he'd not slept well. "Do you trust me?" I said.

He looked up. His eyes sparked into life, lit with love, but also something else. Something that looked almost like fear. Not surprising, I suppose; the question is usually asked before an admission that such trust is misplaced. He swept his hair back from his forehead.

"Of course, darling," he said. He came over and perched on the arm of my chair, taking one of my hands between his. "Of course."

I was suddenly unsure whether I wanted to continue. "Do you talk to Claire?"

He looked down into my eyes. "Claire?" he said. "You remember her?"

I had forgotten that until recently—until the memory of the fireworks party, in fact—Claire had not existed to me at all. "Vaguely," I said.

He glanced away, toward the clock on the mantelpiece.

"No," he said. "I think she moved away. Years ago."

I winced, as if with pain. "Are you sure?" I asked. I could not believe he was still lying to me. It seemed almost worse of him to lie about this than about everything else. This, surely, would be an easy thing to be honest about? The fact that Claire was still local would cause me no pain, might even be something that— were I to see her—would help my memory to improve. So why the dishonesty? A dark thought entered my head—the same black suspicion—but I pushed it away.

"Are you positive? Where did she go?" *Tell me,* I thought. *It's not too late.*

"I don't really remember," he said. "New Zealand, I think. Or Australia."

I felt hope slip farther away, but knew what I had to do. "You're certain?" I said. I took a gamble. "I have this odd memory that she once told me she was thinking of moving to Barcelona for a while. Years and years ago, it must have been." He said nothing. "You're sure it wasn't there?"

"You remembered that?" he said. "When?"

"I don't know," I said. "It's just a feeling."

He squeezed my hand. A consolation. "It's probably your imagination."

"It felt very real, though. You're certain it wasn't Barcelona?"

He sighed. "No. Not Barcelona. It was definitely Australia. Adelaide, I think. I'm not sure. It was a long time ago." He shook his head. "Claire," he said, smiling. "I haven't thought of her for ages. Not for years and years."

I closed my eyes. When I opened them, he was grinning at me. He looked stupid, almost. Pathetic. I wanted to slap him. "Ben," I said, my voice little more than a whisper. "I've spoken to her."

I did not know how he would react. He did nothing, almost as if I hadn't spoken at all, but then his eyes flared.

"When?" he said. His voice was hard as glass.

I could either tell him the truth or admit that I have been writing the story of my days. "This afternoon," I said. "She called me."

"She called you?" he said. "How? How did she call you?"

I decided to lie. "She said you'd given her my number."

"What number? That's ridiculous! How could I? You're sure it was her?"

"She said you spoke together, occasionally. Until fairly recently."

He let go of my hand and it dropped into my lap, a dead weight. He stood up, rounding to face me. "She said what?"

"She told me that the two of you had been in contact. Up until a few years ago."

He leaned in close. I smelled coffee on his breath. "This woman just phoned you out of the blue? You're sure it was even her?"

I rolled my eyes. "Oh, Ben!" I said. "Who else could it have been?" I smiled. I had never thought this conversation might be easy, but it seemed infused with a seriousness I did not like.

He shrugged. "You don't know. There have been people who have tried to get hold of you, in the past. The press. Journalists. People who have read about you, and what happened, and want your side of the story, or even just to nose around and find out just how bad you really are, or see how much you've changed. They've pretended to be other people before, just to get you to talk. There are doctors. Quacks who think they can help you. Homeopathy. Alternative medicine. Even witch doctors."

"Ben," I said. "She was my best friend for years. I recognized her voice." His face sagged, defeated. "You have been speaking to her, haven't you?" I noticed that he was clenching and unclenching his right hand, balling it into a fist, releasing it. "Ben?" I said again.

He looked up. His face was red, his eyes moist. "Okay," he said. "Okay. I have spoken to Claire. She asked me to keep in touch with her, to let her know how you are. We speak every few months, just briefly."

"Why didn't you tell me?" He said nothing. "Ben. Why?" Silence. "You just decided it was easier to keep her from me? To pretend she'd moved away? Is that it? Just like you pretended I'd never written a novel?"

"Chris—" he began, then, "What—"

"It's not fair, Ben," I said. "You have no right to keep these things to yourself. To tell me lies just because it's easier for you. No right."

He stood up. "Easier for me?" he said, his voice rising. "Easier for me? You think I told you that Claire lives abroad because it was easier for me? You're wrong, Christine. Wrong. None of this is easy for me. None of it. I don't tell you you've written a novel because I can't bear to remember how much you wanted to write another, or to see the pain when you realize you never will. I told you that Claire lives abroad because I can't stand to hear the pain in your voice when you realize that she abandoned you in that place. Left you there to rot, like all the others." He waited for a reaction. "Did she tell you that?" he said when none came, and I thought, *No, no she didn't, and, in fact, today I read in my journal that she used to visit me all the time.*

He said it again. "Did she tell you that? That she stopped visiting as soon as she realized that fifteen minutes after she left you'd forgotten she even existed? Sure, she might call up at Christmas to find out how you're doing, but it was me who stood by you, Chris. Me who visited you every single day. Me who was there, who waited, praying for you to be well enough that I could come and take you away from there, and bring you here, to live with me, in safety. Me. I didn't lie to you because it was easy for me. Don't you ever make the mistake of thinking that I did. Don't you ever!"

I remembered reading what Dr. Nash had told me. I looked him in the eye. *Except you didn't,* I thought. *You didn't stand by me.*

"Claire said you divorced me."

He froze, then stepped back, as if punched. His mouth opened, then closed. It was almost comical. At last a single word escaped.

"Bitch."

His face melted into fury. I thought he was going to hit me, but found I didn't care.

"Did you divorce me?" I said. "Is it true?"

"Darling—"

I stood up. "Tell me," I said. "Tell me!" We stood, opposite each other. I didn't know what he was going to do, didn't know what I wanted him to do. I only knew I needed him to be honest. To tell me no more lies. "I just want the truth."

He stepped forward and fell to his knees in front of me, grasping for my hands. "Darling—"

"Did you divorce me? Is it true, Ben? Tell me!" His head dropped, then he looked up at me, his eyes wide, frightened. "Ben!" I shouted. He began to cry. "Ben. She told me about Adam, too. She told me we had a son. I know he's dead."

"I'm sorry," he said. "I'm so sorry. I thought it was for the best." And then, through gentle sobs, he said he would tell me everything.

The light had faded completely, night replacing dusk. Ben switched on a lamp and we sat in its rosy glow, opposite each other, across the dining table. There was a pile of photographs between us, the same ones I had looked at earlier. I feigned surprise as he passed each one to me, telling me of its origins. He lingered on the photos of our wedding—telling me what an amazing day it had been, how special, explaining how beautiful I had looked—but then began to get upset. "I never stopped loving you, Christine," he said. "You have to believe that. It was your illness. You had to go into that place, and, well . . . I couldn't . . . I couldn't bear it. I would've followed you. I would've done anything to get you back. Anything. But they . . . they wouldn't . . . I couldn't see you . . . they said it was for the best . . ."

"Who?" I said. "Who said?" He was silent. "The doctors?"

He looked up at me. He was crying, his eyes circled with red.

"Yes," he said. "Yes. The doctors. They said it was for the best. It was the only way . . ." He wiped away a tear. "I did as they told me. I wish I hadn't. I wish I'd fought for you. I was weak and stupid." His voice softened to a whisper. "I stopped seeing you, yes," he said, "but for your own sake. Even though it nearly killed me, I did it for you, Christine. You have to believe me. For you, and our son. But I never divorced you. Not really. Not here." He leaned over and took my hand, pressing it to his shirt. "Here, we've always been married. We've always been together." I felt warm cotton, damp with sweat. The quick beat of his heart. Love.

*I have been so foolish,* I thought. I have allowed myself to believe he did these things to hurt me, when really he tells me he has done them out of love. I should not condemn him. Instead I should try to understand.

"I forgive you," I said.

# Thursday, November 22

Today, when I woke up, I opened my eyes and saw a man sitting on a chair in the room in which I found myself. He was sitting perfectly still. Watching me. Waiting.

I did not panic. I did not know who he was, but I did not panic. Some part of me knew that everything was all right. That he had a right to be there.

"Who are you?" I said. "How did I get here?" He told me. I felt no horror, no disbelief. I understood. I went to the bathroom and approached my reflection as I might a long-forgotten relative, or the ghost of my mother. Cautious. Curious. I dressed, getting used to my body's new dimensions and unexpected behaviors, and then ate breakfast, dimly aware that, once, there might have been three places at the table. I kissed my husband good-bye and it did not feel wrong to do so, then, without knowing why, I opened the shoebox in the closet and found this journal. I knew straight away what it was. I had been looking for it.

The truth of my situation now sits nearer the surface. It is possible that one day I will wake up and know it already. Things will begin to make sense. Even then, I know, I will never be normal. My history is incomplete. Years have vanished, without trace. There are things about myself, my past, that no one can tell me. Not Dr. Nash—who knows me only through what I have told him, what he has read in my journal, and what is written in my file—and not Ben, either. Things that happened before I met him. Things that happened after but that I chose not to share. Secrets.

But there is one person who might know. One person who might tell me the rest of the truth. Who I had been seeing in Brighton. The real reason my best friend vanished from my life.

I have read this journal. I know that tomorrow I will meet Claire.

# Friday, November 23

---

I am writing this at home. The place I finally understand as mine, somewhere I belong. I have read this journal through, and I have seen Claire, and between them they have told me all I need to know. Claire has promised me that she is back in my life now and will not leave again. In front of me is a tatty envelope with my name on it. An artifact. One that completes me. At last my past makes sense.

Soon, my husband will be home, and I am looking forward to seeing him. I love him. I know that now.

I will get this story down and then, together, we will be able to make everything better.

It was a bright day as I got off the bus. The light was suffused with the blue coolness of winter, the ground was hard. Claire had told me she would wait at the top of the hill, *by the main steps up to the palace*, and so I folded the piece of paper on which I had written her directions and began to climb the gentle incline as it arced around the park. It took longer than I expected, and, still unused to my body's limitations, I had to rest as I neared the top. I must have been fit once, I thought. Or fitter than this, anyway. I wondered if I ought to get some exercise.

The park opened out to an expanse of mowed grass, crisscrossed with tarmac, dotted with garbage pails and women with strollers. I realized I was nervous. I did not know what to expect. How could I? In the images I had of Claire, she was wearing a lot of black. Jeans, T-shirts. I saw her in heavy boots and a trench coat. Or else she was wearing a long skirt, tie-dyed, made of some material that I suppose would be described as *floaty*. I could imagine neither vision representing her now—not at the age we have become—but had no idea what might have taken their place.

I looked at my watch. I was early. Without thinking, I told myself that Claire is always late, then instantly wondered how I knew, what residue of memory had reminded me. There is so much, I thought, just under the surface. So many memories, darting like silvery minnows in a shallow stream. I decided to wait on one of the benches.

Long shadows extended themselves lazily across the grass. Over the trees, rows of houses stretched away from me, packed claustrophobically close. With a start, I realized that one of the houses I could see was the one in which I now lived, looking indistinguishable from the others.

I imagined lighting a cigarette and inhaling an anxious lungful, tried to resist the temptation to stand and pace. I felt nervous, ridiculously so. Yet there was no reason. Claire had been my friend. My best friend. There was nothing to worry about. I was safe.

Paint was flaking off the bench and I picked at it, revealing more of the damp wood beneath. Someone had used the same method to scratch two sets of initials next to where I sat, then surrounded them with a heart and added the date. I closed my eyes. Will I ever get used to the shock of seeing evidence of the year in which I am living? I breathed in: damp grass, the tang of hot dogs, gasoline.

A shadow fell across my face, and I opened my eyes. A woman

stood over me. Tall, with a shock of ginger hair, she was wearing trousers and a sheepskin jacket. A little boy held her hand, a plastic soccer ball in the crook of his other arm. "Sorry," I said, and shuffled along the bench to allow room for them both to sit beside me, but as I did, the woman smiled.

"Chrissy!" she said. The voice was Claire's. Unmistakably so. "Chrissy, darling! It's me." I looked from the child to her face. It was furrowed where once it must have been smooth, her eyes had a downturn to them that was absent from my mental image, but it was *her*. There was no doubt. "Jesus," she said. "I've been so worried about you." She pushed the child toward me. "This is Toby."

The boy looked at me. "Go on," said Claire. "Say hello." For a moment, I thought she was talking to me, but then he took a step forward. I smiled. My only thought was, *Is this Adam?* even though I knew it could not be.

"Hello," I said. Toby shuffled his feet and murmured something I didn't catch, then turned to Claire and said, "Can I go and play now?"

"Don't go out of sight, though. Yes?" She stroked his hair and he ran over to the park.

I stood up and turned to face her. I did not know if I would have preferred to turn and run myself, so vast was the chasm between us, but then she held out her arms. "Chrissy, darling," she said, the plastic bracelets that hung from her wrists clattering into each other. "I've missed you. I've missed you so fucking much." The weight that had been pressing down on me somersaulted, lifted, and vanished, and I fell, sobbing, into her arms.

For the briefest of moments, I felt as if I knew everything about her, and everything about myself, too. It was as if the emptiness, the void that sat at the center of my soul, had been lit with light brighter than the sun. A history—my history—flashed in front of me, but too quickly for me to do anything but snatch at it. "I remember you," I said. "I remember you," and then it was gone and the darkness swept in once more.

We sat on the bench and, for a long time, silently watched Toby playing soccer with a group of boys. I felt happy to be connected with my unknown past, yet there was an awkwardness between us that I could not shake. A phrase kept repeating in my head. *Something to do with Claire.*

"How are you?" I said, in the end, and she laughed.

"I feel like hell," she said. She opened her bag and took out a packet of tobacco. "You haven't started again, have you?" she said, offering it to me, and I shook my head, aware again of how she was someone else who knew so much more about me than I did myself.

"What's wrong?" I said.

She began to roll her cigarette, nodding toward her son. "Oh, you know? Tobes has ADHD. He was up all night, and, hence, so was I."

"ADHD?" I said.

She smiled. "Sorry. It's a fairly new phrase, I suppose. Attention deficit and hyperactivity disorder. We have to give him Ritalin, though I fucking hate it. It's the only way. We've tried just about everything else, and he's an absolute beast without it. A horror."

I looked over at him, running in the distance. Another faulty, fucked-up brain in a healthy body.

"He's okay, though?"

"Yes," she said, sighing. She balanced her cigarette paper on her knee and began sprinkling tobacco along its fold. "He's just exhausting sometimes. It's like the terrible twos never ended."

I smiled. I knew what she meant, but only theoretically. I had no point of reference, no recollection of what Adam might have been like, either at Toby's age, or younger.

"Toby seems quite young?" I said. She laughed.

"You mean I'm quite old!" She licked the gum of her paper. "Yes. I had him late. Pretty sure it wasn't going to happen, so we were being careless . . ."

"Oh," I said. "You mean—?"

She laughed. "I wouldn't say he was an accident, but let's just say he was something of a shock." She put the cigarette in her mouth. "Do you remember Adam?"

I looked at her. She had her head turned away from me, shielding her lighter from the wind, and I could not see her expression, or tell whether the move was deliberately evasive.

"No," I said. "A few weeks ago I remembered that I had a son, and ever since I wrote about it I feel like I've been carrying the knowledge around, like a heavy rock in my chest. But no. I don't remember anything about him."

She sent a cloud of blue-tinged smoke skyward. "That's a shame," she said. "I'm so sorry. Ben shows you pictures, though? Doesn't that help?"

I weighed up how much I should tell her. They seemed to have been in touch, to have been friends, once. I had to be careful, but still, I felt an increasing need to speak, as well as hear, the truth.

"He does show me pictures, yes. Though he doesn't have any up around the house. He says I find them too upsetting. He keeps them hidden." I nearly said *locked away*.

She seemed surprised. "Hidden? Really?"

"Yes," I said. "He thinks I would find it too upsetting if I were to stumble across a picture of him."

Claire nodded. "You might not recognize him? Know who he is?"

"I suppose so."

"I imagine that might be true," she said. She hesitated. "Now that he's gone."

*Gone,* I thought. She said it as though he had just popped out for a few hours, had taken his girlfriend to the movies or to shop for a pair of shoes. I understood it, though. Understood the tacit agreement that we would not talk about Adam's death. Not yet. Understood that Claire is trying to protect me, too.

I said nothing. Instead I tried to imagine what it must have been like, to have seen my child every day, back when the phrase *every day* had some meaning, before every day became severed from the one before it. I tried to imagine waking every morning knowing who he was, being able to plan, to look forward to Christmas, to his birthday.

*How ridiculous,* I thought. *I don't even know when his birthday is.*

"Wouldn't you like to see him—?"

My heart leaped. "You have photographs?" I said. "Could I—"

She looked surprised. "Of course! Loads! At home."

"I'd like one," I said.

"Yes," she said. "But—"

"Please. It'd mean so much to me."

She put her hand on mine. "Of course. I'll bring one next time, but—"

She was interrupted by a cry in the distance. I looked across the park. Toby was running toward us, crying, as, behind him, the game of soccer continued.

"Fuck," said Claire under her breath. She stood up and called out, "Tobes! Toby! What happened?" He kept running. "Shit," she said. "I'll just go and sort him out."

She went to her son, crouching down to ask what was wrong. I looked at the ground. The path was carpeted with moss and the odd blade of grass had poked through the tarmac, fighting toward the light. I felt pleased. Not only that Claire would give me a photograph of Adam, but that she had said she would do so next time we met. We were going to be seeing more of each other. I realized that every time would once again seem like the first. The irony: that I am prone to forgetting that I have no memory.

I realized, too, that something about the way she had spoken of Ben—some wistfulness—made me think that the idea of them having an affair was ridiculous.

She came back.

"Everything's fine," she said. She flicked her cigarette away and ground it out with her heel. "Slight misunderstanding over ownership of the ball. Shall we walk?" I nodded, and she turned to Toby. "Darling! Ice cream?"

He said yes and we began to walk toward the palace. Toby was holding Claire's hand. They looked so alike, I thought, their eyes lit with the same fire.

"I love it up here," said Claire. "The view is so inspiring. Don't you think?"

I looked out at the gray houses, dotted with green. "I suppose. Do you still paint?"

"Hardly," she said. "I dabble. I've become a dabbler. Our own walls are chock-full of my pictures, but nobody else has one. Unfortunately."

I smiled. I did not mention my novel, though I wanted to ask if she'd read it, what she thought. "What do you do now, then?"

"I look after Toby, mostly," she said. "He's homeschooled."

"I see," I said.

"Not through choice," she replied. "None of the schools will take him. They say he's too disruptive. They can't handle him."

I looked at her son as he walked with us. He seemed perfectly calm, holding his mother's hand. He asked if he could have his ice cream, and Claire told him he'd be able to, soon. I could not imagine him being difficult.

"What was Adam like?" I said.

"As a child?" she said. "He was a good boy. Very polite. Well-behaved, you know?"

"Was I a good mother? Was he happy?"

"Oh, Chrissy," she said. "Yes. Yes. Nobody was more loved than that boy. You don't remember, do you? You had been trying for a while. You had an ectopic pregnancy. You were worried you might not be able to get pregnant again, but then along came Adam. You were so happy, both of you. And you loved being pregnant. I hated it. Bloated like a fucking house, and such dreadful sickness. Frightful. But it was different with you. You loved every second of it. You glowed, for the whole time you were carrying him. You lit up rooms when you walked into them, Chrissy."

I closed my eyes, even as we walked, and tried first to remember being pregnant, and then to imagine it. I could do neither. I looked at Claire.

"And then?"

"Then? The birth. It was wonderful. Ben was there, of course. I got there as soon as I could." She stopped walking and turned to look at me. "And you were a great mother, Chrissy. Great. Adam was happy, and cared for, and loved. No child could have wished for more."

I tried to remember motherhood, my son's childhood. Nothing.

"And Ben?"

She paused, then said, "Ben was a great father. Always. He loved that boy. He would race home from work every evening to see him. When he said his first word, he called everyone up and told them. The same when he began to crawl, or took his first step. As soon as he could walk, Ben was taking him to the park, with a football, whatever. And Christmas! So many toys! I think that was just about the only thing I ever saw you argue about—how many toys Ben would buy for Adam. You were worried he'd be spoiled."

I felt a twinge of regret, an urge to apologize for ever having tried to deny my son anything.

"I would let him have anything he wanted, now," I said. "If only I could."

She looked at me sadly. "I know," she said. "I know. But be happy knowing that he didn't want for anything from you, ever."

We carried on walking. A van was parked on the footpath, selling ice creams, and we turned toward it. Toby began to tug at his mother's arm. She leaned down and gave him a bill from her purse before letting him go. "Choose one thing!" she shouted after him. "Just one! And wait for the change!"

I watched him run to the van. "Claire," I said. "How old was Adam when I lost my memory?"

She smiled. "He must have been three. Maybe four, just."

I felt I was stepping into new territory now. Into danger. But it was the place I had to go. The truth I had to discover. "My doctor told me I was attacked," I said. She did not reply. "In Brighton. Why was I there?"

I looked at Claire, scanning her face. She seemed to be making a decision, weighing up options, deciding what to do. "I don't know for sure," she said. "Nobody does."

She stopped speaking, and we both watched Toby for a while.

He had his ice cream now and was unwrapping it; a look of determined concentration scored his face. Silence stretched in front of me. *Unless I say something,* I thought, *this will last forever.*

"I was having an affair, wasn't I?"

There was no reaction. No intake of breath, no gasp of denial or look of shock. Claire looked at me steadily. Calmly. "Yes," she said. "You were cheating on Ben."

Her voice had no emotion. I wondered what she thought of me. Either then, or now.

"Tell me," I said.

"Okay," she said. "But let's sit down. I'm just gasping for a coffee."

We walked up to the main building.

The cafeteria doubled as a bar. The chairs were steel, the tables plain. Palm trees were dotted around, an attempt at atmosphere ruined by the cold air that blasted in whenever someone opened the door. We sat opposite each other across a table that swam with spilled coffee, warming our hands on our drinks.

"What happened?" I said again. "I need to know."

"It's not easy to say," said Claire. She spoke slowly, as if picking her way through a difficult terrain. "I suppose it started not long after you had Adam. Once the initial excitement had worn off, there was a period when things were extremely tough." She paused. "It's so difficult, isn't it? To see what's going on when you're in the absolute middle of something? It's only with hindsight we can see things for what they are." I nodded but didn't understand. Hindsight is something I don't have. She went on. "You cried, awfully. You worried you weren't bonding with the baby. All the usual stuff. Ben and I did what we could, and your mother, when she was around, but it was tough. And even when the absolute worst was over, you still found it hard. You couldn't get back into your work. You'd call me up, in the middle of the day. Upset. You said you felt like a failure. Not a failure at motherhood—you could see how happy Adam was—but a failure as a writer. You thought you'd never be able to write again. I'd come over and see you, and you'd be a mess. Crying, the works." I wondered what was coming next—how bad it would get—then she said, "You and Ben were arguing, too. You resented him, how easy he found life. He offered to pay for a nanny, but, well . . ."

"Well?"

"You said that was typical of him. To throw money at the problem. You had a point, but . . . Perhaps you weren't being terribly fair."

Perhaps not, I thought. It struck me that back then we must have had money—more money than we had after I lost my memory, more money than I guess we have now. What a drain on our resources my illness must have been.

I tried to picture myself, arguing with Ben, looking after a baby, trying to write. I imagined bottles of milk, or Adam at my breast. Dirty diapers. Mornings in which getting both myself and my baby fed were the only ambitions I could reasonably have and afternoons in which I was so exhausted the only thing I craved was sleep—sleep that was still hours away—and the thought of trying to write was pushed far from my mind. I could see it all, and feel the slow, burning resentment.

But that's all they were. Imaginings. I remembered nothing. Claire's story felt like it had nothing to do with me at all.

"So I had an affair?"

She looked up. "I was free. I was doing my painting, then. I said I'd look after Adam, two afternoons a week, so you could write. I insisted." She took my hand in hers. "It was my fault, Chrissy. I even suggested you go to a café."

"A café?" I said.

"I thought it would be a good idea if you got out of the house. Gave yourself space. A few hours a week, away from everything. After a few weeks you seemed to get better. You were happier in yourself, you said your work was going well. You started going to the café almost every day, taking Adam when I couldn't look after him. But then I noticed that you were dressing differently, too. The classic thing, though I didn't realize what it was at the time. I thought it was just because you were feeling better. More confident. But then Ben called me, one evening. He'd been drinking, I think. He said you were arguing, more than ever, and he didn't know what to do. You were off sex, too. I told him it was probably just because of the baby, that he was probably worrying unnecessarily. But—"

I interrupted. "I was seeing someone."

"I asked you. You denied it at first, but then I told you I wasn't stupid, and neither was Ben. We had an argument, but after a while you told me the truth."

The truth. Not glamorous, not exciting. Just the bald facts. I had turned into a living cliché, taken to fucking someone I'd met in a café while my best friend was babysitting my child and my husband was earning the money to pay for the clothes and underwear I was wearing for someone other than him. I pictured the furtive phone calls, the aborted arrangements when something unexpected came up, and, on the days we could get together, the sordid, pathetic afternoons spent in bed with a man who had temporarily seemed better—more exciting? attractive? a better lover? richer?—than my husband. Was this the man I had been waiting for in that hotel room, the man who would eventually attack me, leave me with no past and no future?

I closed my eyes. A flash of memory. Hands gripping my hair, around my throat. My head under water. Gasping, crying. I re-member what I was thinking. *I want to see my son. One last time. I want to see my husband. I should never have done this to him. I should never have betrayed him with this man. I will never be able to tell him I am sorry. Never.*

I opened my eyes. Claire was squeezing my hand. "Are you all right?" she said.

"Tell me," I said.

"I don't know whether—"

"Please," I said. "Tell me. Who was it?"

She sighed. "You said you'd met someone else who went to the café regularly. He was nice, you said. Attractive. You'd tried, but you hadn't been able to stop yourself."

"What was his name?" I said. "Who was he?"

"I don't know."

"You must!" I said. "His name at least! Who did this to me?"

She looked into my eyes. "Chrissy," she said, her voice calm, "you never even told me his name. You just said you'd met him in a coffee shop. I suppose you didn't want me to know any details. Any more than I had to, at least."

I felt another sliver of hope slip away, washed downstream in the river. I would never know who did this to me.

"What happened?"

"I told you that I thought you were being ridiculous. There was Adam to think about, as well as Ben. I thought you ought to call it off. Stop seeing him."

"But I wouldn't listen."

"No," she said. "Not at first. We fought. I told you that you were putting me in an impossible situation. Ben was my friend, too. You were asking me to lie to him."

"What happened? How long did it go on for?"

She was silent, then said, "I don't know. One day—it must have been only a few weeks—you announced that it was all over. You'd told this man that it wasn't working, that you'd made a mistake. You said you were sorry, you'd been foolish. Crazy."

"I was lying?"

"I don't know. I don't think so. You and I didn't lie to each other. We just didn't." She blew across the top of her coffee. "A few weeks later, you were found in Brighton," she said. "I have no idea what happened in that time."

Perhaps it was those words—*I have no idea what happened in that time*—that set it off, the realization that I may never know how I came to be attacked, but a sound suddenly escaped me. I tried to clamp it down, but failed. Something between a gasp and a howl, it was the cry of an animal in pain. Toby looked up from his coloring book. Everyone in the café turned to stare at me, at the madwoman with no memory. Claire grabbed my arm.

"Chrissy!" she said. "What's wrong?"

I was sobbing now, my body heaving, gasping for breath. Crying for all the years that I had lost, and for all those that I would continue to lose between now and the day that I died. Crying because, however hard it had been for her to tell me about the affair, and my marriage, and my son, she would have to do it all again tomorrow. Crying mostly, though, because I had brought all this on myself.

"I'm sorry," I said. "I'm sorry."

Claire stood up and came around the table. She crouched beside me, her arm around my shoulder, and I rested my head against hers. "There, there," she said as I sobbed. "It's all right, Chrissy, darling. I'm here now. I'm here."

We left the café. As if unwilling to be outdone, Toby had become boisterously noisy following my own outburst—he threw his coloring books on the floor, along with a plastic cup of juice. Claire cleaned up and then said, "I need to get some air. Shall we?"

Now we sat on one of the benches that overlooked the park. Our knees were angled toward each other, and Claire held my hands in hers, stroking them as if they were cold.

"Did I—" I began. "Did I have lots of affairs?"

She shook her head. "No. None. We had fun at university, you know? But no more than most. And once you met Ben, that stopped. You were always faithful to him."

I wondered what had been so special about the man in the café. Claire had said that I'd told her he was *nice*. *Attractive*. Was that all it was? Was I really so shallow?

My husband was both of those things, I thought. If only I'd been content with what I had.

"Ben knew I was having an affair?"

"Not at first. No. Not until you were found. It was a dreadful shock for him. For all of us. At first, it looked as though you might not even live. Later, Ben asked me if I knew why you'd been in Brighton. I told him. I had to. I'd already told the police all I knew. I had no choice but to tell Ben."

Guilt punctured me once more as I thought of my husband, of the father of my son, trying to work out why his dying wife had turned up miles away from home. How could I do this to him?

"He forgave you, though," said Claire. "He never held it against you, ever. All he cared about was that you lived, and that you got better. He would have given everything for that. Everything. Nothing else mattered."

I felt a surge of love for my husband. Real. Unforced. Despite everything, he had taken me in. Looked after me.

"Will you talk to him?" I said. She smiled.

"Of course! But about what?"

"He's not telling me the truth," I said. "Or not always, anyway. He's trying to protect me. He tells me what he thinks I can cope with, what he thinks I want to hear."

"Ben wouldn't do that," she said. "He loves you. He always has."

"Well, he is," I said. "He doesn't know I know. He doesn't know I'm writing things down. He doesn't tell me about Adam, other than when I remember him and ask. He doesn't tell me he left me. He tells me you live on the other side of the world. He doesn't think I can cope. He's given up on me, Claire. Whatever he used to be like, he's given up on me. He doesn't want me to see a doctor because he doesn't think I will ever get any better, but I've been seeing one, Claire. A Dr. Nash. In secret. I can't even tell Ben."

Claire's face fell. She looked disappointed. In me, I suppose. "That's not good," she said. "You ought to tell him. He loves you. He trusts you."

"I can't. He only admitted the other day he was still in touch with you. Until then he'd been saying he hadn't spoken to you in years."

Her expression of disapproval changed. For the first time, I could see that she was surprised.

"Chrissy!"

"It's true," I said. "I know he loves me. But I need him to be honest with me. About everything. I don't know my own past. And only he can help me. I need him to help me."

"Then you should just talk to him. Trust him."

"But how can I?" I said. "With all the things he's lied to me about? How can I?"

She squeezed my hands in hers. "Chrissy, Ben loves you. You know he does. He loves you more than life itself. He always has."

"But—" I began, but she interrupted.

"You have to trust him. Believe me. You can sort everything out, but you have to tell him the truth. Tell him about Dr. Nash. Tell him what you've been writing. It's the only way."

Somewhere, deep down, I knew she was right, but still I could not convince myself I should tell Ben about my journal.

"But he might want to read what I've written."

Her eyes narrowed. "There's nothing in there you wouldn't want him to see, is there?" I didn't reply. "Is there? Chrissy?"

I looked away. We didn't speak, and then she opened her bag.

"Chrissy," she said. "I'm going to give you something. Ben gave it to me, when he decided he needed to leave you." She took out an envelope and handed it to me. It was creased but still sealed. "He told me it explained everything." I stared at it. My name was written on the front in capitals. "He asked me to give it to you, if I ever thought you were well enough to read it." I looked up at her, feeling every emotion at once. Excitement and fear. "I think it's time you read it," she said.

I took it from her and put it in my bag. Though I did not know why, I did not want to read it there, in front of Claire. Perhaps I was worried that she would be able to read its contents reflected in my face, and they would no longer be mine to own.

"Thank you," I said. She did not smile.

"Chrissy," she said. She looked down, at her hands. "There's a reason Ben tells you I moved away." I felt my world begin to change, though in what way I was not yet certain. "I have to tell you something. About why we lost touch."

I knew then. Without her saying anything, I knew. The missing piece of the puzzle, the reason Ben had left, the reason my best friend had disappeared from my life and my husband had lied about why this had happened. I had been right. All along. I had been right.

"It's true," I said. "Oh God. It's true. You're seeing Ben. You're fucking my husband."

She looked up, horrified. "No!" she said. "No!"

A certainty overtook me. I wanted to shout *Liar!* But did not. I was about to ask her again what she wanted to tell me when she wiped something from her eye. A tear? I don't know.

"Not now," she whispered, then looked back to the hands in her lap. "But we were once."

Of all the emotions I might have expected to feel, relief wasn't one. But it was true: I felt relieved. Because she was being honest? Because now I had an explanation for everything, one that I could believe? I'm not sure. But the anger that I may have felt was not there, neither was the pain. Perhaps I was happy to feel a tiny spark of jealousy, concrete proof that I loved my husband. Perhaps I was just relieved that Ben had an infidelity to go with my own, that we were equal now. Quits.

"Tell me," I whispered.

She did not look up. "We were always close," she said softly. "The three of us, I mean. You. Me. Ben. But there had never been anything between me and him. You must believe that. Never." I told her to go on. "After your accident I tried to help out in whatever way I could. You can imagine how terribly difficult it was for Ben. Just on a practical level if nothing else. Having to look after Adam . . . I did what I could. We spent a lot of time together. But we didn't sleep together. Not then. I swear, Chrissy."

"So when?" I said. "When did it happen?"

"Just before you were moved to Waring House," she said. "You were at your worst. Adam was being difficult. Things were tough." She looked away. "Ben was drinking. Not too much, but enough. He wasn't coping. One night we got back from visiting you. I put

Adam to bed. Ben was in the living room, crying. 'I can't do it,' he kept saying. 'I can't keep doing this. I love her, but it's killing me.'"

The wind gusted up the hill. Cold. Biting. I pulled my coat around me.

"I sat next to him. And . . ."

I could see it all. The hand on the shoulder, then the hug. The mouths that find each other through the tears, the moment when guilt and the certainty that things must go no further gives way to lust and the certainty that they cannot stop.

And then what? The fucking. On the sofa? The floor? I did not want to know.

"And?"

"I'm sorry," she said. "I never wanted it to happen. But it did, and . . . I felt so bad. So bad. We both did."

"How long?"

"What?"

"How long did it go on for?"

She hesitated, then said, "I don't know. Not long. A few weeks. We only . . . we only had sex a few times. It didn't feel right. We both felt so bad, afterward."

"What happened?" I said. "Who ended it?"

She shrugged, then whispered, "Both of us. We talked. It couldn't go on. I decided I owed it to you—and Ben—to stay away from then on. It was guilt, I suppose."

An awful thought occurred to me.

"Is that when he decided to leave me?"

"Chrissy, no," she said quickly. "Don't think that. He felt awful, too. But he didn't leave you because of me."

*No,* I thought. *Perhaps not directly. But you might have reminded him of just how much he was missing.*

I looked at her. I still did not feel angry. I could not. Perhaps if she had told me that they were still sleeping together, I might have felt differently. What she had told me felt as though it belonged to another time. Prehistory. I found it hard to believe it had anything to do with me at all.

Claire looked up. "At first, I was in touch with Adam, but then Ben must have told him what had happened. Adam said he didn't want to see me again. He told me to stay away from him, and from you, too. But I couldn't, Chrissy. I just couldn't. Ben had given me the letter, asked me to keep an eye on you. So I carried on visiting. At Waring House. Every few weeks at first, then every couple of months. But it upset you. It upset you terribly. I know I was being selfish, but I couldn't just leave you there. On your own. I carried on coming. Just to check you were all right."

"And you told Ben how I was?"

"No. We weren't in touch."

"Is that why you haven't been visiting me lately? At home? Because you don't want to see Ben?"

"No. A few months ago, I visited Waring House and they told me you'd left. You'd gone back to live with Ben. I knew Ben had moved. I asked them to give me your address but they wouldn't. They said it would be a breach of confidentiality. They said they would give you my number and that if I wanted to write to you they would pass the letters on."

"So you wrote?"

"I addressed the letter to Ben. I told him I was sorry, that I regretted what had happened. I begged him to let me see you."

"But he told you you couldn't?"

"No. You wrote back, Chrissy. You said that you were feeling much better. You said you were happy, with Ben." She looked away, across the park. "You said you didn't want to see me. That your memory would sometimes come back and when it did you knew I had betrayed you." She wiped a tear from her eye. "You told me not to come anywhere near you, ever again. That it was better that you forgot me forever, and that I forgot you."

I felt myself go cold. I tried to imagine the anger I must have felt to write a letter like that, but at the same time realized maybe I hadn't felt angry at all. To me, Claire would hardly have existed, any friendship between us forgotten.

"I'm sorry," I said. I could not imagine being able to remember her betrayal. Ben must have helped me write the letter.

She smiled. "No. Don't apologize. You were right. But I didn't stop hoping you'd change your mind. I wanted to see you. I wanted to tell you the truth, to your face." I said nothing. "I'm so sorry," she said then. "Can you ever forgive me?"

I took her hand. How could I be angry with her? Or with Ben? My condition has placed an impossible burden on us all.

"Yes," I said. "Yes. I forgive you."

We left soon after. At the bottom of the slope, she turned to face me.

"Will I see you again?" she said.

I smiled. "I hope so!"

She looked relieved. "I've missed you, Chrissy. You've no idea."

It was true. I did have no idea. But with her, and this journal, there was a chance I could rebuild a life worth living. I thought of the letter in my bag. A message from the past. The final piece of the puzzle. The answers I need.

"I'll see you soon," she said. "Early next week. Okay?"

"Okay," I said. She hugged me, and my voice was lost in the curls of her hair. She felt like my only friend, the only person I could rely on, along with Ben. My sister. I squeezed her hard. "Thank you for telling me the truth," I said. "Thank you. For everything. I love you." When we parted and looked at each other, both of us were crying.

At home, I sat down to read Ben's letter. I felt nervous—would it tell me what I needed to know? Would I finally understand why Ben left me?—but at the same time excited. I felt sure it would. Felt certain that with it, with Ben and Claire, I will have everything I need.

*Darling Christine,*

*This is the hardest thing I have ever had to do. Already I've kicked off with a cliché, but you know I'm not a writer—that was always you!—so I'm sorry, but I'll do my best.*

*By the time you read this, you'll know that I've decided I have to leave you. I can't bear to write it, or even to think it, but I have to. I have tried so hard to find another way, but I can't. Believe me.*

*You have to understand that I love you. I always have. I always will. I don't care what has happened, or why. This isn't about revenge, or anything like that. I haven't met anybody else. When you were in that coma, I realized just how much a part of me you are—I felt like I was dying every time I looked at you. I realized I didn't care what you were doing that night in Brighton, or who you were seeing. I just wanted you to come back to me.*

*And then you did, and I was so happy. You will never know how happy I was, the day they told me you were out of danger, that you wouldn't die. That you weren't going to leave me. Or us. Adam was just little, but I think he understood.*

*When we realized you had no memory of what had happened, I thought it was a good thing. Can you believe that? I feel ashamed now, but I thought it was for the best. But then we realized that you were forgetting other things, too. Gradually, over time. At first it was the names of the people in the beds next to you, the doctors and nurses treating you. But you got worse. You forgot why you were in the hospital, why you weren't being allowed to come home with me. You convinced yourself that the doctors were experimenting on you. When I took you home for a weekend, you didn't recognize our street, our house. Your cousin came to see you and you had no idea who she was. We took you back to the hospital and you had no idea where you were going.*

*I think that's when things started to get difficult. You loved Adam so much. It shone out of your eyes when we arrived, and he would run over to you and into your arms, and you would pick him up, and know who he was, straight away. But then—I'm sorry, Chris, but I have to tell you this—you started to believe that Adam had been taken away from you when he was a baby. Every time you saw him, you thought that it was the first time since he was a few months old. I would ask him to tell you when he last saw you, and he would say, "Yesterday, Mummy," or "last week," but you didn't believe him. "What have you been telling him?" you'd say. "It's a lie." You started accusing me of keeping you locked there. You thought another woman was raising Adam as her own while you were in the hospital.*

*One day, I arrived and you didn't recognize me. You became hysterical. You grabbed Adam when I wasn't looking, and ran to the door, to rescue him, I suppose, but he started screaming. He didn't understand why you'd do that. I took him home and tried to explain, but he didn't understand. He started being really frightened of you.*

*It went on for a while, but got worse. One day, I called the hospital. I asked them what you were like when I wasn't there, when Adam wasn't there. "Describe her, right now," I said. They said you were calm. Happy. You were sitting in the chair next to your bed. "What's she doing?" I said. They said you were talking to one of the other patients, a friend of yours. Sometimes you played cards together.*

*"Played cards?" I said. I couldn't believe it. They said you were good at cards. They had to explain the rules to you every day, but then you could beat just about anybody.*

*"Is she happy?" I said.*

*"Yes," they said. "Yes. She's always happy."*

*"Does she remember me?" I said. "Adam?"*

*"Not unless you're here," they said.*

*I think I knew then that one day I would have to leave you. I've found you a place where you can live for as long as you need to. Somewhere you can be happy. Because you will be happy, without me, without Adam. You won't know us, and so you won't miss us.*

*I love you so much, Chrissy. You must understand that. I love you more than I love anything. But I have to give our son a life, a life he deserves. Soon he will be old enough to understand what's going on. I will not lie to him, Chris. I will explain the choice I have made. I will tell him that although he may want to see you very much it would be enormously upsetting for him to do so. Maybe he will hate me. Blame me. I hope not. But I want him to be happy. And I want you to be happy, too. Even if you can only find that happiness without me.*

*You've been in Waring House for a while now. You don't panic anymore. You have a sense of routine. That's good. And so it's time for me to go.*

*I'm going to give this letter to Claire. I'll ask her to keep it for me, and to show it to you when you're well enough to read it, and to understand it. I can't keep it myself, I'll just brood over it, and won't be able to resist giving it to you next week, or next month, or even next year. Too soon.*

*I cannot pretend I do not hope that one day we can be together again. When you are recovered. The three of us. A family. I have to believe that might happen. I have to, or else I will die from grief.*

*I am not abandoning you, Chris. I will never abandon you. I love you too much.*

*Believe me, this is the right thing, the only thing for me to do.*

*Don't hate me. I love you.*

*Ben*

*X*

———————

I read it again now, and fold the paper. It feels crisp, as though it might have been written yesterday, but the envelope into which I slip it is soft, its edges frayed, with a sweet smell clinging to it, like perfume. Has Claire carried it with her, tucked in a corner of her bag? Or, more likely, has she stored it in a drawer at home, out of sight but never quite forgotten? For years, it waited for the right time to be read. Years that I spent not knowing who my husband was, not even knowing who I was. Years in which I could have never bridged the gap between us, because it was a gap I had never known existed.

I slip the envelope between the pages of my journal. I am crying as I write this, but I do not feel unhappy. I understand everything. Why he left me, why he has been lying to me.

Because *he has* been lying to me. He has not told me about the novel I wrote, so that I will not be devastated that I will never write another. He has been telling me my best friend moved away—to protect me from the fact that the two of them betrayed me. Because he did not trust me to love them both far too much to not forgive them. He has been telling me that I was hit by a car, that this was an accident, so that I don't have to deal with the knowledge that I was attacked and what happened to me was the result of a deliberate act of ferocious hatred. He has been telling me that we never had children, not only to protect me from remembering that my only son is dead but to protect me, too, from having to deal with his death every single day of my life. And he has not told me that, after years of trying to find a way for our family to be together, he had to face the fact that we could not be and take our son and leave, in order to find happiness.

He must have thought that our separation would be forever, when he wrote that letter, but he must also have hoped that it would not, or else why write it? What was he thinking, as he sat there, in his home, our home as it must once have been, and took out his pen and began to try to explain to someone he could never expect to understand why he felt he had no option but to leave her? I am no writer, he said, and yet his words are beautiful to me, profound. They read as if he is talking about someone else, and yet, somewhere inside me, under the skin and bones, the tissue and blood, I know that he is not. He is talking about, and to, me. Christine Lucas. His broken wife.

But it has not been forever. What he hoped for has happened. Somehow my condition has improved, or else he found separation from me even harder than he imagined, and he came back for me.

Everything seems different now. The room I am in looks no more familiar to me than it did this morning when I woke up and stumbled into it, trying to find the kitchen, desperate for a drink of water, desperate to piece together what happened last night. And yet it no longer seems shot through with pain and sadness. It no longer seems emblematic of a life I cannot consider living. The ticking of the clock at my shoulder is no longer just marking time. It speaks to me. *Relax*, it says. *Relax, and take what comes.*

I have been wrong. I have made a mistake. Again and again and again I have made it; who knows how many times? My husband is my protector, yes, but also my lover. And now I realize that I love him. I have always loved him, and if I have to learn to love him again every day, then so be it. That is what I will do.

Ben will be home soon—already I can feel him approach—and when he arrives, I will tell him everything. I will tell him that I have met Claire—and Dr. Nash, and even Dr. Paxton—and that I have read his letter. I will tell him that I understand why he did what he did back then, why he left me, and that I forgive him. I will tell him that I know about the attack, but that I no longer need to know what happened, no longer care who did this to me.

And I will tell him that I know about Adam. I know what happened to him, and though the thought of facing it every day makes me cold with terror, that is what I must do. The memory of our son must be allowed to exist in this house, and in my heart, too, no matter how much pain that causes.

And I will tell him about this journal, that finally I am able to give myself a narrative, a life, and I will show it to him, if he asks to see it. And then I can continue to use it, to tell my story, my autobiography. To create myself from nothing.

"No more secrets," I will say to my husband. "None. I love you, Ben, and I always will. We have wronged each other. But please forgive me. I am sorry that I left you all those years ago to be with somebody else, and I am sorry that we can never know who it was I went to see in that hotel room, or what I found there. But please know that I am determined to make this up to you now."

And then, when there is nothing else between us but love, we can begin to find a way to truly be together.

I have called Dr. Nash. "I want to see you one more time," I said. "I want you to read my journal." I think he was surprised, but he agreed. "When?" he said.

"Next week," I said. "Come for it next week."

He said he would collect it on Tuesday.

# Part III

# Today

I TURN THE PAGE, but there is no more. The story ends there. I have been reading for hours.

I am shaking, can barely breathe. I feel that I have not only lived an entire life in the last few hours, but I have changed. I am not the same person who met Dr. Nash this morning, who sat down to read the journal. I have a past now. A sense of myself. I know what I have, and what I have lost. I realize I am crying.

I close the journal. I force myself to calm down, and the present begins to reassert itself. The darkening room in which I sit. The drilling I can still hear in the street outside. The empty coffee cup at my feet.

I look at the clock next to me and there is a jolt of shock. Only now do I realize that it is the same clock as the one in the journal that I have been reading, that I am in the same living room, am the same person. Only now do I fully understand that the story I have been reading is mine.

I take my journal and mug into the kitchen. There, on the wall, is the same eraser board I had seen this morning, the same list of suggestions in neat capitals, the same note that I had added myself: *Pack bag for tonight?*

I look at it. Something about it troubles me, but I can't work out why.

I think of Ben. How difficult life must have been for him. Never knowing with whom he would wake. Never being certain how much I would remember, how much love I would be able to give him.

But now? Now I understand. Now I know enough for us both to live again. I wonder if I ever had the conversation with him that I had been planning. I must have, so certain was I that it was the right thing to do, but I have not written about it. I have written nothing for a week, in fact. Perhaps I gave my journal to Dr. Nash before I had the opportunity. Perhaps I felt there was no need to write in my book now that I had shared it with Ben.

I turn back to the front of the journal. There it is, in the same blue ink. Those three words, scratched onto the page beneath my name.

### DON'T TRUST BEN.

I take a pen and cross them out. Back in the living room, I see the scrapbook on the table. Still there are no photographs of Adam. Still he did not mention him to me this morning. Still he had not shown me what is in the metal box.

I think of my novel—*For the Morning Birds*—and then look at the journal I am holding. A thought comes, unbidden. *What if I made it all up?*

I stand up. I need evidence. I need a link between what I have read and what I am living, a sign that the past I have been reading about is not one I have invented.

I put the journal in my bag and go out of the living room. The coat stand is there, at the bottom of the stairs, next to a pair of slippers. If I go upstairs, will I find the office, the filing cabinet? Will I find the gray metal box in the bottom drawer, hidden underneath the towel? Will the key be in the bottom drawer by the bed?

And, if it is, will I find my son?

I have to know. I take the stairs two at a time.

The office is smaller than I imagined and even tidier than I expected, but the cabinet is there, gunmetal-gray.

In the bottom drawer is a towel, and beneath it a box. I grip it, preparing to lift it out. I feel stupid, convinced it will be either locked or empty.

It is neither. In it, I find my novel. Not the copy Dr. Nash had given to me—there is no coffee ring on the front, and the pages of this look new. It must be one Ben has been keeping all along. Waiting for the day when I know enough to own it again. I wonder where my copy is, the one that Dr. Nash gave to me.

I take the novel out, and underneath it is a single photograph. Me and Ben, smiling at the camera, though we both look sad. It looks recent, my face is the one I recognize from the mirror and Ben looks as he did when he left this morning. There is a house in the background. A gravel driveway, pots of bright red geraniums. On the back, someone has written, *Waring House*. It must have been taken on the day he collected me, to bring me back here.

That's it, though. There are no other photographs. None of Adam. Not even the ones I have found here before and described in my journal.

There is an explanation, I tell myself. There has to be. I look through the papers that are piled on the desk: magazines, catalogues advertising computer software, a school timetable with some sessions highlighted in yellow. There is a sealed envelope— which, on an impulse, I take—but there are no photographs of Adam.

I go downstairs and make myself a cup of tea. Boiling water, a tea bag. Don't let it stew too long, and don't compress the bag with the back of the spoon or you'll squeeze out too much tannic acid and the tea will be bitter. *Why do I remember this, yet I don't remember giving birth?* A phone rings, somewhere in the living room. I retrieve it from my bag—not the one that flips open, but the one that my husband gave me—and answer it. Ben.

"Christine? Are you okay? Are you at home?"

"Yes," I say. "Yes. Thank you."

"Have you been out today?" he says. His voice sounds familiar, yet somehow cold. I think back to the last time we spoke. I do not remember him mentioning that I had an appointment with Dr. Nash. Perhaps he really does not know, I think. Or perhaps he is testing me, wondering whether I will tell him. I think of the note written next to the appointment. *Don't tell Ben.* I must have written that before I knew I could trust him.

I want to trust him now. No more lies.

"Yes," I say. "I've been to see a doctor." He doesn't speak. "Ben?" I say.

"Sorry, yes," he says. "I heard." I register his lack of surprise. So he had known then, known that I was seeing Dr. Nash. "I'm in traffic," he says. "It's a bit tricky. Listen, I just wanted to make sure you've remembered to pack? We're going away . . ."

"Of course," I say, and then I add, "I'm looking forward to it!" and I realize I am. It will do us good, I think, to get away. It can be another beginning for us.

"I'll be home soon," he says. "Can you try to have our bags packed? I'll help when I get in, but it'd be better if we can set off early."

"I'll try," I say.

"There're two bags in the spare bedroom. In the closet. Use those."

"Okay."

"I love you," he says, and then, after a moment too long, a moment in which he has already ended the call, I tell him that I love him too.

.    .    .

I GO TO the bathroom. I am a woman, I tell myself. An adult. I have a husband. One I love. I think back to what I have read. Of the sex. Of him fucking me. I had not written that I enjoyed it.

Can I enjoy sex? I realize I don't even know that. I flush the toilet and step out of my trousers, my tights, my panties. I sit on the edge of the bath. How alien my body is. How unknown to me. How can I be happy giving it to someone else, when I don't recognize it myself?

I lock the bathroom door, then part my legs. Slightly at first, then more. I lift my blouse and look down. I see the stretch marks I saw the day I remembered Adam, the wiry shock of my pubic hair. I wonder if I ever shave it, whether I choose not to, based on my preference or my husband's. Perhaps those things do not matter anymore. Not now.

I cup my hand and place it over my pubic mound. My fingers rest on my labia, parting them slightly. I brush the tip of what must be my clitoris and press, moving my fingers gently as I do, already feeling a faint tingle. The promise of sensation, rather than sensation itself.

I wonder what will happen later.

The bags are in the spare room, where he said they would be. Both are compact, sturdy, one a little larger than the other. I take them into the bedroom in which I woke this morning, and put them on the bed. I open the top drawer and see my underwear, next to his.

I select clothes for us both, socks for him, tights for me. I remember reading of the night we had sex and realize I must have stockings and garters somewhere. I decide it would be nice to find them now, to take them with me. It might be good for both of us.

I move to the closet. I choose a dress, a skirt. Some trousers, a pair of jeans. I notice the shoebox on the floor—the one that must have hidden my journal—now empty. I wonder what kind of couple we are, when we go on holiday. Whether we spend our evenings in restaurants, or sitting in cozy pubs, relaxing in the rosy heat of a real fire. I wonder whether we walk, exploring the town and its surroundings, or take taxis to carefully selected events. These are the things I don't know yet. These are the things I have the rest of my life to find out. To enjoy.

I select some clothes for both of us, almost randomly, and fold them, placing them into the cases. As I do, I feel a jolt, a surge of energy, and I close my eyes. I see a vision, bright but shimmering. It is unclear at first, as if hovering, out of both reach and focus, and I try to open my mind, to let it come.

I see myself standing in front of a bag; a soft suitcase in worn leather. I am excited. I feel young again, like a child about to go on holiday, or a teenager preparing for a date, wondering how it will go, whether he'll ask me back to his house, whether we'll fuck. I feel that newness, that anticipation, can taste it. I roll it on my tongue, savoring it, because I know it will not last. I open my drawers in turn, selecting blouses, stockings, underwear. Thrilling. Sexy. Underwear that is worn only with the anticipation of its removal. I put in a pair of heels in addition to the flat shoes I am wearing, take them out, put them in again. I do not like them, but this night is about fantasy, about dressing up, about being other than what we are. Only then do I move onto the functional things. I take a quilted toiletries bag in bright red leather and add perfume, shower gel, toothpaste. I want to look beautiful tonight, for the man I love, for the man I have been so close to losing. I add bath salts. Orange blossom. I realize I am remembering the night I packed to go to Brighton.

The memory evaporates. My eyes open. I could not have known, back then, that I was packing for the man who would take everything from me.

I carry on packing for the man I still have.

I hear a car pull up outside. The engine dies. A door opens and then shuts. A key in the lock. Ben. He is here.

I feel nervous. Scared. I am not the same person he left this morning; I have learned my own story. I have discovered myself. What will he think when he sees me? What will he say?

I must ask him if he knows about my journal. If he has read it. What he thinks.

He calls out as he closes the door behind him. "Christine? Chris? I'm home." His voice does not sing, though; he sounds exhausted. I call back, and tell him I am in the bedroom.

The lowest step creaks as it accepts his weight, and I hear an exhalation as first one shoe is removed, and then the other. He will be putting his slippers on, now, and then he will come to find me. I feel a surge of pleasure at knowing his rituals—my journal has clued me in to them, even though my memory cannot—but, as he ascends the stairs, another emotion takes over. Fear. I think of what I wrote in the front of my journal. *Don't trust Ben.*

He opens the bedroom door. "Darling!" he says. I have not moved. I still sit on the edge of the bed, the bags open behind me. He stands by the door until I stand and open my arms, then he comes over and kisses me.

"How was your day?" I say.

He takes off his tie. "Oh," he says. "Let's not talk about that. We're on holiday!"

He begins to unbutton his shirt. I fight the instinct to look away, remind myself that he is my husband, that I love him.

"I packed the bags," I say. "I hope yours is okay. I didn't know what you'd want to take."

He steps out of his trousers and folds them before hanging them in the closet. "I'm sure it's fine."

"Only I wasn't exactly sure where we were going. So I didn't know what to pack."

He turns, and I wonder whether I catch a flash of annoyance in his eyes. "I'll check, before we put the bags in the car. It's fine. Thanks for making a start." He sits on the chair at the dressing table and pulls on a pair of faded blue jeans. I notice a perfect crease ironed down their front, and the twentysomething me has to resist the urge to find him ridiculous.

"Ben?" I say. "You know where I've been today."

He looks at me. "Yes," he says. "I know."

"You know about Dr. Nash?"

He turns away from me. "Yes," he says. "You told me." I can see him, reflected in the mirrors arranged around the dresser. Three versions of the man I married. The man I love. "Everything," he says. "You told me about it all. I know everything."

"You don't mind? About me seeing him?"

He does not look around. "I wish you'd told me. But no. No, I don't mind."

"And my journal? You know about my journal?"

"Yes," he says. "You told me. You said it helped."

A thought comes. "Have you read it?"

"No," he says. "You said it was private. I would never look through your private things."

"But you know about Adam? You know that I know about Adam?"

I see him flinch, as if my words have been hurled at him with violence. I am surprised. I was expecting him to be happy. Happy that he would no longer have to tell me about his death, over and over again.

He looks at me.

"Yes," he says.

"There aren't any pictures," I say. He asks what I mean. "There are photos of me and you, but still none of him."

He stands and comes over to where I am sitting, then sits on the bed beside me. He takes my hand. I wish he would stop treating me as if I am fragile, brittle. As if the truth would break me.

"I wanted to surprise you," he says. He reaches under the bed and retrieves a photo album. "I've put them in here."

He hands me the album. It is heavy, dark, bound in something meant to resemble black leather but does not. I open the cover, and inside it is a pile of photographs.

"I wanted to put them in properly," he says. "To give to you as a present tonight, but I didn't have time. I'm sorry."

I look through the photographs. They are not in any order. There are photographs of Adam as a baby, a young boy. They must be the ones from the metal box. One stands out. In it, he is a young man, sitting next to a woman. "His girlfriend?" I say.

"One of them," says Ben. "The one he was with the longest."

She is pretty, blond, her hair cut short. She reminds me of Claire. In the photograph, Adam is looking directly at the camera, laughing, and she is looking half at him, her face a mixture of joy and disapproval. They have a conspiratorial air, as though they have shared a joke with whoever is behind the lens. They are happy. The thought pleases me. "What was her name?"

"Helen. She's called Helen."

I wince as I realize I had thought of her in the past tense, imagined that she had died, too. A thought stirs; what if she had died instead, but I force it down before it forms and finds a shape.

"Were they still together when he died?"

"Yes," he says. "They were thinking of getting engaged."

She looks so young, so hungry, her eyes full of possibility, of what is in store for her. She does not yet know the impossible amount of pain she still has to face.

"I'd like to meet her," I say. Ben takes the picture from me. He sighs.

"We're not in touch," he says.

"Why?" I say. I had it planned in my head; we would be a support to each other. We would share something, an understanding, a love that pierced all others, if not for each other then at least for the thing we had lost.

"There were arguments," he says. "Difficulties."

I look at him. I can see that he does not want to tell me. The man who wrote the letter, the man who believed in me and cared for me, and who, in the end, loved me enough both to leave me and then to come back for me, seems to have vanished.

"Ben?"

"There were arguments," he says.

"Before Adam died, or after?"

"Both."

The illusion of support vanishes, replaced by a sick feeling. What if Adam and I had fought, too? Surely he would have sided with his girlfriend, over his mother?

"Were Adam and I close?" I say.

"Oh yes," says Ben. "Until you had to go to the hospital. Until you lost your memory. Even then you were close, of course. As close as you could be."

His words hit me like a punch. I realize that Adam was a toddler when he lost his mother to amnesia. Of course I had never known my son's fiancée; every day I saw him would have been like the first.

I close the book.

"Can we bring it with us?" I say. "I'd like to look at it some more later."

.    .    .

WE HAVE CUPS of tea that Ben made in the kitchen as I finished packing for the journey, and then we get into the car. I check that I have my handbag, my journal still within it. Ben has added a few things to the bag I packed for him, and he has brought another bag, too—the leather satchel that he left with this morning—as well as two pairs of walking boots from the back of the closet. I had stood by the door as he loaded these things into the trunk and then waited while he checked the doors were closed, the windows locked. Now, I ask him how long the journey might take.

He shrugs. "Depends on the traffic," he says. "Not too long, once we're out of London."

A refusal to provide an answer, disguised as an answer itself. I wonder if this is what he is always like. I wonder if years of telling me the same thing have worn him down, bored him to the point where he can no longer bring himself to tell me anything.

He is a careful driver, that much I can see. He proceeds slowly, checking his mirror frequently, slowing down at the merest hint of an approaching hazard.

I wonder if Adam drove. I suppose he must have done so to be in the army, but did he ever drive when he was on leave? Did he pick me up, his invalid mother, and take me on trips, to places he thought I might like? Or did he decide there was no point, that whatever enjoyment I might have had at the time would disappear overnight like snow melting on a warm roof?

We are on the highway, heading out of the city. It has begun to rain; huge droplets smack into the windshield, hold their shape for a moment before beginning the swift slide down the glass. In the distance the lights of the city bathe the concrete and glass in a soft orange glow. It is beautiful and terrible, but I am struggling inside. I want so much to think of my son as something other than abstract, but without a concrete memory of him, I cannot. I keep coming back to the single truth: I cannot remember him, and so he might as well have never existed.

I close my eyes. I think back to what I read about our son this afternoon and an image explodes in front of me—Adam as a toddler pushing the blue tricycle along a path. But even as I marvel at it, I know it is not real. I know I am not remembering the thing that happened, I am remembering the image I formed in my mind this afternoon as I read about the thing, and even that was a recollection of an earlier memory. Memories of memories, most people's going back through years, through decades, but, for me, just a few hours.

Failing to remember my son, I do the next best thing, the only thing to quiet my sparking mind. I think of nothing. Nothing at all.

The smell of gasoline, thick and sweet. There is a pain in my neck. I open my eyes. Up close, I see the wet windshield, misted with my breath, and beyond it there are distant lights, blurred, out of focus. I realize that I have been dozing. I am leaning against the glass, my head twisted awkwardly. The car is silent, the engine off. I look over my shoulder.

Ben is there, sitting next to me. He is awake, looking ahead, out of the window. He does not move, does not even seem to have noticed that I have woken up, but instead continues to stare, his expression blank, unreadable in the dark. I turn to see what he is looking at.

Beyond the rain-spattered windshield is the hood of the car, and beyond that a low wooden fence, dimly illuminated in the glow from the streetlamps behind us. Beyond the fence, I see nothing, a blackness, huge and mysterious, in the middle of which hangs the moon, full and low.

"I love the sea," he says, without looking at me, and I realize we are parked on a cliff top, have made it as far as the coast.

"Don't you?" He turns to me. His eyes seem impossibly sad. "You do love the sea, don't you, Chris?" he says.

"I do," I say. "Yes." He is speaking as if he does not know, as if we have never been to the coast before, as if we have never been on holiday together. Fear begins to burn within me, but I resist it. I try to stay here, in the present, with my husband. I try to remember all that I learned from my journal this afternoon. "You know that, darling."

He sighs. "I know. You always used to, but I just don't know anymore. You change. You've changed, over the years. Ever since what happened. Sometimes I don't know who you are. I wake up each day and I don't know how you're going to be."

I am silent. I can think of nothing to say. We both know how senseless it would be for me to try to defend myself, to tell him that he is wrong. We both know that I am the last person who knows how much I change from day to day.

"I'm sorry," I say.

He looks at me. "Oh. It's all right. You don't need to apologize. I know it's not your fault. None of this is your fault. I'm being unfair, I suppose. Thinking of myself."

He looks back out to sea. There is a single light in the distance. A boat, on the waves. Light in a sea of treacly blackness. Ben speaks. "We'll be all right, won't we, Chris?"

"Of course," I say. "Of course we will. This is a new beginning for us. I have my journal now, and Dr. Nash will help me. I'm getting better, Ben. I know I am. I think I'm going to start writing again. There's no reason not to. I should be fine. And anyway, I'm in touch with Claire now, and she can help me." An idea comes to me. "We can all get together, don't you think? Just like old times? Just like at university? The three of us. And her husband, I suppose—I think she said she had a husband. We can all meet up and spend time together. It'll be fine." My mind fixes on the lies I have read, on all the ways I have not been able to trust him, but I force it away. I remind myself that all that has been resolved. It is my turn to be strong now. To be positive. "As long as we promise to always be honest with each other," I say. "Then everything is going to be okay."

He turns back to face me. "You do love me, don't you?"

"Of course. Of course I do."

"And you forgive me? For leaving you? I didn't want to. I had no choice. I'm sorry."

I take his hand. It feels both warm and cold at the same time, slightly damp. I try to hold it between my hands, but he neither assists nor resists my action. Instead, his hand rests, lifeless, on his knee. I squeeze it, and only then does he seem to notice that I am holding him.

"Ben. I understand. I forgive you." I look into his eyes. They, too, seem dull and lifeless, as if they have seen so much horror already that they cannot cope with any more.

"I love you, Ben," I say.

His voice drops to a whisper. "Kiss me."

I do as he asks, and then, when I have drawn back, he whispers, "Again. Kiss me again."

I kiss him a second time. But, even though he asks me to, I cannot kiss him a third. Instead we gaze out over the sea, at the moonlight on the water, at the drops of rain on the windshield reflecting back the yellow glow from the headlights of passing cars. Just the two of us, holding hands. Together.

We sit there for what feels like hours. Ben is beside me, staring out to sea. He scans the water, as if looking for something, some answer in the dark, and he does not speak. I wonder why he has brought us here, what he is hoping to find.

"Is it really our anniversary?" I say. There is no answer. He does not appear to have heard me, and so I say it again.

"Yes," he replies softly.

"Our wedding anniversary?"

"No," he says. "It's the anniversary of the night we met."

I want to ask him whether we are supposed to be celebrating, and to tell him that it doesn't feel like a celebration, but it seems cruel.

The busy road behind us has quieted, the moon is rising high in the sky. I begin to worry that we will stay out all night, looking at the sea while the rain falls around us. I affect a yawn.

"I'm sleepy," I say. "Can we go to our hotel?"

He looks at his watch. "Yes," he says. "Of course. Sorry. Yes." He starts the car. "We'll go there right now."

I am relieved. I am both craving sleep and dreading it.

The coast road dips and rises as we skirt the edges of a village. The lights of another, larger town begin to draw nearer, tightening into focus through the damp glass. The road becomes busier, a marina appears, with its moored boats and shops and nightclubs, and then we are in the town itself. On our right, every building seems to be a hotel, advertising vacancies on white signs that blow in the wind. The streets are busy; it is not as late as I had thought, or else this is the kind of town that is alive night and day.

I look out to sea. A pier juts into the water, flooded with light and with an amusement park at its end. I can see a domed pavilion, a roller coaster. I can almost hear the whoops and cries of the riders as they are spun above the pitch-black sea.

An anxiety I cannot name begins to form in my chest.

"Where are we?" I say. There are words over the entrance to the pier, picked out in bright white lights, but I cannot make them out through the rain-washed windshield.

"We're here," says Ben, as we turn up a side street and stop outside a terraced house. There is lettering on the canopy over the door. RIALTO GUEST HOUSE, it says.

There are steps up to the front door, an ornate fence separating the building from the road. Beside the door is a small, cracked pot that would once have held a shrub but is now empty. I am gripped with an intense fear.

"Have we been here before?" I say. He shakes his head. "You're sure? It looks familiar."

"I'm certain," he says. "We might have stayed somewhere near here, once. You're probably remembering that."

I try to relax. We get out of the car. There is a bar next to the guesthouse, and through its large windows I can see throngs of drinkers and a dance floor, pulsing at the back. Music thuds, muffled by the glass. "We'll check in, and then I'll come back for the luggage. Okay?"

I pull my coat tight around me. The wind is cold now, and the rain heavy. I rush up the steps and open the front door. There is a sign taped to the glass. NO VACANCIES. I go through and into the lobby.

"You've booked?" I say, when Ben joins me. We are standing in a hallway. Farther down, a door is ajar, and from behind it comes the sound of a television, its volume turned up, competing with the music next door. There is no reception desk, but instead a bell sits on a small table, a sign next to it inviting us to ring it to attract attention.

"Yes, of course," says Ben. "Don't worry." He rings the bell.

For a moment, nothing happens, and then a young man comes from a room somewhere at the back of the house. He is tall and awkward, and I notice that, despite it being far too big for his frame, his shirt is untucked. He greets us as though he was expecting us, though not warmly, and I wait while he and Ben complete the formalities.

It is clear the hotel has seen better days. The carpet is threadbare in places, and the paintwork around the doorways scuffed and marked. Opposite the lounge is another door, marked DINING ROOM, and at the back are several more doors, beyond which, I imagine, one would find the kitchen and private rooms of the staff.

"I'll take you to the room, now, shall I?" says the tall man when he and Ben have finished. I realize he is talking to me; Ben is on his way back outside, presumably to get the bags.

"Yes," I say. "Thank you."

He hands me a key and we go up the stairs. On the first landing are several bedrooms, but we walk past them and up another flight of stairs. The house seems to shrink as we go higher; the ceilings are lower, the walls closer. We pass another bedroom and then stand at the bottom of a final flight of stairs that must lead to the very top of the house.

"Your room is up there," he says. "It's the only one."

I thank him, and then he turns and goes back downstairs and I climb to our room.

I open the door. The room is dark, and bigger than I was expecting, up here at the top of the house. I can see a window opposite, and through it a dim gray light is shining, picking out the outline of a dressing table, a bed, a table, and an armchair. The music from the club next door thuds, stripped of its clarity, reduced to a dull, crunching bass.

I stand still. Fear has gripped me again. The same fear that I experienced outside the guesthouse, but worse, somehow. I go cold. Something is wrong, but I cannot say what. I breathe deeply but cannot get enough air into my lungs. I feel as if I am about to drown.

I close my eyes, as if hoping the room will look different when I open them, but it does not. I am filled with an overwhelming terror of what will happen when I switch on the light, as if that simple action will spell disaster, the end of everything.

What will happen if I leave the room shrouded in blackness and instead go back downstairs? I could walk calmly past the tall man, and along the corridor, past Ben if necessary, and out, out of the hotel.

But they would think I had gone mad, of course. They would find me, and bring me back. And what would I tell them? That the woman who remembers nothing had a feeling she didn't like, an inkling? They would think me ridiculous.

I am with my husband. I have come here to be reconciled with him. I am safe with Ben.

And so, I switch on the light.

There is a flash as my eyes adjust, and then I see the room. It is unimpressive. There is nothing to be frightened of. The carpet is a mushroom-gray; the curtains and wallpaper both in a floral pattern, though they don't match. The dresser is battered, with three mirrors on it and a faded painting of a bird above it; the armchair wicker, with yet another floral pattern on the cushion; and the bed covered with an orange bedspread, patterned with a diamond design.

I can see how disappointing it would be to someone who has booked it for their holiday, but, though Ben has booked it for ours, it is not disappointment that I feel. The fear has burned itself down to dread.

I close the door behind me and try to calm myself. I am being stupid. Paranoid. I must keep busy. Do something.

It feels cold in the room, and a slight draft wafts the curtains. The window is open, and I go over to close it. I look out before I do. We are high up; the streetlamps are far below us; seagulls sit silently upon them. I look out across the rooftops, see the cool moon hanging in the sky, and in the distance—the sea. I can make out the pier, the flashing lights.

And then I see them. The words, over the entrance to the pier. BRIGHTON PIER.

Despite the cold, and even though I shiver, I feel a bead of sweat form on my brow. Now it makes sense. Ben has brought me here, to Brighton, to the place of my disaster. But why? Does he think I am more likely to remember what happened if I am back in the town in which my life was ripped from me? Does he think that I will remember who did this to me?

I remember reading that Dr. Nash had once suggested I come here, and I had told him no.

There are footsteps on the stairs, voices. The tall man must be bringing Ben here, to our room. They will be carrying the luggage together, lifting it up the stairs and around the tricky landings. He will be here soon.

What should I tell him? That he is wrong and being here will not help? That I want to go home?

I go back toward the door. I will help to bring the bags inside, and then I will unpack them, and we will sleep, and then tomorrow—

It hits me. Tomorrow I will know nothing again. That must be what Ben has in his satchel. Photographs. The scrapbook. He will have to use everything he has to explain who he is and where we are, all over again.

I wonder if I have brought my journal, then remember packing it, putting it in my bag. I try to calm myself. Tonight I will put it under the pillow, and tomorrow I will find it and read it. Everything will be fine.

I can hear Ben on the landing. He is talking to the tall man, discussing arrangements for breakfast. "We'd probably like it in our room," I hear him say. A gull cries outside the window, startling me.

I go toward the door, and then I see it. To my right. A bathroom; the door is open. A bath, a toilet, a sink. But it is the floor that draws me, fills me with horror. It is tiled, and the pattern is unusual; black and white alternate in crazed diagonals.

My jaw opens. I feel myself go cold. I think I hear myself cry out.

I know, then. I recognize the pattern.

It is not only Brighton that I have recognized.

I have been here before. In this room.

The door opens. I say nothing as Ben comes in, but my mind spins. Is this the room in which I was attacked? Why didn't he tell me we were coming here? How can he go from not even wanting to tell me about the assault to bringing me to the room in which it happened?

I can see the tall man standing just outside the door, and I want to call out to him, to ask him to stay, but he turns to leave and Ben closes the door. It is just the two of us, now.

He looks at me. "Are you all right, love?" he says. I nod and say yes, but the word feels as though it has been forced out of me. I feel the stirrings of hate in my stomach.

He takes my arm. He is squeezing the flesh just a little too tightly; any more and I would say something, any less and I doubt that I would notice. "You're sure?"

"Yes," I say. Why is he doing this? He must know where we are, what this means. All along he must have been planning this. "Yes, I'm fine. I just feel a little tired."

And then it hits me. Dr. Nash. He must have something to do with this. Otherwise, why would Ben—after all these years, when he could have but did not—decide to bring me here now?

They must have been in contact. Perhaps Ben called him, after I told him all about our meetings. Perhaps sometime during the last week—the week I know nothing about—they'd planned it all.

"Why don't you lie down?" says Ben.

I hear myself speak. "I think I will." I turn toward the bed. Perhaps they'd been in touch all along? Dr. Nash might have been lying about everything. I picture him, dialing Ben after he'd said good-bye to me, telling him about my progress, or lack of it.

"Good girl," says Ben. "I meant to bring champagne. I think I'll go and get some. There's a shop, I think. It's not far." He smiles. "Then I'll join you."

I turn to face him, and he kisses me. Now, here, his kiss lingers. He brushes my lips with his, puts his hand in my hair, strokes my back. I fight the urge to pull away. His hand moves lower, down my back, coming to rest on the top of my buttock. I swallow hard.

I cannot trust anybody. Not my husband. Not the man who has claimed to be helping me. They have been working together, building to this day, the day when, clearly, they have decided I am to face the horror in my past.

*How dare they!* I think. *How dare they!*

"Okay," I say. I turn my head away slightly, push him gently so that he lets me go.

He turns and leaves the room. "I'll just lock the door," he says, as he closes it behind him. "You can't be too careful . . ." I hear the key turn in the door outside, and I begin to panic. Is he really going to buy champagne? Or is he meeting Dr. Nash? I cannot believe he has brought me to this room without telling me; another lie to go with all the others. I hear him go down the stairs.

Wringing my hands, I sit on the edge of the bed. I cannot calm my mind, cannot settle on just one thought. Instead, thoughts race, as if, in a mind devoid of memory, each idea has too much space to grow and move, to collide with others in a shower of sparks before spinning off into its own distance.

I stand up. I feel enraged. I cannot face the thought of him coming back, pouring champagne, getting into bed with me. Neither can I face the thought of his skin next to mine, or his hands on me in the night, pawing at me, pressing me, encouraging me to give myself to him. How can I, when there is no me to give?

*I would do anything,* I think. *Anything except for that.*

I cannot stay here, in this place where my life was ruined and everything taken away from me. I try to work out how much time I have. Ten minutes? Five? I go over to Ben's bag and open it. I don't know why; I am not thinking of why, or how, only that I must move, while Ben is away, before he returns and things change again. Perhaps I intend to find the car keys, to force the door and go downstairs, out into the rainy street, to the car. Although I'm not even certain I can drive, perhaps I mean to try, to get in and go far, far away.

Or perhaps I mean to find a picture of Adam; I know they're in there. I will take just one, and then I will leave the room, and run. I will run and run, and then, when I can run no more, I will call Claire, or anybody, and I will tell them that I cannot take it anymore, and beg them to help me.

I dig my hands deep in the bag. I feel metal and plastic. Something soft. And then an envelope. I take it out, thinking it might contain photographs, and see that it is the one I found in the office at home. I must have put it in Ben's bag as I packed, intending to remind him it had not been opened. I turn it over and see that *Private* has been written on the front. Without thinking, I tear it open and remove its contents.

Paper. Pages and pages. I recognize it. The faint blue lines, the red margins. These pages are the same as those in my journal, in the book that I have been writing.

And then I see my own handwriting and begin to understand.

I have not read all of my story. There is more. Pages and pages more.

I find my journal in my bag. I had not noticed before, but after the final page of writing, a whole section has been removed. The pages have been excised neatly, cut with a scalpel or a razor blade, close to the spine.

Cut out by Ben.

I sit on the floor, the pages spread in front of me. This is the missing week of my life. I read the rest of my story.

.    .    .

THE FIRST ENTRY is dated. *Friday, November 23*, it says. The same day I met Claire. I must have written it that evening, after speaking to Ben. Perhaps we had had the conversation I was anticipating, after all. *I sit here*, it begins,

> on the floor of the bathroom, in the house in which, supposedly, I wake up every morning. I have this journal in front of me, this pen in my hand. I write, because it's all I can think of to do.
>
> Tissues are balled around me, soaked with tears, and blood. When I blink, my vision turns red. Blood drips into my eye as fast as I can wipe it away.
>
> When I look in the mirror, I can see that the skin above my eye is cut, and my lip, too. When I swallow, I taste the metallic tang of blood.
>
> I want to sleep. To find a safe place, somewhere, and close my eyes, and rest, like an animal.
>
> That is what I am. An animal. Living from moment to moment, day to day, trying to make sense of the world in which I find myself.

My heart races. I read back over the paragraph, my eyes drawn again and again to the word *blood*. What had happened?

I begin to read quickly, my mind stumbling over words, lurching from line to line. I don't know when Ben will get back and cannot risk him taking these pages before I have read them. Now may be my only chance.

I'd decided it was best to speak to him after dinner. We ate in the den—roast beef and mashed potatoes, our plates balanced on our knees—and when we had both finished, I asked if he would turn the television off. He seemed reluctant. "I need to talk to you," I said.

The room felt too quiet, filled only with the ticking of the clock and the distant hum of the city. And my voice, sounding hollow and empty.

"Darling," said Ben, putting his plate on the coffee table between us. A half-chewed lump of meat sat on the side of the plate, peas floated in thin gravy. "Is everything okay?"

"Yes," I said. "Everything's fine." I did not know how to continue. He looked at me, his eyes wide, waiting. "You do love me, don't you?" I said. I felt almost as if I was gathering evidence, insuring myself against any later disapproval.

"Yes," he said. "Of course. What's this about? What's wrong?"

"Ben," I said. "I love you, too. And I understand your reasons for doing what you've been doing, but I know you've been lying to me."

Almost as soon as I finished the sentence, I regretted starting it. I saw him flinch. He looked at me, his lips pulled back as if to speak, his eyes wounded.

"What do you mean?" he said. "Darling—"

I had to continue now. There was no way out of the stream into which I had begun to wade.

"I know you've been doing it to protect me, not telling me things, but it can't go on. I need to know."

"What do you mean?" he said. "I haven't been lying to you."

I felt a surge of anger. "Ben," I said. "I know about Adam."

His face changed, then. I saw him swallow and look away, toward the corner of the room. He brushed something off the arm of his pullover. "What?"

"Adam," I said. "I know we had a son."

I half-expected him to ask me how I knew, but then realized this conversation was not unusual. We have been here before, on the day I saw my novel, and other days when I have remembered Adam, too.

I saw he was about to speak, but didn't want to hear any more lies.

"I know he died in Afghanistan," I said.

His mouth shut, then opened again, almost comically.

"How do you know that?"

"You told me," I said. "Weeks ago. You were eating a cookie, and I was in the bathroom. I came downstairs and told you that I had remembered we had had a son, even remembered what he was called, and then we sat down and you told me how he'd been killed. You showed me some photographs, from upstairs. Photos of me and him, and letters that he'd written. A letter to Santa Claus—" Grief washed over me again. I stopped talking.

Ben was staring at me. "You remembered? How—?"

"I've been writing things down. For a few weeks. As much as I can remember."

"Where?" he said. He had begun to raise his voice, as

if in anger, though I did not understand what he might be angry about. "Where have you been writing things down? I don't understand, Christine. Where have you been writing things down?"

"I've been keeping a notebook."

"A notebook?" The way he said it made it sound so trivial, as if I have been using it to write shopping lists and record phone numbers.

"A journal," I said.

He shifted forward in his chair, as if he was about to get up. "A journal? For how long?"

"I don't know, exactly. A couple of weeks?"

"Can I see it?"

I felt petulant and angry. I was determined not to show it to him. "No," I said. "Not yet."

He was furious. "Where is it? Show it to me."

"Ben. It's personal."

He shot the word back at me. "Personal? What do you mean, personal?"

"I mean it's private. I wouldn't feel comfortable with you reading it."

"Why not?" he said. "Have you written about me?"

"Of course I have."

"What have you written? What have you said?"

How to answer that? I thought of all the ways I have betrayed him. The things I have said to Dr. Nash, and thought about him. The ways in which I have distrusted my husband, the things I have thought him capable of. I thought of the lies I have told, the days I have seen Dr. Nash—and Claire—and told him nothing.

"Lots of things, Ben. I've written lots of things."

"But why? Why have you been writing things down?"

I could not believe he had to ask me that question. "I want to make sense of my life," I said. "I want to be able to link one day to the next, like you can. Like anybody can."

"But why? Are you unhappy? Don't you love me any-more? Don't you want to be with me, here?"

The question threw me. Why did he feel that wanting to make sense of my fractured life meant that I wanted to change it in some way?

"I don't know," I said. "What is happiness? I'm happy when I wake up, I think, though if this morning is anything to go by, I'm confused. But I'm not happy when I look in the mirror and see that I'm twenty years older than I was expecting, that I have gray hairs and lines around my eyes. I'm not happy when I realize that all those years have been lost, taken from me. So, I suppose a lot of the time I'm not happy, no. But it's not your fault. I'm happy with you. I love you. I need you."

He came and sat next to me, then. His voice softened. "I'm sorry," he said. "I hate the fact that everything was ruined, just because of that car accident."

I felt anger rise in me again, but clamped it down. I had no right to be angry with him; he did not know what I had learned and what I hadn't.

"Ben," I said. "I know what happened. I know it wasn't a car accident. I know I was attacked."

He did not move. He looked at me, his eyes expressionless. I thought he hadn't heard me, and then he said, "What attack?"

I raised my voice. "Ben!" I said. "Stop it!" I could not help it. I had told him I was keeping a journal, told him I was piecing together the details of my story, and yet here he was, still prepared to lie to me when it was obvious I knew the truth. "Don't keep fucking lying to me! I know there was no car accident. I know what happened to me. There's no point in trying to pretend it was anything other than what it was. Denying it doesn't get us anywhere. You have to stop lying to me!"

He stood up. He looked huge, raised above me, blocking my vision.

"Who told you?" he said. "Who? Was it that bitch Claire? Did she go shooting her ugly fat mouth off, telling you lies? Interfering where she isn't wanted?"

"Ben—" I began.

"She's always hated me. She'd do anything to poison you against me. Anything! She's lying, my darling. She's lying!"

"It wasn't Claire," I said. I bowed my head. "It was somebody else."

"Who?" he shouted. "Who?"

"I've been seeing a doctor," I whispered. "We've been talking. He told me."

He was perfectly motionless, apart from the thumb of his right hand, which was tracing slow circles on the knuckle of his left. I could feel the warmth of his body, hear the slow drawing in of his breath, the hold, the release. When he spoke, his voice was so low I struggled to make out the words.

"What do you mean, a doctor?"

"His name is Dr. Nash. Apparently, he contacted me a few weeks ago." Even as I said it, I felt like I wasn't telling my own story but that of someone else.

"Saying what?"

I tried to remember. Had I written about our first conversation?

"I don't know," I said. "I don't think I wrote down what he said."

"And he encouraged you to write things down?"

"Yes."

"Why?" he said.

"I want to get better, Ben."

"And is it working? What have you been doing? Has he been giving you drugs?"

"No," I said. "We've been doing some tests, some exercises. I had a scan—"

The thumb stopped moving. He turned to face me.

"A scan?" His voice was louder again.

"Yes. An MRI. He said it might help. They didn't really have them when I was first ill. Or they weren't as sophisticated as they are now—"

"Where? Where have you been doing these tests? Tell me!"

I was starting to feel confused. "In his office," I said. "In London. The scan was there, too. I don't remember exactly."

"How have you been getting there? How did someone like you get to a doctor's office?" His voice was pinched and urgent, now. "How?"

I tried to speak calmly. "He's been collecting me from here," I said. "And driving me—"

Disappointment flashed on his face, and then anger. I had never wanted the conversation to go like this, never intended it to become difficult.

I needed to try and explain things to him. "Ben—" I began.

What happened next was not what I was expecting. A dull moan began in Ben's throat, somewhere deep. It built quickly until, unable to hold it in anymore, he let out a terrible screech, like nails on glass.

"Ben!" I said. "What's wrong?"

He turned around, staggering as he did so, averting his face from me. I worried he was having some kind of attack. I stood up and put my hand out for him to hold on to. "Ben!" I said again, but he ignored it, steadying himself against the wall. When he turned back to me, his face was bright red, his eyes wide. I could see that spittle had gathered at the corners of his mouth. It looked as though he had put on some kind of grotesque mask, so distorted were his features.

"You stupid fucking bitch," he said, moving up against me as he did so. I flinched. His face was just inches from mine. "How long has this been going on?"

"I—"

"Tell me! Tell me, you slut. How long?"

"Nothing's going on!" I said. Fear welled within me, rising up. It did a slow roll on the surface and then sank beneath. "Nothing!" I said again. I could smell the food on his breath. Meat and onion. Spittle flew, striking me in the face, the lips. I could taste his warm, wet anger.

"You're sleeping with him. Don't lie to me."

The backs of my legs pressed against the edge of the sofa and I tried to move along it, to get away from him, but he grabbed my shoulders and shook them. "You've always been the same," he said. "A stupid lying bitch. I don't know what made me think you'd be any different with me. What have you been doing, eh? Sneaking off while I've been at work? Or have you been having him over here? Or maybe you've been doing it in a car, parked up on the heath?"

I felt his hands grip tight, his fingers and nails digging into my skin even through the cotton of my blouse.

"You're hurting me!" I shouted, hoping to shock him out of his rage. "Ben! Stop it!"

He stopped shaking and loosened his grip a fraction. It did not seem possible that the man gripping my shoulders, his face a mixture of rage and hate, could be the same man who had written the letter that Claire had given me. How could we have reached this level of distrust? How much miscommunication must it have taken to bring us from there to here?

"I'm not sleeping with him," I said. "He's helping me. Helping me to get better so that I can live a normal life. Here, with you. Don't you want that?"

His eyes began darting around the room. "Ben?" I said again. "Talk to me!" He froze. "Don't you want me to get better? Isn't that what you've always wanted, always hoped for?" He began to shake his head, rocking it from side to side. "I know it is," I said. "I know it's what you've wanted all this time." Hot tears ran down my cheeks, but I spoke through them, my voice fracturing into sobs. He was still holding me, but gently now, and I put my hands on his.

"I met Claire," I said. "She gave me your letter. I've read it, Ben. After all these years. I've read it."

There is a stain there, on the page. Ink, mixed with water in a smudge that resembles a star. I must have been crying as I wrote. I carried on reading.

———

I don't know what I expected to happen. Perhaps I thought he'd fall into my arms, sobbing with relief, and we would stand there, holding each other silently for as long as it took for us to relax, to feel our way back into each other again. And then we would sit, and talk things through. Perhaps I would go upstairs and get the letter that Claire had given me, and we would read it together, and begin the slow process of rebuilding our lives on a foundation of truth.

Instead, there was an instant in which nothing at all seemed to move and everything was quiet. There was no sound of breathing, no traffic from the road. I did not even hear the ticking of the clock. It was as if life was suspended, hovering on the cusp between one state and another.

And then it was over. Ben drew away from me. I thought he was going to kiss me, but instead I was aware of a blur out of the corner of my eye and my head cracked to one side. Pain radiated from my jaw. I fell, the sofa coming toward me, and the back of my head connected with something hard and sharp. I cried out. There was another blow, and then another. I closed my eyes, waiting for the next—but nothing came. Instead, I heard footsteps moving away, and a door slamming.

I opened my eyes and inhaled in an angry gasp. The carpet stretched away from me, now vertical. A smashed plate sat near to my head and gravy oozed onto the floor, soaking into the carpet. Green peas had been trodden into the weave of the rug, and the half-chewed lump of meat. The front door swung open, then slammed. Footsteps on the path. Ben had left.

I exhaled. I closed my eyes. *I must not sleep*, I thought. *I must not.*

I opened them again. Dark swirls in the distance and the smell of flesh. I swallowed, and tasted blood.

*What have I done? What have I done?*

I made sure he was gone, then came upstairs and found my journal. Blood dripped onto the carpet from my split lip. I don't know what has happened. I don't know where my husband is, or if he will come back, or whether I want him to.

But I need him to. Without him, I can't live.

*I am scared. I want to see Claire.*

I stop reading and my hand goes to my forehead. It feels tender. The bruise I saw this morning, the one I covered up with makeup. Ben had hit me. I look back at the date. *Friday, November 23*. It was one week ago. One week, spent believing that everything is all right.

I stand up to look in the mirror. It is still there. A faint blue contusion. Proof that what I wrote was true. I wonder what lies I have been telling myself to explain my injury, or what lies he has been telling me.

But now I know the truth. I look at the pages in my hand and it hits me. *He wanted me to find them. He knows that even if I read them today, I will have forgotten them tomorrow.*

Suddenly I hear him on the stairs and, almost for the first time, realize fully that I am here, in this hotel room. With Ben. With the man who has hit me. I hear his key in the lock.

I have to know what happened, so I push the pages under the pillow, and lie on the bed. As he comes into the room, I close my eyes.

"Are you okay, darling?" he says. "Are you awake?"

I open my eyes. He is standing in the doorway, clutching a bottle. "I could only get Cava," he says. "Okay?"

He puts the bottle on the dresser and kisses me. "I think I'll take a shower," he whispers. He goes into the bathroom and turns on the taps.

When he has closed the door, I pull out the pages. I don't have long—surely he will not be more than five minutes—and so I must read as quickly as I can. My eyes flick down the page, not even registering all the words, but seeing enough.

That was hours ago. I have been sitting in the darkened hallway of our empty house, a slip of paper in one hand, a telephone in the other. Ink on paper. A number smudged. There was no answer, just an endless ringing. I wonder if she has turned off her answering machine, or if the tape is full. I try again. And again. I have been here before. My time is circular. Claire is not there to help me.

I looked in my bag and found the phone that Dr. Nash had given me. It is late, I thought. He won't be at work. He'll be with his girlfriend, doing whatever it is that the two of them do during their evenings. Whatever two normal people do. I have no idea what that is.

His home number was written in the front of my journal. It rang and rang, and then was silent. There was no recorded voice to tell me there was an error, no invitation to leave a message. I tried again. The same. His office number was now the only one I had.

I sat there for a while. Helpless. Looking at the front door, half-hoping to see Ben's shadowy figure appear in the frosted glass and insert a key in the lock, half-fearing it.

Eventually, I could wait no more. I went upstairs and

got undressed, and then I got into bed and wrote this. The house is still empty. In a moment, I will close this book and hide it, and then switch off the light and sleep.

And then I will forget, and this journal will be all that is left.

I look at the next page with dread, fearing I will find it blank, but it is not.

*Monday, November 26,* it begins.

He hit me on Friday. Two days, and I have written nothing. For all that time, did I believe things were all right?

My face is bruised and sore. Surely I knew that something was not right?

Today he said that I fell. The biggest cliché in the book, and I believed him. Why wouldn't I? He'd already had to explain who I was, and who he was, and how I'd come to be waking up in a strange house, decades older than I thought I should be, so why would I question his reason for my bruised and swollen eye, my cut lip?

And so, I went ahead with my day. I kissed him as he left for work. I cleared up our breakfast things. I ran a bath.

And then I came in here, found this journal, and learned the truth.

A gap. I realize I have not mentioned Dr. Nash. Had he abandoned me? Had I found the journal without his help?

Or had I stopped hiding it? I read on.

———

Later, I called Claire. The phone that Ben had given me
did not work—the battery was probably dead, I thought—
and so I used the one that Dr. Nash had given me. There
was no answer, and so I sat in the living room. I could not
relax. I picked up magazines, put them down again. I put
the TV on and spent half an hour staring at the screen, not
even noticing what was on. I looked at my journal, unable
to concentrate, unable to write. I tried her again, several
times, each time hearing the same message inviting me to
leave one of my own. It was just after lunchtime when she
answered.

"Chrissy," she said. "How are you?" I could hear Toby
in the background, playing.

"I'm okay," I said, although I wasn't.

"I was going to call you," she said. "I feel like hell, and it's
only Monday!"

Monday. Days meant nothing to me; each melted away,
indistinguishable from the one that had preceded it.

"I need to see you," I said. "Can you come over?"

She sounded surprised. "To your place?"

"Yes," I said. "Please? I want to talk to you."

"Is everything okay, Chrissy? You read the letter?"

I took a deep breath, and my voice dropped to a whisper.
"Ben hit me." I heard a gasp of surprise.

"What?"

"The other night. I'm bruised. He told me I'd fallen, but
I wrote down that he hit me."

"Chrissy, there is no way Ben would hit you. Ever. He
just isn't capable of it."

Doubt flooded me. Was it possible I'd made it all up?

"But I wrote it in my journal," I said.

She said nothing for a moment, and then, "But why do you think he hit you?"

I put my hands to my face, felt the swollen flesh around my eyes. I felt a flash of anger. It was clear she didn't believe me.

I thought back to what I had written. "I told him that I've been keeping a journal. I said I had been seeing you and Dr. Nash. I told him I knew about Adam. I told him you'd given me the letter he'd written, that I'd read it. And then he hit me."

"He just hit you?"

I thought of all the things he'd called me, the things he'd accused me of. "He said I was a bitch." I felt a sob rise in my chest. "He—he accused me of sleeping with Dr. Nash. I said I wasn't, then—"

"Then?"

"Then he hit me."

A silence, then Claire said, "Has he ever hit you before?"

I had no way of knowing. Perhaps he had? It was possible that ours had always been an abusive relationship. My mind flashed on Claire and me, marching, holding homemade placards—WOMEN'S RIGHTS. NO TO DOMESTIC VIOLENCE. I remembered how I had always looked down on women who found themselves with husbands who beat them, and stayed put. They were weak, I thought. Weak and stupid.

Was it possible that I had fallen into the same trap as they had?

"I don't know," I said.

"It's difficult to imagine Ben hurting anything, but I

suppose it's not impossible. Christ! He used to make even me feel guilty. Do you remember?"

"No," I said. "I don't. I don't remember anything."

"Shit," she said. "I'm sorry. I forgot. It's just so hard to imagine. He's the one that convinced me that fish have as much right to life as an animal with legs. He wouldn't even kill a spider!"

The wind gusts the curtains of the room. I hear a train, in the distance. Screams from the pier. Downstairs, on the street, someone shouts "Fuck!" and I hear the sound of breaking glass. I do not want to read on, but know that I must.

I felt a chill. "Ben was a vegetarian?"

"Vegan," she said, laughing. "Don't tell me you didn't know?"

I thought of the night he'd hit me. *A half-chewed lump of meat,* I'd written. *Peas floating in thin gravy.*

I went over to the window. "Ben eats meat . . ." I said, speaking slowly. "He's not a vegetarian . . . Not now, anyway. Maybe he's changed?"

There was another long silence.

"Claire?" She said nothing. "Claire? Are you there?"

"Right," she said. She sounded angry now. "I'm calling him. I'm sorting this out. Where is he?"

I answered without thinking. "He'll be at the school, I suppose. He said he wouldn't be back until five o'clock."

"At the school?" she said. "Do you mean the university? Is he lecturing now?"

Fear began to stir within me. "No," I said. "He works at a school near here. I can't remember the name."

"What does he do there?"

"A teacher. He's head of Chemistry, I think he said." I felt guilty at not knowing what my husband does for a living, not being able to remember how he earns the money to keep us fed and clothed. "I don't remember."

I looked up and caught sight of my swollen face reflected in the window in front of me. The guilt evaporated.

"What school?" she asked.

"I don't know," I said. "I don't think he told me."

"What, never?"

"Not this morning, no," I said. "For me that might as well be never."

"I'm sorry, Chrissy. I didn't mean to upset you. It's just that, well—" I sensed a change of mind, a sentence aborted. "Could you find out the name of the school?"

I thought of the office upstairs. "I guess so. Why?"

"I'd like to speak to Ben, to make sure he's going to be coming home when I'm there this afternoon. I wouldn't want it to be a wasted journey!"

I noticed the humor she was trying to inject into her voice, but did not mention it. I felt out of control, could not work out what was best, what I should do, and so decided to surrender to my friend. "I'll have a look," I said.

I went upstairs. The office was tidy, piles of papers arranged across the desk. It did not take long to find some letterhead: a notice about a parents' evening that had already taken place.

"It's St. Anne's," I said. "You want the number?" She said she'd find it out herself.

"I'll call you back," she said. "Yes?"

Panic hit again. "What are you going to say to him?" I said.

"I'm going to sort this out," she said. "Trust me, Chrissy. There has to be an explanation. Okay?"

"Yes," I said, and ended the call. I sat down, my legs shaking. What if my first hunch had been correct? What if Claire and Ben were still sleeping together? Maybe she was calling him now, warning him. *She suspects,* she might be saying. *Be careful.*

I remembered reading my journal earlier. Dr. Nash had told me that I had once shown symptoms of paranoia. Claiming the doctors were conspiring against you, he'd said. A tendency to confabulate. To invent things.

What if that's all happening again? What if I am inventing this, all of it? Everything in my journal might be fantasy. Paranoia.

I thought of what they'd told me at the ward, and Ben in his letter. *You were occasionally violent.* I realized it might have been me who caused the fight on Friday night. Did I lash out at Ben? Perhaps he hit back and then, upstairs in the bathroom, I took a pen and explained it all away with a fiction.

What if all this journal means is that I'm getting worse again? That soon it really will be time for me to go back to Waring House?

I went cold, suddenly convinced that this was why Dr. Nash had wanted to take me there. To prepare me for my return.

All I can do is wait for Claire to call me back.

———

Another gap. *Is that what's happening now?* I think. Will Ben try to take me back to Waring House? I look over to the bathroom door. I will not let him.

There is one final entry, written later that same day. *Monday, November 26.* I have added the time. *6:55 p.m.*

Claire called me after less than half an hour. And now my mind oscillates. It swings from one thing to the other, then back again. I know what to do. I don't know what to do. I know what to do. But there's a third thought. I shudder as I realize the truth: I am in danger.

I turn to the front of this journal, intending to write *Don't trust Ben*, but I find those words are already there.

I don't remember writing them. But then I don't remember anything.

A gap, and then it continues.

She sounded hesitant, on the phone.

"Chrissy," she said. "Listen."

Her tone frightened me. I sat down. "What?"

"I called Ben. At school."

I had the overwhelming sensation of being on an uncontrollable journey, of being in unnavigable waters. "What did he say?"

"I didn't speak to him. I just wanted to make sure he worked there."

"Why?" I said. "Don't you trust him?"

"He's lied about other things."

I had to agree. "But why did you think he'd tell me he worked somewhere if he didn't?" I said.

"I was just surprised he was working in a school. You know he trained to be an architect? The last time I spoke to him he was looking into setting up his own practice. I just thought it was a bit odd he should be working in a school."

"What did they say?"

"They said they couldn't disturb him. He was busy, in a class." I felt relief. He hadn't lied about that, at least.

"He must have changed his mind," I said. "About his career."

"Chrissy? I told them I wanted to send him some documents. A letter. I asked for his official title."

"And?" I said.

"He's not head of Chemistry. Or Science. Or anything else. They said he was a lab assistant."

I felt my body jerk. I may have gasped; I don't remember.

"Are you sure?" I said. My mind raced to think of a reason for this new lie. Was it possible he was embarrassed? Worried about what I would think if I knew he had gone from being a successful architect to a lab assistant in a local school? Did he really think I was so shallow that I would love him any more or less based on what he did for a living?

Everything made sense.

"Oh God," I said. "It's my fault!"

"No!" she said. "It's not your fault!"

"It is!" I said. "It's the strain of having to look after me. Of having to deal with me, day in and day out. He must be having a breakdown. Maybe he doesn't even know himself what's true and what's not." I began to cry. "It must be unbearable," I said. "He even has to go through all that grief on his own, every day."

The line was silent, and then Claire said, "Grief? What grief?"

"Adam," I said. I felt pain at having to say his name.

"What about Adam?"

It came to me. Wild. Unbidden. *Oh God*, I thought. *She doesn't know. Ben hasn't told her.*

"He's dead," I said.

She gasped. "Dead? When? How?"

"I don't know when, exactly," I said. "I think Ben told me it was last year. He was killed in the war."

"The war? What war?"

"Afghanistan?"

And then she said it. "Chrissy, what would he be doing in Afghanistan?" Her voice was strange. She almost sounded pleased.

"He was in the army," I said, but even as I spoke, I was starting to doubt what I was saying. It was as if I was finally facing something I had known all along.

I heard Claire snort, almost as if she was finding something amusing. "Chrissy," she said. "Chrissy, darling. Adam hasn't been in the army. He's never been to Afghanistan. He's living in Birmingham, with someone called Helen. He works with computers. He hasn't forgiven me for what happened between me and his father, but I still call him occasionally. He'd probably rather I didn't, but I am his godmother, remember?" It took me a moment to work out why she was still using the present tense, and even as I did so, she said it.

"I called him after we met last week," she said. She was almost laughing, now. "He wasn't there, but I spoke to Helen. She said she'd ask him to call me back. Adam is alive."

I stop reading. I feel light. Empty. I feel I might fall backward, or else float away. Dare I believe it? Do I want to? I steady myself against the dresser and read on, only dimly aware that no longer do I hear the sound of Ben's shower.

I must have stumbled, grabbed hold of the chair. "He's alive?" My stomach rolled, I remember feeling vomit rise in my throat and having to swallow it down. "He's really alive?"

"Yes," she said. "Yes!"

"But—" I began. "But— I saw a newspaper. A clipping. It said he'd been killed."

"It can't have been real, Chrissy," she said. "It can't have been. He's alive."

I began to speak, but then everything hit me at once, every emotion bound up in every other. Joy. I remember joy. The sheer pleasure of knowing that Adam was alive fizzed on my tongue, but mixed into it was the bitter, acid tang of fear. I thought of my bruises, of the force with which Ben must have struck me to cause them. Perhaps his abuse is not only physical, perhaps some days he takes delight in telling me that my son is dead so that he can see the pain that thought inflicts. Was it really possible that on other days, in which I remember the fact of my pregnancy, or giving birth to my baby, he simply tells me that Adam has moved away, is working abroad, living on the other side of town?

And, if so, why did I never write down any of those alternative stories that he fed me?

Images entered my head, of Adam as he might be now, fragments of scenes I may have missed, but none would hold. Each image slid through me and then vanished. The only thing I could think about was he's alive. Alive. My son is alive. I can meet him.

"Where is he?" I said. "Where is he? I want to see him!"

"Chrissy," Claire said. "Stay calm."

"But—"

"Chrissy!" she interrupted. "I'm coming over. Stay there."

"Claire! Tell me where he is!"

"I'm really worried about you, Chrissy. Please—"

"But—"

She raised her voice. "Chrissy, calm down!" she said, and then a single thought pierced through the fog of my confusion: I am hysterical. I took a breath and tried to settle, as Claire began to speak again.

"Adam is living in Birmingham," she said.

"But he must know where I am now," I said. "Why doesn't he come to see me?"

"Chrissy . . ." she began.

"Why? Why doesn't he visit me? Does he not get on with Ben? Is that why he stays away?"

"Chrissy," she said, her voice soft. "Birmingham is a fair way away. He has a busy life . . ."

"You mean—"

"Maybe he can't get down to London that often?"

"But—"

"Chrissy. You think Adam doesn't visit. But I can't believe that. Maybe he does come, when he can."

I fell silent. Nothing made sense. Yet she was right. I have only been keeping my journal for a couple of weeks. Before that, anything could have happened.

"I need to see him," I said. "I want to see him. Do you think that can be arranged?"

"I don't see why not. But if Ben is really telling you that he's dead, then we ought to speak to him first."

Of course, I thought. But what will he say? He thinks that I still believe his lies.

"He'll be here soon," I said. "Will you still come over? Will you help me to sort this out?"

"Of course," she said. "Of course. I don't know what's going on. But we'll talk to Ben. I promise. I'll come now."

"Now? Right now?"

"Yes. I'm worried, Chrissy. Something's not right."

Her tone bothered me, but at the same time I felt relieved, and excited at the thought that I might soon be able to meet my son. I wanted to see him, to see his photograph, right away. I remembered that we had hardly any, and those we did have were locked away. A thought began to form.

"Claire," I said. "Did we have a fire?"

She sounded confused. "A fire?"

"Yes. We have hardly any photographs of Adam. And almost none of our wedding. Ben said we lost them in a fire."

"A fire?" she said. "What fire?"

"Ben said there was a fire in our old home. We lost lots of things."

"When?"

"I don't know. Years ago."

"And you have no photographs of Adam?"

I felt myself getting annoyed. "We have some. But not many. Hardly any of him other than when he was a baby.

A toddler. And none of holidays, not even our honeymoon. None of Christmases. Nothing like that."

"Chrissy," she said. Her voice was quiet, measured. I thought I detected something in it, some new emotion. Fear. "Describe Ben to me."

"What?"

"Describe him to me. Ben. What does he look like?"

"What about the fire?" I said. "Tell me about that."

"There was no fire," she said.

"But I wrote down that I remembered it," I said. "A chip pan. The phone rang . . ."

"You must have been imagining it," she said.

"But—"

I sensed her anxiety. "Chrissy! There was no fire. Not years ago. Ben would have told me. Now, describe Ben. What does he look like? Is he tall?"

"Not particularly."

"Black hair?"

My mind went blank. "Yes. No. I don't know. He's beginning to go gray. He has a paunch, I think. Maybe not." I stood up. "I need to see his photograph."

I went back upstairs. They were there, pinned around the mirror. Me and my husband. Happy. Together.

"His hair looks kind of brown," I said. I heard a car pull up outside the house.

"You're sure?"

"Yes," I said. The engine was switched off, the door slammed. A loud beep. I lowered my voice. "I think Ben's home."

"Shit," said Claire. "Quick. Does he have a scar?"

"A scar?" I said. "Where?"

"On his face, Chrissy. A scar, across one cheek. He had an accident. Rock climbing."

I scanned the photographs, choosing the one of me and my husband sitting at a breakfast table in our dressing gowns. In it, he was smiling happily and, apart from a hint of stubble, his cheeks were unblemished. Fear rushed to hit me.

I heard the front door open. A voice. "Christine! Darling! I'm home!"

"No," I said. "No, he doesn't."

A sound. Somewhere between a gasp and a sigh.

"The man you're living with," Claire said. "I don't know who it is. But it's not Ben."

Terror hits. I hear the toilet flush, but can do nothing but read on.

I don't know what happened then. I cannot piece it together. Claire began talking, almost shouting. "Fuck!" she said, over and over. My mind was spinning with panic. I heard the front door shut, the click of the lock.

"I'm in the bathroom," I shouted to the man who I had thought was my husband. My voice sounded cracked. Desperate. "I'll be down in a minute."

"I'll come over," said Claire. "I'm getting you out of there."

"Everything okay, darling?" shouted the man who was not Ben. I heard his footsteps on the stairs and realized I had not locked the bathroom door. I lowered my voice.

"He's here," I said. "Come tomorrow. While he's at work. I'll pack my things. I'll call you."

"Shit," she said. "Okay. But write in your journal. Write in it as soon as you can. Don't forget."

I thought of my journal, hidden in the closet. *I must stay calm,* I thought. *I must pretend nothing is wrong, at least until I can get to it and write down the danger I am in.*

"Help me," I said. "Help me."

I ended the call as he pushed open the bathroom door.

It ends there. Frantic, I riffle the last few pages, but they are blank, scored only with their faint blue lines. Waiting for the rest of my story. But there is no more. Ben had found the journal, removed the pages, and Claire had not come for me. When Dr. Nash collected the journal—on Tuesday, it must have been—I had not known anything was wrong.

In a single rush, I see it all, realize why the board in the kitchen so disturbed me. The handwriting. Its neat, even capitals looked totally different from the scrawl of the letter Claire had given me. Somewhere, deep down, I had known then that they were not written by the same person.

I look up. Ben, or the man pretending to be Ben, has come out of the shower. He is standing in the doorway, dressed as he was before, looking at me. I don't know how long he has been there, watching me read. His eyes hold nothing more than a sort of vacant emptiness, as if he is barely interested in what he is seeing, as if it doesn't concern him.

I hear myself gasp. I drop the papers. Unbound, they fan onto the floor.

"You!" I say. "Who are you?" He says nothing. He is looking at the papers in front of me. "Answer me!" I say. My voice has an authority to it, but one that I do not feel.

My mind reels as I try to work out who he could be. Someone from Waring House, perhaps. A patient? Nothing makes any sense. I feel the stirrings of panic as another thought begins to form and then vanishes.

He looks up at me then. "I'm Ben," he says. He speaks slowly, as if trying to make me understand the obvious. "Ben. Your husband."

I move back along the floor, away from him, as I fight to remember what I have read, what I know.

"No," I say, and then again, louder. "No!"

He moves forward. "I am, Christine. You know I am."

Fear takes me. Terror. It lifts me up, holds me suspended, and then slams me back into its own horror. Claire's words come back to me. *But it's not Ben.* A strange thing happens then. I realize I am not remembering reading about her saying those words, I am remembering the incident itself. I can remember the panic in her voice, the way she said *fuck* before telling me what she'd realized, and repeated, *It's not Ben.*

I am remembering.

"You're not," I say. "You're not Ben. Claire told me! Who are you?"

"Remember the pictures though, Christine? The ones from around the bathroom mirror? Look, I brought them, to show you."

He takes a step toward me, and then reaches for his bag on the floor beside the bed. He picks out a few curled photographs. "Look!" he says, and when I shake my head, he takes the first one and, glancing at it, holds it up to me.

"This is us," he says. "Look. Me and you." The photograph shows us sitting on some sort of boat, on a river, or canal. Behind us there is dark, muddy water, with unfocused reeds beyond that. We both look young, our skin taut where now it sags, our eyes unlined and wide with happiness. "Don't you see?" he says. "Look! That's us. Me and you. Years ago. We've been together for years, Chris. Years and years."

I focus on the picture. Images come to me; the two of us, a sunny afternoon. We'd hired a boat somewhere. I don't know where.

He holds up another picture. We are much older now. It looks recent. We are standing outside a church. The day is overcast, and he is wearing a suit and shaking hands with a man, also in a suit. I am wearing a hat, which I seem to be having difficulty with; I am holding it as if it is in danger of blowing off in the wind. I am not looking at the camera.

"That was just a few weeks ago," he says. "Some friends of ours invited us to their daughter's wedding. You remember?"

"No," I say angrily. "No, I don't remember!"

"It was a lovely day," he says, turning the picture back to look at it himself. "Lovely—"

I remember reading what Claire had said when I told her I had found a newspaper clipping about Adam's death. *It can't have been real.*

"Show me one of Adam," I say. "Go on! Show me just one picture of him."

"Adam is dead," he says. "A soldier's death. Noble. He died a hero—"

I shout, "You should still have a picture of him! Show me!"

He takes out the picture of Adam with Helen. The one I have already seen. Fury rises in me. "Show me just one picture of Adam with you in it. Just one. You must have some, surely? If you're his father?"

He looks through the photographs in his hand, and I think he will produce a picture of the two of them, but he does not. His arms hang at his side. "I don't have one with me," he says. "They must be at the house."

"You're not his father, are you?" I say. "What father wouldn't have pictures of himself with his son?" His eyes narrow, as if in rage, but I cannot stop. "And what kind of father would tell his wife that their son was dead when he isn't? Admit it! You're not Adam's father! Ben is." Even as I said the name, an image came to me. A man with narrow, dark-rimmed glasses and black hair. *Ben.* I say his name again, as if to lock the image in my mind. "Ben."

The name has an effect on the man standing in front of me. He says something, but too quietly for me to hear it, and so I ask him to repeat it. "You don't need Adam," he says.

"What?" I say, and he speaks more firmly, looking into my eyes as he does so.

"You don't need Adam. You have me now. We're together. You don't need Adam. You don't need Ben."

At his words, I feel all the strength I had within me disappear, and, as it goes, he seems to recover. I sink to the floor. He smiles.

"Don't be upset," he says brightly. "What does it matter? I love you. That's all that's important. Surely? I love you, and you love me."

He crouches down, holding out his hands toward me. He is smiling, as if I am an animal that he is trying to coax out of the hole in which it has hidden.

"Come," he says. "Come to me."

I shift farther backward, sliding on my haunches. I hit something solid and feel the warm, sticky radiator behind me. I realize I am under the window at the far end of the room. He advances slowly.

"Who are you?" I say again, trying to keep my voice even, calm. "What do you want?"

He stops moving. He is crouched in front of me. If he were to reach out, he could touch my foot, my knee. If he were to move closer, I may be able to kick him, should I need to, though I am not sure I could reach and, in any case, am barefoot.

"What do I want?" he says. "I don't want anything. I just want us to be happy, Chris. Like we used to be. Do you remember?"

That word again. *Remember.* For a moment, I think perhaps he is being sarcastic.

"I don't know who you are," I say, near hysterical. "How can I remember? I've never met you before!"

His smile vanishes then. I see his face collapse in on itself with pain. There is a moment of limbo, as if the balance of power is shifting from him to me and, for a fraction of a second, it is equal between us.

He becomes animated again. "But you love me," he says. "I read it, in your journal. You said you love me. I know you want us to be together. Why can't you remember that?"

"My journal!" I say. I know he must have known about it—how else did he remove those vital pages?—but I realize he must have been reading it for a while, at least since I first told him about it a week ago. "How long have you been reading my journal?"

He doesn't seem to have heard me. He raises his voice, as if in triumph. "Tell me you don't love me," he says. I say nothing. "See? You can't, can you? You can't say it. Because you do. You always have done, Chris. Always."

He rocks back, and the two of us sit on the floor, opposite each other. "I remember when we met," he says. I think of what he's told me—spilled coffee in the university library—and wonder what is coming now.

"You were working on something. You used to go to the same café every day. You always used to sit in the window, in the same seat. Sometimes you would have a child with you, but usually not. You would sit with a notebook open in front of you, either writing or sometimes just looking out of the window. I thought you looked so beautiful. I used to walk past you, every day, on my way to catch the bus, and I started to look forward to my walk home so that I could catch a glimpse of you. I used to try and guess what you might be wearing, or whether you'd have your hair pulled back or loose, or whether you'd have a snack, a cake, or a sandwich. Sometimes you'd have a whole brownie in front of you, sometimes just a plate of crumbs, or even nothing at all, just the tea."

He laughs, shaking his head sadly, and I remember Claire telling me about the café and know that he is speaking the truth. "I would pass by at exactly the same time every day," he says, "and no matter how hard I tried I just couldn't work out how you decided when to eat your snack. At first I thought maybe it depended on the day of the week, but it didn't seem to follow any pattern there, so then I thought perhaps it was related to the date. But that didn't seem to work, either. I started to wonder what time you actually ordered your snack. I thought maybe that was related to the time that you got to the café, so I started to leave work earlier and run so that I could maybe see you arriving. And then, one day, you weren't there. I waited until I saw you coming down the street. You were pushing a stroller, and when you got to the café door, you seemed to have trouble getting it in. You looked so helpless and stuck, and, without thinking, I walked over the road and held the door for you. And you smiled at me, and said, 'Thank you so much.' You looked so beautiful, Christine. I wanted to kiss you, there and then, but I couldn't, and because I didn't want you to think that I'd run across the road just to help you, I went into the café, too, and stood behind you in the line. You spoke to me as we waited. 'Busy today, isn't it?' you said, and I said, 'Yes,' even though it wasn't particularly busy for that time of day. I just wanted to carry on making conversation. I ordered tea, and I had the same cake as you, too, and I wondered if I should ask you whether it would be okay for me to sit with you, but by the time I'd got my tea, you were chatting to someone, one of the people who ran the café, I think, and so I sat on my own in the corner.

"After that, I used to go to the café almost every day. It's always easier to do something when you've done it once. Sometimes I'd wait for you to arrive, or make sure you were there before I went in, but sometimes I'd just go in anyway. And you noticed me. I know you did. You began to say hello to me, or you'd comment on the weather. And then one time I was held up, and when I arrived, you actually said, 'You're late today!' as I walked past, holding my tea and my muffin, and when you saw that there were no free tables, you said, 'Why don't you sit here?' and you pointed to the chair at your table, opposite you. The baby wasn't there that day, so I said, 'Are you sure you don't mind? I won't disturb you?' and then I felt bad for saying that, and I dreaded you saying that yes, actually, on second thought, it would disturb you. But you didn't, you said, 'No! Not at all! To be honest it's not going too well anyway. I'd be glad of a distraction!' and that was how I knew that you wanted me to speak to you rather than just have my tea and eat my cake in silence. Do you remember?"

I shake my head. I have decided to let him speak. I want to find out everything he has to say.

"So I sat, and we chatted. You told me you were a writer. You said you'd had a book published, but you were struggling with your second one. I asked what it was about, but you wouldn't tell me. 'It's fiction,' you said, and then you said, 'supposedly,' and you suddenly looked very sad, so I offered to buy you another cup of coffee. You said that would be nice, but that you didn't have any money with you to buy me one. 'I don't bring my purse when I come here,' you said. 'I just bring enough money to buy one drink and one snack. That way I'm not tempted to pig out!' I thought it was an odd thing to say. You didn't look as though you needed to worry about how much you ate at all. You were always so slim. But anyway, I was glad, as it meant you must be enjoying speaking to me, and you would owe me a drink, so we'd have to see each other again. I said that it didn't matter about the money, or buying me one back, and I got us some more tea and coffee. After that, we started to meet quite regularly."

I begin to see it all. Though I have no memory, somehow I know how these things work. The casual meeting, the exchange of a drink. The appeal of talking to—confiding in—a stranger, one who does not judge or take sides, because he can't. The gradual acceptance into confidence, leading . . . to what?

I have seen the photographs of the two of us, taken years ago. We look happy. It is obvious where those confidences led us. He was attractive, too. Not film-star handsome, but better-looking than most; it is not difficult to see what drew me. At some point, I must have started scanning the door anxiously as I sat trying to work, thinking more carefully about what clothes I would wear when I went to the café, whether to add a dash of perfume. And, one day, one or the other of us must have suggested we go for a walk, or to a bar, or maybe even to catch a film, and our friendship slipped over a line, into something else, something infinitely more dangerous.

I close my eyes and try to imagine it, and as I do, I begin to remember. The two of us, in bed, naked. Semen drying on my stomach, in my hair, me turning to him as he begins to laugh and kiss me again. "Mike!" I am saying. "Stop it! You have to leave soon. Ben's back later today and I have to pick Adam up. Stop it!" But he doesn't listen. Instead he leans in, his mustachioed face in mine, and we are kissing again, forgetting about everything, about my husband, about my child. With a sickening plunge, I realize that a memory of this day has come to me before. That day, as I had stood in the kitchen of the house I once shared with my husband, I had not been remembering my husband but my lover. The man I was fucking while my husband was at work. That's why he had to leave that day. Not just to catch a train—but because the man I was married to would be returning home.

I open my eyes. I am back in the hotel room and he is still crouching in front of me.

"Mike," I say. "Your name is Mike."

"You remember!" he says. He is pleased. "Chris! You remember!"

Hate bubbles up in me. "I remember your name," I say. "Nothing else. Just your name."

"You don't remember how much in love we were?"

"No," I say. "I don't think I could ever have loved you, or surely I would remember more."

I say it to hurt him, but his reaction surprises me. "You don't remember Ben, though, do you? You can't have loved him. And not Adam, either."

"You're sick," I say. "How fucking dare you! Of course I loved him! He was my son!"

"Is. Is your son. But you wouldn't recognize him if he walked in, now. Would you? You think that's love? And where is he? And where is Ben? They walked out on you, Christine. Both of them. I'm the only one who never stopped loving you. Not even when you left me."

It is then that it hits me, finally, properly. How else could he have known about this room, about so much of my past?

"Oh my God," I say. "It was you! It was you who did this to me! You who attacked me!"

He moves over to me then. He wraps his arms around me, as if to embrace me, and begins to stroke my hair. "Christine, darling," he murmurs, "don't say that. Don't think about it. It'll just upset you."

I try to push him off me, but he is strong. He squeezes me tighter.

"Let me go!" I say. "Please, let me go!" My words are lost in the folds of his shirt.

"My love," he says. He has begun to rock me, as if soothing a baby. "My love. My sweet, my darling. You should never have left me. Don't you see? None of this would have happened if you hadn't left."

Memory comes again. *We are sitting in a car, at night. I am crying, and he is staring out of the window, utterly silent. "Say something," I am saying. "Anything. Mike?"*

*"You don't mean it," he says. "You can't."*

*"I'm sorry. I love Ben. We have our problems, yes, but I love him. He's the person I am meant to be with. I'm sorry."*

*I am aware that I am trying to keep things simple, so that he will understand. I have come to realize, over the past few months with Mike, that it is better this way. Complicated things confuse him. He likes order. Routine. Things mixing in precise proportions with predictable results. Plus, I don't want to get too mired in details.*

*"It's because I came over to your house, isn't it? I'm sorry, Chris. I won't do that again. I promise. I just wanted to see you, and I wanted to explain to your husband—"*

*I interrupt him. "Ben. You can say his name. It's Ben."*

"Ben," he says, as if trying the word for the first time and finding it unpleasant. "I wanted to explain things to him. I wanted to tell him the truth."

"What truth?"

"That you don't love him anymore. That you love me now. That you want to be with me. That was all I was going to say."

I sigh. "Don't you see that, even if it were true—which it isn't—it's not you who should be saying that to him? It's me. You had no right to just turn up at the house."

As I speak, I think about what a lucky escape I have had. Ben was in the shower, Adam playing in the dining room, and I was able to persuade Mike that he ought to go home before either of them were aware of his presence. That was the night I decided I had to end the affair.

"I have to go now," I say. I open the car door, step out onto the gravel. "I'm sorry."

He leans across to look at me. I think how attractive he is, that if he had been less damaged, my marriage might have been in real trouble. "Will I see you again?" he says.

"No," I reply. "No. It's over."


Yet here we are now, all these years later. He is holding me again, and I understand that no matter how scared I was of him, I was not scared enough. I begin to scream.

"Darling," he says. "Calm down." He puts his hand over my mouth and I scream louder. "Calm down! Someone will hear you!" My head smacks backward, connects with the radiator behind me. There is no change in the music from the club next door—if anything, it is louder now. *They won't,* I think. *They will never hear me.* I scream again.

"Stop it!" he says. He has hit me, I think, or else shaken me. I begin to panic. "Stop it!" My head hits the warm metal again and I am stunned into silence. I begin to sob.

"Let me go," I say, pleading with him. "Please—" He relaxes his grip a little, though not enough for me to wriggle free. "How did you find me? All these years later? How did you find me?"

"Find you?" he says. "I never lost you." My mind whirs, uncomprehending. "I watched over you. Always. I protected you."

"You visited me? In those places? The hospital, Waring House?" I begin. "But—?"

He sighs. "Not always. They wouldn't have let me. But I would sometimes tell them I was there to see someone else, or that I was a volunteer. Just so that I could see you, and make sure you were all right. At that last place it was easier. All those windows . . ."

I go cold. "You watched me?"

"I had to know you were all right, Chris. I had to protect you."

"So you came back for me? Is that it? Wasn't what you did here, in this room, enough?"

"When I found out that bastard had left you, I couldn't just leave you in that place. I knew you'd want to be with me. I knew it was the best thing for you. I had to wait for a while, wait until I knew there was no one still there to try and stop me, but who else would have looked after you?"

"And they just let me go with you?" I say. "Surely they wouldn't have let me go with a stranger!"

I wonder what lies he must have told for them to let him take me, then remember reading what Dr. Nash had told me about the woman from Waring House. *She was so happy when she found out you'd gone back to live with Ben.* An image forms, a memory. My hand in Mike's as he signs a form. A woman behind a desk smiles at me. "We'll miss you, Christine," she says. "But you'll be happy at home." She looks at Mike. "With your husband."

I follow her gaze. I don't recognize the man whose hand I am holding, but I know he is the man I married. He must be. He has told me he is.

"Oh my God!" I say now. "How long have you been pretending to be Ben?"

He looks surprised. "Pretending?"

"Yes," I say. "Pretending to be my husband."

He looks confused. I wonder if he has forgotten that he is not Ben. Then his face falls. He looks upset.

"Do you think I wanted to do that? I had to. It was the only way."

His arms relax slightly, and an odd thing happens. My mind stops spinning, and, although I remain terrified, I am infused with a bizarre sense of complete calm. A thought comes from nowhere. *I will beat him. I will get away. I have to.*

"Mike?" I say. "I do understand, you know? It must have been difficult."

He looks up at me. "You do?"

"Yes, of course. I'm grateful to you for coming for me. For giving me a home. For looking after me."

"Really?"

"Yes. Just think where I'd be if you hadn't? I couldn't bear it." I sense him soften. The pressure on my arms and shoulder lessens and is accompanied by a subtle yet definite sensation of stroking that I find almost more distasteful but I know is more likely to lead to my escape. Because escape is all I can think of. I need to get away. How stupid of me, I think now, to have sat there on the floor while he was in the bathroom, to read what he had stolen of my journal. Why hadn't I taken it with me and left? Then I remember that it was not until I read the end of the journal that I had any real idea of how much danger I was in. That same small voice comes in again. *I will escape. I have a son I cannot remember having met.*

*I will escape.* I move my head to face him, and begin to stroke the back of his hand where it rests on my shoulder.

"Why not let me go, and then we can talk about what we should do?"

"How about Claire, though?" he says. "She knows I'm not Ben. You told her."

"She won't remember that," I say desperately.

He laughs, a hollow, choked sound. "You always treated me like I was stupid. I'm not, you know? I know what's going to happen! You told her. You ruined everything!"

"No," I say quickly. "I can call her. I can tell her I was confused. That I'd forgotten who you were. I can tell her that I thought you were Ben, but I was wrong."

I almost believe he thinks this is possible, but then he says, "She'd never believe you."

"She would," I say, even though I know that she would not. "I promise."

"Why did you have to go and call her?" His face clouds with anger, his hands begin to grip me tighter. "Why? Why, Chris? We were doing fine, until then. Fine." He begins to shake me again. "Why?" he shouts. "Why?"

"Ben," I say. "You're hurting me."

He hits me then. I hear the sound of his hand against my face before I feel the flash of pain. My head twists around, my lower jaw cracks up, connecting painfully with its companion.

"Don't you ever fucking call me that again," he spits.

"Mike," I say quickly, as if I can erase my mistake. "Mike—"

He ignores me.

"I'm sick of being Ben," he says. "You can call me Mike, from now on. Okay? It's Mike. That's why we came back here. So that we can put all that behind us. You wrote in your book that if you could only remember what happened here all those years ago then you'd get your memory back. Well, we're here now. I made it happen, Chris. So remember!"

I am incredulous. "You *want* me to remember?"

"Yes! Of course I do! I love you, Christine. I want you to remember how much you love me. I want us to be together again. Properly. As we should be." He pauses, his voice drops to a whisper. "I don't want to be Ben anymore."

"But—"

He looks back at me. "When we go back home tomorrow, you can call me Mike." He shakes me again, his face inches from mine. "Okay?" I can smell sourness on his breath, and another smell, too. I wonder if he's been drinking. "We're going to be okay, aren't we, Christine? We're going to move on."

"Move on?" I say. My head is sore, and something is coming out of my nose. Blood, I think, though I am not sure. The calmness disappears. I raise my voice, shouting as loud as I can. "You want me to go back home? Move on? Are you absolutely fucking crazy?" He moves his hand to clamp it over my mouth, and I realize that has left my arm free. I hit out at him, catching him on the side of his face, though not hard. Still, it takes him by surprise. He falls backward, letting go of my other arm as he does.

I stumble to my feet. "Bitch!" he says, but I step forward, over him, and head toward the door.

I manage three steps before he grabs my ankle. I come crashing down. There is a stool sitting tucked under the dressing table, and my head hits its edge as I go down. I am lucky; the stool is padded and breaks my fall, but it causes my body to twist awkwardly as I land. Pain shoots up my back and through my neck, and I am afraid I have broken something. I begin to crawl toward the door, but he still holds my ankle. He pulls me toward him with a grunt, and then his crushing weight is on top of me, his lips inches from my ear.

"Mike," I sob. "Mike—"

In front of me is the photograph of Adam and Helen, lying on the floor where he had dropped it. Even in the middle of everything else, I wonder how he had got it, and then it hits me. Adam had sent it to me at Waring House and Mike had taken it, along with all the other photographs, when he'd come for me.

"You stupid, stupid bitch," he says, spitting into my ear. One of his hands is around my throat; with the other, he has grabbed a handful of my hair. He pulls my head back, jerking my neck up. "What did you have to go and do that for?"

"I'm sorry," I sob. I cannot move. One of my hands is trapped beneath my body, the other clamped between my back and his leg.

"Where did you think you were going to go, eh?" he says. He is snarling now, an animal. Something like hate floods out of him.

"I'm sorry," I say again, because it is all I can think of to say. "I'm sorry." I remember the days when those words would always work, always be enough, be what was needed to get me out of whatever trouble I was in.

"Stop saying you're fucking sorry," he says. My head jerks back, and then slams forward. My forehead, nose, mouth all connect with the carpeted floor. There is a noise, a sickening crunch, and the smell of stale cigarettes. I cry out. There is blood in my mouth. I have bitten my tongue. "Where do you think you're going to run to? You can't drive. You don't know anybody. You don't even know who you are most of the time. You have nowhere to go, nowhere at all. You're pathetic."

I start to cry, because he is right. I am pathetic. Claire never came; I have no friends. I am utterly alone, relying totally on the man who did this to me, and, tomorrow morning, if I survive, I will have forgotten even this.

*If I survive.* The words echo through me as I realize what this man is capable of, and that, this time, I may not get out of this room alive. Terror slams into me, but then I hear the tiny voice again. *This is not the place you die. Not with him. Not now. Anything but that.*

I arch my back painfully and manage to free my arm. Lunging forward, I grab the leg of the stool. It is heavy, and the angle of my body wrong, but I manage to twist around and heave it back over my head, where I imagine Mike's head will be. It strikes something with a satisfying crack, and there is a gasp in my ear. He lets go of my hair.

I look around. He has rocked backward, his hand to his forehead. Blood is beginning to trickle between his fingers. He looks up at me, uncomprehending.

Later, I will think how I should have hit him again. With the stool, or with my bare hands. With anything. I should have made sure he was incapacitated, that I could get away, get downstairs, even far enough away that I could open the door and scream for help.

But I do not. I pull myself upright and then I stand, looking at him on the floor in front of me. No matter what I do now, I think, he has won. He will always have won. He has taken everything from me, even the ability to remember exactly what he did to me. I turn, and begin to move toward the door.

With a grunt, he launches himself at me. His whole body collides with mine. Together we slam into the dresser, stumble toward the door. "Christine!" he says, "Chris! Don't leave me!"

I reach out. If I can just open the door, then surely, despite the noise from the club, someone will hear us and come?

He clings to my waist. Like some grotesque, two-headed monster, we inch forward, me dragging him. "Chris! I love you!" he says. He is wailing, and this, plus the ridiculousness of his words, spurs me on. I am nearly there. Soon I will reach the door.

And then it happens. I remember that night, all those years ago. Me, in this room, standing in the same spot. I am reaching out a hand toward the same door. I am happy, ridiculously so. The walls resonate with the soft orange glow of the lit candles that were dotted around the room when I arrived, the air is tinged with the sweet smell of the roses in the bouquet that was on the bed. *I'll be upstairs at around seven, my darling,* said the note that was pinned to them, and though I wondered briefly what Ben was doing downstairs, I am glad of the few minutes I have had alone before he arrives. It has given me the opportunity to gather my thoughts, to reflect on how close I came to losing him, what a relief it has been to end the affair with Mike, how fortunate I am that Ben and I are now set on a new trajectory. How could I have thought that I wanted to be with Mike? Mike would never have done what Ben has done: arrange a surprise night away in a hotel at the coast, to show me how much he loves me and that, despite our recent differences, this will never change. Mike was too inward-looking for that, I have learned. With him, everything is a test, affection is measured, that given weighed against that which has been received, and the balance, more often than not, disappointing him.

I am touching the handle of the door, twisting it, pulling it toward me. Ben has taken Adam to stay with his grandparents. We have a whole weekend in front of us, with nothing to worry about. Just the two of us.

"Darling," I am starting to say, but the word is choked off in my throat. It's not Ben at the door. It's Mike. He is pushing past me, coming into the room, and even as I am asking him what he thinks he is doing—what right he has to lure me here, to this room, what he thinks he can achieve—I am thinking, *You devious bastard. How dare you pretend to be my husband. Do you have no pride left at all?*

I think of Ben and Adam, at home. By now Ben will be wondering where I am. Possibly he will soon call the police. How stupid I was to get on a train and come here without mentioning it to anybody. How stupid to believe that a typewritten note, even one sprayed with my favorite perfume, was from my husband.

Mike speaks. "Would you have come, if you'd known it was to meet me?"

I laugh. "Of course not! It's over. I told you that before."

I look at the flowers, the bottle of champagne he still holds in his hand. Everything carries the smack of romance, of seduction. "My God!" I am saying. "You really thought you could just lure me here, give me flowers and a bottle of champagne and that would be it? That I would just fall into your arms and everything would go back to being like it was before? You're crazy, Mike. Crazy. I'm leaving now. Going back to my husband and my son."

I don't want to remember any more. I suppose that must have been when he first hit me, but, after that, I don't know what happened, what led me from there to the hospital. And now I am here again, in this room. We have turned a full circle, though for me all the days between have been stolen. It is as though I never left.

I cannot reach the door. He is pulling himself up. I begin to shout. "Help! Help!"

"Quiet!" he says. "Shut up!"

I shout louder, and he swings me around, at the same time pushing me backward. I fall, and the ceiling and his face slide down in front of me like a curtain descending. My skull hits something hard and unyielding. I realize he has pushed me into the bathroom. I twist my head and see the tiled floor stretching away from me, the bottom of the toilet, the edge of the bath. There is a bar of soap on the floor, sticky and mashed. "Mike!" I say. "Don't . . ." but he is crouching over me, his hands around my throat.

"Shut up!" he is saying, over and over, even though I am not saying anything now, just crying. I am gasping for breath, my eyes and mouth are wet, with blood, and tears, and I don't know what else.

"Mike—" I gasp. I cannot breathe. His hands are around my throat and I cannot breathe. Memory floods back. I can remember him holding my head under water. I remember waking up, in a white bed, wearing a hospital gown, and Ben sitting next to me, the real Ben, the one I married. I remember a policewoman asking me questions I cannot answer. A man in pale blue pajamas sitting on the edge of my hospital bed, laughing with me even as he tells me that I greet him every day as if I have never seen him before. A little boy with blond hair and a tooth missing, calling me Mummy. One after another, the images come. They flood through me. The effect is violent. I shake my head, trying to clear it, but Mike grips me tighter. His head is above mine, his eyes wild and unblinking as he squeezes my throat, and I can remember it being so once before, in this room. I close my eyes. "How dare you?" he is saying, and I cannot work out which Mike it is who is speaking: the one here, now, or the one who exists only in my memory. "How dare you?" he says again. "How dare you take my child?"

It is then that I remember. When he had attacked me all those years ago, I had been carrying a baby. Not Mike's, but Ben's. The child that was going to be our new start together.

Neither of us had survived.

I must have blacked out. When I regain consciousness, I am sitting in a chair. I cannot move my hands, the inside of my mouth tastes furry. I open my eyes. The room is dim, lit only by the moonlight streaming in through the open curtains and the reflected yellow streetlights. Mike is sitting opposite me, on the edge of the bed. He is holding something in his hand.

I try to speak, but cannot. I realize something is in my mouth. A sock, perhaps. It has been secured, somehow, tied in place, and my wrists are tied together, and also my ankles.

This is what he wanted all along, I think. Me, silent and un-moving. I struggle, and he notices that I have woken up. He looks up, his face a mask of pain and sadness, and stares at me, right into my eyes. I feel nothing but hate.

"You're awake." I wonder if he intends to say anything else, whether he is capable of saying anything else. "This isn't what I wanted. I thought we would come here and it might help you to remember. Remember how things used to be between us. And then we could talk, and I could explain what happened here, all those years ago. I never meant for it to happen, Chris. I just get so mad, sometimes. I can't help it. I'm sorry. I never wanted to hurt you, ever. I ruined everything."

He looks down, into his lap. There is so much more I used to want to know, yet I am exhausted, and it is too late. I feel as though I could close my eyes and will myself into oblivion, erasing everything.

Yet I do not want to sleep tonight. And if I must sleep, then I do not want to wake up tomorrow.

"It was when you told me you were having a baby." He does not lift his head. Instead, he speaks softly into the folds of his clothes, and I have to strain to hear what he is saying. "I never thought I'd have a child. Never. They all said—" he hesitates, as if changing his mind, deciding that some things are better not shared. "You said it wasn't mine. But I knew it was. And I couldn't cope with the thought that you were still going to leave me, going to take my baby away from me, that I might never see him. I couldn't cope, Chris."

I still don't know what he wants from me.

"You think I'm not sorry? For what I did? Every day. I see you so bewildered and lost and unhappy. Sometimes I lie there, in bed. I hear you wake up. And you look at me, and I know you don't know who I am, and I can feel the disappointment and shame. It comes off you in waves. That hurts. Knowing that you'd never sleep with me now, if you had the choice. And then you get out of bed and go to the bathroom, and I know that in a few minutes you will come back and you'll be so confused and so unhappy and in so much pain."

He pauses. "And now I know even that will be over soon. I've read your journal. I know your doctor will have worked it out by now. Or he will do soon. Claire, too. I know they'll come for me." He looks up. "And they'll try to take you away from me. But Ben doesn't want you. I do. I want to look after you. Please, Chris. Please remember how much you loved me. Then you can tell them that you want to be with me." He points to the last few pages of my journal, scattered on the floor. "You can tell them that you forgive me. For this. And then we can be together."

I shake my head. I cannot believe he *wants* me to remember. He *wants* me to know what he has done.

He smiles. "You know, sometimes I think it might have been kinder if you'd died that night. Kinder for both of us." He looks out of the window. "I would join you, Chris. If that's what you wanted." He looks down again. "It would be easy enough. You could go first. And I promise you I would follow. You do trust me, don't you?"

He looks at me expectantly. "Would you like that?" he says. "It would be painless."

I shake my head, try to speak, fail. My eyes are burning, and I can hardly breathe.

"No?" He looks disappointed. "No. I suppose any life is better than none. Very well. You're probably right." I begin to cry. He shakes his head. "Chris. This will all be fine. You see? This book is the problem." He holds up my journal. "We were happy, before you started writing this. Or as happy as we could be, anyway. And that was happy enough, wasn't it? We should just get rid of this, and then maybe you could tell them you were confused, and we could go back to how it was before. For a little while, at least."

He stands up and slides the metal bin from beneath the dresser, taking out the empty liner and discarding it. "It'll be easy, then," he says. He puts the bin on the floor between his legs. "Easy." He drops my journal into the bin, and gathers the last few pages that are still littering the floor and adds those. "We have to get rid of it," he says. "All of it. Once and for all."

He takes a box of matches out of his pocket, strikes one, and retrieves a single page from the bin.

I look at him in horror. "No!" I try to say, but nothing comes apart from a muffled grunt. He does not look at me as he sets fire to the single page and then drops it into the bin.

"No!" I say again, but this time it is a silent scream in my head. I watch my history begin to burn to ash, my memories reduced to carbon. My journal, the letter from Ben, everything. *I am nothing without that journal*, I think. *Nothing. And he has won.*

I do not plan to do what I do next. It is instinctive. I launch my body at the bin. With my hands tied, I cannot break my fall, and

I hit it awkwardly, hearing something snap as I twist. Pain shoots from my arm and I think I will faint, but do not. The bin falls over, scattering burning paper across the floor.

Mike cries out—a shriek—and falls to his knees, slapping the ground, trying to put out the flames. I notice a burning shred has come to rest under the bed, unnoticed by Mike. Flames are beginning to lick at the edge of the bedspread, but I can neither reach it nor cry out, and so I simply lie there, watching the bedspread catch fire. It begins to smoke, and I close my eyes. The room will burn, I think, and Mike will burn, and I will burn, and no one will ever really know what happened here, in this room, just like no one will ever really know what happened here all those years ago, and history will turn to ash and be replaced by conjecture.

I cough, a dry, heaving retch, swallowed by the sock balled in my throat. I am beginning to choke. I think of my son. I will never see him, now, though at least I'll die knowing I had one, and that he is alive and happy. For that I am glad. I think of Ben. The man I married and then forgot. I want to see him. I want to tell him that now, at the end, I can remember him. I can remember meeting him at the rooftop party, and him proposing to me on a hill looking out over a city, and I can remember marrying him in the church in Manchester, having our photographs taken in the rain.

And, yes, I can remember loving him. I know that I do love him, and I always have.

Things go dark. I cannot breathe. I can hear the lap of flames, and feel their heat on my lips and eyes.

There were never going to be any happy endings for me. I know that now. But that is all right.

That is all right.

I am lying down. I have been asleep, but not for long. I can remember who I am, where I have been. I can hear noise, the roar of traffic, a siren that is neither rising nor falling in pitch but remaining constant. Something is over my mouth—I think of a balled sock—yet I find I can breathe. I am too frightened to open my eyes. I do not know what I will see.

But I must. I have no choice but to face whatever my reality has become.

The light is bright. I can see a fluorescent tube on the low ceiling, and two metal bars running parallel to it. The walls are close by on each side, and they are hard, shiny with metal and plastic. I can make out drawers and shelves stocked with bottles and packets, and there are machines, blinking. Everything is moving slightly, vibrating, including, I realize, the bed in which I am lying.

A man's face appears from somewhere behind me, over my head. He is wearing a green shirt. I do not recognize him.

"She's awake, everybody," he says, and then more faces appear. I scan them quickly. Mike is not among them, and I relax, a little.

"Christine," comes a voice. "Chrissy. It's me." It is a woman's voice, one I recognize. "We're on our way to the hospital. You've broken your collarbone, but you're going to be all right. Everything's going to be fine. He's dead. That man is dead. He can't hurt you anymore."

I see the person speaking, then. She is smiling and holding my hand. It's Claire. The same Claire I saw just the other day, not the young Claire I might expect to see after just waking up, and I notice her earrings are the same pair that she had on the last time I saw her.

"Claire?" I say, but she interrupts.

"Don't speak," she says. "Just try to relax." She leans forward and strokes my hair, and whispers something in my ear, but I don't hear what. It sounds like "I'm sorry."

"I remember," I say. "I remember."

She smiles, and then she steps back and a young man takes her place. He has a narrow face and is wearing thick-rimmed glasses. For a moment, I think it is Ben, until I realize that Ben would be my age now.

"Mum?" he says. "Mum?"

He looks the same as he did in the picture of him and Helen, and I realize I remember him, too.

"Adam?" I say. Words choke in my throat as he hugs me.

"Mum," he says. "Dad's coming. He'll be here soon."

I pull him to me, and breathe in the smell of my boy, and I am happy.


I can wait no longer. It is time. I must sleep. I have a private room and so there is no need for me to observe the strict routines of the hospital, but I am exhausted, my eyes already beginning to close. It is time.

I have spoken to Ben. To the man I really married. We talked for hours, it seems, though it may only have been a few minutes. He told me that he flew in as soon as the police contacted him.

"The police?"

"Yes," he said. "When they realized you weren't living with the person Waring House thought you were, they traced me. I'm not sure how. I suppose they had my old address and went from there."

"So where were you?"

He pushed his glasses up the bridge of his nose. "I've been in Italy for a few months," he said. "I've been working out there."

He paused. "I thought you were okay." He took my hand. "I'm sorry . . ."

"You couldn't have known," I said.

He looked away. "I left you, Chrissy."

"I know. I know everything. Claire told me. I read your letter."

"I thought it was for the best," he said. "I really did. I thought it would help. Help you. Help Adam. I tried to get on with my life. I really did." He hesitated. "I thought I could only do that if I divorced you. I thought it would free me. Adam didn't understand, even when I explained to him that you wouldn't even know, wouldn't even remember being married to me."

"Did it?" I said. "Did it help you to move on?"

He turned to me. "I won't lie to you, Chrissy. There have been other women. Not many, but some. It's been a long time, years and years. At first nothing serious, but then I met someone a couple of years ago. I moved in with her. But—"

"But?"

"Well, that ended. She said I didn't love her. That I'd never stopped loving you . . ."

"And was she right?"

He did not reply, and so, fearing his answer, I said, "So what happens now? Tomorrow? Will you take me back to Waring House?"

He looked up at me.

"No," he said. "She was right. I never stopped loving you. And I won't take you there again. Tomorrow, I want you to come home."

Now I look at him. He sits in a chair next to me, and although he is already snoring, his head tipped forward at an awkward angle, he still holds my hand. I can just make out his glasses, the scar running down the side of his face. My son has left the room to phone his girlfriend and whisper a good-night to his unborn daughter, and my best friend is outside in the parking lot, smoking a cigarette. No matter what, I am surrounded by the people I love.

Earlier, I spoke to Dr. Nash. He told me I had left the care home almost four months ago, a little while after Mike had started visiting, claiming to be Ben. I had discharged myself, signed all the paperwork. I had left voluntarily. They couldn't have stopped me, even if they'd believed there was a reason for them to try. When I left, I took with me the few photographs and personal possessions that I still had.

"That was why Mike had those pictures?" I said. "The ones of me, and Adam. That's why he had the letter that Adam had written to Santa Claus? His birth certificate?"

"Yes," said Dr. Nash. "They were with you at Waring House, and they went with you when you left. At some point, Mike must have destroyed all the pictures that showed you with Ben. Possibly even before you were discharged from Waring House—the staff turnover is fairly high and they had no idea what your husband really looked like."

"But how would he have got access to the photographs?"

"They were in an album in a drawer in your room. It would have been easy enough for him to get to them once he started visiting you. He might even have slipped in a few photographs of himself. He must have had some of the two of you taken during . . . well, when you were seeing each other, years ago. The staff at Waring House were convinced that the man who had been visiting you was the same one as in the photo album."

"So I brought my photos back to Mike's house and he hid them in a metal box? Then he invented a fire, to explain why there were so few?"

"Yes," he said. He looked tired, and guilty. I wondered whether he blamed himself for any of what had happened, and hoped he didn't. He had helped me, after all. He had rescued me. I hoped he would still be able to write his paper and present my case. I hoped he would be recognized for what he had done for me. After all, without him I'd—

I don't want to think about where I'd be.

"How did you find me?" I said. He explained that Claire had been frantic with worry after we'd spoken, but she had waited for me to call the next day. "Mike must have removed the pages from your journal that night. That was why you didn't think anything was wrong when you gave me the journal on Tuesday, and neither did I. When you didn't call her, Claire tried to phone you, but she only had the number for the mobile phone I had given you, and Mike had taken that, too. I should have known something was wrong when I called you on that number this morning and you didn't answer. But I didn't think. I just called you on your other phone . . ." He shook his head.

"It's okay," I said. "Go on . . ."

"It's fair to assume he'd been reading your journal for at least the last week or so, probably longer. At first Claire couldn't get hold of Adam and didn't have Ben's number, so she called Waring House. They only had one number, which they thought was for Ben but, in fact, it was Mike's. Claire didn't have my number. She called the school he worked at and persuaded them to give her Mike's address and phone number, but both were false. She was at a dead end."

I think of this man discovering my journal, reading it every day. Why didn't he destroy it?

Because I'd written that I loved him. And because that was what he wanted me to carry on believing.

Or maybe I am being too kind to him. Maybe he just wanted me to see it burn.

"Claire didn't call the police?"

"She did," he nodded. "But it was a few days before they really took it seriously. In the meantime she'd got hold of Adam and he'd told her that Ben had been abroad for a while and that as far as he knew you were still in Waring House. She contacted them and, though they wouldn't give her your home address, they eventually relented and gave Adam my number. They must have thought that was a good compromise, as I am a doctor. Claire only got through to me this afternoon."

"This afternoon?"

"Yes. Claire convinced me something was wrong, and of course finding out that Adam was alive confirmed it. We came to see you at home, but by then you'd already left for Brighton."

"How did you know to find me there?"

"You told me this morning that Ben—sorry, Mike—had told you that you were going away for the weekend. You said he'd told you that you were going to the coast. Once Claire told me what was going on, I guessed where he was taking you."

I lay back. I felt tired. Exhausted. I wanted only to sleep, but was frightened to. Frightened of what I might forget.

"But you told me Adam was dead," I said. "You said he'd been killed. When we were sitting in the parking lot. And the fire, too. You told me there'd been a fire."

He smiled sadly. "Because that's what you told me." I told him I didn't understand. "One day, a couple of weeks after we first met, you told me Adam was dead. Evidently, Mike had told you, and you had believed him and told me. When you asked me in the parking lot, I told you the truth as I believed it. It was the same with the fire. I believed there'd been one, because that's what you told me."

"But I remembered Adam's funeral," I said. "His coffin . . ."

Again the sad smile. "Your imagination . . ."

"But I saw pictures," I said. "That man"—I found it impossible to say Mike's name—"he showed me pictures of me and him together, of us getting married. I found a picture of a gravestone. It had Adam's name—"

"He must have faked them," he said.

"Faked them?"

"Yes. On a computer. It's really quite easy to mock-up photos these days. He must have guessed you were suspecting the truth and left them where he knew you'd find them. It's quite likely that some of the photos you thought were of the two of you were also faked."

I thought of the times I had written that Mike was in his office. Working. Is that what he'd been doing? How thoroughly he had betrayed me.

"Are you okay?" said Dr. Nash.

I smiled. "Yes," I said. "I think so." I looked at him, and realized I could picture him in a different suit, with his hair cut much shorter.

"I can remember things," I said.

His expression did not change. "What things?" he said.

"I remember you with a different haircut," I said. "And I recognized Ben, too. And Adam and Claire, in the ambulance. And I can remember seeing her the other day. We went to the café at Alexandra Palace. We had coffee. She has a son, called Toby."

His eyes were sad.

"Have you read your journal today?" he said.

"Yes," I said. "But don't you see? I can remember things that I didn't write down. I can remember the earrings that she was wearing. They're the same ones she has on now. I asked her. She said I was right. And I can remember that Toby was wearing a blue parka, and he had cartoons on his socks, and I remember he was upset because he wanted apple juice and they only had orange or blackcurrant. Don't you see? I didn't write those things down. I can remember them."

He looked pleased then, though still cautious.

"Dr. Paxton did say that he could find no obvious organic cause for your amnesia. That it seemed likely that it was at least partly caused by the emotional trauma of what had happened to you, as well as the physical. I suppose it's possible that another trauma might reverse that, at least to some degree."

I leaped on what he was suggesting. "So I might be cured?" I said.

He looked at me intently. I had the feeling he was weighing up what to say, how much of the truth I could stand.

"I have to say it's unlikely," he said. "There's been a degree of improvement over the last few weeks, but nothing like a complete return of memory. But it is possible."

I felt a rush of joy. "Doesn't the fact that I remember what happened a week ago mean that I can form new memories again? And keep them?"

He spoke hesitantly. "It would suggest that, yes. But Christine, I want you to be prepared for the fact that the effect may well be temporary. We won't know until tomorrow."

"When I wake up?"

"Yes. It's entirely possible that after you sleep tonight, all the memories you have from today will be gone. All the new ones, and all the old ones."

"It might be exactly the same as when I woke up this morning?"

"Yes," he said. "It might."

That I might wake up and have forgotten Adam and Ben seemed too much to contemplate. It felt like it would be a living death.

"But—" I began.

"Keep your journal, Christine," he said. "You still have it?"

I shook my head. "He burned it. That's what caused the fire."

Dr. Nash looked disappointed. "That's a shame," he said. "But it doesn't really matter. Christine, you'll be fine. You can begin another. The people who love you have come back to you."

"But I want to have come back to them, too," I said. "I want to have come back to them."

We talked for a little while longer, but he was keen to leave me with my family. I know he was only trying to prepare me for the worst—for the possibility that I will wake up tomorrow with no idea where I am, or who this man sitting next to me is, or who the person is who is claiming to be my son—but I have to believe that he is wrong. That my memory is back. I have to believe that.

I look at my sleeping husband, silhouetted in the dim room. I remember us meeting, that night of the party, the night I watched the fireworks with Claire on the roof. I remember him asking me to marry him, on holiday in Verona, and the rush of excitement I'd felt as I said yes. And our wedding, too, our marriage, our life. I remember it all. I smile.

"I love you," I whisper, and I close my eyes, and I sleep.

## Author's Note

This book was inspired in part by the lives of several amnesiac patients, most notably Henry Gustav Molaison and Clive Wearing, whose story has been told by his wife, Deborah Wearing, in her book *Forever Today: A Memoir of Love and Amnesia*.

However, events in *Before I Go to Sleep* are entirely fictitious.

# Acknowledgments

Endless gratitude to my wonderful agent, Clare Conville, to Jake Smith-Bosanquet and all at C&W, and to my editors, Claire Wachtel, Selina Walker, Michael Heyward, and Iris Tupholme.

Thanks and love to all my family and friends, for starting me on this journey, for reading early drafts, and for their constant support. Particular thanks to Margaret and Alistair Peacock, Jennifer Hill, Samantha Lear, and Simon Graham, who believed in me before I believed in myself; to Andrew Dell, Anzel Britz, Gillian Ib, and Jamie Gambino, who came later; and to Nicholas Ib, who has been there always. Thanks also to all at GSTT.

Thank you to all at the Faber Academy, and in particular to Patrick Keogh. Finally, this book would not have been written without the input of my gang—Richard Skinner, Amy Cunnah, Damien Gibson, Antonia Hayes, Simon Murphy, and Richard Reeves. Huge gratitude for your friendship and support, and long may the FAGs keep control of their feral narrators.